Little Brother

Little Brother

CORY DOCTOROW

TOR®

A Tom Doherty Associates Book

New York

LITTLE BROTHER

Copyright © 2008 by Cory Doctorow

Afterword copyright © 2008 by Bruce Schneier

Afterword copyright © 2008 by Andrew Huang

Edited by Patrick Nielsen Hayden
Book design by Spring Hoteling

A Tor Teen Book
Published by Tom Doherty Associates, LLC
175 Fifth Avenue
New York, NY 10010

www.tor-forge.com

Tor® is a registered trademark of Tom Doherty Associates, LLC.

ISBN-13: 978-0-7653-1985-2
ISBN-10: 0-7653-1985-3

First Edition: May 2008

Printed in the United States of America

0 9 8 7 6 5 4 3 2 1

For Alice, who makes me whole

Little Brother

Chapter 1

I'm a senior at Cesar Chavez High in San Francisco's sunny Mission district, and that makes me one of the most surveilled people in the world. My name is Marcus Yallow, but back when this story starts, I was going by w1n5t0n. Pronounced "Winston."

Not pronounced "Double-you-one-enn-five-tee-zero-enn"—unless you're a clueless disciplinary officer who's far enough behind the curve that you still call the Internet "the information superhighway."

I know just such a clueless person, and his name is Fred Benson, one of three vice-principals at Cesar Chavez. He's a sucking chest wound of a human being. But if you're going to have a jailer, better a clueless one than one who's really on the ball.

"Marcus Yallow," he said over the PA one Friday morning. The PA isn't very good to begin with, and when you combine that with Benson's habitual mumble, you get something that sounds more like someone struggling to digest a bad burrito than a school announcement. But human beings are good at picking their names out of audio confusion—it's a survival trait.

I grabbed my bag and folded my laptop three-quarters

shut—I didn't want to blow my downloads—and got ready for the inevitable.

"Report to the administration office immediately."

My social studies teacher, Ms. Galvez, rolled her eyes at me and I rolled my eyes back at her. The Man was always coming down on me, just because I go through school firewalls like wet kleenex, spoof the gait-recognition software, and nuke the snitch chips they track us with. Galvez is a good type, anyway, never holds that against me (especially when I'm helping get with her webmail so she can talk to her brother who's stationed in Iraq).

My boy Darryl gave me a smack on the ass as I walked past. I've known Darryl since we were still in diapers and escaping from play-school, and I've been getting him into and out of trouble the whole time. I raised my arms over my head like a prizefighter and made my exit from Social Studies and began the perp-walk to the office.

I was halfway there when my phone went. That was another no-no—phones are muy prohibido at Chavez High—but why should that stop me? I ducked into the toilet and shut myself in the middle stall (the farthest stall is always grossest because so many people head straight for it, hoping to escape the smell and the squick—the smart money and good hygiene is down the middle). I checked the phone—my home PC had sent it an email to tell it that there was something new up on Harajuku Fun Madness, which happens to be the best game ever invented.

I grinned. Spending Fridays at school was teh suck anyway, and I was glad of the excuse to make my escape.

I ambled the rest of the way to Benson's office and tossed him a wave as I sailed through the door.

"If it isn't Double-you-one-enn-five-tee-zero-enn," he said. Fredrick Benson—Social Security number 545–03–2343, date of birth August 15 1962, mother's maiden name Di Bona, home-town Petaluma—is a lot taller than me. I'm a runty 5'8", while he stands 6'7", and his college basketball days are far enough be-hind him that his chest muscles have turned into saggy man-boobs that were painfully obvious through his freebie dot-com polo shirts. He always looks like he's about to slam-dunk your ass, and he's really into raising his voice for dramatic effect. Both these start to lose their efficacy with repeated application.

"Sorry, nope," I said. "I never heard of this R2D2 character of yours."

"W1n5t0n," he said, spelling it out again. He gave me a hairy eyeball and waited for me to wilt. Of course it was my handle, and had been for years. It was the identity I used when I was post-ing on message boards where I was making my contributions to the field of applied security research. You know, like sneaking out of school and disabling the minder-tracer on my phone. But he didn't know that this was my handle. Only a small number of people did, and I trusted them all to the end of the earth.

"Um, not ringing any bells," I said. I'd done some pretty cool stuff around school using that handle—I was very proud of my work on snitch-tag killers—and if he could link the two identities, I'd be in trouble. No one at school ever called me w1n5t0n or even Winston. Not even my pals. It was Marcus or nothing.

Benson settled down behind his desk and tapped his class ring nervously on his blotter. He did this whenever things started to go bad for him. Poker players call stuff like this a "tell"—something that lets you know what's going on in the other guy's head. I knew Benson's tells backwards and forwards.

"Marcus, I hope you realize how serious this is."

"I will just as soon as you explain what this is, sir." I always say "sir" to authority figures when I'm messing with them. It's my own tell.

He shook his head at me and looked down, another tell. Any second now, he was going to start shouting at me. "Listen, kiddo! It's time you came to grips with the fact that we know about what you've been doing, and that we're not going to be lenient about it. You're going to be lucky if you're not expelled before this meeting is through. Do you want to graduate?"

"Mr. Benson, you still haven't explained what the problem is—"

He slammed his hand down on the desk and then pointed his finger at me. "The *problem,* Mr. Yallow, is that you've been engaged in criminal conspiracy to subvert this school's security system, and you have supplied security countermeasures to your fellow students. You know that we expelled Graciella Uriarte last week for using one of your devices." Uriarte had gotten a bad rap. She'd bought a radio-jammer from a head shop near the 16th Street BART station and it had set off the countermeasures in the school hallway. Not my doing, but I felt for her.

"And you think I'm involved in that?"

"We have reliable intelligence indicating that you are w1n5t0n"—again, he spelled it out, and I began to wonder if he hadn't figured out that the 1 was an I and the 5 was an S. "We know that this w1n5t0n character is reponsible for the theft of last year's standardized tests." That actually hadn't been me, but it was a sweet hack, and it was kind of flattering to hear it attributed to me. "And therefore liable for several years in prison unless you cooperate with me."

"You have 'reliable intelligence'? I'd like to see it."

He glowered at me. "Your attitude isn't going to help you."

"If there's evidence, sir, I think you should call the police and turn it over to them. It sounds like this is a very serious matter, and I wouldn't want to stand in the way of a proper investigation by the duly constituted authorities."

"You want me to call the police."

"And my parents, I think. That would be for the best."

We stared at each other across the desk. He'd clearly expected me to fold the second he dropped the bomb on me. I don't fold. I have a trick for staring down people like Benson. I look slightly to the left of their heads, and think about the lyrics to old Irish folk songs, the kind with three hundred verses. It makes me look perfectly composed and unworried.

And the wing was on the bird and the bird was on the egg and the egg was in the nest and the nest was on the leaf and the leaf was on the twig and the twig was on the branch and the branch was on the limb and the limb was in the tree and the tree was in the bog—the bog down in the valley-oh! High-ho the rattlin' bog, the bog down in the valley-oh—

"You can return to class now," he said. "I'll call on you once the police are ready to speak to you."

"Are you going to call them now?"

"The procedure for calling in the police is complicated. I'd hoped that we could settle this fairly and quickly, but since you insist—"

"I can wait while you call them is all," I said. "I don't mind."

He tapped his ring again and I braced for the blast.

"Go!" he yelled. "Get the hell out of my office, you miserable little—"

I got out, keeping my expression neutral. He wasn't going to call the cops. If he'd had enough evidence to go to the police with, he would have called them in the first place. He hated my guts. I figured he'd heard some unverified gossip and hoped to spook me into confirming it.

I moved down the corridor lightly and sprightly, keeping my gait even and measured for the gait-recognition cameras. These had been installed only a year before, and I loved them for their sheer idiocy. Beforehand, we'd had face-recognition cameras covering nearly every public space in school, but a court ruled that was unconstitutional. So Benson and a lot of other paranoid school administrators had spent our textbook dollars on these idiot cameras that were supposed to be able to tell one person's walk from another. Yeah, right.

I got back to class and sat down again, Ms. Galvez warmly welcoming me back. I unpacked the school's standard-issue machine and got back into classroom mode. The SchoolBooks were the snitchiest technology of them all, logging every keystroke, watching all the network traffic for suspicious keywords, counting every click, keeping track of every fleeting thought you put out over the net. We'd gotten them in my junior year, and it only took a couple months for the shininess to wear off. Once people figured out that these "free" laptops worked for the man—and showed a never-ending parade of obnoxious ads to boot—they suddenly started to feel very heavy and burdensome.

Cracking my SchoolBook had been easy. The crack was online within a month of the machine showing up, and there was nothing to it—just download a DVD image, burn it, stick it in the SchoolBook, and boot it while holding down a bunch of different keys at the same time. The DVD did the rest, installing a whole bunch of hidden programs on the machine, programs that would stay hidden even when the Board of Ed did its daily remote integrity checks of the machines. Every now and again I had to get an update for the software to get around the Board's latest tests, but it was a small price to pay to get a little control over the box.

I fired up IMParanoid, the secret instant messenger that I used when I wanted to have an off-the-record discussion right in the middle of class. Darryl was already logged in.

> **The game's afoot! Something big is going down with Harajuku Fun Madness, dude. You in?**

> **No. Freaking. Way. If I get caught ditching a third time, I'm expelled. Man, you know that. We'll go after school.**

> **You've got lunch and then study hall, right? That's two hours. Plenty of time to run down this clue and get back before anyone misses us. I'll get the whole team out.**

Harajuku Fun Madness is the best game ever made. I know I already said that, but it bears repeating. It's an ARG, an Alternate Reality Game, and the story goes that a gang of Japanese fashion-teens discovered a miraculous healing gem at the temple in Harajuku, which is basically where cool Japanese teenagers invented every major subculture for the past ten years. They're being hunted by evil monks, the Yakuza (aka the Japanese mafia), aliens, tax inspectors, parents, and a rogue artificial intelligence. They slip the players coded messages that we have to decode and use to track down clues that lead to more coded messages and more clues.

Imagine the best afternoon you've ever spent prowling the streets of a city, checking out all the weird people, funny handbills, street maniacs, and funky shops. Now add a scavenger hunt to that, one that requires you to research crazy old films and songs and teen culture from around the world and across time and space. And it's a competition, with the winning team of four taking a grand prize of ten days in Tokyo, chilling on Harajuku bridge, geeking out in Akihabara, and taking home all the Astro Boy merchandise you can eat. Except that he's called "Atom Boy" in Japan.

That's Harajuku Fun Madness, and once you've solved a puzzle or two, you'll never look back.

> No man, just no. NO. Don't even ask.

> I need you D. You're the best I've got. I swear I'll get us in and out without anyone knowing it. You know I can do that, right?

> I know you can do it

> So you're in?

> Hell no

> Come on, Darryl. You're not going to your deathbed wishing you'd spent more study periods sitting in school

> I'm not going to go to my deathbed wishing I'd spent more time playing ARGs either

> Yeah but don't you think you might go to your deathbed wishing you'd spent more time with Vanessa Pak?

Van was part of my team. She went to a private girl's school in the East Bay, but I knew she'd ditch to come out and run the mission with me. Darryl has had a crush on her literally for years—even before puberty endowed her with many lavish gifts. Darryl had fallen in love with her mind. Sad, really.

> You suck

> You're coming?

He looked at me and shook his head. Then he nodded. I winked at him and set to work getting in touch with the rest of my team.

I wasn't always into ARGing. I have a dark secret: I used to be a LARPer. LARPing is Live Action Role Playing, and it's just about what it sounds like: running around in costume, talking in a funny accent, pretending to be a superspy or a vampire or a medieval knight. It's like Capture the Flag in monster-drag, with a bit of Drama Club thrown in, and the best games were the ones we played in Scout Camps out of town in Sonoma or down on the Peninsula. Those three-day epics could get pretty hairy, with all-day hikes, epic battles with foam-and-bamboo swords, casting spells by throwing beanbags and shouting "Fireball!" and so on. Good fun, if a little goofy. Not nearly as geeky as talking about what your elf planned on doing as you sat around a table loaded with Diet Coke cans and painted miniatures, and more physically active than going into a mouse-coma in front of a massively multiplayer game at home.

The thing that got me into trouble were the minigames in the hotels. Whenever a science fiction convention came to town, some LARPer would convince them to let us run a couple of six-hour minigames at the con, piggybacking on their rental of the space. Having a bunch of enthusiastic kids running around in costume lent color to the event, and we got to have a ball among people even more socially deviant than us.

The problem with hotels is that they have a lot of nongamers in them, too—and not just sci-fi people. Normal people. From states that begin and end with vowels. On holidays.

And sometimes those people misunderstand the nature of a game.

Let's just leave it at that, okay?

Class ended in ten minutes, and that didn't leave me with much time to prepare. The first order of business was those pesky gait-recognition cameras. Like I said, they'd started out as face-recognition cameras, but those had been ruled unconstitutional. As far as I know, no court has yet determined whether these gait-cams are any more legal, but until they do, we're stuck with them.

"Gait" is a fancy word for the way you walk. People are pretty good at spotting gaits—next time you're on a camping trip, check out the bobbing of the flashlight as a distant friend approaches you. Chances are you can identify him just from the movement of the light, the characteristic way it bobs up and down that tells our monkey brains that this is a person approaching us.

Gait-recognition software takes pictures of your motion, tries to isolate you in the pics as a silhouette, and then tries to match the silhouette to a database to see if it knows who you are. It's a biometric identifier, like fingerprints or retina-scans, but it's got a lot more "collisions" than either of those. A biometric "collision" is when a measurement matches more than one person. Only you have your fingerprint, but you share your gait with plenty other people.

Not exactly, of course. Your personal, inch-by-inch walk is yours and yours alone. The problem is your inch-by-inch walk changes based on how tired you are, what the floor is made of, whether you pulled your ankle playing basketball, and whether you've changed your shoes lately. So the system kind of fuzzes out your profile, looking for people who walk kind of like you.

There are a lot of people who walk kind of like you. What's more, it's easy not to walk kind of like you—just take one shoe off. Of course, you'll always walk like you-with-one-shoe-off in that case, so the cameras will eventually figure out that it's still you. Which is why I prefer to inject a little randomness into my attacks on gait-recognition: I put a handful of gravel into each shoe. Cheap and effective, and no two steps are the same. Plus you get a great reflexology foot massage in the process. (I kid. Reflexology is about as scientifically useful as gait-recognition.)

The cameras used to set off an alert every time someone they didn't recognize stepped onto campus.

This did *not* work.

The alarm went off every ten minutes. When the mailman came by. When a parent dropped in. When the groundspeople went to work fixing up the basketball court. When a student showed up wearing new shoes.

So now it just tries to keep track of who's where, when. If someone leaves by the school gates during classes, their gait is checked to see if it kinda-sorta matches any student gait and if it does, whoop-whoop-whoop, ring the alarm!

Chavez High is ringed with gravel walkways. I like to keep a couple handsful of rocks in my shoulder bag, just in case. I silently passed Darryl ten or fifteen pointy little bastards and we both loaded our shoes.

Class was about to finish up—and I realized that I still hadn't checked the Harajuku Fun Madness site to see where the next clue was! I'd been a little hyperfocused on the escape, and hadn't bothered to figure out where we were escaping *to*.

I turned to my SchoolBook and hit the keyboard. The web browser we used was supplied with the machine. It was a locked-down spyware version of Internet Explorer, Microsoft's crash-ware turd that no one under the age of forty used voluntarily.

I had a copy of Firefox on the USB drive built into my watch, but that wasn't enough—the SchoolBook ran Windows Vista4Schools, an antique operating system designed to give school administrators the illusion that they controlled the programs their students could run.

But Vista4Schools is its own worst enemy. There are a lot of programs that Vista4Schools doesn't want you to be able to shut down—keyloggers, censorware—and these programs run in a special mode that makes them invisible to the system. You can't quit them because you can't even see they're there.

Any program whose name starts with SYS is invisible to the operating system. It doesn't show up on listings of the hard drive, nor in the process monitor. So my copy of Firefox was called SYSFirefox—and as I launched it, it became invisible to Windows, and thus invisible to the network's snoopware.

Now that I had an indie browser running, I needed an indie network connection. The school's network logged every click in and out of the system, which was bad news if you were planning on surfing over to the Harajuku Fun Madness site for some extracurricular fun.

The answer is something ingenious called TOR—The Onion Router. An onion router is an Internet site that takes requests for web pages and passes them onto other onion routers, and on to other onion routers, until one of them finally decides to fetch the page and pass it back through the layers of the onion until it reaches you. The traffic to the onion routers is encrypted, which means that the school can't see what you're asking for, and the layers of the onion don't know who they're working for. There are millions of nodes—the program was set up by the U.S. Office of Naval Research to help their people get around the censorware in countries like Syria and China, which means that it's perfectly designed for operating in the confines of an average American high school.

TOR works because the school has a finite blacklist of naughty addresses we aren't allowed to visit, and the addresses of the nodes change all the time—no way could the school keep track of them all. Firefox and TOR together made me into the invisible man, impervious to Board of Ed snooping, free to check out the Harajuku FM site and see what was up.

There it was, a new clue. Like all Harajuku Fun Madness

clues, it had a physical, online and mental component. The online component was a puzzle you had to solve, one that required you to research the answers to a bunch of obscure questions. This batch included a bunch of questions on the plots in dōjinshi—those are comic books drawn by fans of manga, Japanese comics. They can be as big as the official comics that inspire them, but they're a lot weirder, with crossover storylines and sometimes really silly songs and action. Lots of love stories, of course. Everyone loves to see their favorite toons hook up.

I'd have to solve those riddles later, when I got home. They were easiest to solve with the whole team, downloading tons of dōjinshi files and scouring them for answers to the puzzles.

I'd just finished scrap-booking all the clues when the bell rang and we began our escape. I surreptitiously slid the gravel down the side of my short boots—ankle-high Blundstones from Australia, great for running and climbing, and the easy slip-on/slip-off laceless design makes them convenient at the never-ending metal detectors that are everywhere now.

We also had to evade physical surveillance, of course, but that gets easier every time they add a new layer of physical snoopery—all the bells and whistles lull our beloved faculty into a totally false sense of security. We surfed the crowd down the hallways, heading for my favorite side-exit. We were halfway along when Darryl hissed, "Crap! I forgot, I've got a library book in my bag."

"You're kidding me," I said, and hauled him into the next bathroom we passed. Library books are bad news. Every one of them has an arphid—Radio Frequency ID tag—glued into its binding, which makes it possible for the librarians to check out the books by waving them over a reader, and lets a library shelf tell you if any of the books on it are out of place.

But it also lets the school track where you are at all times. It was another of those legal loopholes: the courts wouldn't let the schools track *us* with arphids, but they could track *library books,* and use the school records to tell them who was likely to be carrying which library book.

I had a little Faraday pouch in my bag—these are little wallets lined with a mesh of copper wires that effectively block radio energy, silencing arphids. But the pouches were made for neutralizing ID cards and toll-book transponders, not books like—

"Introduction to Physics?" I groaned. The book was the size of a dictionary.

Chapter 2

"I'm thinking of majoring in physics when I go to Berkeley," Darryl said. His dad taught at the University of California at Berkeley, which meant he'd get free tuition when he went. And there'd never been any question in Darryl's household about whether he'd go.

"Fine, but couldn't you research it online?"

"My dad said I should read it. Besides, I didn't plan on committing any crimes today."

"Skipping school isn't a crime. It's an infraction. They're totally different."

"What are we going to do, Marcus?"

"Well, I can't hide it, so I'm going to have to nuke it." Killing arphids is a dark art. No merchant wants malicious customers going for a walk around the shop floor and leaving behind a bunch of lobotomized merchandise that is missing its invisible bar code, so the manufacturers have refused to implement a "kill signal" that you can radio to an arphid to get it to switch off. You can reprogram arphids with the right box, but I hate doing that to library books. It's not exactly tearing pages out of a book, but it's still bad, since a book with a reprogrammed arphid can't be shelved and can't be found. It just becomes a needle in a haystack.

That left me with only one option: nuking the thing. Literally. Thirty seconds in a microwave will do in pretty much every arphid on the market. And because the arphid wouldn't answer at all when D checked it back in at the library, they'd just print a fresh one for it and recode it with the book's catalog info, and it would end up clean and neat back on its shelf.

All we needed was a microwave.

"Give it another two minutes and the teachers' lounge will be empty," I said.

Darryl grabbed his book and headed for the door. "Forget it, no way. I'm going to class."

I snagged his elbow and dragged him back. "Come on, D, easy now. It'll be fine."

"The *teachers' lounge*? Maybe you weren't listening, Marcus. If I get busted *just once more,* I am *expelled*. You hear that? *Expelled.*"

"You won't get caught," I said. The one place a teacher wouldn't be after this period was the lounge. "We'll go in the back way." The lounge had a little kitchenette off to one side, with its own entrance for teachers who just wanted to pop in and get a cup of joe. The microwave—which always reeked of popcorn and spilled soup—was right in there, on top of the miniature fridge.

Darryl groaned. I thought fast. "Look, the bell's *already rung*. If you go to study hall now, you'll get a late slip. Better not to show at all at this point. I can infiltrate and exfiltrate any room on this campus, D. You've seen me do it. I'll keep you safe, bro."

He groaned again. That was one of Darryl's tells: once he starts groaning, he's ready to give in.

"Let's roll," I said, and we took off.

It was flawless. We skirted the classrooms, took the back stairs into the basement, and came up the front stairs right in front of the teachers' lounge. Not a sound came from the door, and I quietly turned the knob and dragged Darryl in before silently closing the door.

The book just barely fit in the microwave, which was looking even less sanitary than it had the last time I'd popped in here to use it. I conscientiously wrapped it in paper towels before I set it down. "Man, teachers are *pigs,*" I hissed. Darryl, white-faced and tense, said nothing.

The arphid died in a shower of sparks, which was really quite lovely (though not nearly as pretty as the effect you get when you nuke a frozen grape, which has to be seen to be believed).

Now, to exfiltrate the campus in perfect anonymity and make our escape.

Darryl opened the door and began to move out, me on his heels. A second later, he was standing on my toes, elbows jammed into my chest, as he tried to backpedal into the closet-sized kitchen we'd just left.

"Get back," he whispered urgently. "Quick—it's Charles!"

Charles Walker and I don't get along. We're in the same grade, and we've known each other as long as I've known Darryl, but that's where the resemblance ends. Charles has always been big for his age, and now that he's playing football and on the juice, he's even bigger. He's got anger management problems—I lost a milk tooth to him in the third grade—and he's managed to keep from getting in trouble over them by becoming the most active snitch in school.

It's a bad combination, a bully who also snitches, taking great pleasure in going to the teachers with whatever infractions he's found. Benson *loved* Charles. Charles liked to let on that he had some kind of unspecified bladder problem, which gave him a ready-made excuse to prowl the hallways at Chavez, looking for people to fink on.

The last time Charles had caught some dirt on me, it had ended with me giving up LARPing. I had no intention of being caught by him again.

"What's he doing?"

"He's coming this way is what he's doing," Darryl said. He was shaking.

"Okay," I said. "Okay, time for emergency countermeasures." I got my phone out. I'd planned this well in advance. Charles would never get me again. I emailed my server at home, and it got into motion.

A few seconds later, Charles's phone spazzed out spectacularly. I'd had tens of thousands of simultaneous random calls and text messages sent to it, causing every chirp and ring it had to go off and keep going off. The attack was accomplished by means of a botnet, and for that I felt bad, but it was in the service of a good cause.

Botnets are where infected computers spend their afterlives. When you get a worm or a virus, your computer sends a message to a chat channel on IRC—the Internet Relay Chat. That message tells the botmaster—the guy who deployed the worm—that the computer in there is ready to do his bidding. Botnets are supremely powerful, since they can comprise thousands, even hundreds of thousands of computers, scattered all over the Internet, connected to juicy high-speed connections and running on fast home PCs. Those PCs normally function on behalf of their owners, but when the botmaster calls them, they rise like zombies to do his bidding.

There are so many infected PCs on the Internet that the price of hiring an hour or two on a botnet has crashed. Mostly these things work for spammers as cheap, distributed spambots, filling your mailbox with come-ons for boner-pills or with new viruses that can infect you and recruit your machine to join the botnet.

I'd just rented ten seconds' time on three thousand PCs and had each of them send a text message or voice-over-IP call to Charles's phone, whose number I'd extracted from a sticky note on Benson's desk during one fateful office visit.

Needless to say, Charles's phone was not equipped to handle this. First the SMSes filled the memory on his phone, causing it to start choking on the routine operations it needed to do things like manage the ringer and log all those incoming calls' bogus return numbers (did you know that it's *really easy* to fake the return number on a caller ID? There are about fifty ways of doing it—just google "spoof caller id").

Charles stared at it dumbfounded, and jabbed at it furiously, his thick eyebrows knotting and wiggling as he struggled with the demons that had possessed his most personal of devices. The plan was working so far, but he wasn't doing what he was supposed to be doing next—he was supposed to go find some place to sit down and try to figure out how to get his phone back.

Darryl shook me by the shoulder, and I pulled my eye away from the crack in the door.

"What's he doing?" Darryl whispered.

"I totaled his phone, but he's just staring at it now instead of moving on." It wasn't going to be easy to reboot that thing. Once the memory was totally filled, it would have a hard time loading the code it needed to delete the bogus messages—and there was no bulk-erase for texts on his phone, so he'd have to manually delete all of the thousands of messages.

Darryl shoved me back and stuck his eye up to the door. A moment later, his shoulders started to shake. I got scared, thinking he was panicking, but when he pulled back, I saw that he was laughing so hard that tears were streaming down his cheeks.

"Galvez just totally busted him for being in the halls during class *and* for having his phone out—you should have seen her tear into him. She was really enjoying it."

We shook hands solemnly and snuck back out of the corridor, down the stairs, around the back, out the door, past the fence and out into the glorious sunlight of afternoon in the Mission. Valencia Street had never looked so good. I checked my watch and yelped.

"Let's move! The rest of the gang is meeting us at the cable cars in twenty minutes!"

Van spotted us first. She was blending in with a group of Korean tourists, which is one of her favorite ways of camouflaging herself when she's ditching school. Ever since the truancy moblog went live, our world is full of nosy shopkeepers and pecksniffs who take it upon themselves to snap our piccies and put them on the net where they can be perused by school administrators.

She came out of the crowd and bounded toward us. Darryl has had a thing for Van since forever, and she's sweet enough to pretend she doesn't know it. She gave me a hug and then moved onto Darryl, giving him a quick sisterly kiss on the cheek that made him go red to the tops of his ears.

The two of them made a funny pair: Darryl is a little on the heavy side, though he wears it well, and he's got a kind of pink complexion that goes red in the cheeks whenever he runs or gets excited. He's been able to grow a beard since we were fourteen, but thankfully he started shaving after a brief period known to our gang as "the Lincoln years." And he's tall. Very, very tall. Like basketball player tall.

Meanwhile, Van is half a head shorter than me, and skinny, with straight black hair that she wears in crazy, elaborate braids that she researches on the net. She's got pretty coppery skin and dark eyes, and she loves big glass rings the size of radishes, which click and clack together when she dances.

"Where's Jolu?" she said.

"How are you, Van?" Darryl asked in a choked voice. He always ran a step behind the conversation when it came to Van.

"I'm great, D. How's your every little thing?" Oh, she was a bad, bad person. Darryl nearly fainted.

Jolu saved him from social disgrace by showing up just then, in an oversize leather baseball jacket, sharp sneakers, and a mesh-back cap advertising our favorite Mexican masked wrestler, El Santo Junior. Jolu is Jose-Luis Torrez, the completing member of our foursome. He went to a super-strict Catholic school in the Outer Richmond, so it wasn't easy for him to get out. But he always did: no one exfiltrated like our Jolu. He liked his jacket because it hung down low—which was pretty stylish in parts of the city—and covered up all his Catholic school crap, which was like a bull's-eye for nosy jerks with the truancy moblog bookmarked on their phones.

"Who's ready to go?" I asked, once we'd all said hello. I pulled out my phone and showed them the map I'd downloaded to it on the BART. "Near as I can work out, we wanna go up to the Nikko again, then one block past it to O'Farrell, then left up toward Van Ness. Somewhere in there we should find the wireless signal."

Van made a face. "That's a nasty part of the Tenderloin." I couldn't argue with her. That part of San Francisco is one of the weird bits—you go in through the Hilton's front entrance and it's all touristy stuff like the cable car turnaround and family restaurants. Go through to the other side and you're in the 'Loin, where every tracked out transvestite hooker, hard-case pimp, hissing drug dealer and cracked up homeless person in town was concentrated. What they bought and sold, none of us were old enough to be a part of (though there were plenty of hookers our age plying their trade in the 'Loin).

"Look on the bright side," I said. "The only time you want to go up around there is broad daylight. None of the other players are going to go near it until tomorrow at the earliest. This is what we in the ARG business call a *monster head start*."

Jolu grinned at me. "You make it sound like a good thing," he said.

"Beats eating uni," I said.

"We going to talk or we going to win?" Van said. After me, she was hands down the most hardcore player in our group. She took winning very, very seriously.

We struck out, four good friends, on our way to decode a clue, win the game—and lose everything we cared about, forever.

The physical component of today's clue was a set of GPS coordinates—there were coordinates for all the major cities where Harajuku Fun Madness was played—where we'd find a WiFi access point's signal. That signal was being deliberately jammed by another, nearby WiFi point that was hidden so that it couldn't be spotted by conventional wifinders, little key-fobs that told you when you were within range of someone's open access point, which you could use for free.

We'd have to track down the location of the "hidden" access point by measuring the strength of the "visible" one, finding the spot where it was most mysteriously weakest. There we'd find another clue—last time it had been in the special of the day at Anzu, the swanky sushi restaurant in the Nikko hotel in the Tenderloin. The Nikko was owned by Japan Airlines, one of Harajuku Fun Madness's sponsors, and the staff had all made a big fuss over us when we finally tracked down the clue. They'd given us bowls of miso soup and made us try uni, which is sushi made from sea urchin, with the texture of very runny cheese and a smell like very runny dog droppings. But it tasted *really* good. Or so Darryl told me. I wasn't going to eat that stuff.

I picked up the WiFi signal with my phone's wifinder about three blocks up O'Farrell, just before Hyde Street, in front of a dodgy "Asian Massage Parlor" with a red blinking CLOSED sign in the window. The network's name was HarajukuFM, so we knew we had the right spot.

"If it's in there, I'm not going," Darryl said.

"You all got your wifinders?" I said.

Darryl and Van had phones with built-in wifinders, while Jolu, being too cool to carry a phone bigger than his pinky finger, had a separate little directional fob.

"Okay, fan out and see what we see. You're looking for a sharp drop-off in the signal that gets worse the more you move along it."

I took a step backwards and ended up standing on someone's toes. A female voice said "oof" and I spun around, worried that some crack ho was going to stab me for breaking her heels.

Instead, I found myself face to face with another kid my age. She had a shock of bright pink hair and a sharp, rodentlike face, with big sunglasses that were practically Air Force goggles. She was dressed in striped tights beneath a black granny dress, with lots of little Japanese decorer toys safety pinned to it—anime characters, old world leaders, emblems from foreign soda pop.

She held up a camera and snapped a picture of me and my crew.

"Cheese," she said. "You're on candid snitch-cam."

"No way," I said. "You wouldn't—"

"I will," she said. "I will send this photo to truant watch in thirty seconds unless you four back off from this clue and let me and my friends here run it down. You can come back in one hour and it'll be all yours. I think that's more than fair."

I looked behind her and noticed three other girls in similar garb—one with blue hair, one with green, and one with purple. "Who are you supposed to be, the Popsicle Squad?"

"We're the team that's going to kick your team's ass at Harajuku Fun Madness," she said. "And I'm the one who's *right this second* about to upload your photo and get you in *so much trouble*—"

Behind me I felt Van start forward. Her all-girls school was notorious for its brawls, and I was pretty sure she was ready to knock this chick's block off.

Then the world changed forever.

We felt it first, that sickening lurch of the cement under your feet that every Californian knows instinctively—*earthquake*. My first inclination, as always, was to get away: "When in trouble or in doubt, run in circles, scream and shout." But the fact was, we were already in the safest place we could be, not in a building that could fall in on us, not out toward the middle of the road where bits of falling mortice could brain us.

Earthquakes are eerily quiet—at first, anyway—but this wasn't quiet. This was loud, an incredible roaring sound that was louder than anything I'd ever heard before. The sound was so punishing it drove me to my knees, and I wasn't the only one.

Darryl shook my arm and pointed over the buildings and we saw it then: a huge black cloud rising from the northeast, from the direction of the Bay.

There was another rumble, and the cloud of smoke spread out, that spreading black shape we'd all grown up seeing in movies. Someone had just blown up something, in a big way.

There were more rumbles and more tremors. Heads appeared at windows up and down the street. We all looked at the mushroom cloud in silence.

Then the sirens started.

I'd heard sirens like these before—they test the civil defense sirens at noon on Tuesdays. But I'd only heard them go off unscheduled in old war movies and video games, the kind where someone is bombing someone else from above. Air raid sirens. The wooooooo sound made it all less real.

"Report to shelters immediately." It was like the voice of God, coming from all places at once. There were speakers on some of the electric poles, something I'd never noticed before, and they'd all switched on at once.

"Report to shelters immediately." Shelters? We looked at each other in confusion. What shelters? The cloud was rising steadily, spreading out. Was it nuclear? Were we breathing our last breaths?

The girl with the pink hair grabbed her friends and they tore ass downhill, back toward the BART station and the foot of the hills.

"REPORT TO SHELTERS IMMEDIATELY." There was screaming now, and a lot of running around. Tourists—you can always spot the tourists, they're the ones who think CALIFOR-NIA = WARM and spend their San Francisco holidays freezing in shorts and T-shirts—scattered in every direction.

"We should go!" Darryl hollered in my ear, just barely audible over the shrieking of the sirens, which had been joined by traditional police sirens. A dozen SFPD cruisers screamed past us.

"REPORT TO SHELTERS IMMEDIATELY."

"Down to the BART station," I hollered. My friends nodded. We closed ranks and began to move quickly downhill.

Chapter 3

We passed a lot of people in the road on the way to the Powell Street BART. They were running or walking, white-faced and silent or shouting and panicked. Homeless people cowered in doorways and watched it all, while a tall black tranny hooker shouted at two mustached young men about something.

The closer we got to the BART, the worse the press of bodies became. By the time we reached the stairway down into the station, it was a mob scene, a huge brawl of people trying to crowd their way down a narrow staircase. I had my face crushed up against someone's back, and someone else was pressed into my back.

Darryl was still beside me—he was big enough that he was hard to shove, and Jolu was right behind him, kind of hanging on to his waist. I spied Vanessa a few yards away, trapped by more people.

"Screw you!" I heard Van yell behind me. "Pervert! Get your hands off of me!"

I strained around against the crowd and saw Van looking with disgust at an older guy in a nice suit who was kind of smirking at her. She was digging in her purse and I knew what she was digging for.

"Don't mace him!" I shouted over the din. "You'll get us all, too."

At the mention of the word mace, the guy looked scared and kind of melted back, though the crowd kept him moving forward. Up ahead, I saw someone, a middle-aged lady in a hippie dress, falter and fall. She screamed as she went down, and I saw her thrashing to get up, but she couldn't, the crowd's pressure was too strong. As I neared her, I bent to help her up, and was nearly knocked over her. I ended up stepping on her stomach as the crowd pushed me past her, but by then I don't think she was feeling anything.

I was as scared as I'd ever been. There was screaming everywhere now, and more bodies on the floor, and the press from behind was as relentless as a bulldozer. It was all I could do to keep on my feet.

We were in the open concourse where the turnstiles were. It was hardly any better here—the enclosed space sent the voices around us echoing back in a roar that made my head ring, and the smell and feeling of all those bodies made me feel a claustrophobia I'd never known I was prone to.

People were still cramming down the stairs, and more were squeezing past the turnstiles and down the escalators onto the platforms, but it was clear to me that this wasn't going to have a happy ending.

"Want to take our chances up top?" I said to Darryl.

"Yes, hell yes," he said. "This is vicious."

I looked to Vanessa—there was no way she'd hear me. I managed to get my phone out and I texted her.

> **We're getting out of here**

I saw her feel the vibe from her phone, then look down at it and then back at me and nod vigorously. Darryl, meanwhile, had clued Jolu in.

"What's the plan?" Darryl shouted in my ear.

"We're going to have to go back!" I shouted back, pointing at the remorseless crush of bodies.

"It's impossible!" he said.

"It's just going to get more impossible the longer we wait!"

He shrugged. Van worked her way over to me and grabbed hold of my wrist. I took Darryl's and Darryl took Jolu by the other hand and we pushed out.

It wasn't easy. We moved about three inches a minute at first, then slowed down even more when we reached the stairway. The people we passed were none too happy about us shoving them out of the way, either. A couple people swore at us and there was a guy who looked like he'd have punched me if he'd been able to get his arms loose. We passed three more crushed people beneath us, but there was no way I could have helped them. By that point, I wasn't even thinking of helping anyone. All I could think of was finding the spaces in front of us to move into, of Darryl's mighty straining on my wrist, of my death grip on Van behind me.

We popped free like champagne corks an eternity later, blinking in the gray smoky light. The air raid sirens were still blaring, and the sound of emergency vehicles' sirens as they tore down Market Street was even louder. There was almost no one on the streets anymore—just the people trying hopelessly to get underground. A lot of them were crying. I spotted a bunch of empty benches—usually staked out by skanky winos—and pointed toward them.

We moved for them, the sirens and the smoke making us duck and hunch our shoulders. We got as far as the benches before Darryl fell forward.

We all yelled and Vanessa grabbed him and turned him over. The side of his shirt was stained red, and the stain was spreading.

She tugged his shirt up and revealed a long, deep cut in his pudgy side.

"Someone freaking *stabbed* him in the crowd," Jolu said, his hands clenching into fists. "Christ, that's vicious."

Darryl groaned and looked at us, then down at his side, then he groaned and his head went back again.

Vanessa took off her jean jacket and then pulled off the cotton hoodie she was wearing underneath it. She wadded it up and pressed it to Darryl's side. "Take his head," she said to me. "Keep it elevated." To Jolu she said, "Get his feet up—roll up your coat or something." Jolu moved quickly. Vanessa's mother is a nurse and she'd had first aid training every summer at camp. She loved to watch people in movies get their first aid wrong and make fun of them. I was so glad to have her with us.

We sat there for a long time, holding the hoodie to Darryl's side. He kept insisting that he was fine and that we should let him up, and Van kept telling him to shut up and lie still before she kicked his ass.

"What about calling 911?" Jolu said.

I felt like an idiot. I whipped my phone out and punched 911. The sound I got wasn't even a busy signal—it was like a whimper of pain from the phone system. You don't get sounds like that unless there's three million people all dialing the same number at once. Who needs botnets when you've got terrorists?

"What about Wikipedia?" Jolu said.

"No phone, no data," I said.

"What about them?" Darryl said, and pointed at the street. I looked where he was pointing, thinking I'd see a cop or a paramedic, but there was no one there.

"It's okay buddy, you just rest," I said.

"No, you idiot, what about *them,* the cops in the cars? There!"

He was right. Every five seconds, a cop car, an ambulance or a firetruck zoomed past. They could get us some help. I was such an idiot.

"Come on, then," I said, "let's get you where they can see you and flag one down."

Vanessa didn't like it, but I figured a cop wasn't going to stop for a kid waving his hat in the street, not that day. They just might stop if they saw Darryl bleeding there, though. I argued briefly with her and Darryl settled it by lurching to his feet and dragging himself down toward Market Street.

The first vehicle that screamed past—an ambulance—didn't even slow down. Neither did the cop car that went past, nor the fire truck, nor the next three cop cars. Darryl wasn't in good shape—he was white-faced and panting. Van's sweater was soaked in blood.

I was sick of cars driving right past me. The next time a car appeared down Market Street, I stepped right out into the road, waving my arms over my head, shouting *"STOP."* The car slowed to a stop and only then did I notice that it wasn't a cop car, ambulance or fire engine.

It was a military-looking Jeep, like an armored Hummer, only it didn't have any military insignia on it. The car skidded to a stop just in front of me, and I jumped back and lost my balance and ended up on the road. I felt the doors open near me, and then saw a confusion of booted feet moving close by. I looked up and saw a bunch of military-looking guys in coveralls, holding big, bulky rifles and wearing hooded gas masks with tinted faceplates.

I barely had time to register them before those rifles were pointed at me. I'd never looked down the barrel of a gun before, but everything you've heard about the experience is true. You freeze where you are, time stops, and your heart thunders in your ears. I opened my mouth, then shut it, then, very slowly, I held my hands up in front of me.

The faceless, eyeless armed man above me kept his gun very level. I didn't even breathe. Van was screaming something and Jolu was shouting and I looked at them for a second and that was when someone put a coarse sack over my head and cinched it tight around my windpipe, so quick and so fiercely I barely had time to gasp before it was locked on me. I was pushed roughly but dispassionately onto my stomach and something went twice around my wrists and then tightened up as well, feeling like baling wire and biting cruelly. I cried out and my own voice was muffled by the hood.

I was in total darkness now and I strained my ears to hear what was going on with my friends. I heard them shouting through the muffling canvas of the bag, and then I was being impersonally hauled to my feet by my wrists, my arms wrenched up behind my back, my shoulders screaming.

I stumbled some, then a hand pushed my head down and I was inside the Hummer. More bodies were roughly shoved in beside me.

"Guys?" I shouted, and earned a hard thump on my head for my trouble. I heard Jolu respond, then felt the thump he was dealt, too. My head rang like a gong.

"Hey," I said to the soldiers. "Hey, listen! We're just high school students. I wanted to flag you down because my friend was bleeding. Someone stabbed him." I had no idea how much of this was making it through the muffling bag. I kept talking. "Listen—this is some kind of misunderstanding. We've got to get my friend to a hospital—"

Someone went upside my head again. It felt like they used a baton or something—it was harder than anyone had ever hit me in the head before. My eyes swam and watered and I literally couldn't breathe through the pain. A moment later, I caught my breath, but I didn't say anything. I'd learned my lesson.

Who were these clowns? They weren't wearing insignia. Maybe they were terrorists! I'd never really believed in terrorists before—I mean, I knew that in the abstract there were terrorists somewhere in the world, but they didn't really represent any risk to me. There were millions of ways that the world could kill me— starting with getting run down by a drunk burning his way down Valencia—that were infinitely more likely and immediate than terrorists. Terrorists killed a lot less people than bathroom falls and accidental electrocutions. Worrying about them always struck me as about as useful as worrying about getting hit by lightning.

Sitting in the back of that Hummer, my head in a hood, my hands lashed behind my back, lurching back and forth while the bruises swelled up on my head, terrorism suddenly felt a lot riskier.

The car rocked back and forth and tipped uphill. I gathered we were headed over Nob Hill, and from the angle, it seemed we were taking one of the steeper routes—I guessed Powell Street.

Now we were descending just as steeply. If my mental map was right, we were heading down to Fisherman's Wharf. You could get on a boat there, get away. That fit with the terrorism hypothesis. Why the hell would terrorists kidnap a bunch of high school students?

We rocked to a stop still on a downslope. The engine died and then the doors swung open. Someone dragged me by my arms out onto the road, then shoved me, stumbling, down a paved road. A few seconds later, I tripped over a steel staircase, bashing my shins. The hands behind me gave me another shove. I went up the stairs cautiously, not able to use my hands. I got up the third step and reached for the fourth, but it wasn't there.

I nearly fell again, but new hands grabbed me from in front and dragged me down a steel floor and then forced me to my knees and locked my hands to something behind me.

More movement, and the sense of bodies being shackled in alongside of me. Groans and muffled sounds. Laughter. Then a long, timeless eternity in the muffled gloom, breathing my own breath, hearing my own breath in my ears.

I actually managed a kind of sleep there, kneeling with the circulation cut off to my legs, my head in canvas twilight. My body had squirted a year's supply of adrenaline into my bloodstream in the space of thirty minutes, and while that stuff can give you the strength to lift cars off your loved ones and leap over tall buildings, the payback's always a bitch.

I woke up to someone pulling the hood off my head. They were neither rough nor careful—just . . . impersonal. Like someone at McDonald's putting together burgers.

The light in the room was so bright I had to squeeze my eyes shut, but slowly I was able to open them to slits, then cracks, then all the way and look around.

We were all in the back of a truck, a big 16-wheeler. I could see the wheel wells at regular intervals down the length. But the back of this truck had been turned into some kind of mobile command-post/jail. Steel desks lined the walls with banks of slick flat-panel displays climbing above them on articulated arms that let them be repositioned in a halo around the operators. Each desk had a gorgeous office chair in front of it, festooned with user-interface knobs for adjusting every millimeter of the sitting surface, as well as height, pitch and yaw.

Then there was the jail part—at the front of the truck, farthest away from the doors, there were steel rails bolted into the

sides of the vehicle, and attached to these steel rails were the prisoners.

I spotted Van and Jolu right away. Darryl might have been in
the remaining dozen shackled up back here, but it was impossible
to say—many of them were slumped over and blocking my view.
It stank of sweat and fear back there.

Vanessa looked at me and bit her lip. She was scared. So was I.
So was Jolu, his eyes rolling crazily in their sockets, the whites
showing. I was scared. What's more, I had to piss like a *racehorse*.

I looked around for our captors. I'd avoided looking at them
up until now, the same way you don't look into the dark of a
closet where your mind has conjured up a boogeyman. You
don't want to know if you're right.

But I had to get a better look at these jerks who'd kidnapped
us. If they were terrorists, I wanted to know. I didn't know what
a terrorist looked like, though TV shows had done their best to
convince me that they were brown Arabs with big beards and
knit caps and loose cotton dresses that hung down to their
ankles.

Not so our captors. They could have been halftime-show
cheerleaders on the Super Bowl. They looked *American* in a way
I couldn't exactly define. Good jawlines, short, neat haircuts that
weren't quite military. They came in white and brown, male and
female, and smiled freely at one another as they sat down at the
other end of the truck, joking and drinking coffee out of go-
cups. These weren't Ay-rabs from Afghanistan: they looked like
tourists from Nebraska.

I stared at one, a young white woman with brown hair who
barely looked older than me, kind of cute in a scary office-
power-suit way. If you stare at someone long enough, they'll
eventually look back at you. She did, and her face slammed into

a totally different configuration, dispassionate, even robotic. The smile vanished in an instant.

"Hey," I said. "Look, I don't understand what's going on here, but I really need to take a leak, you know?"

She looked right through me as if she hadn't heard.

"I'm serious, if I don't get to a can soon, I'm going to have an ugly accident. It's going to get pretty smelly back here, you know?"

She turned to her colleagues, a little huddle of three of them, and they held a low conversation I couldn't hear over the fans from the computers.

She turned back to me. "Hold it for another ten minutes, then you'll each get a piss-call."

"I don't think I've got another ten minutes in me," I said, letting a little more urgency than I was really feeling creep into my voice. "Seriously, lady, it's now or never."

She shook her head and looked at me like I was some kind of pathetic loser. She and her friends conferred some more, then another one came forward. He was older, in his early thirties, and pretty big across the shoulders, like he worked out. He looked like he was Chinese or Korean—even Van can't tell the difference sometimes—but with that bearing that said *American* in a way I couldn't put my finger on.

He pulled his sports coat aside to let me see the hardware strapped there: I recognized a pistol, a tazer and a can of either mace or pepper spray before he let it fall again.

"No trouble," he said.

"None," I agreed.

He touched something at his belt and the shackles behind me let go, my arms dropping suddenly behind me. It was like he was wearing Batman's utility belt—wireless remotes for shackles!

I guessed it made sense, though: you wouldn't want to lean over your prisoners with all that deadly hardware at their eye level—they might grab your gun with their teeth and pull the trigger with their tongues or something.

My hands were still lashed together behind me by the plastic strapping, and now that I wasn't supported by the shackles, I found that my legs had turned into lumps of cork while I was stuck in one position. Long story short, I basically fell onto my face and kicked my legs weakly as they went pins-and-needles, trying to get them under me so I could rock up to my feet.

The guy jerked me to my feet and I clown-walked to the very back of the truck, to a little boxed-in porta-john there. I tried to spot Darryl on the way back, but he could have been any of the five or six slumped people. Or none of them.

"In you go," the guy said.

I jerked my wrists. "Take these off, please?" My fingers felt like purple sausages from the hours of bondage in the plastic cuffs.

The guy didn't move.

"Look," I said, trying not to sound sarcastic or angry (it wasn't easy). "Look. You either cut my wrists free or you're going to have to aim for me. A toilet visit is not a hands-free experience." Someone in the truck sniggered. The guy didn't like me, I could tell from the way his jaw muscles ground around. Man, these people were wired tight.

He reached down to his belt and came up with a very nice set of multipliers. He flicked out a wicked-looking knife and sliced through the plastic cuffs and my hands were my own again.

"Thanks," I said.

He shoved me into the bathroom. My hands were useless, like lumps of clay on the ends of my wrists. As I wiggled my fingers limply, they tingled, then the tingling turned to a burning feeling that almost made me cry out. I put the seat down, dropped my pants and sat down. I didn't trust myself to stay on my feet.

As my bladder cut loose, so did my eyes. I wept, crying silently and rocking back and forth while the tears and snot ran down my face. It was all I could do to keep from sobbing—I covered my mouth and held the sounds in. I didn't want to give them the satisfaction.

Finally, I was peed out and cried out and the guy was pounding on the door. I cleaned my face as best as I could with wads of toilet paper, stuck it all down the john and flushed, then looked around for a sink but only found a pump-bottle of heavy-duty hand-sanitizer covered in small-print lists of the bio-agents it worked on. I rubbed some into my hands and stepped out of the john.

"What were you doing in there?" the guy said.

"Using the facilities," I said. He turned me around and grabbed my hands and I felt a new pair of plastic cuffs go around them. My wrists had swollen since the last pair had come off and the new ones bit cruelly into my tender skin, but I refused to give him the satisfaction of crying out.

He shackled me back to my spot and grabbed the next person down, who, I saw now, was Jolu, his face puffy and an ugly bruise on his cheek.

"Are you okay?" I asked him, and my friend with the utility belt abruptly put his hand on my forehead and shoved hard, bouncing the back of my head off the truck's metal wall with a sound like a clock striking one. "No talking," he said as I struggled to refocus my eyes.

I didn't like these people. I decided right then that they would pay a price for all this.

One by one, all the prisoners went to the can and came back, and when they were done, my guard went back to his friends and had another cup of coffee—they were drinking out of a big cardboard urn of Starbucks, I saw—and they had an indistinct conversation that involved a fair bit of laughter.

Then the door at the back of the truck opened and there was fresh air—not smoky the way it had been before, but tinged with ozone. In the slice of outdoors I saw before the door closed, I caught that it was dark out, and raining, with one of those San Francisco drizzles that's part mist.

The man who came in was wearing a military uniform. A U.S. military uniform. He saluted the people in the truck and they saluted him back and that's when I knew that I wasn't a prisoner of some terrorists—I was a prisoner of the United States of America.

They set up a little screen at the end of the truck and then came for us one at a time, unshackling us and leading us to the back of the truck. As close as I could work it—counting seconds off in my head, one hippopotami, two hippopotami—the interviews lasted about seven minutes each. My head throbbed with dehydration and caffeine withdrawal.

I was third, brought back by the woman with the severe haircut. Up close, she looked tired, with bags under her eyes and grim lines at the corners of her mouth.

"Thanks," I said, automatically, as she unlocked me with a remote and then dragged me to my feet. I hated myself for the automatic politeness, but it had been drilled into me.

She didn't twitch a muscle. I went ahead of her to the back of the truck and behind the screen. There was a single folding chair and I sat in it. Two of them—severe haircut lady and utility belt man—looked at me from their ergonomic superchairs.

They had a little table between them with the contents of my wallet and backpack spread out on it.

"Hello, Marcus," severe haircut lady said. "We have some questions for you."

"Am I under arrest?" I asked. This wasn't an idle question. If you're not under arrest, there are limits on what the cops can and can't do to you. For starters, they can't hold you forever without arresting you, giving you a phone call, and letting you talk to a lawyer. And hoo-boy, was I ever going to talk to a lawyer.

"What's this for?" she said, holding up my phone. The screen was showing the error message you got if you kept trying to get into its data without giving the right password. It was a bit of a rude message—an animated hand giving a certain universally recognized gesture—because I liked to customize my gear.

"Am I under arrest?" I repeated. They can't make you answer any questions if you're not under arrest, and when you ask if you're under arrest, they have to answer you. It's the rules.

"You're being detained by the Department of Homeland Security," the woman snapped.

"Am I under arrest?"

"You're going to be more cooperative, Marcus, starting right now." She didn't say, "or else," but it was implied.

"I would like to contact an attorney," I said. "I would like to know what I've been charged with. I would like to see some form of identification from both of you."

The two agents exchanged looks.

"I think you should really reconsider your approach to this situation," severe haircut lady said. "I think you should do that right now. We found a number of suspicious devices on your person. We found you and your confederates near the site of the worst terrorist attack this country has ever seen. Put those two facts together and things don't look very good for you, Marcus. You can cooperate, or you can be very, very sorry. Now, what is this for?"

"You think I'm a terrorist? I'm seventeen years old!"

"Just the right age—Al Qaeda loves recruiting impressionable, idealistic kids. We googled you, you know. You've posted a lot of very ugly stuff on the public Internet."

"I would like to speak to an attorney," I said.

Severe haircut lady looked at me like I was a bug. "You're under the mistaken impression that you've been picked up by the police for a crime. You need to get past that. You are being detained as a potential enemy combatant by the government of the United States. If I were you, I'd be thinking very hard about how to convince us that you are not an enemy combatant. Very hard. Because there are dark holes that enemy combatants can disappear into, very dark deep holes, holes where you can just vanish. Forever. Are you listening to me young man? I want you to unlock this phone and then decrypt the files in its memory. I want you to account for yourself: Why were you out on the street? What do you know about the attack on this city?"

"I'm not going to unlock my phone for you," I said, indignant. My phone's memory had all kinds of private stuff on it: photos, emails, little hacks and mods I'd installed. "That's private stuff."

"What have you got to hide?"

"I've got the right to my privacy," I said. "And I want to speak to an attorney."

"This is your last chance, kid. Honest people don't have anything to hide."

"I want to speak to an attorney." My parents would pay for it. All the FAQs on getting arrested were clear on this point. Just keep asking to see an attorney, no matter what they say or do. There's no good that comes of talking to the cops without your lawyer present. These two said they weren't cops, but if this wasn't an arrest, what was it?

In hindsight, maybe I should have unlocked my phone for them.

Chapter 4

They reshackled and rehooded me and left me there. A long time later, the truck started to move, rolling down-hill, and then I was hauled back to my feet. I immediately fell over. My legs were so asleep they felt like blocks of ice, all except my knees, which were swollen and tender from all the hours of kneeling.

Hands grabbed my shoulders and feet and I was picked up like a sack of potatoes. There were indistinct voices around me. Someone crying. Someone cursing.

I was carried a short distance, then set down and reshackled to another railing. My knees wouldn't support me anymore and I pitched forward, ending up twisted on the ground like a pretzel, straining against the chains holding my wrists.

Then we were moving again, and this time, it wasn't like driving in a truck. The floor beneath me rocked gently and vibrated with heavy diesel engines and I realized I was on a ship! My stomach turned to ice. I was being taken off America's shores to somewhere *else,* and who the hell knew where that was? I'd been scared before, but this thought *terrified* me, left me paralyzed and wordless with fear. I realized that I might never see my parents again and I actually tasted a little vomit burn up my throat. The bag over my head closed in on me and I could barely breathe, something that was compounded by the weird position I was twisted into.

But mercifully we weren't on the water for very long. It felt like an hour, but I know now that it was a mere fifteen minutes, and then I felt us docking, felt footsteps on the decking around me and felt other prisoners being unshackled and carried or led away. When they came for me, I tried to stand again, but couldn't, and they carried me again, impersonally, roughly.

When they took the hood off again, I was in a cell.

The cell was old and crumbled, and smelled of sea air. There was one window high up, and rusted bars guarded it. It was still dark outside. There was a blanket on the floor and a little metal toilet without a seat, set into the wall. The guard who took off my hood grinned at me and closed the solid steel door behind him.

I gently massaged my legs, hissing as the blood came back into them and into my hands. Eventually I was able to stand, and then to pace. I heard other people talking, crying, shouting. I did some shouting too: "Jolu! Darryl! Vanessa!" Other voices on the cell-block took up the cry, shouting out names, too, shouting out obscenities. The nearest voices sounded like drunks losing their minds on a street corner. Maybe I sounded like that, too.

Guards shouted at us to be quiet and that just made everyone yell louder. Eventually we were all howling, screaming our heads off, screaming our throats raw. Why not? What did we have to lose?

The next time they came to question me, I was filthy and tired, thirsty and hungry. Severe haircut lady was in the new questioning party, as were three big guys who moved me around like a cut of meat. One was black, the other two were white, though one might have been hispanic. They all carried guns. It was like a Benneton's ad crossed with a game of Counter-Strike.

They'd taken me from my cell and chained my wrists and ankles together. I paid attention to my surroundings as we went. I heard water outside and thought that maybe we were on Alcatraz—it was a prison, after all, even if it had been a tourist attraction for generations, the place where you went to see where Al Capone and his gangster contemporaries did their time. But I'd been to Alcatraz on a school trip. It was old and rusted, medieval. This place felt like it dated back to World War Two, not colonial times.

There were bar codes laser-printed on stickers and placed on each of the cell doors, and numbers, but other than that, there was no way to tell who or what might be behind them.

The interrogation room was modern, with fluorescent lights, ergonomic chairs—not for me, though, I got a folding plastic garden chair—and a big wooden boardroom table. A mirror lined one wall, just like in the cop shows, and I figured someone or other must be watching from behind it. Severe haircut lady and her friends helped themselves to coffee from an urn on a side table (I could have torn her throat out with my teeth and taken her coffee just then), and then set a styrofoam cup of water down next to me—without unlocking my wrists from behind my back, so I couldn't reach it. Hardy har har.

"Hello, Marcus," severe haircut lady said. "How's your 'tude doing today?"

I didn't say anything.

"This isn't as bad as it gets you know," she said. "This is as *good* as it gets from now on. Even once you tell us what we want to know, even if that convinces us that you were just in the wrong place at the wrong time, you're a marked man now. We'll be watching you everywhere you go and everything you do. You've acted like you've got something to hide, and we don't like that."

It's pathetic, but all my brain could think about was that phrase, "convince us that you were in the wrong place at the wrong time." This was the worst thing that had ever happened to me. I had never, ever felt this bad or this scared before. Those words, "wrong place at the wrong time," those six words, they were like a lifeline dangling before me as I thrashed to stay on the surface.

"Hello, Marcus?" She snapped her fingers in front of my face. "Over here, Marcus." There was a little smile on her face and I hated myself for letting her see my fear. "Marcus, it can be a lot worse than this. This isn't the worst place we can put you, not by a damned sight." She reached down below the table and came out with a briefcase, which she snapped open. From it, she withdrew my phone, my arphid sniper/cloner, my wifinder and my memory keys. She set them down on the table one after the other.

"Here's what we want from you. You unlock the phone for us today. If you do that, you'll get outdoor and bathing privileges. You'll get a shower and you'll be allowed to walk around in the exercise yard. Tomorrow, we'll bring you back and ask you to decrypt the data on these memory sticks. Do that, and you'll get to eat in the mess hall. The day after, we're going to want your email passwords, and that will get you library privileges."

The word "no" was on my lips, like a burp trying to come up, but it wouldn't come. "Why?" is what came out instead.

"We want to be sure that you're what you seem to be. This is about your security, Marcus. Say you're innocent. You might be, though why an innocent man would act like he's got so much to hide is beyond me. But say you are: you could have been on that bridge when it blew. Your parents could have been. Your friends. Don't you want us to catch the people who attacked your home?"

It's funny, but when she was talking about my getting "privileges" it scared me into submission. I felt like I'd done *something* to end up where I was, like maybe it was partially my fault, like I could do something to change it.

But as soon as she switched to this BS about "safety" and "security," my spine came back. "Lady," I said, "you're talking about attacking my home, but as far as I can tell, you're the only one who's attacked me lately. I thought I lived in a country with a constitution. I thought I lived in a country where I had *rights*. You're talking about defending my freedom by tearing up the Bill of Rights."

A flicker of annoyance passed over her face, then went away. "So melodramatic, Marcus. No one's attacked you. You've been detained by your country's government while we seek details on the worst terrorist attack ever perpetrated on our nation's soil. You have it within your power to help us fight this war on our nation's enemies. You want to preserve the Bill of Rights? Help us stop bad people from blowing up your city. Now, you have exactly thirty seconds to unlock that phone before I send you back to your cell. We have lots of other people to interview today."

She looked at her watch. I rattled my wrists, rattled the chains that kept me from reaching around and unlocking the phone. Yes, I was going to do it. She'd told me what my path was to freedom—to the world, to my parents—and that had given me hope. Now she'd threatened to send me away, to take me off that path, and my hope had crashed and all I could think of was how to get back on it.

So I rattled my wrists, wanting to get to my phone and unlock it for her, and she just looked at me coldly, checking her watch.

"The password," I said, finally understanding what she wanted of me. She wanted me to say it out loud, here, where she could record it, where her pals could hear it. She didn't want me to just unlock the phone. She wanted me to submit to her. To put her in charge of me. To give up every secret, all my privacy. "The password," I said again, and then I told her the password. God help me, I submitted to her will.

She smiled a little prim smile, which had to be her ice-queen equivalent of a touchdown dance, and the guards led me away. As the door closed, I saw her bend down over the phone and key the password in.

I wish I could say that I'd anticipated this possibility in advance and created a fake password that unlocked a completely innocuous partition on my phone, but I wasn't nearly that paranoid/ clever.

You might be wondering at this point what dark secrets I had locked away on my phone and memory sticks and email. I'm just a kid, after all.

The truth is that I had everything to hide, and nothing. Between my phone and my memory sticks, you could get a pretty good idea of who my friends were, what I thought of them, all the goofy things we'd done. You could read the transcripts of the electronic arguments we'd carried out and the electronic reconciliations we'd arrived at.

You see, I don't delete stuff. Why would I? Storage is cheap, and you never know when you're going to want to go back to that stuff. Especially the stupid stuff. You know that feeling you get sometimes where you're sitting on the subway and there's no one to talk to and you suddenly remember some bitter fight you had, some terrible thing you said? Well, it's usually never as bad as you remember. Being able to go back and see it again is a great way to remind yourself that you're not as horrible a person as you think you are. Darryl and I have gotten over more fights that way than I can count.

And even that's not it. I know my phone is private. I know my memory sticks are private. That's because of cryptography—message scrambling. The math behind crypto is good and solid, and you and me get access to the same crypto that banks and the National Security Agency use. There's only one kind of crypto that anyone uses: crypto that's public, open and can be deployed by anyone. That's how you know it works.

There's something really liberating about having some corner of your life that's *yours,* that no one gets to see except you. It's a little like nudity or taking a dump. Everyone gets naked every once in a while. Everyone has to squat on the toilet. There's nothing shameful, deviant or weird about either of them. But what if I decreed that from now on, every time you went to evacuate some solid waste, you'd have to do it in a glass room perched in the middle of Times Square, and you'd be buck naked?

Even if you've got nothing wrong or weird with your body—and how many of us can say that?—you'd have to be pretty strange to like that idea. Most of us would run screaming. Most of us would hold it in until we exploded.

It's not about doing something shameful. It's about doing something *private.* It's about your life belonging to you.

They were taking that from me, piece by piece. As I walked back to my cell, that feeling of deserving it came back to me. I'd broken a lot of rules all my life and I'd gotten away with it, by and large. Maybe this was justice. Maybe this was my past coming back to me. After all, I had been where I was because I'd snuck out of school.

I got my shower. I got to walk around the yard. There was a

patch of sky overhead, and it smelled like the Bay Area, but beyond that, I had no clue where I was being held. No other prisoners were visible during my exercise period, and I got pretty bored with walking in circles. I strained my ears for any sound that might help me understand what this place was, but all I heard was the occasional vehicle, some distant conversations, a plane landing somewhere nearby.

They brought me back to my cell and fed me, a half a pepperoni pie from Goat Hill Pizza, which I knew well, up on Potrero Hill. The carton with its familiar graphic and 415 phone number was a reminder that only a day before, I'd been a free man in a free country and that now I was a prisoner. I worried constantly about Darryl and fretted about my other friends. Maybe they'd been more cooperative and had been released. Maybe they'd told my parents and they were frantically calling around.

Maybe not.

The cell was fantastically spare, empty as my soul. I fantasized that the wall opposite my bunk was a screen that I could be hacking right now, opening the cell door. I fantasized about my workbench and the projects there—the old cans I was turning into a ghetto surround-sound rig, the aerial photography kitecam I was building, my home-brew laptop.

I wanted to get out of there. I wanted to go home and have my friends and my school and my parents and my life back. I wanted to be able to go where I wanted to go, not be stuck pacing and pacing and pacing.

They took my passwords for my USB keys next. Those held some interesting messages I'd downloaded from one online discussion group or another, some chat transcripts, things where people had helped me out with some of the knowledge I needed to do the things I did. There was nothing on there you couldn't find with Google, of course, but I didn't think that would count in my favor.

I got exercise again that afternoon, and this time there were others in the yard when I got there, four other guys and two women, of all ages and racial backgrounds. I guess lots of people were doing things to earn their "privileges."

They gave me half an hour, and I tried to make conversation with the most normal-seeming of the other prisoners, a black guy about my age with a short afro. But when I introduced myself and stuck my hand out, he cut his eyes toward the cameras mounted ominously in the corners of the yard and kept walking without ever changing his facial expression.

But then, just before they called my name and brought me back into the building, the door opened and out came—Vanessa! I'd never been more glad to see a friendly face. She looked tired and grumpy, but not hurt, and when she saw me, she shouted my name and ran to me. We hugged each other hard and I realized I was shaking. Then I realized she was shaking, too.

"Are you okay?" she said, holding me at arms' length.

"I'm okay," I said. "They told me they'd let me go if I gave them my passwords."

"They keep asking me questions about you and Darryl."

There was a voice blaring over the loudspeaker, shouting at us to stop talking, to walk, but we ignored it.

"Answer them," I said, instantly. "Anything they ask, answer them. If it'll get you out."

"How are Darryl and Jolu?"

"I haven't seen them."

The door banged open and four big guards boiled out. Two took me and two took Vanessa. They forced me to the ground and turned my head away from Vanessa, though I heard her getting the same treatment. Plastic cuffs went around my wrists and then I was yanked to my feet and brought back to my cell.

No dinner came that night. No breakfast came the next morning. No one came and brought me to the interrogation room to extract more of my secrets. The plastic cuffs didn't come off, and my shoulders burned, then ached, then went numb, then burned again. I lost all feeling in my hands.

I had to pee. I couldn't undo my pants. I really, really had to pee.

I pissed myself.

They came for me after that, once the hot piss had cooled and gone clammy, making my already filthy jeans stick to my legs. They came for me and walked me down the long hall lined with doors, each door with its own bar code, each bar code a prisoner like me. They walked me down the corridor and brought me to the interrogation room and it was like a different planet when I entered there, a world where things were normal, where everything didn't reek of urine. I felt so dirty and ashamed, and all those feelings of deserving what I got came back to me.

Severe haircut lady was already sitting. She was perfect: coifed and with just a little makeup. I smelled her hair stuff. She wrinkled her nose at me. I felt the shame rise in me.

"Well, you've been a very naughty boy, haven't you? Aren't you a filthy thing?"

Shame. I looked down at the table. I couldn't bear to look up. I wanted to tell her my email password and get gone.

"What did you and your friend talk about in the yard?"

I barked a laugh at the table. "I told her to answer your questions. I told her to cooperate."

"So do you give the orders?"

I felt the blood sing in my ears. "Oh come on," I said. "We play a *game* together, it's called Harajuku Fun Madness. I'm the *team captain*. We're not terrorists, we're high school students. I don't give her orders. I told her that we needed to be *honest* with you so that we could clear up any suspicion and get out of here."

She didn't say anything for a moment.

"How is Darryl?" I said.

"Who?"

"Darryl. You picked us up together. My friend. Someone had stabbed him in the Powell Street BART. That's why we were up on the surface. To get him help."

"I'm sure he's fine, then," she said.

My stomach knotted and I almost threw up. "You don't *know*? You haven't got him here?"

"Who we have here and who we don't have here is not something we're going to discuss with you, ever. That's not something you're going to know. Marcus, you've seen what happens when you don't cooperate with us. You've seen what happens when you disobey our orders. You've been a little cooperative, and it's gotten you almost to the point where you might go free again. If you want to make that possibility into a reality, you'll stick to answering my questions."

I didn't say anything.

"You're learning, that's good. Now, your email passwords, please."

I was ready for this. I gave them everything: server address, login, password. This didn't matter. I didn't keep any email on my server. I downloaded it all and kept it on my laptop at home, which downloaded and deleted my mail from the server every sixty seconds. They wouldn't get anything out of my mail—it got cleared off the server and stored on my laptop at home.

Back to the cell, but they cut loose my hands and they gave me a shower and a pair of orange prison pants to wear. They were too big for me and hung down low on my hips, like a Mexican gang kid in the Mission. That's where the baggy-pants-down-your-ass look comes from you know that? From prison. I tell you what, it's less fun when it's not a fashion statement.

They took away my jeans, and I spent another day in the cell. The walls were scratched cement over a steel grid. You could tell, because the steel was rusting in the salt air, and the grid shone through the green paint in red-orange. My parents were out that window, somewhere.

They came for me again the next day.

"We've been reading your mail for a day now. We changed the password so that your home computer couldn't fetch it."

Well, of course they had. I would have done the same, now that I thought of it.

"We have enough on you now to put you away for a very long time, Marcus. Your possession of these articles"—she gestured at all my little gizmos—"and the data we recovered from your phone and memory sticks, as well as the subversive material we'd no doubt find if we raided your house and took your computer. It's enough to put you away until you're an old man. Do you understand that?"

I didn't believe it for a second. There's no way a judge would say that all this stuff constituted any kind of real crime. It was free speech, it was technological tinkering. It wasn't a crime.

But who said that these people would ever put me in front of a judge.

"We know where you live, we know who your friends are. We know how you operate and how you think."

It dawned on me then. They were about to let me go. The

room seemed to brighten. I heard myself breathing, short little breaths.

"We just want to know one thing: what was the delivery mechanism for the bombs on the bridge?"

I stopped breathing. The room darkened again.

"What?"

"There were ten charges on the bridge, all along its length. They weren't in car trunks. They'd been placed there. Who placed them there, and how did they get there?"

"What?" I said it again.

"This is your last chance, Marcus," she said. She looked sad. "You were doing so well until now. Tell us this and you can go home. You can get a lawyer and defend yourself in a court of law. There are doubtless extenuating circumstances that you can use to explain your actions. Just tell us this thing, and you're gone."

"I don't know what you're talking about!" I was crying and I didn't even care. Sobbing, blubbering. "I have *no idea what you're talking about!*"

She shook her head. "Marcus, please. Let us help you. By now you know that we always get what we're after."

There was a gibbering sound in the back of my mind. They were *insane*. I pulled myself together, working hard to stop the tears. "Listen, lady, this is nuts. You've been into my stuff, you've seen it all. I'm a seventeen-year-old high school student, not a terrorist! You can't seriously think—"

"Marcus, haven't you figured out that we're serious yet?" She shook her head. "You get pretty good grades. I thought you'd be smarter than that." She made a flicking gesture and the guards picked me up by the armpits.

Back in my cell, a hundred little speeches occurred to me. The French call this *esprit d'escalier*—the spirit of the staircase, the snappy rebuttals that come to you after you leave the room and slink down the stairs. In my mind, I stood and delivered, telling her that I was a citizen who loved my freedom, which made me the patriot and made her the traitor. In my mind, I shamed her for turning my country into an armed camp. In my mind, I was eloquent and brilliant and reduced her to tears.

But you know what? None of those fine words came back to me when they pulled me out the next day. All I could think of was freedom. My parents.

"Hello, Marcus," she said. "How are you feeling?"

I looked down at the table. She had a neat pile of documents in front of her, and her ubiquitous go-cup of Starbucks beside her. I found it comforting somehow, a reminder that there was a real world out there somewhere, beyond the walls.

"We're through investigating you, for now." She let that hang there. Maybe it meant that she was letting me go. Maybe it meant that she was going to throw me in a pit and forget that I existed.

"And?" I said finally.

"And I want to impress on you again that we are very serious about this. Our country has experienced the worst attack ever committed on its soil. How many 9/11s do you want us to suffer before you're willing to cooperate? The details of our investigation are secret. We won't stop at anything in our efforts to bring the perpetrators of these heinous crimes to justice. Do you understand that?"

"Yes," I mumbled.

"We are going to send you home today, but you are a marked man. You have not been found to be above suspicion—we're only releasing you because we're done questioning you for now. But from now on, you *belong* to us. We will be watching you.

We'll be waiting for you to make a misstep. Do you understand that we can watch you closely, all the time?"

"Yes," I mumbled.

"Good. You will never speak of what happened here to anyone, ever. This is a matter of national security. Do you know that the death penalty still holds for treason in time of war?"

"Yes," I mumbled.

"Good boy," she purred. "We have some papers here for you to sign." She pushed the stack of papers across the table to me. Little Post-its with SIGN HERE printed on them had been stuck throughout them. A guard undid my cuffs.

I paged through the papers and my eyes watered and my head swam. I couldn't make sense of them. I tried to decipher the legalese. It seemed that I was signing a declaration that I had been voluntarily held and submitted to voluntary questioning, of my own free will.

"What happens if I don't sign this?" I said.

She snatched the papers back and made that flicking gesture again. The guards jerked me to my feet.

"Wait!" I cried. "Please! I'll sign them!" They dragged me to the door. All I could see was that door, all I could think of was it closing behind me.

I lost it. I wept. I begged to be allowed to sign the papers. To be so close to freedom and have it snatched away, it made me ready to do anything. I can't count the number of times I've heard someone say, "Oh, I'd rather die than do something-or-other"—I've said it myself now and again. But that was the first time I understood what it really meant. I would have rather died than go back to my cell.

I begged as they took me out into the corridor. I told them I'd sign anything.

She called out to the guards and they stopped. They brought me back. They sat me down. One of them put the pen in my hand.

Of course, I signed, and signed and signed.

My jeans and T-shirt were back in my cell, laundered and folded. They smelled of detergent. I put them on and washed my face and sat on my cot and stared at the wall. They'd taken everything from me. First my privacy, then my dignity. I'd been ready to sign anything. I would have signed a confession that said I'd assassinated Abraham Lincoln.

I tried to cry, but it was like my eyes were dry, out of tears.

They got me again. A guard approached me with a hood, like the hood I'd been put in when they picked us up, whenever that was, days ago, weeks ago.

The hood went over my head and cinched tight at my neck. I was in total darkness and the air was stifling and stale. I was raised to my feet and walked down corridors, up stairs, on gravel. Up a gangplank. On a ship's steel deck. My hands were chained behind me, to a railing. I knelt on the deck and listened to the thrum of the diesel engines.

The ship moved. A hint of salt air made its way into the hood. It was drizzling and my clothes were heavy with water. I was outside, even if my head was in a bag. I was outside, in the world, moments from my freedom.

They came for me and led me off the boat and over uneven ground. Up three metal stairs. My wrists were unshackled. My hood was removed.

I was back in the truck. Severe haircut woman was there, at the little desk she'd sat at before. She had a Ziploc bag with her, and inside it were my phone and other little devices, my wallet and the change from my pockets. She handed them to me wordlessly.

I filled my pockets. It felt so weird to have everything back in its familiar place, to be wearing my familiar clothes. Outside the truck's back door, I heard the familiar sounds of my familiar city.

A guard passed me my backpack. The woman extended her hand to me. I just looked at it. She put it down and gave me a wry smile. Then she mimed zipping up her lips and pointed to me, and opened the door.

It was daylight outside, gray and drizzling. I was looking down an alley toward cars and trucks and bikes zipping down the road. I stood transfixed on the truck's top step, staring at freedom.

My knees shook. I knew now that they were playing with me again. In a moment, the guards would grab me and drag me back inside, the bag would go over my head again, and I would be back on the boat and sent off to the prison again, to the endless, unanswerable questions. I barely held myself back from stuffing my fist in my mouth.

Then I forced myself to go down one stair. Another stair. The last stair. My sneakers crunched down on the crap on the alley's floor, broken glass, a needle, gravel. I took a step. Another. I reached the mouth of the alley and stepped onto the sidewalk.

No one grabbed me.

I was free.

Then strong arms threw themselves around me. I nearly cried.

Chapter 5

But it was Van, and she *was* crying, and hugging me so hard I couldn't breathe. I didn't care. I hugged her back, my face buried in her hair.

"You're okay!" she said.

"I'm okay," I managed.

She finally let go of me and another set of arms wrapped themselves around me. It was Jolu! They were both there. He whispered, "You're safe, bro," in my ear and hugged me even tighter than Vanessa had.

When he let go, I looked around. "Where's Darryl?" I asked.

They both looked at each other. "Maybe he's still in the truck," Jolu said.

We turned and looked at the truck at the alley's end. It was a nondescript white 18-wheeler. Someone had already brought the little folding staircase inside. The rear lights glowed red, and the truck rolled backwards toward us, emitting a steady eep, eep, eep.

"Wait!" I shouted as it accelerated toward us. "Wait! What about Darryl?" The truck drew closer. I kept shouting. "What about Darryl?"

Jolu and Vanessa each had me by an arm and were dragging

me away. I struggled against them, shouting. The truck pulled
out of the alley's mouth and reversed into the street and pointed
itself downhill and drove away. I tried to run after it, but Van and
Jolu wouldn't let me go.

I sat down on the sidewalk and put my arms around my
knees and cried. I cried and cried and cried, loud sobs of the sort
I hadn't done since I was a little kid. They wouldn't stop coming.
I couldn't stop shaking.

Vanessa and Jolu got me to my feet and moved me a little
ways up the street. There was a Muni bus stop with a bench and
they sat me on it. They were both crying, too, and we held each
other for a while, and I knew we were crying for Darryl, whom
none of us ever expected to see again.

We were north of Chinatown, at the part where it
starts to become North Beach, a neighborhood with a bunch of
neon strip clubs and the legendary City Lights counterculture
bookstore, where the Beat poetry movement had been founded
back in the 1950s.

I knew this part of town well. My parents' favorite Italian
restaurant was here and they liked to take me here for big plates
of linguine and huge Italian ice cream mountains with candied
figs and lethal little espressos afterward.

Now it was a different place, a place where I was tasting freedom for the first time in what seemed like an enternity.

We checked our pockets and found enough money to get a
table at one of the Italian restaurants, out on the sidewalk, under
an awning. The pretty waitress lighted a gas heater with a barbe-
cue lighter, took our orders and went inside. The sensation of
giving orders, of controlling my destiny, was the most amazing
thing I'd ever felt.

"How long were we in there?" I asked.

"Six days," Vanessa said.

"I got five," Jolu said.

"I didn't count."

"What did they do to you?" Vanessa said. I didn't want to talk about it, but they were both looking at me. Once I started, I couldn't stop. I told them everything, even when I'd been forced to piss myself, and they took it all in silently. I paused when the waitress delivered our sodas and waited until she got out of earshot, then finished. In the telling, it receded into the distance. By the end of it, I couldn't tell if I was embroidering the truth or if I was making it all seem *less* bad. My memories swam like little fish that I snatched at, and sometimes they wriggled out of my grasp.

Jolu shook his head. "They were hard on you, dude," he said. He told us about his stay there. They'd questioned him, mostly about me, and he'd kept on telling them the truth, sticking to a plain telling of the facts about that day and about our friendship. They had gotten him to repeat it over and over again, but they hadn't played games with his head the way they had with me. He'd eaten his meals in a mess hall with a bunch of other people, and been given time in a TV room where they were shown last year's blockbusters on video.

Vanessa's story was only slightly different. After she'd gotten them angry by talking to me, they'd taken away her clothes and made her wear a set of orange prison coveralls. She'd been left in her cell for two days without contact, though she'd been fed regularly. But mostly it was the same as Jolu: the same questions, repeated again and again.

"They really hated you," Jolu said. "Really had it in for you. Why?"

I couldn't imagine why. Then I remembered.

You can cooperate, or you can be very, very sorry.

"It was because I wouldn't unlock my phone for them, that first night. That's why they singled me out." I couldn't believe it, but there was no other explanation. It had been sheer vindictiveness. My mind reeled at the thought. They had done all that as a mere punishment for defying their authority.

I had been scared. Now I was angry. "Those bastards," I said, softly. "They did it to get back at me for mouthing off."

Jolu swore and then Vanessa cut loose in Korean, something she only did when she was really, really angry.

"I'm going to get them," I whispered, staring at my soda. "I'm going to get them."

Jolu shook his head. "You can't, you know. You can't fight back against that."

None of us much wanted to talk about revenge then. Instead, we talked about what we would do next. We had to go home. Our phones' batteries were dead and it had been years since this neighborhood had any pay phones. We just needed to go home. I even thought about taking a taxi, but there wasn't enough money between us to make that possible.

So we walked. On the corner, we pumped some quarters into a *San Francisco Chronicle* newspaper box and stopped to read the front section. It had been five days since the bombs went off, but it was still all over the front cover.

Severe haircut woman had talked about "the bridge" blowing up, and I'd just assumed that she was talking about the Golden Gate bridge, but I was wrong. The terrorists had blown up the *Bay Bridge*.

"Why the hell would they blow up the Bay Bridge?" I said.

"The Golden Gate is the one on all the postcards." Even if you've never been to San Francisco, chances are you know what the Golden Gate looks like: it's that big orange suspension bridge that swoops dramatically from the old military base called the Presidio to Sausalito, where all the cutesy wine-country towns are with their scented candle shops and art galleries. It's picturesque as hell, and it's practically the symbol for the state of California. If you go to the Disneyland California Adventure park, there's a replica of it just past the gates, with a monorail running over it.

So naturally I assumed that if you were going to blow up a bridge in San Francisco, that's the one you'd blow.

"They probably got scared off by all the cameras and stuff," Jolu said. "The National Guard's always checking cars at both ends and there's all those suicide fences and junk all along it." People have been jumping off the Golden Gate since it opened in 1937—they stopped counting after the thousandth suicide in 1995.

"Yeah," Vanessa said. "Plus the Bay Bridge actually goes somewhere." The Bay Bridge goes from downtown San Francisco to Oakland and thence to Berkeley, the East Bay townships that are home to many of the people who live and work in town. It's one of the only parts of the Bay Area where a normal person can afford a house big enough to really stretch out in, and there's also the university and a bunch of light industry over there. The BART goes under the Bay and connects the two cities, too, but it's the Bay Bridge that sees most of the traffic. The Golden Gate was a nice bridge if you were a tourist or a rich retiree living out in wine country, but it was mostly ornamental. The Bay Bridge is—was—San Francisco's workhorse bridge.

I thought about it for a minute. "You guys are right," I said. "But I don't think that's all of it. We keep acting like terrorists attack landmarks because they hate landmarks. Terrorists don't hate landmarks or bridges or airplanes. They just want to screw stuff up and make people scared. To make terror. So of course they went after the Bay Bridge after the Golden Gate got all those cameras—after airplanes got all metal-detected and X-rayed." I thought about it some more, staring blankly at the cars rolling down the street, at the people walking down the sidewalks, at the city all around me. "Terrorists don't hate airplanes or bridges. They love terror." It was so obvious I couldn't believe I'd never thought of it before. I guess that being treated like a terrorist for a few days was enough to clarify my thinking.

The other two were staring at me. "I'm right, aren't I? All this crap, all the X-rays and ID checks, they're all useless, aren't they?"

They nodded slowly.

"Worse than useless," I said, my voice going up and cracking. "Because they ended up with us in prison, with Darryl—" I hadn't thought of Darryl since we sat down and now it came back to me: my friend, missing, disappeared. I stopped talking and ground my jaws together.

"We have to tell our parents," Jolu said.

"We should get a lawyer," Vanessa said.

I thought of telling my story. Of telling the world what had become of me. Of the videos that would no doubt come out, of me weeping, reduced to a groveling animal.

"We can't tell them anything," I said, without thinking.

"What do you mean?" Van said.

"We can't tell them anything," I repeated. "You heard her. If we talk, they'll come back for us. They'll do to us what they did to Darryl."

"You're joking," Jolu said. "You want us to—"

"I want us to fight back," I said. "I want to stay free so that I can do that. If we go out there and blab, they'll just say that we're kids, making it up. We don't even know where we were held! No one will believe us. Then, one day, they'll come for us.

"I'm telling my parents that I was in one of those camps on the other side of the Bay. I came over to meet you guys there and we got stranded, and just got loose today. They said in the papers that people were still wandering home from them."

"I can't do that," Vanessa said. "After what they did to you, how can you even think of doing that?"

"It happened to *me*, that's the point. This is me and them, now. I'll beat them, I'll get Darryl. I'm not going to take this lying down. But once our parents are involved, that's it for us. No one will believe us and no one will care. If we do it my way, people will care."

"What's your way?" Jolu said. "What's your plan?"

"I don't know yet," I admitted. "Give me until tomorrow morning, give me that, at least." I knew that once they'd kept it a secret for a day, it would have to be a secret forever. Our parents would be even more skeptical if we suddenly "remembered" that we'd been held in a secret prison instead of taken care of in a refugee camp.

Van and Jolu looked at each other.

"I'm just asking for a chance," I said. "We'll work out the story on the way, get it straight. Give me one day, just one day."

The other two nodded glumly and we set off downhill again, heading back toward home. I lived on Potrero Hill, Vanessa lived in the North Mission and Jolu lived in Noe Valley—three wildly different neighborhoods just a few minutes' walk from one another.

We turned onto Market Street and stopped dead. The street was barricaded at every corner, the cross streets reduced to a single lane, and parked down the whole length of Market Street were big, nondescript 18-wheelers like the one that had carried us, hooded, away from the ship's docks and to Chinatown.

Each one had three steel steps leading down from the back and they buzzed with activity as soldiers, people in suits and cops went in and out of them. The suits wore little badges on their lapels and the soldiers scanned them as they went in and out—wireless authorization badges. As we walked past one, I got a look at it, and saw the familiar logo: Department of Homeland Security. The soldier saw me staring and stared back hard, glaring at me.

I got the message and moved on. I peeled away from the gang at Van Ness. We clung to each other and cried and promised to call each other.

The walk back to Potrero Hill has an easy route and a hard route, the latter taking you over some of the steepest hills in the city, the kind of thing that you see car chases on in action movies, with cars catching air as they soar over the zenith. I always take the hard way home. It's all residential streets, and the old Victorian houses they call "painted ladies" for their gaudy, elaborate paint jobs, and front gardens with scented flowers and tall grasses. Housecats stare at you from hedges, and there are hardly any homeless.

It was so quiet on those streets that it made me wish I'd taken the *other* route, through the Mission, which is . . . *raucous* is probably the best word for it. Loud and vibrant. Lots of rowdy drunks and angry crackheads and unconscious junkies, and also lots of families with strollers, old ladies gossiping on stoops, lowriders with boom-cars going thumpa-thumpa-thumpa down the streets. There were hipsters and mopey emo art students and even a couple old-school punk rockers, old guys with pot bellies bulging out beneath their Dead Kennedys shirts. Also drag queens, angry gang kids, graffiti artists and bewildered gentrifiers trying not to get killed while their real estate investments matured.

I went up Goat Hill and walked past Goat Hill Pizza, which made me think of the jail I'd been held in, and I had to sit down on the bench out in front of the restaurant until my shakes passed. Then I noticed the truck up the hill from me, a nondescript 18-wheeler with three metal steps coming down from the back end. I got up and got moving. I felt the eyes watching me from all directions.

I hurried the rest of the way home. I didn't look at the painted ladies or the gardens or the housecats. I kept my eyes down.

Both my parents' cars were in the driveway, even though it was the middle of the day. Of course. Dad works in the East Bay, so he'd be stuck at home while they worked on the bridge. Mom—well, who knew why Mom was home.

They were home for me.

Even before I'd finished unlocking the door it had been jerked out of my hand and flung wide. There were both of my parents, looking gray and haggard, bug-eyed and staring at me. We stood there in frozen tableau for a moment, then they both rushed forward and dragged me into the house, nearly tripping me up. They were both talking so loud and fast all I could hear was a wordless, roaring gabble and they both hugged me and cried and I cried, too, and we just stood there like that in the little foyer, crying and making almost-words until we ran out of steam and went into the kitchen.

I did what I always did when I came home: got myself a glass of water from the filter in the fridge and dug a couple cookies out of the "biscuit barrel" that Mom's sister had sent us from England. The normalcy of this made my heart stop hammering, my heart catching up with my brain, and soon we were all sitting at the table.

"Where have you been?" they both said, more or less in unison.

I had given this some thought on the way home. "I got trapped," I said. "In Oakland. I was there with some friends, doing a project, and we were all quarantined."

"For five days?"

"Yeah," I said. "Yeah. It was really bad." I'd read about the quarantines in the *Chronicle* and I cribbed shamelessly from the quotes they'd published. "Yeah. Everyone who got caught in the cloud. They thought we had been attacked with some kind of superbug and they packed us into shipping containers in the docklands, like sardines. It was really hot and sticky. Not much food, either."

"Christ," Dad said, his fists balling up on the table. Dad teaches in Berkeley three days a week, working with a few grad students in the library science program. The rest of the time he consults for clients in the city and down the Peninsula, third-wave dotcoms that are doing various things with archives. He's a mild-mannered librarian by profession, but he'd been a real radical in the sixties and wrestled a little in high school. I'd seen him get crazy angry now and again—I'd even made him that angry now and again—and he could seriously lose it when he was Hulking out. He once threw a swing-set from Ikea across my granddad's whole lawn when it fell apart for the fiftieth time while he was assembling it.

"Barbarians," Mom said. She's been living in America since she was a teenager, but she still comes over all British when she encounters American cops, health care, airport security or homelessness. Then the word is "barbarians," and her accent comes back strong. We'd been to London twice to see her family and I can't say as it felt any more civilized than San Francisco, just more cramped.

"But they let us go, and ferried us over today." I was improvising now.

"Are you hurt?" Mom said. "Hungry?"

"Sleepy?"

"Yeah, a little of all that. Also Dopey, Doc, Sneezy and Bashful." We had a family tradition of Seven Dwarfs jokes. They both smiled a little, but their eyes were still wet. I felt really bad for them. They must have been out of their minds with worry. I was glad for a chance to change the subject. "I'd totally love to eat."

"I'll order a pizza from Goat Hill," Dad said.

"No, not that," I said. They both looked at me like I'd sprouted antennae. I normally have a thing about Goat Hill Pizza—as in, I can normally eat it like a goldfish eats his food, gobbling until it either runs out or I pop. I tried to smile. "I just don't feel like pizza," I said, lamely. "Let's order some curry, okay?" Thank heaven that San Francisco is take-out central.

Mom went to the drawer of take-out menus (more normalcy, feeling like a drink of water on a dry, sore throat) and riffled through them. We spent a couple of distracting minutes going through the menu from the halal Pakistani place on Valencia. I settled on a mixed tandoori grill and creamed spinach with farmer's cheese, a salted mango lassi (much better than it sounds) and little fried pastries in sugar syrup.

Once the food was ordered, the questions started again. They'd heard from Van's, Jolu's and Darryl's families (of course) and had tried to report us missing. The police were taking names, but there were so many "displaced persons" that they weren't going to open files on anyone unless they were still missing after seven days.

Meanwhile, millions of have-you-seen sites had popped up on the net. A couple of the sites were old MySpace clones that had run out of money and saw a new lease on life from all the attention. After all, some venture capitalists had missing family in the Bay Area. Maybe if they were recovered, the site would attract some new investment. I grabbed Dad's laptop and looked through them. They were plastered with advertising, of course, and pictures of missing people, mostly grad photos, wedding pictures and that sort of thing. It was pretty ghoulish.

I found my pic and saw that it was linked to Van's, Jolu's and Darryl's. There was a little form for marking people found and another one for writing up notes about other missing people. I filled in the fields for me and Jolu and Van, and left Darryl blank.

"You forgot Darryl," Dad said. He didn't like Darryl much—once he'd figured out that a couple inches were missing out of one of the bottles in his liquor cabinet, and to my enduring shame I'd blamed it on Darryl. In truth, of course, it had been both of us, just fooling around, trying out vodka-and-Cokes during an all-night gaming session.

"He wasn't with us," I said. The lie tasted bitter in my mouth.

"Oh my God," my mom said. She squeezed her hands together. "We just assumed when you came home that you'd all been together."

"No," I said, the lie growing. "No, he was supposed to meet us but we never met up. He's probably just stuck over in Berkeley. He was going to take the BART over."

Mom made a whimpering sound. Dad shook his head and closed his eyes. "Don't you know about the BART?" he said.

I shook my head. I could see where this was going. I felt like the ground was rushing up to me.

"They blew it up," Dad said. "The bastards blew it up at the same time as the bridge."

That hadn't been on the front page of the *Chronicle*, but then, a BART blowout under the water wouldn't be nearly as picturesque as the images of the bridge hanging in tatters and pieces over the Bay. The BART tunnel from the Embarcadero in San Francisco to the West Oakland station was submerged.

I went back to Dad's computer and surfed the headlines. No one was sure, but the body count was in the thousands. Between the cars that plummeted 191 feet to the sea and the people drowned in the trains, the deaths were mounting. One reporter claimed to have interviewed an "identity counterfeiter" who'd helped "dozens" of people walk away from their old lives by simply vanishing after the attacks, getting new ID made up and slipping away from bad marriages, bad debts and bad lives.

Dad actually got tears in his eyes, and Mom was openly crying. They each hugged me again, patting me with their hands as if to assure themselves that I was really there. They kept telling me they loved me. I told them I loved them, too.

We had a weepy dinner and Mom and Dad had each had a couple glasses of wine, which was a lot for them. I told them that I was getting sleepy, which was true, and mooched up to my room. I wasn't going to bed, though. I needed to get online and find out what was going on. I needed to talk to Jolu and Vanessa. I needed to get working on finding Darryl.

I crept up to my room and opened the door. I hadn't seen my old bed in what felt like a thousand years. I lay down on it and reached over to my bedstand to grab my laptop. I must have not plugged it in all the way—the electrical adapter needed to be jiggled just right—so it had slowly discharged while I was away. I plugged it back in and gave it a minute or two to charge up before trying to power it up again. I used the time to get undressed and throw my clothes in the trash—I never wanted to see them again—and put on a clean pair of boxers and a fresh T-shirt. The fresh-laundered clothes, straight out of my drawers, felt so familiar and comfortable, like getting hugged by my parents.

I powered up my laptop and punched a bunch of pillows into place behind me at the top of the bed. I scooched back and opened my computer's lid and settled it onto my thighs. It was still booting, and man, those icons creeping across the screen looked *good*. It came all the way up and then it started giving me more low-power warnings. I checked the power cable again and wiggled it and they went away. The power jack was really flaking out.

In fact, it was so bad that I couldn't actually get anything done. Every time I took my hand off the power cable it lost contact and the computer started to complain about its battery. I took a closer look at it.

The whole case of my computer was slightly misaligned, the seam split in an angular gape that started narrow and widened toward the back.

Sometimes you look at a piece of equipment and discover something like this and you wonder, "Was it always like that?" Maybe you just never noticed.

But with my laptop, that wasn't possible. You see, I built it. After the Board of Ed issued us all SchoolBooks, there was no way my parents were going to buy me a computer of my own, even though technically the SchoolBook didn't belong to me, and I wasn't supposed to install software on it or mod it.

I had some money saved—odd jobs, Christmases and birthdays, a little bit of judicious ebaying. Put it all together and I had enough money to buy a totally crappy, five-year-old machine.

So Darryl and I built one instead. You can buy laptop cases

just like you can buy cases for desktop PCs, though they're a little more specialized than plain old PCs. I'd built a couple PCs with Darryl over the years, scavenging parts from Craigslist and garage sales and ordering stuff from cheap Taiwanese vendors we found on the net. I figured that building a laptop would be the best way to get the power I wanted at the price I could afford.

To build your own laptop, you start by ordering a "bare-book"—a machine with just a little hardware in it and all the right slots. The good news was, once I was done, I had a machine that was a whole pound lighter than the Dell I'd had my eye on, ran faster and cost a third of what I would have paid Dell. The bad news was that assembling a laptop is like building one of those ships in a bottle. It's all finicky work with tweezers and magnifying glasses, trying to get everything to fit in that little case. Unlike a full-sized PC—which is mostly air—every cubic millimeter of space in a laptop is spoken for. Every time I thought I had it, I'd go to screw the thing back together and find that something was keeping the case from closing all the way, and it'd be back to the drawing board.

So I knew *exactly* how the seam on my laptop was supposed to look when the thing was closed, and it was *not* supposed to look like this.

I kept jiggling the power adapter, but it was hopeless. There was no way I was going to get the thing to boot without taking it apart. I groaned and put it beside the bed. I'd deal with it in the morning.

That was the theory, anyway. Two hours later, I was still staring at the ceiling, playing back movies in my head of what they'd done to me, what I should have done, all regrets and *esprit d'escalier*.

I rolled out of bed. It had gone midnight and I'd heard my parents hit the sack at eleven. I grabbed the laptop and cleared some space on my desk and clipped the little LED lamps to the temples of my magnifying glasses and pulled out a set of little precision screwdrivers. A minute later, I had the case open and the keyboard removed and I was staring at the guts of my laptop. I got a can of compressed air and blew out the dust that the fan had sucked in and looked things over.

Something wasn't right. I couldn't put my finger on it, but then it had been months since I'd had the lid off this thing. Luckily, the third time I'd had to open it up and struggle to close it again, I'd gotten smart: I'd taken a photo of the guts with everything in place. I hadn't been totally smart: at first, I'd just left that pic on my hard drive, and naturally I couldn't get to it when I had the laptop in parts. But then I'd printed it out and stuck it in my messy drawer of papers, the dead-tree graveyard where I kept all the warranty cards and pin-out diagrams. I shuffled them—they seemed messier than I remembered—and brought out my photo. I set it down next to the computer and kind of unfocused my eyes, trying to find things that looked out of place.

Then I spotted it. The ribbon cable that connected the keyboard to the logic board wasn't connected right. That was a weird one. There was no torque on that part, nothing to dislodge it in the course of normal operations. I tried to press it back down again and discovered that the plug wasn't just badly mounted—there was something between it and the board. I tweezed it out and shone my light on it.

There was something new in my keyboard. It was a little chunk of hardware, only a sixteenth of an inch thick, with no markings. The keyboard was plugged into it, and it was plugged into the board. It other words, it was perfectly situated to capture all the keystrokes I made while I typed on my machine.

It was a bug.

My heart thudded in my ears. It was dark and quiet in the house, but it wasn't a comforting dark. There were eyes out there, eyes and ears, and they were watching me. Surveilling me. The surveillance I faced at school had followed me home, but this time, it wasn't just the Board of Education looking over my shoulder: the Department of Homeland Security had joined them.

I almost took the bug out. Then I figured that whoever put it there would know that it was gone. I left it in. It made me sick to do it.

I looked around for more tampering. I couldn't find any, but did that mean there hadn't been any? Someone had broken into my room and planted this device—had disassembled my laptop and reassembled it. There were lots of other ways to wiretap a computer. I could never find them all.

I put the machine together with numb fingers. This time, the case wouldn't snap shut just right, but the power cable stayed in. I booted it up and set my fingers on the keyboard, thinking that I would run some diagnostics and see what was what.

But I couldn't do it.

Hell, maybe my room was wiretapped. Maybe there was a camera spying on me now.

I'd been feeling paranoid when I got home. Now I was nearly out of my skin. It felt like I was back in jail, back in the interrogation room, stalked by entities who had me utterly in their power. It made me want to cry.

Only one thing for it.

I went into the bathroom and took off the toilet paper roll and replaced it with a fresh one. Luckily, it was almost empty already. I unrolled the rest of the paper and dug through my parts box until I found a little plastic envelope full of ultrabright white LEDs I'd scavenged out of a dead bike lamp. I punched their leads through the cardboard tube carefully, using a pin to make the holes, then got out some wire and connected them all in series with little metal clips. I twisted the wires into the leads for a nine-volt battery and connected the battery. Now I had a tube ringed with ultrabright, directional LEDs, and I could hold it up to my eye and look through it.

I'd built one of these last year as a science fair project and had been thrown out of the fair once I showed that there were hidden cameras in half the classrooms at Chavez High. Pinhead video cameras cost less than a good restaurant dinner these days, so they're showing up everywhere. Sneaky store clerks put them in changing rooms or tanning salons and get pervy with the hidden footage they get from their customers—sometimes they just put it on the net. Knowing how to turn a toilet paper roll and three bucks' worth of parts into a camera-detector is just good sense.

This is the simplest way to catch a spy-cam. They have tiny lenses, but they reflect light like the dickens. It works best in a dim room: stare through the tube and slowly scan all the walls and other places someone might have put a camera until you see the glint of a reflection. If the reflection stays still as you move around, that's a lens.

There wasn't a camera in my room—not one I could detect, anyway. There might have been audio bugs, of course. Or better cameras. Or nothing at all. Can you blame me for feeling paranoid?

I loved that laptop. I called it the Salmagundi, which means anything made out of spare parts.

Once you get to naming your laptop, you know that you're really having a deep relationship with it. Now, though, I felt like

I didn't want to ever touch it again. I wanted to throw it out the window. Who knew what they'd done to it? Who knew how it had been tapped?

I put it in a drawer with the lid shut and looked at the ceiling. It was late and I should have been in bed. There was no way I was going to sleep now, though. I was tapped. Everyone might be tapped. The world had changed forever.

"I'll find a way to get them," I said. It was a vow, I knew it when I heard it, though I'd never made a vow before.

I couldn't sleep after that. And besides, I had an idea.

Somewhere in my closet was a shrink-wrapped box containing one still-sealed, mint-in-package Xbox Universal. Every Xbox has been sold way below cost—Microsoft makes most of its money charging games companies money for the right to put out Xbox games—but the Universal was the first Xbox that Microsoft decided to give away entirely for free.

Last Christmas season, there'd been poor losers on every corner dressed as warriors from the Halo series, handing out bags of these game machines as fast as they could. I guess it worked—everyone says they sold a whole butt-load of games. Naturally, there were countermeasures to make sure you only played games from companies that had bought licenses from Microsoft to make them.

Hackers blow through those countermeasures. The Xbox was cracked by a kid from MIT who wrote a best-selling book about it, and then the 360 went down, and then the short-lived Xbox Portable (which we all called the "luggable"—it weighed three pounds!) succumbed. The Universal was supposed to be totally bulletproof. The high school kids who broke it were Brazilian Linux hackers who lived in a *favela*—a kind of squatter's slum.

Never underestimate the determination of a kid who is time-rich and cash-poor.

Once the Brazilians published their crack, we all went nuts on it. Soon there were dozens of alternate operating systems for the Xbox Universal. My favorite was ParanoidXbox, a flavor of ParanoidLinux. ParanoidLinux is an operating system that assumes that its operator is under assault from the government (it was intended for use by Chinese and Syrian dissidents), and it does everything it can to keep your communications and documents a secret. It even throws up a bunch of "chaff" communications that are supposed to disguise the fact that you're doing anything covert. So while you're receiving a political message one character at a time, ParanoidLinux is pretending to surf the Web and fill in questionnaires and flirt in chat rooms. Meanwhile, one in every five hundred characters you receive is your real message, a needle buried in a huge haystack.

I'd burned a ParanoidXbox DVD when they first appeared, but I'd never gotten around to unpacking the Xbox in my closet, finding a TV to hook it up to and so on. My room is crowded enough as it is without letting Microsoft crashware eat up valuable workspace.

Tonight, I'd make the sacrifice. It took about twenty minutes to get up and running. Not having a TV was the hardest part, but eventually I remembered that I had a little overhead LCD projector that had standard TV RCA connectors on the back. I connected it to the Xbox and shone it on the back of my door and got ParanoidLinux installed.

Now I was up and running, and ParanoidLinux was looking for other Xbox Universals to talk to. Every Xbox Universal comes with built-in wireless for multiplayer gaming. You can connect to your neighbors on the wireless link and to the Internet, if you have a wireless Internet connection. I found three different sets of neighbors in range. Two of them had their Xbox Universals also connected to the Internet. ParanoidXbox loved that configuration: it could siphon off some of my neighbors' Internet connections and use them to get online through the gaming network. The neighbors would never miss the packets: they were paying for flat-rate Internet connections, and they weren't exactly doing a lot of surfing at 2 A.M.

The best part of all of this is how it made me *feel*: in control. My technology was working for me, serving me, protecting me. It wasn't spying on me. This is why I loved technology: if you used it right, it could give you power and privacy.

My brain was really going now, running like sixty. There were lots of reasons to run ParanoidXbox—the best one was that anyone could write games for it. Already there was a port of MAME, the Multiple Arcade Machine Emulator, so you could play practically any game that had ever been written, all the way back to Pong—games for the Apple][+ and games for the Colecovision, games for the NES and the Dreamcast, and so on.

Even better were all the cool multiplayer games being built specifically for ParanoidXbox—totally free hobbyist games that anyone could run. When you combined it all, you had a free console full of free games that could get you free Internet access.

And the best part—as far as I was concerned—was that ParanoidXbox was *paranoid*. Every bit that went over the air was scrambled to within an inch of its life. You could wiretap it all you wanted, but you'd never figure out who was talking, what they were talking about or who they were talking to. Anonymous Web, email and IM. Just what I needed.

All I had to do now was convince everyone I knew to use it, too.

Chapter 6

Believe it or not, my parents made me go to school the next day. I'd only fallen into feverish sleep at three in the morning, but at seven the next day, my dad was standing at the foot of my bed, threatening to drag me out by the ankles. I managed to get up—something had died in my mouth after painting my eyelids shut—and into the shower.

I let my mom force a piece of toast and a banana into me, wishing fervently that my parents would let me drink coffee at home. I could sneak one on the way to school, but watching them sip down their black gold while I was drag-assing around the house, getting dressed and putting my books in my bag—it was awful.

I've walked to school a thousand times, but today it was different. I went up and over the hills to get down into the Mission, and everywhere there were trucks. I saw new sensors and traffic cameras installed at many of the stop signs. Someone had a lot of surveillance gear lying around, waiting to be installed at the first opportunity. The attack on the Bay Bridge had been just what they needed.

It all made the city seem more subdued, like being inside an elevator, embarrassed by the close scrutiny of your neighbors and the ubiquitous cameras.

The Turkish coffee shop on 24th Street fixed me up good with a go-cup of Turkish coffee. Basically, Turkish coffee is mud, pretending to be coffee. It's thick enough to stand a spoon up in, and it has way more caffeine than the kiddee-pops like Red Bull. Take it from someone who's read the Wikipedia entry: this is how the Ottoman Empire was won: maddened horsemen fueled by lethal jet-black coffee-mud.

I pulled out my debit card to pay and he made a face. "No more debit," he said.

"Huh? Why not?" I'd paid for my coffee habit on my card for years at the Turk's. He used to hassle me all the time, telling me I was too young to drink the stuff, and he still refused to serve me at all during school hours, convinced that I was skipping class. But over the years, the Turk and me have developed a kind of gruff understanding.

He shook his head sadly. "You wouldn't understand. Go to school, kid."

There's no surer way to make me want to understand than to tell me I won't. I wheedled him, demanding that he tell me. He looked like he was going to throw me out, but when I asked him if he thought I wasn't good enough to shop there, he opened up.

"The security," he said, looking around his little shop with its tubs of dried beans and seeds, its shelves of Turkish groceries. "The government. They monitor it all now, it was in the papers. PATRIOT Act II, the Congress passed it yesterday. Now they can monitor every time you use your card. I say no. I say my shop will not help them spy on my customers."

My jaw dropped.

"You think it's no big deal maybe? What is the problem with

government knowing when you buy coffee? Because it's one way they know where you are, where you been. Why you think I left Turkey? Where you have government always spying on the people, is no good. I move here twenty years ago for freedom— I no help them take freedom away."

"You're going to lose so many sales," I blurted. I wanted to tell him he was a hero and shake his hand, but that was what came out. "Everyone uses debit cards."

"Maybe not so much anymore. Maybe my customers come here because they know I love freedom, too. I am making sign for window. Maybe other stores do the same. I hear the ACLU will sue them for this."

"You've got all my business from now on," I said. I meant it. I reached into my pocket. "Um, I don't have any cash, though."

He pursed his lips and nodded. "Many peoples say the same thing. Is okay. You give today's money to the ACLU."

In two minutes, the Turk and I had exchanged more words than we had in all the time I'd been coming to his shop. I had no idea he had all these passions. I just thought of him as my friendly neighborhood caffeine dealer. Now I shook his hand and when I left his store, I felt like he and I had joined a team. A secret team.

I'd missed two days of school but it seemed like I hadn't missed much class. They'd shut the school on one of those days while the city scrambled to recover. The next day had been devoted, it seemed, to mourning those missing and presumed dead. The newspapers published biographies of the lost, personal memorials. The Web was filled with these capsule obituaries, thousands of them.

Embarrassingly, I was one of those people. I stepped into the schoolyard, not knowing this, and then there was a shout and a moment later there were a hundred people around me, pounding me on the back, shaking my hand. A couple girls I didn't even know kissed me, and they were more than friendly kisses. I felt like a rock star.

My teachers were only a little more subdued. Ms. Galvez cried as much as my mother had and hugged me three times before she let me go to my desk and sit down. There was something new at the front of the classroom. A camera. Ms. Galvez caught me staring at it and handed me a permission slip on smeary xeroxed school letterhead.

The Board of the San Francisco Unified School District had held an emergency session over the weekend and unanimously voted to ask the parents of every kid in the city for permission to put closed circuit television cameras in every classroom and corridor. The law said they couldn't force us to go to school with cameras all over the place, but it didn't say anything about us *volunteering* to give up our Constitutional rights. The letter said that the Board was sure that they would get complete compliance from the city's parents, but that they would make arrangements to teach those kids whose parents objected in a separate set of "unprotected" classrooms.

Why did we have cameras in our classrooms now? Terrorists. Of course. Because by blowing up a bridge, terrorists had indicated that schools were next. Somehow that was the conclusion that the Board had reached anyway.

I read this note three times and then I stuck my hand up.

"Yes, Marcus?"

"Ms. Galvez, about this note?"

"Yes, Marcus."

"Isn't the point of terrorism to make us afraid? That's why it's called *terror*ism, right?"

"I suppose so." The class was staring at me. I wasn't the best student in school, but I did like a good in-class debate. They were waiting to hear what I'd say next.

"So aren't we doing what the terrorists want from us? Don't they win if we act all afraid and put cameras in the classrooms and all of that?"

There was some nervous tittering. One of the others put his hand up. It was Charles. Ms. Galvez called on him.

"Putting cameras in makes us safe, which makes us less afraid."

"Safe from what?" I said, without waiting to be called on.

"Terrorism," Charles said. The others were nodding their heads.

"How do they do that? If a suicide bomber rushed in here and blew us all up—"

"Ms. Galvez, Marcus is violating school policy. We're not supposed to make jokes about terrorist attacks—"

"Who's making jokes?"

"Thank you, both of you," Ms. Galvez said. She looked really unhappy. I felt kind of bad for hijacking her class. "I think that this is a really interesting discussion, but I'd like to hold it over for a future class. I think that these issues may be too emotional for us to have a discussion about them today. Now, let's get back to the suffragists, shall we?"

So we spent the rest of the hour talking about suffragists and the new lobbying strategies they'd devised for getting four women into every congresscritter's office to lean on him and let him know what it would mean for his political future if he kept on denying women the vote. It was normally the kind of thing I really liked—little guys making the big and powerful be honest. But today I couldn't concentrate. It must have been Darryl's absence. We both liked Social Studies and we would have had our SchoolBooks out and an IM session up seconds after sitting down, a back channel for talking about the lesson.

I'd burned twenty ParanoidXbox discs the night before and I had them all in my bag. I handed them out to people I knew were really, really into gaming. They'd all gotten an Xbox Universal or two the year before, but most of them had stopped using them. The games were really expensive and not a lot of fun. I took them aside between periods, at lunch and study hall, and sang the praises of the ParanoidXbox games to the sky. Free and fun—addictive social games with lots of cool people playing them from all over the world.

Giving away one thing to sell another is what they call a "razor blade business"—companies like Gillette give you free razor blade handles and then stiff you by charging you a small fortune for the blades. Printer cartridges are the worst for that—the most expensive champagne in the world is cheap when compared with inkjet ink, which costs all of a penny a gallon to make wholesale.

Razor blade businesses depend on you not being able to get the "blades" from someone else. After all, if Gillette can make nine bucks on a ten-dollar replacement blade, why not start a competitor that makes only four bucks selling an identical blade: an 80 percent profit margin is the kind of thing that makes your average businessguy go all drooly and round-eyed.

So razor blade companies like Microsoft pour a lot of effort into making it hard and/or illegal to compete with them on the blades. In Microsoft's case, every Xbox has had countermeasures to keep you from running software that was released by people who didn't pay the Microsoft blood money for the right to sell Xbox programs.

The people I met didn't think much about this stuff. They perked up when I told them that the games were unmonitored. These days, any online game you play is filled with all kinds of unsavory sorts. First there are the pervs who try to get you to come out to some remote location so they can go all weird and Silence of the Lambs on you. Then there are the cops, who are pretending to be gullible kids so they can bust the pervs. Worst of all, though, are the monitors who spend all their time spying on our discussions and snitching on us for violating their Terms of Service, which say no flirting, no cussing and no "clear or masked language which insultingly refers to any aspect of sexual orientation or sexuality."

I'm no 24/7 horn-dog, but I'm a seventeen-year-old boy. Sex does come up in conversation every now and again. But God help you if it came up in chat while you were gaming. It was a real buzz-kill. No one monitored the ParanoidXbox games, because they weren't run by a company: they were just games that hackers had written for the hell of it.

So these game-kids loved the story. They took the discs greedily, and promised to burn copies for all their friends—after all, games are most fun when you're playing them with your buddies.

When I got home, I read that a group of parents was suing the school board over the surveillance cameras in the classrooms, but that they'd already lost their bid to get a preliminary injunction against them.

I don't know who came up with the name Xnet, but it stuck. You'd hear people talking about it on the Muni. Van called me up to ask me if I'd heard of it and I nearly choked once I figured out what she was talking about: the discs I'd started distributing last week had been sneakernetted and copied all the way to Oakland in the space of two weeks. It made me look over my shoulder—like I'd broken a rule and now the DHS would come and take me away forever.

They'd been hard weeks. The BART had completely abandoned cash fares now, switching them for arphid "contactless" cards that you waved at the turnstiles to go through. They were cool and convenient, but every time I used one, I thought about how I was being tracked. Someone on Xnet posted a link to an Electronic Frontier Foundation white paper on the ways that these things could be used to track people, and the paper had tiny stories about little groups of people that had protested at the BART stations.

I used the Xnet for almost everything now. I'd set up a fake email address through the Pirate Party, a Swedish political party that hated Internet surveillance and promised to keep their mail accounts a secret from everyone, even the cops. I accessed it strictly via Xnet, hopping from one neighbor's Internet connection to the next, staying anonymous—I hoped—all the way to Sweden. I wasn't using w1n5t0n anymore. If Benson could figure it out, anyone could. My new handle, come up with on the spur of the moment, was M1k3y, and I got a *lot* of email from people who heard in chat rooms and message boards that I could help them troubleshoot their Xnet configurations and connections.

I missed Harajuku Fun Madness. The company had suspended the game indefinitely. They said that for "security reasons" they didn't think it would be a good idea to hide things and then send people off to find them. What if someone thought it was a bomb? What if someone put a bomb in the same spot?

What if I got hit by lightning while walking with an umbrella? Ban umbrellas! Fight the menace of lightning!

I kept on using my laptop, though I got a skin-crawly feeling when I used it. Whoever had wiretapped it would wonder why I didn't use it. I figured I'd just do some random surfing with it every day, a little less each day, so that anyone watching would see me slowly changing my habits, not doing a sudden reversal. Mostly I read those creepy obits—all those thousands of my friends and neighbors dead at the bottom of the Bay.

Truth be told, I *was* doing less and less homework every day. I had business elsewhere. I burned new stacks of ParanoidXbox every day, fifty or sixty, and took them around the city to people I'd heard were willing to burn sixty of their own and hand them out to their friends.

I wasn't too worried about getting caught doing this, because I had good crypto on my side. Crypto is cryptography, or "secret writing," and it's been around since Roman times (literally: Augustus Caesar was a big fan and liked to invent his own codes, some of which we use today for scrambling joke punch lines in email).

Crypto is math. Hard math. I'm not going to try to explain it in detail because I don't have the math to really get my head around it, either—look it up on Wikipedia if you really want.

But here's the Cliff's Notes version: Some kinds of mathematical functions are really easy to do in one direction and really hard to do in the other direction. It's easy to multiply two big prime numbers together and make a giant number. It's really, really hard to take any given giant number and figure out which primes multiply together to give you that number.

That means that if you can come up with a way of scrambling something based on multiplying large primes, unscrambling it without knowing those primes will be hard. Wicked hard. Like, a trillion years of all the computers ever invented working 24/7 won't be able to do it.

There are four parts to any crypto message: the original message, called the "cleartext." The scrambled message, called the "ciphertext." The scrambling system, called the "cipher." And finally there's the key: secret stuff you feed into the cipher along with the cleartext to make ciphertext.

It used to be that crypto people tried to keep all of this a secret. Every agency and government had its own ciphers *and* its own keys. The Nazis and the Allies didn't want the other guys to know how they scrambled their messages, let alone the keys that they could use to descramble them. That sounds like a good idea, right?

Wrong.

The first time anyone told me about all this prime factoring stuff, I immediately said, "No way, that's BS. I mean, *sure* it's hard to do this prime factorization stuff, whatever you say it is. But it used to be impossible to fly or go to the moon or get a hard drive with more than a few kilobytes of storage. Someone *must* have invented a way of descrambling the messages." I had visions of a hollow mountain full of National Security Agency mathematicians reading every email in the world and snickering.

In fact, that's pretty much what happened during World War II. That's the reason that life isn't more like Castle Wolfenstein, where I've spent many days hunting Nazis.

The thing is, ciphers are hard to keep secret. There's a lot of math that goes into one, and if they're widely used, then everyone who uses them has to keep them a secret, too, and if someone changes sides, you have to find a new cipher.

The Nazi cipher was called Enigma, and they used a little mechanical computer called an Enigma Machine to scramble and unscramble the messages they got. Every sub and boat and station needed one of these, so it was inevitable that eventually the Allies would get their hands on one.

When they did, they cracked it. That work was led by my personal all-time hero, a guy named Alan Turing, who pretty much invented computers as we know them today. Unfortunately for him, he was gay, so after the war ended, the stupid British government forced him to get shot up with hormones to "cure" his homosexuality and he killed himself. Darryl gave me a biography of Turing for my fourteenth birthday—wrapped in twenty layers of paper and in a recycled Batmobile toy, he was like that with presents—and I've been a Turing junkie ever since.

Now the Allies had the Enigma Machine, and they could intercept lots of Nazi radio messages, which shouldn't have been that big a deal, since every captain had his own secret key. Since the Allies didn't have the keys, having the machine shouldn't have helped.

Here's where secrecy hurts crypto. The Enigma cipher was flawed. Once Turing looked hard at it, he figured out that the Nazi cryptographers had made a mathematical mistake. By getting his hands on an Enigma Machine, Turing could figure out how to crack *any* Nazi message, no matter what key it used.

That cost the Nazis the war. I mean, don't get me wrong. That's good news. Take it from a Castle Wolfenstein veteran. You wouldn't want the Nazis running the country.

After the war, cryptographers spent a lot of time thinking about this. The problem had been that Turing was smarter than the guy who thought up Enigma. Any time you had a cipher, you were vulnerable to someone smarter than you coming up with a way of breaking it.

And the more they thought about it, the more they realized that *anyone* can come up with a security system that he can't figure out how to break. But *no one* can figure out what a smarter person might do.

You have to publish a cipher to know that it works. You have to tell *as many people as possible* how it works, so that they can thwack on it with everything they have, testing its security. The longer you go without anyone finding a flaw, the more secure you are.

Which is how it stands today. If you want to be safe, you don't use crypto that some genius thought of last week. You use the stuff that people have been using for as long as possible without anyone figuring out how to break them. Whether you're a bank, a terrorist, a government or a teenager, you use the same ciphers.

If you tried to use your own cipher, there'd be the chance that someone out there had found a flaw you missed and was doing a Turing on your butt, deciphering all your "secret" messages and chuckling at your dumb gossip, financial transactions and military secrets.

So I knew that crypto would keep me safe from eavesdroppers, but I wasn't ready to deal with histograms.

I got off the BART and waved my card over the turnstile as I headed up to the 24th Street station. As usual, there were lots of weirdos hanging out in the station, drunks and Jesus freaks and intense Mexican men staring at the ground and a few gang kids. I looked straight past them as I hit the stairs and jogged up to the surface. My bag was empty now, no longer bulging with the ParanoidXbox discs I'd been distributing, and it made my shoulders feel light and put a spring in my step as I came up the street. The preachers were at work still, exhorting in Spanish and English about Jesus and so on.

The counterfeit sunglass sellers were gone, but they'd been replaced by guys selling robot dogs that barked the national anthem and would lift their legs if you showed them a picture of

Osama bin Laden. There was probably some cool stuff going on in their little brains and I made a mental note to pick a couple of them up and take them apart later. Face-recognition was pretty new in toys, having only recently made the leap from the military to casinos trying to find cheats to law enforcement.

I started down 24th Street toward Potrero Hill and home, rolling my shoulders and smelling the burrito smells wafting out of the restaurants and thinking about dinner.

I don't know why I happened to glance back over my shoulder, but I did. Maybe it was a little bit of subconscious sixth sense stuff. I knew I was being followed.

They were two beefy white guys with little mustaches that made me think of either cops or the gay bikers who rode up and down the Castro, but gay guys usually had better haircuts. They had on windbreakers the color of old cement and blue jeans, with their waistbands concealed. I thought of all the things a cop might wear on his waistband, of the utility belt that DHS guy in the truck had worn. Both guys were wearing Bluetooth headsets.

I kept walking, my heart thumping in my chest. I'd been expecting this since I started. I'd been expecting the DHS to figure out what I was doing. I took every precaution, but severe haircut lady had told me that she'd be watching me. She'd told me I was a marked man. I realized that I'd been waiting to get picked up and taken back to jail. Why not? Why should Darryl be in jail and not me? What did I have going for me? I hadn't even had the guts to tell my parents—or his—what had really happened to us.

I quickened my step and took a mental inventory. I didn't have anything incriminating in my bag. Not too incriminating, anyway. My SchoolBook was running the crack that let me IM and stuff, but half the people in school had that. I'd changed the way I encrypted the stuff on my phone—now I *did* have a fake partition that I could turn back into cleartext with one password, but all the good stuff was hidden, and needed another password to open up. That hidden section looked just like random junk—when you encrypt data, it becomes indistinguishable from random noise—and they'd never even know it was there.

There were no discs in my bag. My laptop was free of incriminating evidence. Of course, if they thought to look hard at my Xbox, it was game over. So to speak.

I stopped where I was standing. I'd done as good a job as I could of covering myself. It was time to face my fate. I stepped into the nearest burrito joint and ordered one with carnitas—shredded pork—and extra salsa. Might as well go down with a full stomach. I got a bucket of horchata, too, an ice-cold rice drink that's like watery, semisweet rice pudding (better than it sounds).

I sat down to eat, and a profound calm fell over me. I was about to go to jail for my "crimes," or I wasn't. My freedom since they'd taken me in had been just a temporary holiday. My country was not my friend anymore: we were now on different sides and I'd known I could never win.

The two guys came into the restaurant as I was finishing the burrito and going up to order some churros—deep-fried dough with cinnamon sugar—for dessert. I guess they'd been waiting outside and got tired of my dawdling.

They stood behind me at the counter, boxing me in. I took my churro from the pretty granny and paid her, taking a couple of quick bites of the dough before I turned around. I wanted to eat at least a little of my dessert. It might be the last dessert I got for a long, long time.

Then I turned around. They were both so close I could see the zit on the cheek of the one on the left, the little booger up the nose of the other.

" 'Scuse me," I said, trying to push past them. The one with the booger moved to block me.

"Sir," he said, "can you step over here with us?" He gestured toward the restaurant's door.

"Sorry, I'm eating," I said and moved again. This time he put his hand on my chest. He was breathing fast through his nose, making the booger wiggle. I think I was breathing hard, too, but it was hard to tell over the hammering of my heart.

The other one flipped down a flap on the front of his windbreaker to reveal a SFPD insignia. "Police," he said. "Please come with us."

"Let me just get my stuff," I said.

"We'll take care of that," he said. The booger one stepped right up close to me, his foot on the inside of mine. You do that in some martial arts, too. It lets you feel if the other guy is shifting his weight, getting ready to move.

I wasn't going to run, though. I knew I couldn't outrun fate.

Chapter 7

They took me outside and around the corner to a waiting unmarked police car. It wasn't like anyone in that neighborhood would have had a hard time figuring out that it was a cop car, though. Only police drove big Crown Victorias now that gas had hit seven bucks a gallon. What's more, only cops could double-park in the middle of Van Ness Street without getting towed by the schools of predatory tow operators that circled endlessly, ready to enforce San Francisco's incomprehensible parking regulations and collect a bounty for kidnapping your car.

Booger blew his nose. I was sitting in the back seat, and so was he. His partner was sitting in the front, typing with one finger on an ancient, ruggedized laptop that looked like Fred Flintstone had been its original owner.

Booger looked closely at my ID again. "We just want to ask you a few routine questions."

"Can I see your badges?" I said. These guys were clearly cops, but it couldn't hurt to let them know I knew my rights.

Booger flashed his badge at me too fast for me to get a good look at it, but Zit in the front seat gave me a long look at his. I got their division number and memorized the four-digit badge number. It was easy: 1337 is also the way hackers write "leet," or "elite."

They were both being very polite and neither of them was trying to intimidate me the way that the DHS had done when I was in their custody.

"Am I under arrest?"

"You've been momentarily detained so that we can ensure your safety and the general public safety," Booger said.

He passed my driver's license to Zit, who pecked it slowly into his computer. I saw him make a typo and almost corrected him, but figured it was better to just keep my mouth shut.

"Is there anything you want to tell me, Marcus? Do they call you Marc?"

"Marcus is fine," I said. Booger looked like he might be a nice guy. Except for the part about kidnapping me into his car, of course.

"Marcus. Anything you want to tell me?"

"Like what? Am I under arrest?"

"You're not under arrest right now," Booger said. "Would you like to be?"

"No," I said.

"Good. We've been watching you since you left the BART. Your Fast Pass says that you've been riding to a lot of strange places at a lot of funny hours."

I felt something let go inside my chest. This wasn't about the Xnet at all, then, not really. They'd been watching my subway use and wanted to know why it had been so freaky lately. How totally stupid.

"So you guys follow everyone who comes out of the BART station with a funny ride history? You must be busy."

"Not everyone, Marcus. We get an alert when anyone with an uncommon ride profile comes out and that helps us assess whether we want to investigate. In your case, we came along because we wanted to know why a smart-looking kid like you had such a funny ride profile."

Now that I knew I wasn't about to go to jail, I was getting pissed. These guys had no business spying on me—Christ, the BART had no business *helping* them to spy on me. Where the hell did my subway pass get off on finking me out for having a "nonstandard ride pattern"?

"I think I'd like to be arrested now," I said.

Booger sat back and raised his eyebrow at me.

"Really? On what charge?"

"Oh, you mean riding public transit in a nonstandard way isn't a crime?"

Zit closed his eyes and scrubbed them with his thumbs.

Booger sighed a put-upon sigh. "Look, Marcus, we're on your side here. We use this system to catch bad guys. To catch terrorists and drug dealers. Maybe you're a drug dealer yourself. Pretty good way to get around the city, a Fast Pass. Anonymous."

"What's wrong with anonymous? It was good enough for Thomas Jefferson. And by the way, am I under arrest?"

"Let's take him home," Zit said. "We can talk to his parents."

"I think that's a great idea," I said. "I'm sure my parents will be anxious to hear how their tax dollars are being spent—"

I'd pushed it too far. Booger had been reaching for the door handle but now he whirled on me, all Hulked out and throbbing veins. "Why don't you shut up right now, while it's still an option? After everything that's happened in the past two weeks, it wouldn't kill you to cooperate with us. You know what, maybe we *should* arrest you. You can spend a day or two in jail while your lawyer looks for you. A lot can happen in that time. A *lot*. How'd you like that?"

I didn't say anything. I'd been giddy and angry. Now I was scared witless.

"I'm sorry," I managed, hating myself again for saying it.

Booger got in the front seat and Zit put the car in gear, cruising up 24th Street and over Potrero Hill. They had my address from my ID.

Mom answered the door after they rang the bell, leaving the chain on. She peeked around it, saw me and said, "Marcus? Who are these men?"

"Police," Booger said. He showed her his badge, letting her get a good look at it—not whipping it away the way he had with me. "Can we come in?"

Mom closed the door and took the chain off and let them in. They brought me in and Mom gave the three of us one of her looks.

"What's this about?"

Booger pointed at me. "We wanted to ask your son some routine questions about his movements, but he declined to answer them. We felt it might be best to bring him here."

"Is he under arrest?" Mom's accent was coming on strong. Good old Mom.

"Are you a United States citizen, ma'am?" Zit said.

She gave him a look that could have stripped paint. "I shore am, hyuck," she said, in a broad southern accent. "Am *I* under arrest?"

The two cops exchanged a look.

Zit took the fore. "We seem to have gotten off to a bad start. We identified your son as someone with a nonstandard public transit usage pattern, as part of a new proactive enforcement program. When we spot people whose travels are unusual, or that match a suspicious profile, we investigate further."

"Wait," Mom said. "How do you know how my son uses the Muni?"

"The Fast Pass," he said. "It tracks voyages."

"I see," Mom said, folding her arms. Folding her arms was a bad sign. It was bad enough she hadn't offered them a cup of tea—in Mom-land, that was practically like making them shout through the mail slot—but once she folded her arms, it was not going to end well for them. At that moment, I wanted to go and buy her a big bunch of flowers.

"Marcus here declined to tell us why his movements had been what they were."

"Are you saying you think my son is a terrorist because of how he rides the bus?"

"Terrorists aren't the only bad guys we catch this way," Zit said. "Drug dealers. Gang kids. Even shoplifters smart enough to hit a different neighborhood with every run."

"You think my son is a drug dealer?"

"We're not saying that—" Zit began. Mom clapped her hands at him to shut him up.

"Marcus, please pass me your backpack."

I did.

Mom unzipped it and looked through it, turning her back to us first.

"Officers, I can now affirm that there are no narcotics, explosives or shoplifted gewgaws in my son's bag. I think we're done here. I would like your badge numbers before you go, please."

Booger sneered at her. "Lady, the ACLU is suing three hundred cops on the SFPD, you're going to have to get in line."

Mom made me a cup of tea and then chewed me out for eating dinner when I knew that she'd been making falafel. Dad came home while we were still at the table and Mom and I took turns telling him the story. He shook his head.

"Lillian, they were just doing their jobs." He was still wearing the blue blazer and khakis he wore on the days that he was consulting in Silicon Valley. "The world isn't the same place it was last week."

Mom set down her teacup. "Drew, you're being ridiculous. Your son is not a terrorist. His use of the public transit system is not cause for a police investigation."

Dad took off his blazer. "We do this all the time at my work. It's how computers can be used to find all kinds of errors, anomalies and outcomes. You ask the computer to create a profile of an average record in a database and then ask it to find out which records in the database are furthest away from average. It's part of something called Bayesian analysis and it's been around for centuries now. Without it, we couldn't do spam-filtering—"

"So you're saying that you think the police should suck as hard as my spam filter?" I said.

Dad never got angry at me for arguing with him, but tonight I could see the strain was running high in him. Still, I couldn't resist. My own father, taking the police's side!

"I'm saying that it's perfectly reasonable for the police to conduct their investigations by starting with data-mining, and then following it up with legwork where a human being actually intervenes to see why the abnormality exists. I don't think that a

computer should be telling the police whom to arrest, just helping them sort through the haystack to find a needle."

"But by taking in all that data from the transit system, they're
creating the haystack," I said. "That's a gigantic mountain of data
and there's almost nothing worth looking at there, from the police's point of view. It's a total waste."

"I understand that you don't like that this system caused you
some inconvenience, Marcus. But you of all people should ap-
preciate the gravity of the situation. There was no harm done,
was there? They even gave you a ride home."

They threatened to send me to jail, I thought, but I could see
there was no point in saying it.

"Besides, you still haven't told us where the blazing hells
you've been to create such an unusual traffic pattern."

That brought me up short.

"I thought you relied on my judgment, that you didn't want
to spy on me." He'd said this often enough. "Do you really want
me to account for every trip I've ever taken?"

I hooked up my Xbox as soon as I got to my room. I'd
bolted the projector to the ceiling so that it could shine on the
wall over my bed (I'd had to take down my awesome mural of
punk rock handbills I'd taken down off telephone poles and
glued to big sheets of white paper).

I powered up the Xbox and watched as it came onto the
screen. I was going to email Van and Jolu to tell them about the
hassle with the cops, but as I put my fingers to the keyboard, I
stopped again.

A feeling crept over me, one not unlike the feeling I'd had
when I realized that they'd turned poor old Salmagundi into a
traitor. This time, it was the feeling that my beloved Xnet might

be broadcasting the location of every one of its users to the DHS.

It was what Dad had said: *You ask the computer to create a profile of an average record in a database and then ask it to find out which records in the database are furthest away from average.*

The Xnet was secure because its users weren't directly connected to the Internet. They hopped from Xbox to Xbox until they found one that was connected to the Internet, then they injected their material as undecipherable, encrypted data. No one could tell which of the Internet's packets were Xnet and which ones were just plain old banking and e-commerce and other encrypted communication. You couldn't find out who was tying the Xnet, let alone who was using the Xnet.

But what about Dad's "Bayesian statistics?" I'd played with Bayesian math before. Darryl and I once tried to write our own better spam filter and when you filter spam, you need Bayesian math. Thomas Bayes was an 18th-century British mathematician that no one cared about until a couple hundred years after he died, when computer scientists realized that his technique for statistically analyzing mountains of data would be super-useful for the modern world's info-Himalayas.

Here's some of how Bayesian stats work. Say you've got a bunch of spam. You take every word that's in the spam and count how many times it appears. This is called a "word-frequency histogram" and it tells you what the probability is that any bag of words is likely to be spam. Now, take a ton of email that's not spam—in the biz, they call that "ham"—and do the same.

Wait until a new email arrives and count the words that appear in it. Then use the word-frequency histogram in the candidate message to calculate the probability that it belongs in the "spam" pile or the "ham" pile. If it turns out to be spam, you adjust the "spam" histogram accordingly. There are lots of ways to refine the technique—looking at words in pairs, throwing away old data—but this is how it works at core. It's one of those great, simple ideas that seems obvious after you hear about it.

It's got lots of applications—you can ask a computer to count the lines in a picture and see if it's more like a "dog" line-frequency histogram or a "cat" line-frequency histogram. It can find porn, bank fraud and flamewars. Useful stuff.

And it was bad news for the Xnet. Say you had the whole Internet wiretapped—which, of course, the DHS has. You can't tell who's passing Xnet packets by looking at the contents of those packets, thanks to crypto.

What you *can* do is find out who is sending way, way more encrypted traffic out than everyone else. For a normal Internet surfer, a session online is probably about 95 percent cleartext, 5 percent ciphertext. If someone is sending out 95 percent ciphertext, maybe you could dispatch the computer-savvy equivalents of Booger and Zit to ask them if they're terrorist drug dealer Xnet users.

This happens all the time in China. Some smart dissident will get the idea of getting around the Great Firewall of China, which is used to censor the whole country's Internet connection, by using an encrypted connection to a computer in some other country. Now, the Party there can't tell what the dissident is surfing: maybe it's porn, or bomb-making instructions, or dirty letters from his girlfriend in the Philippines, or political material, or good news about Scientology. They don't have to know. All they have to know is that this guy gets way more encrypted traffic than his neighbors. At that point, they send him to a forced labor camp just to set an example so that everyone can see what happens to smart-asses.

So far, I was willing to bet that the Xnet was under the

DHS's radar, but it wouldn't be the case forever. And after to-night, I wasn't sure that I was in any better shape than a Chinese dissident. I was putting all the people who signed onto the Xnet in jeopardy. The law didn't care if you were actually doing any-thing bad; they were willing to put you under the microscope just for being statistically abnormal. And I couldn't even stop it—now that the Xnet was running, it had a life of its own.

I was going to have to fix it some other way.

I wished I could talk to Jolu about this. He worked at an In-ternet Service Provider called Pigspleen Net that had hired him when he was twelve, and he knew way more about the net than I did. If anyone knew how to keep our butts out of jail, it would be him.

Luckily, Van and Jolu and I were planning to meet for coffee the next night at our favorite place in the Mission after school. Officially, it was our weekly Harajuku Fun Madness team meet-ing, but with the game canceled and Darryl gone, it was pretty much just a weekly weepfest, supplemented by about six phone calls and IMs a day that went, "Are you okay? Did it really hap-pen?" It would be good to have something else to talk about.

"You're out of your mind," Vanessa said. "Are you actually, totally, really, for-real crazy or what?"

She had shown up in her girl's school uniform because she'd been stuck going the long way home, all the way down to the San Mateo bridge then back up into the city, on a shuttle bus service that her school was operating. She hated being seen in public in her gear, which was totally Sailor Moon—a pleated skirt and a tu-nic and kneesocks. She'd been in a bad mood ever since she turned up at the cafe, which was full of older, cooler, mopey emo art students who snickered into their lattes when she turned up.

"What do you want me to do, Van?" I said. I was getting exasperated myself. School was unbearable now that the game wasn't on, now that Darryl was missing. All day long, in my classes, I consoled myself with the thought of seeing my team, what was left of it. Now we were fighting.

"I want you to stop putting yourself at risk, M1k3y." The hairs on the back of my neck stood up. Sure, we always used our team handles at team meetings, but now that my handle was also associated with my Xnet use, it scared me to hear it said aloud in a public place.

"Don't use that name in public anymore," I snapped.

Van shook her head. "That's just what I'm taking about. You could end up going to jail for this, Marcus, and not just you. Lots of people. After what happened to Darryl—"

"I'm doing this for Darryl!" Art students swiveled to look at us and I lowered my voice. "I'm doing this because the alternative is to let them get away with it all."

"You think you're going to stop them? You're out of your mind. They're the government."

"It's still our country," I said. "We still have the right to do this."

Van looked like she was going to cry. She took a couple of deep breaths and stood up. "I can't do it, I'm sorry. I can't watch you do this. It's like watching a car wreck in slow motion. You're going to destroy yourself, and I love you too much to watch it happen."

She bent down and gave me a fierce hug and a hard kiss on the cheek that caught the edge of my mouth. "Take care of yourself, Marcus," she said. My mouth burned where her lips had pressed it. She gave Jolu the same treatment, but square on the cheek. Then she left.

Jolu and I stared at each other after she'd gone.

I put my face in my hands. "Dammit," I said, finally.

Jolu patted me on the back and ordered me another latte. "It'll be okay," he said.

"You'd think Van, of all people, would understand." Van's parents were North Korean refugees. They'd lived under a crazy dictator for decades before escaping to America, determined to give their daughter a better life.

Jolu shrugged. "Maybe that's why she's so freaked out. Because she knows how dangerous it can get."

I knew what he was talking about. Two of Van's uncles had gone to jail after her parents got out and had never reappeared.

"Yeah," I said.

"So how come you weren't on Xnet last night?"

I was grateful for the distraction. I explained it all to him, the Bayesian stuff and my fear that we couldn't go on using Xnet the way we had been without getting nabbed. He listened thoughtfully.

"I see what you're saying. The problem is that if there's too much crypto in someone's Internet connection, they'll stand out as unusual. But if you don't encrypt, you'll make it easy for the bad guys to wiretap you."

"Yeah," I said. "I've been trying to figure it out all day. Maybe we could slow the connection down, spread it out over more peoples' accounts—"

"Won't work," he said. "To get it slow enough to vanish into the noise, you'd have to basically shut down the network, which isn't an option."

"You're right," I said. "But what else can we do?"

"What if we changed the definition of normal?"

And that was why Jolu got hired to work at Pigspleen when

he was twelve. Give him a problem with two bad solutions and he'd figure out a third totally different solution based on throwing away all your assumptions. I nodded vigorously. "Go on, tell me."

"What if the average San Francisco Internet user had a *lot* more crypto in his average day on the Internet? If we could change the split so it's more like fifty-fifty cleartext to ciphertext, then the users that supply the Xnet would just look like normal."

"But how do we do that? People just don't care enough about their privacy to surf the net through an encrypted link. They don't see why it matters if eavesdroppers know what they're googling for."

"Yeah, but Web pages are small amounts of traffic. If we got people to routinely download a few giant encrypted files every day, that would create as much ciphertext as thousands of Web pages."

"You're talking about indienet," I said.

"You got it," he said.

indienet—all lower case, always—was the thing that made Pigspleen Net into one of the most successful independent ISPs in the world. Back when the major record labels started suing their fans for downloading their music, a lot of the independent labels and their artists were aghast. How can you make money by suing your customers?

Pigspleen's founder had the answer: she opened up a deal for any act that wanted to work with their fans instead of fighting them. Give Pigspleen a license to distribute your music to its customers and it would give you a share of the subscription fees based on how popular your music was. For an indie artist, the big problem isn't piracy, it's obscurity: no one even cares enough about your tunes to steal 'em.

It worked. Hundreds of independent acts and labels signed

up with Pigspleen, and the more music there was, the more fans switched to getting their Internet service from Pigspleen, and the more money there was for the artists. Inside of a year, the ISP had a hundred thousand new customers and now it had a million—more than half the broadband connections in the city.

"An overhaul of the indienet code has been on my plate for months now," Jolu said. "The original programs were written really fast and dirty and they could be made a lot more efficient with a little work. But I just haven't had the time. One of the high-marked to-do items has been to encrypt the connections, just because Trudy likes it that way." Trudy Doo was the founder of Pigspleen. She was an old-time San Francisco punk legend, the singer/frontwoman of the anarcho-feminist band Speedwhores, and she was crazy about privacy. I could totally believe that she'd want her music service encrypted on general principles.

"Will it be hard? I mean, how long would it take?"

"Well, there's tons of crypto code for free online, of course," Jolu said. He was doing the thing he did when he was digging into a meaty code problem—getting that faraway look, drumming his fingers on the table, making the coffee slosh into the saucers. I wanted to laugh—everything might be destroyed and crap and scary, but Jolu would write that code.

"Can I help?"

He looked at me. "What, you don't think I can manage it?"

"What?"

"I mean, you did this whole Xnet thing without even telling me. Without talking to me. I kind of thought that you didn't need my help with this stuff."

I was brought up short. "What?" I said again. Jolu was looking really steamed now. It was clear that this had been eating at him for a long time. "Jolu—"

He looked at me and I could see that he was furious. How had I missed this? God, I was such an idiot sometimes. "Look dude, it's not a big deal"—by which he clearly meant that it was a really big deal—"it's just that you know, you never even *asked*. I hate the DHS. Darryl was my friend, too. I could have really helped with it."

I wanted to stick my head between my knees. "Listen Jolu, that was really stupid of me. I did it at like two in the morning. I was just crazy when it was happening. I—" I couldn't explain it. Yeah, he was right, and that was the problem. It had been two in the morning but I could have talked to Jolu about it the next day or the next. I hadn't because I'd known what he'd say—that it was an ugly hack, that I needed to think it through better. Jolu was always figuring out how to turn my 2 A.M. ideas into real code, but the stuff that he came out with was always a little different from what I'd come up with. I'd wanted the project for myself. I'd gotten totally into being M1k3y.

"I'm sorry," I said at last. "I'm really, really sorry. You're totally right. I just got freaked out and did something stupid. I really need your help. I can't make this work without you."

"You mean it?"

"Of course I mean it," I said. "You're the best coder I know. You're a goddamned genius, Jolu. I would be honored if you'd help me with this."

He drummed his fingers some more. "It's just— You know. You're the leader. Van's the smart one. Darryl was . . . He was your second-in-command, the guy who had it all organized, who watched the details. Being the programmer, that was *my* thing. It felt like you were saying you didn't need me."

"Oh man, I am such an idiot. Jolu, you're the best-qualified person I know to do this. I'm really, really, really—"

"All right, already. Stop. Fine. I believe you. We're all really screwed up right now. So yeah, of course you can help. We can probably even pay you—I've got a little budget for contract programmers."

"Really?" No one had ever paid me for writing code.

"Sure. You're probably good enough to be worth it." He grinned and slugged me in the shoulder. Jolu's really easygoing most of the time, which is why he'd freaked me out so much.

I paid for the coffees and we went out. I called my parents and let them know what I was doing. Jolu's mom insisted on making us sandwiches. We locked ourselves in his room with his computer and the code for indienet and we embarked on one of the great all-time marathon programming sessions. Once Jolu's family went to bed around 11:30, we were able to kidnap the coffee machine up to his room and go IV with our magic coffee bean supply.

If you've never programmed a computer, you should. There's nothing like it in the whole world. When you program a computer, it does *exactly* what you tell it to do. It's like designing a machine—any machine, like a car, like a faucet, like a gas hinge for a door—using math and instructions. It's awesome in the truest sense: it can fill you with awe.

A computer is the most complicated machine you'll ever use. It's made of billions of microminiaturized transistors that can be configured to run any program you can imagine. But when you sit down at the keyboard and write a line of code, those transistors do what you tell them to.

Most of us will never build a car. Pretty much none of us will ever create an aviation system. Design a building. Lay out a city.

Those are complicated machines, those things, and they're off-limits to the likes of you and me. But a computer is like, ten times more complicated, and it will dance to any tune you play.

You can learn to write simple code in an afternoon. Start with a language like Python, which was written to give nonprogrammers an easier way to make the machine dance to their tune. Even if you only write code for one day, one afternoon, you have to do it. Computers can control you or they can lighten your work—if you want to be in charge of your machines, you have to learn to write code.

We wrote a lot of code that night.

Chapter 8

I wasn't the only one who got screwed up by the histograms. There are lots of people who have abnormal traffic patterns, abnormal usage patterns. Abnormal is so common, it's practically normal.

The Xnet was full of these stories, and so were the newspapers and the TV news. Husbands were caught cheating on their wives; wives were caught cheating on their husbands; kids were caught sneaking out with illicit girlfriends and boyfriends. A kid who hadn't told his parents he had AIDS got caught going to the clinic for his drugs.

Those were the people with something to hide—not guilty people, but people with secrets. There were even more people with nothing to hide at all, but who nevertheless resented being picked up and questioned. Imagine if someone locked you in the back of a police car and demanded that you prove that you're *not* a terrorist.

It wasn't just public transit. Most drivers in the Bay Area have a FasTrak pass clipped to their sun-visors. This is a little radio-based "wallet" that pays your tolls for you when you cross the bridges, saving you the hassle of sitting in a line for hours at

the toll plazas. They'd tripled the cost of using cash to get across
the bridge (though they always fudged this, saying that FasTrak
was cheaper, not that anonymous cash was more expensive).
Whatever holdouts were left afterward disappeared after the
number of cash lanes was reduced to just one per bridgehead, so
that the cash lines were even longer.

So if you're a local, or if you're driving a rental car from a
local agency, you've got a FasTrak. It turns out that toll plazas
aren't the only place that your FasTrak gets read, though. The
DHS had put FasTrak readers all over town—when you drove
past them, they logged the time and your ID number, building an
ever more perfect picture of who went where and when, in a
database that was augmented by "speeding cameras," "red light
cameras" and all the other license plate cameras that had popped
up like mushrooms.

No one had given it much thought. And now that people
were paying attention, we were all starting to notice little things,
like the fact that the FasTrak doesn't have an off switch.

So if you drove a car, you were just as likely to be pulled over
by an SFPD cruiser that wanted to know why you were taking
so many trips to the Home Depot lately, and what was that midnight drive up to Sonoma last week about?

The little demonstrations around town on the weekend were
growing. Fifty thousand people marched down Market Street after a week of this monitoring. I couldn't care less. The people
who'd occupied my city didn't care what the natives wanted.
They were a conquering army. They knew how we felt about
that.

One morning I came down to breakfast just in time to hear
Dad tell Mom that the two biggest taxi companies were going to
give a "discount" to people who used special cards to pay their

fares, supposedly to make drivers safer by reducing the amount of cash they carried. I wondered what would happen to the information about who took which cabs where.

I realized how close I'd come. The new indienet client had been pushed out as an automatic update just as this stuff started to get bad, and Jolu told me that 80 percent of the traffic he saw at Pigspleen was now encrypted. The Xnet just might have been saved.

Dad was driving me nuts, though.

"You're being paranoid, Marcus," he told me over breakfast one day as I told him about the guys I'd seen the cops shaking down on the BART the day before.

"Dad, it's ridiculous. They're not catching any terrorists, are they? It's just making people scared."

"They may not have caught any terrorists yet, but they're sure getting a lot of scumbags off the streets. Look at the drug dealers—it says they've put dozens of them away since this all started. Remember when those druggies robbed you? If we don't bust their dealers, it'll only get worse." I'd been mugged the year before. They'd been pretty civilized about it. One skinny guy who smelled bad told me he had a gun, the other one asked me for my wallet. They even let me keep my ID, though they got my debit card and Fast Pass. It had still scared me witless and left me paranoid and checking my shoulder for weeks.

"But most of the people they hold up aren't doing anything wrong, Dad," I said. This was getting to me. My own father! "It's crazy. For every guilty person they catch, they have to punish thousands of innocent people. That's just not good."

"Innocent? Guys cheating on their wives? Drug dealers? You're defending them, but what about all the people who died? If you don't have anything to hide—"

"So you wouldn't mind if they pulled *you* over?" My dad's histograms had proven to be depressingly normal so far.

"I'd consider it my duty," he said. "I'd be proud. It would make me feel safer."

Easy for him to say.

Vanessa didn't like me talking about this stuff, but she was too smart about it for me to stay away from the subject for long. We'd get together all the time and talk about the weather and school and stuff, and then, somehow, I'd be back on this subject. Vanessa was cool when it happened—she didn't Hulk out on me again—but I could see it upset her.

Still.

"So my dad says, 'I'd consider it my duty.' Can you freaking *believe* it? I mean, God! I almost told him then about going to jail, asking him if he thought that was our 'duty'!"

We were sitting in the grass in Dolores Park after school, watching the dogs chase Frisbees.

Van had stopped at home and changed into an old T-shirt for one of her favorite Brazilian tecno-brega bands, Carioca Probidão—the forbidden guy from Rio. She'd gotten the shirt at a live show we'd all gone to two years before, sneaking out for a grand adventure down at the Cow Palace, and she'd sprouted an inch or two since, so it was tight and rode up her tummy, showing her flat little belly button.

She lay back in the weak sun with her eyes closed behind her shades, her toes wiggling in her flip-flops. I'd known Van since forever, and when I thought of her, I usually saw the little kid I'd known with hundreds of jangly bracelets made out of sliced-up soda cans, who played the piano and couldn't dance to save her life. Sitting out there in Dolores Park, I suddenly saw her as she was.

She was totally h4wt—that is to say, hot. It was like looking at that picture of a vase and noticing that it was also two faces. I could see that Van was just Van, but I could also see that she was hella pretty, something I'd never noticed.

Of course, Darryl had known it all along, and don't think that I wasn't bummed out anew when I realized this.

"You can't tell your dad, you know," she said. "You'd put us all at risk." Her eyes were closed and her chest was rising up and down with her breath, which was distracting in a really embarrassing way.

"Yeah," I said, glumly. "But the problem is that I know he's just totally full of it. If you pulled my dad over and made him prove he wasn't a child-molesting, drug-dealing terrorist, he'd go berserk. Totally off the rails. He hates being put on hold when he calls about his credit card bill. Being locked in the back of a car and questioned for an hour would give him an aneurism."

"They only get away with it because the normals feel smug compared to the abnormals. If everyone was getting pulled over, it'd be a disaster. No one would ever get anywhere, they'd all be waiting to get questioned by the cops. Total gridlock."

Whoa.

"Van, you are a total genius," I said.

"Tell me about it," she said. She had a lazy smile and she looked at me through half-lidded eyes, almost romantic.

"Seriously. We can do this. We can mess up the profiles easily. Getting people pulled over is easy."

She sat up and pushed her hair off her face and looked at me. I felt a little flip in my stomach, thinking that she was really impressed with me.

"It's the arphid cloners," I said. "They're totally easy to make. Just flash the firmware on a ten-dollar Radio Shack reader/writer and you're done. What we do is go around and randomly swap the tags on people, overwriting their Fast Passes and FasTraks with other people's codes. That'll make *everyone* skew all weird and screwy, and make everyone look guilty. Then: total gridlock."

Van pursed her lips and lowered her shades and I realized she was so angry she couldn't speak.

"Good-bye, Marcus," she said, and got to her feet. Before I knew it, she was walking away so fast she was practically running.

"Van!" I called, getting to my feet and chasing after her. "Van! Wait!"

She picked up speed, making me run to catch up with her.

"Van, what the hell," I said, catching her arm. She jerked it away so hard I punched myself in the face.

"You're psycho, Marcus. You're going to put all your little Xnet buddies in danger for their lives, and on top of it, you're going to turn the whole city into terrorism suspects. Can't you stop before you hurt these people?"

I opened and closed my mouth a couple times. "Van, *I'm* not the problem, *they* are. I'm not arresting people, jailing them, making them disappear. The Department of Homeland Security are the ones doing that. I'm fighting back to make them stop."

"How, by making it worse?"

"Maybe it has to get worse to get better, Van. Isn't that what you were saying? If everyone was getting pulled over—"

"That's not what I meant. I didn't mean you should get everyone arrested. If you want to protest, join the protest movement. Do something positive. Didn't you learn *anything* from Darryl? *Anything?*"

"You're damned right I did," I said, losing my cool. "I learned that they can't be trusted. That if you're not fighting them, you're helping them. That they'll turn the country into a prison if we let them. What did you learn, Van? To be scared all the time, to sit tight and keep your head down and hope you don't get noticed? You think it's going to get better? If we don't do anything, this is as *good as it's going to get*. It will only get worse and worse from now on. You want to help Darryl? Help me bring them down!"

There it was again. My vow. Not to get Darryl free, but to bring down the entire DHS. That was crazy, even I knew it. But it was what I planned to do. No question about it.

Van shoved me hard with both hands. She was strong from school athletics—fencing, lacrosse, field hockey, all the girls-school sports—and I ended up on my ass on the disgusting San Francisco sidewalk. She took off and I didn't follow.

> **The important thing about security systems isn't how they work, it's how they fail.**

That was the first line of my first blog post on Open Revolt, my Xnet site. I was writing as M1k3y, and I was ready to go to war.

> **Maybe all the automatic screening is supposed to catch terrorists. Maybe it will catch a terrorist sooner or later. The problem is that it catches _us_ too, even though we're not doing anything wrong.**

> **The more people it catches, the more brittle it gets. If it catches too many people, it dies.**

> **Get the idea?**

I pasted in my HOWTO for building an arphid cloner, and some tips for getting close enough to people to read and write their tags. I put my own cloner in the pocket of my vintage black leather motocross jacket with the armored pockets and left for school. I managed to clone six tags between home and Chavez High.

It was war they wanted. It was war they'd get.

If you ever decide to do something as stupid as build an automatic terrorism detector, here's a math lesson you need to learn first. It's called "the paradox of the false positive," and it's a doozy.

Say you have a new disease, called Super-AIDS. Only one in a million people gets Super-AIDS. You develop a test for Super-AIDS that's 99 percent accurate. I mean, 99 percent of the time, it gives the correct result—true if the subject is infected, and false if the subject is healthy. You give the test to a million people.

One in a million people have Super-AIDS. One in a hundred people that you test will generate a "false positive"—the test will say he has Super-AIDS even though he doesn't. That's what "99 percent accurate" means: one percent wrong.

What's one percent of one million?

$1,000,000 / 100 = 10,000$.

One in a million people has Super-AIDS. If you test a million random people, you'll probably only find one case of real Super-AIDS. But your test won't identify *one* person as having Super-AIDS. It will identify *ten thousand* people as having it.

Your 99 percent accurate test will perform with 99.99 percent *inaccuracy*.

That's the paradox of the false positive. When you try to find something really rare, your test's accuracy has to match the rarity of the thing you're looking for. If you're trying to point at a single pixel on your screen, a sharp pencil is a good pointer: the pencil tip is a lot smaller (more accurate) than the pixels. But a pencil tip is no good at pointing at a single *atom* in your screen. For that, you need a pointer—a test—that's one atom wide or less at the tip.

This is the paradox of the false positive, and here's how it applies to terrorism:

Terrorists are really rare. In a city of twenty million like New York, there might be one or two terrorists. Maybe ten of them at the outside. $10/20,000,000 = 0.00005$ percent. One twenty-thousandth of a percent.

That's pretty rare all right. Now, say you've got some software that can sift through all the bank records, or toll pass records, or public transit records, or phone call records in the city and catch terrorists 99 percent of the time.

In a pool of twenty million people, a 99 percent accurate test will identify two hundred thousand people as being terrorists. But only ten of them are terrorists. To catch ten bad guys, you have to haul in and investigate two hundred thousand innocent people.

Guess what? Terrorism tests aren't anywhere *close* to 99 percent accurate. More like 60 percent accurate. Even 40 percent accurate, sometimes.

What this all meant was that the Department of Homeland Security had set itself up to fail badly. They were trying to spot incredibly rare events—a person is a terrorist—with inaccurate systems.

Is it any wonder we were able to make such a mess?

I stepped out the front door whistling on a Tuesday morning one week into Operation False Positive. I was rockin' out to some new music I'd downloaded from the Xnet the night before—lots of people sent M1k3y little digital gifts to say thank you for giving them hope.

I turned onto 23rd Street and carefully took the narrow stone steps cut into the side of the hill. As I descended, I passed Mr. Wiener Dog. I don't know Mr. Wiener Dog's real name, but I see him nearly every day, walking his three panting wiener dogs up the staircase to the little parkette. Squeezing past them all on the stairs is pretty much impossible and I always end up tangled in a leash, knocked into someone's front garden or perched on the bumper of one of the cars parked next to the curb.

Mr. Wiener Dog is clearly Someone Important, because he has a fancy watch and always wears a nice suit. I had mentally assumed that he worked down in the financial district.

Today as I brushed up against him, I triggered my arphid cloner, which was already loaded in the pocket of my leather jacket. The cloner sucked down the numbers off his credit cards and his car keys, his passport and the hundred-dollar bills in his wallet.

Even as it was doing that, it was flashing some of them with new numbers, taken from other people I'd brushed against. It was like switching the license plates on a bunch of cars, but invisible and instantaneous. I smiled apologetically at Mr. Wiener Dog and continued down the stairs. I stopped at three of the cars long enough to swap their FasTrak tags with numbers taken off cars I'd gone past the day before.

You might think I was being a little aggro here, but I was cautious and conservative compared to a lot of the Xnetters. A couple girls in the Chemical Engineering program at UC Berkeley had figured out how to make a harmless substance out of kitchen products that would trip an explosive sniffer. They'd had a merry time sprinkling it on their profs' briefcases and jackets, then hiding out and watching the same profs try to get into the auditoriums and libraries on campus, only to get flying-tackled by the new security squads that had sprung up everywhere.

Other people wanted to figure out how to dust envelopes with substances that would test positive for anthrax, but everyone else thought they were out of their minds. Luckily, it didn't seem like they'd be able to figure it out.

I passed by San Francisco General Hospital and nodded with satisfaction as I saw the huge lines at the front doors. They had a police checkpoint, too, of course, and there were enough Xnetters working as interns and cafeteria workers and whatnot there that everyone's badges had been snarled up and swapped around. I'd read the security checks had tacked an hour onto everyone's work day, and the unions were threatening to walk out unless the hospital did something about it.

A few blocks later, I saw an even longer line for the BART. Cops were walking up and down the line pointing people out and calling them aside for questioning, bag searches and pat downs. They kept getting sued for doing this, but it didn't seem to be slowing them down.

I got to school a little ahead of time and decided to walk down to 22nd Street to get a coffee—and I passed a police checkpoint where they were pulling over cars for secondary inspection.

School was no less wild—the security guards on the metal detectors were also wanding our school IDs and pulling out students with odd movements for questioning. Needless to say, we all had pretty weird movements. Needless to say, classes were starting an hour or more later.

Classes were crazy. I don't think anyone was able to concentrate. I overheard two teachers talking about how long it had taken them to get home from work the day before, and planning to sneak out early that day.

It was all I could do to keep from laughing. The paradox of the false positive strikes again!

Sure enough, they let us out of class early and I headed home the long way, circling through the Mission to see the havoc. Long lines of cars. BART stations lined up around the blocks. People swearing at ATMs that wouldn't dispense their money because they'd had their accounts frozen for suspicious activity (that's the danger of wiring your checking account straight into your Fas-Trak and Fast Pass!).

I got home and made myself a sandwich and logged into the Xnet. It had been a good day. People from all over town were crowing about their successes. We'd brought the city of San Francisco to a standstill. The news reports confirmed it—they were calling it the DHS gone haywire, blaming it all on the fake-ass "security" that was supposed to be protecting us from terrorism. The Business section of the San Francisco *Chronicle* gave its whole front page to an estimate of the economic cost of the DHS security resulting from missed work hours, meetings and so on. According to the *Chronicle*'s economist, a week of this crap would cost the city more than the Bay Bridge bombing had.

Mwa-ha-ha-ha.

The best part: Dad got home that night late. Very late. Three *hours* late. Why? Because he'd been pulled over, searched, questioned. Then it happened *again*. Twice.

Twice!

Chapter 9

He was so angry I thought he was going to pop. You know I said I'd only seen him lose his cool rarely? That night, he lost it more than he ever had.

"You wouldn't believe it. This cop, he was like eighteen years old and he kept saying, 'But sir, why were you in Berkeley yesterday if your client is in Mountain View?' I kept explaining to him that I teach at Berkeley and then he'd say, 'I thought you were a consultant,' and we'd start over again. It was like some kind of sitcom where the cops have been taken over by the stupidity ray.

"What's worse was he kept insisting that I'd been in Berkeley today as well, and I kept saying no, I hadn't been, and he said I had been. Then he showed me my FasTrak billing and it said I'd driven the San Mateo bridge three times that day!

"That's not all," he said, and drew in a breath that let me know he was really steamed. "They had information about where I'd been, places that *didn't have a toll plaza*. They'd been polling my pass just on the street, at random. And it was *wrong*! Holy crap, I mean, they're spying on us all and they're not even competent!"

I'd drifted down into the kitchen as he railed there, and now I was watching him from the doorway. Mom met my eye and we both raised our eyebrows as if to say, *Who's going to say 'I told you so' to him?* I nodded at her. She could use her spousular powers to nullify his rage in a way that was out of my reach as a mere filial unit.

"Drew," she said, and grabbed him by the arm to make him stop stalking back and forth in the kitchen, waving his arms like a street preacher.

"What?" he snapped.

"I think you owe Marcus an apology." She kept her voice even and level. Dad and I are the spazzes in the household—Mom's a total rock.

Dad looked at me. His eyes narrowed as he thought for a minute. "All right," he said at last. "You're right. I was talking about competent surveillance. These guys were total amateurs. I'm sorry, son," he said. "You were right. That was ridiculous." He stuck his hand out and shook my hand, then gave me a firm, unexpected hug.

"God, what are we doing to this country, Marcus? Your generation deserves to inherit something better than this." When he let me go, I could see the deep wrinkles in his face, lines I'd never noticed.

I went back up to my room and played some Xnet games. There was a good multiplayer thing, a clockwork pirate game where you had to quest every day or two to wind up your whole crew's mainsprings before you could go plundering and pillaging again. It was the kind of game I hated but couldn't stop playing: lots of repetitive quests that weren't all that satisfying to complete, a little bit of player-versus-player combat (scrapping to see who would captain the ship) and not that many cool puzzles that you had to figure out. Mostly, playing this kind of game made me homesick for Harajuku Fun Madness, which balanced out running around in the real world, figuring out online puzzles and strategizing with your team.

But today it was just what I needed. Mindless entertainment. My poor dad.

I'd done that to him. He'd been happy before, confident that his tax dollars were being spent to keep him safe. I'd destroyed that confidence. It was false confidence, of course, but it had kept him going. Seeing him now, miserable and broken, I wondered if it was better to be clear-eyed and hopeless or to live in a fool's paradise. That shame—the shame I'd felt since I gave up my pass-words, since they'd broken me—returned, leaving me listless and wanting to just get away from myself.

My character was a swabbie on the pirate ship *Zombie Charger*, and he'd wound down while I'd been offline. I had to IM all the other players on my ship until I found one willing to wind me up. That kept me occupied. I liked it, actually. There was something magic about a total stranger doing you a favor. And since it was the Xnet, I knew that all the strangers were friends, in some sense.

> **Where u located?**

The character who wound me up was called Lizanator, and it was female, though that didn't mean that it was a girl. Guys had some weird affinity for playing female characters.

> **San Francisco**

I said.

> **No stupe, where you located in San Fran?**
> **Why, you a pervert?**

That usually shut down that line of conversation. Of course every gamespace was full of pedos and pervs, and cops pretend-ing to be pedo- and perv-bait (though I sure hoped there weren't any cops on the Xnet!). An accusation like that was enough to change the subject nine out of ten times.

> **Mission? Potrero Hill? Noe? East Bay?**
> **Just wind me up k thx?**
She stopped winding.
> **You scared?**
> **Safe—why do you care?**
> **Just curious**

I was getting a bad vibe off her. She was clearly more than just curious. Call it paranoia. I logged off and shut down my Xbox.

Dad looked at me over the table the next morning and said, "It looks like it's going to get better, at least." He handed me a copy of the *Chronicle* open to the third page.

> A Department of Homeland Security spokesman has confirmed that the San Francisco office has requested a 300 percent budget and personnel increase from Washington, DC.

What?

> Major General Graeme Sutherland, the commanding officer for Northern California DHS operations, confirmed the request at a press conference yesterday, noting that a spike in suspicious activity in the Bay Area prompted the request. "We are tracking a spike in underground chatter and activity and believe that saboteurs are deliberately manufacturing false security alerts to undermine our efforts."

My eyes crossed. No freaking way.

> "These false alarms are potentially 'radar chaff' intended to disguise real attacks. The only effective way of combatting them is to step up staffing and analyst levels so that we can fully investigate every lead."
>
> Sutherland noted the delays experienced all over the city were "unfortunate" and committed to eliminating them.

I had a vision of the city with four or five times as many DHS enforcers, brought in to make up for my own stupid ideas. Van was right. The more I fought them, the worse it was going to get.

Dad pointed at the paper. "These guys may be fools, but they're methodical fools. They'll just keep throwing resources at this problem until they solve it. It's tractable, you know. Mining all the data in the city, following up on every lead. They'll catch the terrorists."

I lost it. "Dad! Are you *listening to yourself*? They're talking about investigating practically every person in the city of San Francisco!"

"Yeah," he said, "that's right. They'll catch every alimony cheat, every dope dealer, every dirtbag and every terrorist. You just wait. This could be the best thing that ever happened to this country."

"Tell me you're joking," I said. "I beg you. You think that that's what they intended when they wrote the Constitution? What about the Bill of Rights?"

"The Bill of Rights was written before data-mining," he said. He was awesomely serene, convinced of his rightness. "The right to freedom of association is fine, but why shouldn't the cops be allowed to mine your social network to figure out if you're hanging out with gangbangers and terrorists?"

"Because it's an invasion of my privacy!" I said.

"What's the big deal? Would you rather have privacy or terrorists?"

Agh. I hated arguing with my dad like this. I needed a coffee. "Dad, come on. Taking away our privacy isn't catching terrorists: it's just inconveniencing normal people."

"How do you know it's not catching terrorists?"

"Where are the terrorists they've caught?"

"I'm sure we'll see arrests in good time. You just wait."

"Dad, what the hell has happened to you since last night? You were ready to go nuclear on the cops for pulling you over—"

"Don't use that tone with me, Marcus. What's happened since last night is that I've had the chance to think it over and to read *this*." He rattled his paper. "The reason they caught me is that the bad guys are actively jamming them. They need to adjust their techniques to overcome the jamming. But they'll get there. Meanwhile the occasional road stop is a small price to pay. This isn't the time to be playing lawyer about the Bill of Rights. This is the time to make some sacrifices to keep our city safe."

I couldn't finish my toast. I put the plate in the dishwasher and left for school. I had to get out of there.

The Xnetters weren't happy about the stepped-up police surveillance, but they weren't going to take it lying down. Someone called a phone-in show on KQED and told them that the police were wasting their time, that we could monkey-wrench the system faster than they could untangle it. The recording was a top Xnet download that night.

"This is California Live and we're talking to an anonymous caller at a pay phone in San Francisco. He has his own information about the slowdowns we've been facing around town this week. Caller, you're on the air."

"Yeah, yo, this is just the beginning, you know? I mean, like, we're just getting started. Let them hire a billion pigs and put a checkpoint on every corner. We'll jam them all! And like, all this crap about terrorists? We're not terrorists! Give me a break, I mean, really! We're jamming up the system because we hate the Homeland Security, and because we love our city. Terrorists? I can't even spell jihad. Peace out."

He sounded like an idiot. Not just the incoherent words, but also his gloating tone. He sounded like a kid who was indecently proud of himself. He *was* a kid who was indecently proud of himself.

The Xnet flamed out over this. Lots of people thought he was an idiot for calling in, while others thought he was a hero. I worried that there was probably a camera aimed at the pay phone he'd used. Or an arphid reader that might have sniffed his Fast Pass. I hoped he'd had the smarts to wipe his fingerprints off the quarter, keep his hood up and leave all his arphids at home. But I doubted it. I wondered if he'd get a knock on the door sometime soon.

The way I knew when something big had happened on Xnet was that I'd suddenly get a million emails from people who wanted M1k3y to know about the latest haps. It was just as I was reading about Mr. Can't-Spell-Jihad that my mailbox went crazy. Everyone had a message for me—a link to a LiveJournal on the Xnet—one of the many anonymous blogs that were based on the Freenet document publishing system that was also used by Chinese democracy advocates.

> Close call

> We were jamming at the Embarcadero tonite and goofing around giving everyone a new car key or door key or Fast Pass or FasTrak, tossing around a little fake gunpowder. There were cops everywhere but we were smarter than them; we're there pretty much every night and we never get caught.

> So we got caught tonight. It was a stupid mistake we got sloppy we got busted. It was an undercover who caught my pal and then got the rest of us. They'd been watching the crowd for a long time and they had one of those trucks nearby and they took four of us in but missed the rest.

> The truck was JAMMED like a can of sardines with every kind of person, old young black white rich poor all suspects, and there were two cops trying to ask us questions and the undercovers kept bringing in more of us. Most people were trying to get to the front of the line to get through questioning so we kept on moving back and it was like hours in there and really hot and it was getting more crowded not less.

> At like 8PM they changed shifts and two new cops came in and bawled out the two cops who were there all like wtf? aren't you doing anything here. They had a real fight and then the two old cops left and the new cops sat down at their desks and whispered to each other for a while.

> Then one cop stood up and started shouting EVERYONE JUST GO HOME JESUS CHRIST WE'VE GOT BETTER THINGS TO DO THAN BOTHER YOU WITH MORE QUESTIONS IF

YOU'VE DONE SOMETHING WRONG JUST DON'T DO IT AGAIN
AND LET THIS BE A WARNING TO YOU ALL.

> A bunch of the suits got really pissed which
was HILARIOUS because I mean ten minutes before they
were buggin about being held there and now they were
wicked pissed about being let go, like make up your
minds!

> We split fast though and got out and came home
to write this. There are undercovers everywhere, believe. If you're jamming, be open-eyed and get ready
to run when problems happen. If you get caught try to
wait it out they're so busy they'll maybe just let
you go.

> We made them that busy! All those people in that
truck were there because we'd jammed them. So jam on!

I felt like I was going to throw up. Those four people—kids
I'd never met—they nearly went away forever because of something I'd started.

Because of something I'd told them to do. I was no better
than a terrorist.

The DHS got their budget requisition approved. The
President went on TV with the Governor to tell us that no price
was too high for security. We had to watch it the next day in
school at assembly. My dad cheered. He'd hated the President since
the day he was elected, saying he wasn't any better than the last guy
and the last guy had been a complete disaster, but now all he could
do was talk about how decisive and dynamic the new guy was.

"You have to take it easy on your father," Mom said to me
one night after I got home from school. She'd been working from

home as much as possible. Mom's a freelance relocation specialist who helps British people get settled in in San Francisco. The UK High Commission pays her to answer emails from mystified British people across the country who are totally confused by how freaky we Americans are. She explains Americans for a living, and she said that these days it was better to do that from home, where she didn't have to actually see any Americans or talk to them.

I don't have any illusions about Britain. America may be willing to trash its Constitution every time some jihadist looks cross-eyed at us, but as I learned in my ninth-grade Social Studies independent project, the Brits don't even *have* a Constitution. They've got laws there that would curl the hair on your toes: they can put you in jail for an entire year if they're really sure that you're a terrorist but don't have enough evidence to prove it. Now, how sure can they be if they don't have enough evidence to prove it? How'd they get that sure? Did they see you committing terrorist acts in a really vivid dream?

And the surveillance in Britain makes America look like amateur hour. The average Londoner is photographed five hundred times a day, just walking around the streets. Every license plate is photographed at every corner in the country. Everyone from the banks to the public transit company is enthusiastic about tracking you and snitching on you if they think you're remotely suspicious.

But Mom didn't see it that way. She'd left Britain halfway through high school and she'd never felt at home here, no matter that she'd married a boy from Petaluma and raised a son here. To her, this was always the land of barbarians, and Britain would always be home.

"Mom, he's just wrong. You of all people should know that. Everything that makes this country great is being flushed down the toilet and he's going along with it. Have you noticed that they haven't *caught any terrorists*? Dad's all like, 'We need to be safe,' but he needs to know that most of us don't feel safe. We feel endangered all the time."

"I know this all, Marcus. Believe me, I'm not a fan of what's been happening to this country. But your father is—" She broke off. "When you didn't come home after the attacks, he thought—"

She got up and made herself a cup of tea, something she did whenever she was uncomfortable or disconcerted.

"Marcus," she said. "Marcus, we thought you were dead. Do you understand that? We were mourning you for days. We were imagining you blown to bits, at the bottom of the ocean. Dead because some bastard decided to kill hundreds of strangers to make some point."

That sank in slowly. I mean, I understood that they'd been worried. Lots of people died in the bombings—four thousand was the present estimate—and practically everyone knew someone who didn't come home that day. There were two people from my school who had disappeared.

"Your father was ready to kill someone. Anyone. He was out of his mind. You've never seen him like this. I've never seen him like it, either. He was out of his mind. He'd just sit at this table and curse and curse and curse. Vile words, words I'd never heard him say. One day—the third day—someone called and he was sure it was you, but it was a wrong number and he threw the phone so hard it disintegrated into thousands of pieces." I'd wondered about the new kitchen phone.

"Something broke in your father. He loves you. We both love you. You are the most important thing in our lives. I don't think you realize that. Do you remember when you were ten, when I went home to London for all that time? Do you remember?"

I nodded silently.

"We were ready to get a divorce, Marcus. Oh, it doesn't matter why anymore. It was just a bad patch, the kind of thing that happens when people who love each other stop paying attention for a few years. He came and got me and convinced me to come back for you. We couldn't bear the thought of doing that to you. We fell in love again for you. We're together today because of you."

I had a lump in my throat. I'd never known this. No one had ever told me.

"So your father is having a hard time right now. He's not in his right mind. It's going to take some time before he comes back to us, before he's the man I love again. We need to understand him until then."

She gave me a long hug, and I noticed how thin her arms had gotten, how saggy the skin on her neck was. I always thought of my mother as young, pale, rosy-cheeked and cheerful, peering shrewdly through her metal-rim glasses. Now she looked a little like an old woman. I had done that to her. The terrorists had done that to her. The Department of Homeland Security had done that to her. In a weird way, we were all on the same side, and Mom and Dad and all those people we'd spoofed were on the other side.

I couldn't sleep that night. Mom's words kept running through my head. Dad had been tense and quiet at dinner and we'd barely spoken, because I didn't trust myself not to say the wrong thing and because he was all wound up over the latest news, that Al Qaeda was definitely responsible for the bombing. Six different terrorist groups had claimed responsibility for the attack, but only Al Qaeda's Internet video disclosed information that the DHS said they hadn't disclosed to anyone.

I lay in bed and listened to a late-night call-in radio show.

The topic was sex problems, with this gay guy who I normally loved to listen to, he would give people such raw advice, but good advice, and he was really funny and campy.

Tonight I couldn't laugh. Most of the callers wanted to ask what to do about the fact that they were having a hard time getting busy with their partners ever since the attack. Even on sextalk radio, I couldn't get away from the topic.

I switched the radio off and heard a purring engine on the street below.

My bedroom is in the top floor of our house, one of the painted ladies. I have a sloping attic ceiling and windows on both sides—one overlooks the whole Mission, the other looks out into the street in front of our place. There were often cars cruising at all hours of the night, but there was something different about this engine noise.

I went to the street window and pulled up my blinds. Down on the street below me was a white, unmarked van whose roof was festooned with radio antennas, more antennas than I'd ever seen on a car. It was cruising very slowly down the street, a little dish on top spinning around and around.

As I watched, the van stopped and one of the back doors popped open. A guy in a DHS uniform—I could spot one from a hundred yards now—stepped out into the street. He had some kind of handheld device, and its blue glow lit his face. He paced back and forth, first scouting my neighbors, making notes on his device, then heading for me. There was something familiar in the way he walked, looking down—

He was using a wifinder! The DHS was scouting for Xnet nodes. I let go of the blinds and dove across my room for my Xbox. I'd left it up while I downloaded some cool animations one of the Xnetters had made of the President's no-price-too-high speech. I yanked the plug out of the wall, then scurried back to the window and cracked the blind a fraction of an inch.

The guy was looking down into his wifinder again, walking back and forth in front of our house. A moment later, he got back into his van and drove away.

I got out my camera and took as many pictures as I could of the van and its antennas. Then I opened them in a free image-editor called the GIMP and edited out everything from the photo except the van, erasing my street and anything that might identify me.

I posted them to Xnet and wrote down everything I could about the vans. These guys were definitely looking for the Xnet, I could tell.

Now I really couldn't sleep.

Nothing for it but to play windup pirates. There'd be lots of players even at this hour. The real name for windup pirates was Clockwork Plunder, and it was a hobbyist project that had been created by teenaged death metal freaks from Finland. It was totally free to play, and offered just as much fun as any of the $15/month services like Ender's Universe and Middle Earth Quest and Discworld Dungeons.

I logged back in and there I was, still on the deck of the *Zombie Charger,* waiting for someone to wind me up. I hated this part of the game.

> **Hey you**

I typed to a passing pirate.

> **Wind me up?**

He paused and looked at me.

> **y should i?**

> **We're on the same team. Plus you get experience points.**

What a jerk.

> **Where are you located?**

> **San Francisco**

This was starting to feel familiar.

> **Where in San Francisco?**

I logged out. There was something weird going on in the game. I jumped onto the LiveJournals and began to crawl from blog to blog. I got through half a dozen before I found something that froze my blood.

LiveJournalers love quizzes. What kind of hobbit are you? Are you a great lover? What planet are you most like? Which character from some movie are you? What's your emotional type? They fill them in and their friends fill them in and everyone compares their results. Harmless fun.

But the quiz that had taken over the blogs of the Xnet that night was what scared me, because it was anything but harmless:

> _ **What's your sex**

> _ **What grade are you in?**

> _ **What school do you go to?**

> _ **Where in the city do you live?**

The quizzes plotted the results on a map with colored push-pins for schools and neighborhoods, and made lame recommendations for places to buy pizza and stuff.

But look at those questions. Think about my answers:

> _ **Male**

> _ **17**

> _ **Chavez High**

> _ **Potrero Hill**

There were only two people in my whole school who matched that profile. Most schools it would be the same. If you wanted to figure out who the Xnetters were, you could use these quizzes to find them all.

That was bad enough, but what was worse was what it implied: someone from the DHS was using the Xnet to get at us. The Xnet was compromised by the DHS.

We had spies in our midst.

I'd given Xnet discs to hundreds of people, and they'd done the same. I knew the people I gave the discs to pretty well. Some of them I knew very well. I've lived in the same house all my life and I've made hundreds and hundreds of friends over the years, from people who went to day care with me to people I played soccer with, people who LARPed with me, people I met clubbing, people I knew from school. My ARG team were my closest friends, but there were plenty of people I knew and trusted enough to hand an Xnet disc to.

I needed them now.

I woke Jolu up by ringing his cell phone and hanging up after the first ring, three times in a row. A minute later, he was up on Xnet and we were able to have a secure chat. I pointed him to my blog-post on the radio vans and he came back a minute later all freaked out.

> `You sure they're looking for us?`

In response I sent him to the quiz.

> `OMG we're doomed`

> `No it's not that bad but we need to figure out who we can trust`

> `How?`

> `That's what I wanted to ask you—how many people can you totally vouch for like trust them to the ends of the earth?`

> Um 20 or 30 or so

> I want to get a bunch of really trustworthy people together and do a key-exchange web-of-trust thing

Web of trust is one of those cool crypto things that I'd read about but never tried. It was a nearly foolproof way to make sure that you could talk to the people you trusted, but that no one else could listen in. The problem is that it requires you to physically meet with the people in the Web at least once, just to get started.

> I get it sure. That's not bad. But how you going to get everyone together for the key-signing?

> That's what I wanted to ask you about—how can we do it without getting busted?

Jolu typed some words and erased them, typed more and erased them.

> Darryl would know

I typed.

> God, this was the stuff he was great at.

Jolu didn't type anything. Then,

> How about a party?

he typed.

> How about if we all get together somewhere like we're teenagers having a party and that way we'll have a ready-made excuse if anyone shows up asking us what we're doing there?

> That would totally work! You're a genius, Jolu.

> I know it. And you're going to love this: I know just where to do it, too

> Where?

> Sutro Baths!

Chapter 10

What would you do if you found out you had a spy in
your midst? You could denounce him, put him up against the
wall and take him out. But then you might end up with another
spy in your midst, and the new spy would be more careful than
the last one and maybe not get caught quite so readily.

Here's a better idea: start intercepting the spy's communications and feed him and his masters misinformation. Say his masters instruct him to gather information on your movements. Let
him follow you around and take all the notes he wants, but steam
open the envelopes that he sends back to HQ and replace his account of your movements with a fictitious one. If you want, you
can make him seem erratic and unreliable so they get rid of him.
You can manufacture crises that might make one side or the
other reveal the identities of other spies. In short, you own them.

This is called the man-in-the-middle attack and if you think
about it, it's pretty scary. Someone who man-in-the-middles
your communications can trick you in any of a thousand ways.

Of course, there's a great way to get around the man-in-the-
middle attack: use crypto. With crypto, it doesn't matter if the
enemy can see your messages, because he can't decipher them,

change them and resend them. That's one of the main reasons to use crypto.

But remember: for crypto to work, you need to have keys for the people you want to talk to. You and your partner need to share a secret or two, some keys that you can use to encrypt and decrypt your messages so that men-in-the-middle get locked out.

That's where the idea of public keys comes in. This is a little hairy, but it's so unbelievably elegant, too.

In public-key crypto, each user gets two keys. They're long strings of mathematical gibberish, and they have an almost magic property. Whatever you scramble with one key, the other will unlock, and vice versa. What's more, they're the *only* keys that can do this—if you can unscramble a message with one key, you *know* it was scrambled with the other (and vice versa).

So you take either one of these keys (it doesn't matter which one) and you just *publish* it. You make it a total *nonsecret*. You want anyone in the world to know what it is. For obvious reasons, they call this your "public key."

The other key, you hide in the darkest reaches of your mind. You protect it with your life. You never let anyone ever know what it is. That's called your "private key." (Duh.)

Now say you're a spy and you want to talk with your bosses. Their public key is known by everyone. Your public key is known by everyone. No one knows your private key but you. No one knows their private key but them.

You want to send them a message. First, you encrypt it with your private key. You could just send that message along, and it would work pretty well, since they would know when the message arrived that it came from you. How? Because if they can decrypt it with your public key, it can *only* have been encrypted with your private key. This is the equivalent of putting your seal or signature on the bottom of a message. It says, "I wrote this, and no one else. No one could have tampered with it or changed it."

Unfortunately, this won't actually keep your message a *secret*. That's because your public key is really well known (it has to be, or you'll be limited to sending messages to those few people who have your public key). Anyone who intercepts the message can read it. They can't change it and make it seem like it came from you, but if you don't want people to know what you're saying, you need a better solution.

So instead of just encrypting the message with your private key, you *also* encrypt it with your boss's public key. Now it's been locked twice. The first lock—the boss's public key—only comes off when combined with your boss's private key. The second lock—your private key—only comes off with your public key. When your bosses receive the message, they unlock it with both keys and now they know for sure that: a) you wrote it, and b) only they can read it.

It's very cool. The day I discovered it, Darryl and I immediately exchanged keys and spent months cackling and rubbing our hands as we exchanged our military-grade secret messages about where to meet after school and whether Van would ever notice him.

But if you want to understand security, you need to consider the most paranoid possibilities. Like, what if I tricked you into thinking that *my* public key was your boss's public key? You'd encrypt the message with your private key and my public key. I'd decrypt it, read it, reencrypt it with your boss's *real* public key and send it on. As far as your boss knows, no one but you could have written the message and no one but him could have read it.

And I get to sit in the middle, like a fat spider in a web, and all your secrets belong to me.

Now, the easiest way to fix this is to really widely advertise your public key. If it's *really* easy for anyone to know what your real key is, man-in-the-middle gets harder and harder. But you know what? Making things well known is just as hard as keeping them secret. Think about it—how many billions of dollars are spent on shampoo ads and other crap, just to make sure that as many people know about something that some advertiser wants them to know?

There's a cheaper way of fixing man-in-the-middle: the web of trust. Say that before you leave HQ, you and your bosses sit down over coffee and actually tell each other your keys. No more man-in-the-middle! You're absolutely certain whose keys you have, because they were put into your own hands.

So far, so good. But there's a natural limit to this: how many people can you physically meet with and swap keys? How many hours in the day do you want to devote to the equivalent of writing your own phone book? How many of those people are willing to devote that kind of time to you?

Thinking about this like a phone book helps. The world was once a place with a lot of phone books, and when you needed a number, you could look it up in the book. But for many of the numbers that you wanted to refer to on a given day, you would either know it by heart or you'd be able to ask someone else. Even today, when I'm out with my cell phone, I'll ask Jolu or Darryl if they have a number I'm looking for. It's faster and easier than looking it up online and they're more reliable, too. If Jolu has a number, I trust him, so I trust the number, too. That's called "transitive trust"—trust that moves across the web of our relationships.

A web of trust is a bigger version of this. Say I meet Jolu and get his key. I can put it on my "keyring"—a list of keys that I've signed with my private key. That means you can unlock it with my public key and know for sure that me—or someone with my key, anyway—says that "this key belongs to this guy."

So I hand you my keyring and provided that you trust me to have actually met and verified all the keys on it, you can take it and add it to your keyring. Now, you meet someone else and you hand the whole ring to him. Bigger and bigger the ring grows, and provided that you trust the next guy in the chain, and he trusts the next guy in his chain and so on, you're pretty secure.

Which brings me to keysigning parties. These are *exactly* what they sound like: a party where everyone gets together and signs everyone else's keys. Darryl and I, when we traded keys, that was kind of a mini keysigning party, one with only two sad and geeky attendees. But with more people, you create the seed of the web of trust, and the web can expand from there. As everyone on your keyring goes out into the world and meets more people, they can add more and more names to the ring. You don't have to meet the new people, just trust that the signed key you get from the people in your web is valid.

So that's why web of trust and parties go together like peanut butter and chocolate.

"Just tell them it's a superprivate party, invitational only," I said. "Tell them not to bring anyone along or they won't be admitted."

Jolu looked at me over his coffee. "You're joking, right? You tell people that, and they'll bring *extra* friends."

"Argh," I said. I spent a night a week at Jolu's these days, keeping the code up to date on indienet. Pigspleen actually paid me a nonzero sum of money to do this, which was really weird. I never thought I'd be paid to write code.

"So what do we do? We only want people we really trust there, and we don't want to mention why until we've got everyone's keys and can send them messages in secret."

Jolu debugged and I watched over his shoulder. This used to be called "extreme programming," which was a little embarrassing. Now we just call it "programming." Two people are much better at spotting bugs than one. As the cliche goes, "With enough eyeballs, all bugs are shallow."

We were working our way through the bug reports and getting ready to push out the new rev. It all autoupdated in the background, so our users didn't really need to do anything, they just woke up once a week or so with a better program. It was pretty freaky to know that the code I wrote would be used by hundreds of thousands of people, *tomorrow*!

"What do we do? Man, I don't know. I think we just have to live with it."

I thought back to our Harajuku Fun Madness days. There were lots of social challenges involving large groups of people as part of that game.

"Okay, you're right. But let's at least try to keep this secret. Tell them that they can bring a maximum of one person, and it has to be someone they've known personally for a minimum of five years."

Jolu looked up from the screen. "Hey," he said. "Hey, that would totally work. I can really see it. I mean, if you told me not to bring anyone, I'd be all, 'Who the hell does he think he is?' But when you put it that way, it sounds like some awesome 007 stuff."

I found a bug. We drank some coffee. I went home and played a little Clockwork Plunder, trying not to think about keywinders with nosy questions, and slept like a baby.

Sutro Baths are San Francisco's authentic fake
Roman ruins. When it opened in 1896, it was the largest in-
door bathing house in the world, a huge Victorian glass solar-
ium filled with pools and tubs and even an early water slide. It
went downhill by the fifties, and the owners torched it for the
insurance in 1966. All that's left is a labyrinth of weathered
stone set into the sere cliff face at Ocean Beach. It looks for all
the world like a Roman ruin, crumbled and mysterious, and
just beyond it is a set of caves that let out into the sea. In rough
tides, the waves rush through the caves and over the ruins—
they've even been known to suck in and drown the occasional
tourist.

Ocean Beach is way out past Golden Gate Park, a stark cliff
lined with expensive, doomed houses, plunging down to a narrow beach studded with jellyfish and brave (insane) surfers.
There's a giant white rock that juts out of the shallows off the
shore. That's called Seal Rock, and it used to be the place where
the sea lions congregated until they were relocated to the more
tourist-friendly environs of Fisherman's Wharf.

After dark, there's hardly anyone out there. It gets very cold,
with a salt spray that'll soak you to your bones if you let it. The
rocks are sharp and there's broken glass and the occasional junkie
needle.

It is an awesome place for a party.

Bringing along the tarpaulins and chemical glove-warmers
was my idea. Jolu figured out where to get the beer—his older
brother, Javier, had a buddy who actually operated a whole un-
derage drinking service: pay him enough and he'd back up to
your secluded party spot with ice chests and as many brews as you
wanted. I blew a bunch of my indienet programming money, and
the guy showed up right on time—8 P.M., a good hour after

sunset—and lugged the six foam ice chests out of his pickup truck and down into the ruins of the baths. He even brought a spare chest for the empties.

"You kids play safe now," he said, tipping his cowboy hat. He was a fat Samoan guy with a huge smile, and a scary tank top that you could see his armpit- and belly- and shoulder-hair escaping from. I peeled twenties off my roll and handed them to him—his markup was 150 percent. Not a bad racket.

He looked at my roll. "You know, I could just take that from you," he said, still smiling. "I'm a criminal, after all."

I put my roll in my pocket and looked him levelly in the eye. I'd been stupid to show him what I was carrying, but I knew that there were times when you should just stand your ground.

"I'm just messing with you," he said, at last. "But you be careful with that money. Don't go showing it around."

"Thanks," I said. "Homeland Security'll get my back though."

His smile got even bigger. "Ha! They're not even real five-oh. Those peckerwoods don't know nothin'."

I looked over at his truck. Prominently displayed in his windscreen was a FasTrak. I wondered how long it would be until he got busted.

"You got girls coming tonight? That why you got all the beer?"

I smiled and waved at him as though he was walking back to his truck, which he should have been doing. He eventually got the hint and drove away. His smile never faltered.

Jolu helped me hide the coolers in the rubble, working with little white LED torches on headbands. Once the coolers were in place, we threw little white LED keychains into each one, so it would glow when you took the styrofoam lid off, making it easier to see what you were doing.

It was a moonless night and overcast, and the distant street-lights barely illuminated us. I knew we'd stand out like blazes on an infrared scope, but there was no chance that we'd be able to get a bunch of people together without being observed. I'd settle for being dismissed as a little drunken beach party.

I don't really drink much. There's been beer and pot and ecstasy at the parties I've been going to since I was fourteen, but I hated smoking (though I'm quite partial to a hash brownie every now and again), ecstasy took too long—who's got a whole weekend to get high and come down—and beer, well, it was all right, but I didn't see what the big deal was. My favorite was big, elaborate cocktails, the kind of thing served in a ceramic volcano, with six layers, on fire, and a plastic monkey on the rim, but that was mostly for the theater of it all.

I actually like being drunk. I just don't like being hungover, and boy, do I ever get hungover. Though again, that might have to do with the kind of drinks that come in a ceramic volcano.

But you can't throw a party without putting a case or two of beer on ice. It's expected. It loosens things up. People do stupid things after too many beers, but it's not like my friends are the kind of people who have cars. And people do stupid things no matter what—beer or grass or whatever are all incidental to that central fact.

Jolu and I each cracked beers—Anchor Steam for him, a Bud Lite for me—and clinked the bottles together, sitting down on a rock.

"You told them nine P.M.?"

"Yeah," he said.

"Me too."

We drank in silence. The Bud Lite was the least alcoholic thing in the ice chest. I'd need a clear head later.

"You ever get scared?" I said, finally.

He turned to me. "No man, I don't get scared. I'm always scared. I've been scared since the minute the explosions happened. I'm so scared sometimes, I don't want to get out of bed."

"Then why do you do it?"

He smiled. "About that," he said. "Maybe I won't, not for much longer. I mean, it's been great helping you. Great. Really excellent. I don't know when I've done anything so important. But Marcus, bro, I have to say . . ." He trailed off.

"What?" I said, though I knew what was coming next.

"I can't do it forever," he said at last. "Maybe not even for another month. I think I'm through. It's too much risk. The DHS, you can't go to war on them. It's crazy. Really actually crazy."

"You sound like Van," I said. My voice was much more bitter than I'd intended.

"I'm not criticizing you, man. I think it's great that you've got the bravery to do this all the time. But I haven't got it. I can't live my life in perpetual terror."

"What are you saying?"

"I'm saying I'm out. I'm going to be one of those people who acts like it's all okay, like it'll all go back to normal some day. I'm going to use the Internet like I always did, and only use the Xnet to play games. I'm going to get out is what I'm saying. I won't be a part of your plans anymore."

I didn't say anything.

"I know that's leaving you on your own. I don't want that, believe me. I'd much rather you give up with me. You can't declare war on the government of the USA. It's not a fight you're going to win. Watching you try is like watching a bird fly into a window again and again."

He wanted me to say something. What *I* wanted to say was, *Jesus Jolu, thanks so very much for abandoning me! Do you forget what it was like when they took us away? Do you forget what the country used to be like before they took it over?* But that's not what he wanted me to say. What he wanted me to say was:

I understand, Jolu. I respect your choice.

He drank the rest of his beer and pulled out another one and twisted off the cap.

"There's something else," he said.

"What?"

"I wasn't going to mention it, but I want you to understand why I have to do this."

"Jesus, Jolu, *what?*"

"I hate to say it, but you're *white*. I'm not. White people get caught with cocaine and do a little rehab time. Brown people get caught with crack and go to prison for twenty years. White people see cops on the street and feel safer. Brown people see cops on the street and wonder if they're about to get searched. The way the DHS is treating you? The law in this country has always been like that for us."

It was so unfair. I didn't ask to be white. I didn't think I was being braver just because I'm white. But I knew what Jolu was saying. If the cops stopped someone in the Mission and asked to see some ID, chances were that person wasn't white. Whatever risk I ran, Jolu ran more. Whatever penalty I'd pay, Jolu would pay more.

"I don't know what to say," I said.

"You don't have to say anything," he said. "I just wanted you to know, so you could understand."

I could see people walking down the side trail toward us. They were friends of Jolu's, two Mexican guys and a girl I knew from around, short and geeky, always wearing cute black Buddy

Holly glasses that made her look like the outcast art student in a teen movie who comes back as the big success.

Jolu introduced me and gave them beers. The girl didn't take one, but instead produced a small silver flask of vodka from her purse and offered me a drink. I took a swallow—warm vodka must be an acquired taste—and complimented her on the flask, which was embossed with a repeating motif of Parappa the Rapper characters.

"It's Japanese," she said as I played another LED keyring over it. "They have all these great booze-toys based on kids' games. Totally twisted."

I introduced myself and she introduced herself. "Ange," she said, and shook my hand with hers—dry, warm, with short nails. Jolu introduced me to his pals, whom he'd known since computer camp in the fourth grade. More people showed up—five, then ten, then twenty. It was a seriously big group now.

We'd told people to arrive by 9:30 sharp, and we gave it until 9:45 to see who all would show up. About three quarters were Jolu's friends. I'd invited all the people I really trusted. Either I was more discriminating than Jolu or less popular. Now that he'd told me he was quitting, it made me think that he was less discriminating. I was really pissed at him, but trying not to let it show by concentrating on socializing with other people. But he wasn't stupid. He knew what was going on. I could see that he was really bummed. Good.

"Okay," I said, climbing up on a ruin. "Okay, hey, hello?" A few people nearby paid attention to me, but the ones in the back kept on chatting. I put my arms in the air like a referee, but it was too dark. Eventually I hit on the idea of turning my LED keychain on and pointing it at each of the talkers in turn, then at me. Gradually, the crowd fell quiet.

I welcomed them and thanked them all for coming, then asked them to close in so I could explain why we were there. I could tell they were into the secrecy of it all, intrigued and a little warmed up by the beer.

"So here it is. You all use the Xnet. It's no coincidence that the Xnet was created right after the DHS took over the city. The people who did that are an organization devoted to personal liberty, who created the network to keep us safe from DHS spooks and enforcers." Jolu and I had worked this out in advance. We weren't going to cop to being behind it all, not to anyone. It was way too risky. Instead, we'd put it out that we were merely lieutenants in "M1k3y"'s army, acting to organize the local resistance.

"The Xnet isn't pure," I said. "It can be used by the other side just as readily as by us. We know that there are DHS spies who use it now. They use social engineering hacks to try to get us to reveal ourselves so that they can bust us. If the Xnet is going to succeed, we need to figure out how to keep them from spying on us. We need a network within the network."

I paused and let this sink in. Jolu had suggested that this might be a little heavy—learning that you're about to be brought into a revolutionary cell.

"Now, I'm not here to ask you to do anything active. You don't have to go out jamming or anything. You've been brought here because we know you're cool, we know you're trustworthy. It's that trustworthiness I want to get you to contribute tonight. Some of you will already be familiar with the web of trust and keysigning parties, but for the rest of you, I'll run it down quickly—" Which I did.

"Now what I want from you tonight is to meet the people here and figure out how much you can trust them. We're going to help you generate key-pairs and share them with each other."

This part was tricky. Asking people to bring their own laptops wouldn't have worked out, but we still needed to do something hella complicated that wouldn't exactly work with paper and pencil.

I held up a laptop Jolu and I had rebuilt the night before, from the ground up. "I trust this machine. Every component in it was laid by our own hands. It's running a fresh-out-of-the-box version of ParanoidLinux, booted off of the DVD. If there's a trustworthy computer left anywhere in the world, this might well be it.

"I've got a key-generator loaded here. You come up here and give it some random input—mash the keys, wiggle the mouse— and it will use that as the seed to create a random public and private key for you, which it will display on the screen. You can take a picture of the private key with your phone, and hit any key to make it go away forever—it's not stored on the disc at all. Then it will show you your public key. At that point, you call over all the people here you trust and who trust you, and *they* take a picture of the screen with you standing next to it, so they know whose key it is.

"When you get home, you have to convert the photos to keys. This is going to be a lot of work, I'm afraid, but you'll only have to do it once. You have to be super-careful about typing these in—one mistake and you're screwed. Luckily, we've got a way to tell if you've got it right: beneath the key will be a much shorter number, called the 'fingerprint.' Once you've typed in the key, you can generate a fingerprint from it and compare it to the fingerprint, and if they match, you've got it right."

They all boggled at me. Okay, so I'd asked them to do something pretty weird, it's true, but still.

Chapter 11

Jolu stood up.

"This is where it starts, guys. This is how we know which side you're on. You might not be willing to take to the streets and get busted for your beliefs, but if you *have* beliefs, this will let us know it. This will create the web of trust that tells us who's in and who's out. If we're ever going to get our country back, we need to do this. We need to do something like this."

Someone in the audience—it was Ange—had a hand up, holding a beer bottle.

"So call me stupid but I don't understand this at all. Why do you want us to do this?"

Jolu looked at me, and I looked back at him. It had all seemed so obvious when we were organizing it. "The Xnet isn't just a way to play free games. It's the last open communications network in America. It's the last way to communicate without being snooped on by the DHS. For it to work we need to know that the person we're talking to isn't a snoop. That means that we need to know that the people we're sending messages to are the people we think they are.

"That's where you come in. You're all here because we trust you. I mean, really trust you. Trust you with our lives."

Some of the people groaned. It sounded melodramatic and stupid.

I got back to my feet.

"When the bombs went off," I said, and then something welled up in my chest, something painful. "When the bombs went off, there were four of us caught up by Market Street. For whatever reason, the DHS decided that made us suspicious. They put bags over our heads, put us on a ship and interrogated us for days. They humiliated us. Played games with our minds. Then they let us go.

"All except one person. My best friend. He was with us when they picked us up. He'd been hurt and he needed medical care. He never came out again. They say they never saw him. They say that if we ever tell anyone about this, they'll arrest us and make us disappear.

"Forever."

I was shaking. The shame. The goddamned shame. Jolu had the light on me.

"Oh Christ," I said. "You people are the first ones I've told. If this story gets around, you can bet they'll know who leaked it. You can bet they'll come knocking on my door." I took some more deep breaths. "That's why I volunteered on the Xnet. That's why my life, from now on, is about fighting the DHS. With every breath. Every day. Until we're free again. Any one of you could put me in jail now, if you wanted to."

Ange put her hand up again. "We're not going to rat on you," she said. "No way. I know pretty much everyone here and I can promise you that. I don't know how to know who to trust, but I know who *not* to trust: old people. Our parents. Grown-ups.

When they think of someone being spied on, they think of someone *else,* a bad guy. When they think of someone being caught and sent to a secret prison, it's someone *else*—someone brown, someone young, someone foreign.

"They forget what it's like to be our age. To be the object of suspicion *all the time*! How many times have you gotten on the bus and had every person on it give you a look like you'd been gargling turds and skinning puppies?

"What's worse, they're turning into adults younger and younger out there. Back in the day, they used to say, 'Never trust anyone over 30.' I say, 'Don't trust any bastard over 25!'"

That got a laugh, and she laughed, too. She was pretty, in a weird, horsey way, with a long face and a long jaw. "I'm not really kidding, you know? I mean, think about it. Who elected these ass-clowns? Who let them invade our city? Who voted to put the cameras in our classrooms and follow us around with creepy spyware chips in our transit passes and cars? It wasn't a sixteen-year-old. We may be dumb, we may be young, but we're not scum."

"I want that on a T-shirt," I said.

"It would be a good one," she said. We smiled at each other.

"Where do I go to get my keys?" she said, and pulled out her phone.

"We'll do it over there, in the secluded spot by the caves. I'll take you in there and set you up, then you do your thing and take the machine around to your friends to get photos of your public key so they can sign it when they get home."

I raised my voice. "Oh! One more thing! Jesus, I can't believe I forgot this. *Delete those photos once you've typed in the keys!* The last thing we want is a Flickr stream full of pictures of all of us conspiring together."

There was some good-natured, nervous chuckling, then Jolu turned out the light and in the sudden darkness I could see nothing. Gradually, my eyes adjusted and I set off for the cave. Someone was walking behind me. Ange. I turned and smiled at her, and she smiled back, luminous teeth in the dark.

"Thanks for that," I said. "You were great."

"You mean what you said about the bag on your head and everything?"

"I meant it," I said. "It happened. I never told anyone, but it happened." I thought about it for a moment. "You know, with all the time that went by since, without saying anything, it started to feel like a bad dream. It was real though." I stopped and climbed up into the cave. "I'm glad I finally told people. Any longer and I might have started to doubt my own sanity."

I set up the laptop on a dry bit of rock and booted it from the DVD with her watching. "I'm going to reboot it for every person. This is a standard ParanoidLinux disc, though I guess you'd have to take my word for it."

"Hell," she said. "This is all about trust, right?"

"Yeah," I said. "Trust."

I retreated some distance as she ran the key-generator, listening to her typing and mousing to create randomness, listening to the crash of the surf, listening to the party noises from over where the beer was.

She stepped out of the cave, carrying the laptop. On it, in huge white luminous letters, were her public key and her fingerprint and email address. She held the screen up beside her face and waited while I got my phone out.

"Cheese," she said. I snapped her pic and dropped the camera back in my pocket. She wandered off to the revelers and let them each get pics of her and the screen. It was festive. Fun. She really had a lot of charisma—you didn't want to laugh at her, you just wanted to laugh *with* her. And hell, it *was* funny! We were declaring a secret war on the secret police. Who the hell did we think we were?

So it went, through the next hour or so, everyone taking pictures and making keys. I got to meet everyone there. I knew a lot of them—some were my invitees—and the others were friends of my pals or my pals' pals. We should all be buddies. We were, by the time the night was out. They were all good people.

Once everyone was done, Jolu went to make a key, and then turned away, giving me a sheepish grin. I was past my anger with him, though. He was doing what he had to do. I knew that no matter what he said, he'd always be there for me. And we'd been through the DHS jail together. Van, too. No matter what, that would bind us together forever.

I did my key and did the perp-walk around the gang, letting everyone snap a pic. Then I climbed up on the high spot I'd spoken from earlier and called for everyone's attention.

"So a lot of you have noted that there's a vital flaw in this procedure: What if this laptop can't be trusted? What if it's secretly recording our instructions? What if it's spying on us? What if Jose-Luis and I can't be trusted?"

More good-natured chuckles. A little warmer than before, more beery.

"I mean it," I said. "If we were on the wrong side, this could get all of us—all of *you*—into a heap of trouble. Jail, maybe."

The chuckles turned more nervous.

"So that's why I'm going to do this," I said, and picked up a hammer I'd brought from my dad's toolkit. I set the laptop down beside me on the rock and swung the hammer, Jolu following the swing with his keychain light. Crash—I'd always dreamt of killing a laptop with a hammer, and here I was doing it. It felt pornographically good. And bad.

Smash! The screen-panel fell off, shattered into millions of pieces, exposing the keyboard. I kept hitting it, until the keyboard fell off, exposing the motherboard and the hard drive. Crash! I aimed square for the hard drive, hitting it with everything I had. It took three blows before the case split, exposing the fragile media inside. I kept hitting it until there was nothing bigger than a cigarette lighter, then I put it all in a garbage bag. The crowd was cheering wildly—loud enough that I actually got worried that someone far above us might hear over the surf and call the law.

"All right!" I called. "Now, if you'd like to accompany me, I'm going to march this down to the sea and soak it in salt water for ten minutes."

I didn't have any takers at first, but then Ange came forward and took my arm in her warm hand and said, "That was beautiful," in my ear and we marched down to the sea together.

It was perfectly dark by the sea, and treacherous, even with our keychain lights. Slippery, sharp rocks that were difficult enough to walk on even without trying to balance six pounds of smashed electronics in a plastic bag. I slipped once and thought I was going to cut myself up, but Ange caught me with a surprisingly strong grip and kept me upright. I was pulled in right close to her, close enough to smell her perfume, which smelled like new cars. I love that smell.

"Thanks," I managed, looking into the big eyes that were further magnified by her mannish, black-rimmed glasses. I couldn't tell what color they were in the dark, but I guessed something dark, based on her dark hair and olive complexion. She looked Mediterranean, maybe Greek or Spanish or Italian.

I crouched down and dipped the bag in the sea, letting it fill with salt water. I managed to slip a little and soak my shoe, and I swore and she laughed. We'd hardly said a word since we lit out for the ocean. There was something magical in our wordless silence.

At that point, I had kissed a total of three girls in my life, not counting that moment when I went back to school and got a hero's welcome. That's not a gigantic number, but it's not a minuscule one, either. I have reasonable girl radar, and I think I could have kissed her. She wasn't h4wt in the traditional sense, but there's something about a girl and a night and a beach, plus she was smart and passionate and committed.

But I didn't kiss her, or take her hand. Instead we had a moment that I can only describe as spiritual. The surf, the night, the sea and the rocks, and our breathing. The moment stretched. I sighed. This had been quite a ride. I had a lot of typing to do tonight, putting all those keys into my keychain, signing them and publishing the signed keys. Starting the web of trust.

She sighed, too.

"Let's go," I said.

"Yeah," she said.

Back we went. It was a good night, that night.

Jolu waited after for his brother's friend to come by and pick up his coolers. I walked with everyone else up the road to the nearest Muni stop and got on board. Of course, none of us was using an issued Muni pass. By that point, Xnetters habitually cloned someone else's Muni pass three or four times a day, assuming a new identity for every ride.

It was hard to stay cool on the bus. We were all a little drunk, and looking at our faces under the bright bus lights was kind of hilarious. We got pretty loud and the driver used his intercom to tell us to keep it down twice, then told us to shut up right now or he'd call the cops.

That set us to giggling again and we disembarked in a mass before he did call the cops. We were in North Beach now, and there were lots of buses, taxis, the BART at Market Street, neon-lit clubs and cafes to pull apart our grouping, so we drifted away.

I got home and fired up my Xbox and started typing in keys from my phone's screen. It was dull, hypnotic work. I was a little drunk, and it lulled me into a half-sleep.

I was about ready to nod off when a new IM window popped up.

> **herro!**

I didn't recognize the handle—spexgril—but I had an idea who might be behind it.

> **hi**

I typed, cautiously.

> **it's me, from tonight**

Then she paste-bombed a block of crypto. I'd already entered her public key into my keychain, so I told the IM client to try decrypting the code with the key.

> **it's me, from tonight**

It was her!

> **Fancy meeting you here**

I typed, then encrypted it to my public key and mailed it off.

> **It was great meeting you**

I typed.

> **You too. I don't meet too many smart guys who are also cute and also socially aware. Good god, man, you don't give a girl much of a chance.**

My heart hammered in my chest.

> Hello? Tap tap? This thing on? I wasn't born here folks, but I'm sure dying here. Don't forget to tip your waitresses, they work hard. I'm here all week.

I laughed aloud.

> Im here, I'm here. Laughing too hard to type is all

> Well at least my IM comedy-fu is still mighty

Um.

> It was really great to meet you too

> Yeah, it usually is. Where are you taking me?

> Taking you?

> On our next adventure?

> I didnt really have anything planned

> Oki—then I'll take YOU. Friday. Dolores Park. Illegal open air concert. Be there or be a dodecahedron

> Wait what?

> Dont you even read Xnet? Its all over the place. You ever hear of the Speedwhores?

I nearly choked. That was Trudy Doo's band—as in Trudy Doo, the woman who had paid me and Jolu to update the indienet code.

> Yeah Ive heard of them

> They're putting on a huge show and they've got like fifty bands signed to play the bill, going to set up on the tennis courts and bring out their own amp trucks and rock out all night

I felt like I'd been living under a rock. How had I missed that? There was an anarchist bookstore on Valencia that I sometimes passed on the way to school that had a poster of an old revolutionary named Emma Goldman with the caption "If I can't dance, I don't want to be a part of your revolution." I'd been spending all my energies on figuring out how to use the Xnet to organize dedicated fighters so they could jam the DHS, but this was so much cooler. A big concert—I had no idea how to do one of those, but I was glad someone did.

And now that I thought of it, I was damned proud that they were using the Xnet to do it.

The next day I was a zombie. Ange and I had chatted—flirted—until 4 a.m. Lucky for me, it was a Saturday and I was able to sleep in, but between the hangover and the sleep-dep, I could barely put two thoughts together.

By lunchtime, I managed to get up and get my ass out onto the streets. I staggered down toward the Turk's to buy my coffee—these days, if I was alone, I always bought my coffee there, like the Turk and I were part of a secret club.

On the way, I passed a lot of fresh graffiti. I liked Mission graffiti; a lot of the times, it came in huge, luscious murals, or sarcastic art-student stencils. I liked that the Mission's taggers kept right on going, under the nose of the DHS. Another kind of Xnet, I supposed—they must have all kinds of ways of knowing what was going on, where to get paint, what cameras worked. Some of the cameras had been spray-painted over, I noticed.

Maybe they used Xnet!

Painted in ten-foot-high letters on the side of an auto yard's fence were the drippy words: DON'T TRUST ANYONE OVER 25.

I stopped. Had someone left my "party" last night and come here with a can of paint? A lot of those people lived in the neighborhood.

I got my coffee and had a little wander around town. I kept thinking I should be calling someone, seeing if they wanted to get a movie or something. That's how it used to be on a lazy Saturday like this. But who was I going to call? Van wasn't talking to me, I didn't think I was ready to talk to Jolu, and Darryl—

Well, I couldn't call Darryl.

I got my coffee and went home and did a little searching around on the Xnet's blogs. These anonablogs were untraceable to any author—unless that author was stupid enough to put her name on it—and there were a lot of them. Most of them were apolitical, but a lot of them weren't. They talked about schools and the unfairness there. They talked about the cops. Tagging.

Turned out there'd been plans for the concert in the park for weeks. It had hopped from blog to blog, turning into a full-blown movement without my noticing. And the concert was called "DON'T TRUST ANYONE OVER 25."

Well, that explained where Ange got it. It was a good slogan.

Monday morning, I decided I wanted to check out that anarchist bookstore again, see about getting one of those Emma Goldman posters. I needed the reminder.

I detoured down to 16th and Mission on my way to school, then up to Valencia and across. The store was shut, but I got the hours off the door and made sure they still had that poster up.

As I walked down Valencia, I was amazed to see how much of the DON'T TRUST ANYONE OVER 25 stuff there was. Half the shops had DON'T TRUST merch in the windows: lunchboxes, babydoll tees, pencil boxes, trucker hats. The hipster stores have been getting faster and faster, of course. As new memes sweep the net in the course of a day or two, stores have gotten better at putting merch in the windows to match. Some funny little youtube of a guy launching himself with jet-packs made of carbonated water would land in your inbox on Monday and by Tuesday you'd be able to buy T-shirts with stills from the video on it.

But it was amazing to see something make the leap from Xnet to the head shops. Distressed designer jeans with the slogan written in careful high school ballpoint ink. Embroidered patches.

Good news travels fast.

It was written on the blackboard when I got to Ms. Galvez's Social Studies class. We all sat at our desks, smiling at it. It seemed to smile back. There was something profoundly cheering about the idea that we could all trust each other, that the enemy could be identified. I knew it wasn't entirely true, but it wasn't entirely false, either.

Ms. Galvez came in and patted her hair and set down her SchoolBook on her desk and powered it up. She picked up her chalk and turned around to face the board. We all laughed. Good-naturedly, but we laughed.

She turned around and was laughing, too. "Inflation has hit the nation's slogan-writers, it seems. How many of you know where this phrase comes from?"

We looked at each other. "Hippies?" someone said, and we laughed. Hippies are all over San Francisco, both the old stoner kinds with giant skanky beards and tie-dyes, and the new kind, who are more into dress-up and maybe playing Hacky Sack than protesting anything.

"Well, yes, hippies. But when we think of hippies these days, we just think of the clothes and the music. Clothes and music were incidental to the main part of what made that era, the sixties, important.

"You've heard about the civil rights movement to end segregation, white and black kids like you riding buses into the South to sign up black voters and protest against official state racism.

California was one of the main places where the civil rights leaders came from. We've always been a little more political than the rest of the country, and this is also a part of the country where black people have been able to get the same union factory jobs as white people, so they were a little better off than their cousins in the Southland.

"The students at Berkeley sent a steady stream of freedom riders south, and they recruited them from information tables on campus, at Bancroft and Telegraph Avenue. You've probably seen that there are still tables there to this day.

"Well, the campus tried to shut them down. The president of the university banned political organizing on campus, but the civil rights kids wouldn't stop. The police tried to arrest a guy who was handing out literature from one of these tables, and they put him in a van, but three thousand students surrounded the van and refused to let it budge. They wouldn't let them take this kid to jail. They stood on top of the van and gave speeches about the First Amendment and Free Speech.

"That galvanized the Free Speech Movement. That was the start of the hippies, but it was also where more radical student movements came from. Black power groups like the Black Panthers—and later gay rights groups like the Pink Panthers, too. Radical women's groups, even 'lesbian separatists' who wanted to abolish men altogether! And the Yippies. Anyone ever hear of the Yippies?"

"Didn't they levitate the Pentagon?" I said. I'd once seen a documentary about this.

She laughed. "I forgot about that, but yes, that was them! Yippies were like very political hippies, but they weren't serious the way we think of politics these days. They were very playful. Pranksters. They threw money into the New York Stock Exchange. They circled the Pentagon with hundreds of protestors and said a magic spell that was supposed to levitate it. They invented a fictional kind of LSD that you could spray onto people with squirt guns and shot each other with it and pretended to be stoned. They were funny and they made great TV—one Yippie, a clown called Wavy Gravy, used to get hundreds of protestors to dress up like Santa Claus so that the cameras would show police officers arresting and dragging away Santa on the news that night—and they mobilized a lot of people.

"Their big moment was the Democratic National Convention in 1968, where they called for demonstrations to protest the Vietnam War. Thousands of demonstrators poured into Chicago, slept in the parks, and picketed every day. They had lots of bizarre stunts that year, like running a pig called Pigasus for the presidential nomination. The police and the demonstrators fought in the streets—they'd done that many times before, but the Chicago cops didn't have the smarts to leave the reporters alone. They beat up the reporters, and the reporters retaliated by finally showing what really went on at these demonstrations, so the whole country watched their kids being really savagely beaten down by the Chicago police. They called it a 'police riot.'

"The Yippies loved to say, 'Never trust anyone over thirty.' They meant that people who were born before a certain time, when America had been fighting enemies like the Nazis, could never understand what it meant to love your country enough to refuse to fight the Vietnamese. They thought that by the time you hit thirty, your attitudes would be frozen and you couldn't ever understand why the kids of the day were taking to the streets, dropping out, freaking out.

"San Francisco was ground zero for this. Revolutionary armies were founded here. Some of them blew up buildings or robbed banks for their cause. A lot of those kids grew up to be more or less normal, while others ended up in jail. Some of the university dropouts did amazing things—for example, Steve Jobs and Steve Wozniak, who founded Apple Computers and invented the PC."

I was really getting into this. I knew a little of it, but I'd never heard it told like this. Or maybe it had never mattered as much as it did now. Suddenly, those lame, solemn, grown-up street demonstrations didn't seem so lame after all. Maybe there was room for that kind of action in the Xnet movement.

I put my hand up. "Did they win? Did the Yippies win?"

She gave me a long look, like she was thinking it over. No one said a word. We all wanted to hear the answer.

"They didn't lose," she said. "They kind of imploded a little. Some of them went to jail for drugs or other things. Some of them changed their tunes and became yuppies and went on the lecture circuit telling everyone how stupid they'd been, talking about how good greed was and how dumb they'd been.

"But they did change the world. The war in Vietnam ended, and the kind of conformity and unquestioning obedience that people had called patriotism went out of style in a big way. Black rights, women's rights and gay rights came a long way. Chicano rights, rights for disabled people, the whole tradition of civil liberties was created or strengthened by these people. Today's protest movement is the direct descendant of those struggles."

"I can't believe you're talking about them like this," Charles said. He was leaning so far out of his seat he was half standing, and his sharp, skinny face had gone red. He had wet, large eyes and big lips, and when he got excited he looked a little like a fish.

Ms. Galvez stiffened a little, then said, "Go on, Charles."

"You've just described terrorists. Actual terrorists. They

blew up buildings, you said. They tried to destroy the stock exchange. They beat up cops, and stopped cops from arresting people who were breaking the law. They attacked us!"

Ms. Galvez nodded slowly. I could tell she was trying to figure out how to handle Charles, who really seemed like he was ready to pop. "Charles raises a good point. The Yippies weren't foreign agents, they were American citizens. When you say 'They attacked us,' you need to figure out who 'they' and 'us' are. When it's your fellow countrymen—"

"Crap!" he shouted. He was on his feet now. "We were at war then. These guys were giving aid and comfort to the enemy. It's easy to tell who's us and who's them: if you support America, you're us. If you support the people who are shooting at Americans, you're *them*."

"Does anyone else want to comment on this?"

Several hands shot up. Ms. Galvez called on them. Some people pointed out that the reason that the Vietnamese were shooting at Americans is that the Americans had flown to Vietnam and started running around the jungle with guns. Others thought that Charles had a point, that people shouldn't be allowed to do illegal things.

Everyone had a good debate except Charles, who just shouted at people, interrupting them when they tried to get their points out. Ms. Galvez tried to get him to wait for his turn a couple times, but he wasn't having any of it.

I was looking something up on my SchoolBook, something I knew I'd read.

I found it. I stood up. Ms. Galvez looked expectantly at me. The other people followed her gaze and went quiet. Even Charles looked at me after a while, his big wet eyes burning with hatred for me.

"I wanted to read something," I said. "It's short. 'Governments are instituted among men, deriving their just powers from the consent of the governed, that whenever any form of government becomes destructive of these ends, it is the right of the people to alter or abolish it, and to institute new government, laying its foundation on such principles, and organizing its powers in such form, as to them shall seem most likely to effect their safety and happiness.' "

Chapter 12

Ms. Galvez's smile was wide.

"Does anyone know what that comes from?"

A bunch of people chorused, "The Declaration of Independence."

I nodded.

"Why did you read that to us, Marcus?"

"Because it seems to me that the founders of this country said that governments should only last for so long as we believe that they're working for us, and if we stop believing in them, we should overthrow them. That's what it says, right?"

Charles shook his head. "That was hundreds of years ago!" he said. "Things are different now!"

"What's different?"

"Well, for one thing, we don't have a king anymore. They were talking about a government that existed because some old jerk's great-great-great-grandfather believed that God put him in charge and killed everyone who disagreed with him. We have a democratically elected government—"

"I didn't vote for them," I said.

"So that gives you the right to blow up a building?"

"What? Who said anything about blowing up a building? The Yippies and hippies and all those people believed that the government no longer listened to them—look at the way people who tried to sign up voters in the South were treated! They were beaten up, arrested—"

"Some of them were killed," Ms. Galvez said. She held up her hands and waited for Charles and me to sit down. "We're almost out of time for today, but I want to commend you all on one of the most interesting classes I've ever taught. This has been an excellent discussion and I've learned much from you all. I hope you've learned from each other, too. Thank you all for your contributions.

"I have an extra-credit assignment for those of you who want a little challenge. I'd like you to write up a paper comparing the political response to the antiwar and civil rights movements in the Bay Area to the present day civil rights responses to the War on Terror. Three pages minimum, but take as long as you'd like. I'm interested to see what you come up with."

The bell rang a moment later and everyone filed out of the class. I hung back and waited for Ms. Galvez to notice me.

"Yes, Marcus?"

"That was amazing," I said. "I never knew all that stuff about the sixties."

"The seventies, too. This place has always been an exciting place to live in politically charged times. I really liked your reference to the Declaration—that was very clever."

"Thanks," I said. "It just came to me. I never really appreciated what those words all meant before today."

"Well, those are the words every teach loves to hear, Marcus," she said, and shook my hand. "I can't wait to read your paper."

———

I bought the Emma Goldman poster on the way home and stuck it up over my desk, tacked over a vintage black-light poster. I also bought a NEVER TRUST T-shirt that had a photoshop of Grover and Elmo kicking the grown-ups Gordon and Susan off Sesame Street. It made me laugh. I later found out that there had already been about six photoshop contests for the slogan online in places like Fark and Worth1000 and B3ta and there were hundreds of readymade pics floating around to go on whatever merch someone churned out.

Mom raised an eyebrow at the shirt, and Dad shook his head and lectured me about not looking for trouble. I felt a little vindicated by his reaction.

Ange found me online again and we IM-flirted until late at night again. The white van with the antennas came back and I switched off my Xbox until it had passed. We'd all gotten used to doing that.

Van was really excited by this party. It looked like it was going to be monster. There were so many bands signed up they were talking about setting up a B-stage for the secondary acts.

> How'd they get a permit to blast sound all night in that park? There's houses all around there

> Per-mit? What is "per-mit"? Tell me more of your hu-man per-mit.

> Woah, it's illegal?

> Um, hello? _You're_ worried about breaking the law?

> Fair point

> LOL

I felt a little premonition of nervousness though. I mean, I was taking this perfectly awesome girl out on a date that weekend—well, she was taking me, technically—to an illegal rave being held in the middle of a busy neighborhood.

It was bound to be interesting at least.

Interesting.

People started to drift into Dolores Park through the long Saturday afternoon, showing up among the ultimate frisbee players and the dog-walkers. Some of them played frisbee or walked dogs. It wasn't really clear how the concert was going to work, but there were a lot of cops and undercovers hanging around. You could tell the undercovers because, like Zit and Booger, they had Castro haircuts and Nebraska physiques: tubby guys with short hair and untidy mustaches. They drifted around, looking awkward and uncomfortable in their giant shorts and loose-fitting shirts that no doubt hung down to cover the chandelier of gear hung around their midriffs.

Dolores Park is pretty and sunny, with palm trees, tennis courts and lots of hills and regular trees to run around on, or hang out on. Homeless people sleep there at night, but that's true everywhere in San Francisco.

I met Ange down the street at the anarchist bookstore. That had been my suggestion. In hindsight, it was a totally transparent move to seem cool and edgy to this girl, but at the time I would have sworn that I picked it because it was a convenient place to meet up. She was reading a book called *Up Against the Wall Moth-erf___er* when I got there.

"Nice," I said. "You kiss your mother with that mouth?"

"Your mama don't complain," she said. "Actually, it's a history of a group of people like the Yippies, but from New York. They all used that word as their last names, like 'Ben M-F.' The idea was to have a group out there, making news, but with a totally unprintable name. Just to screw around with the news media. Pretty funny, really." She put the book back on the shelf and now I wondered if I should hug her. People in California hug to say hello and good-bye all the time. Except when they don't. And sometimes they kiss on the cheek. It's all very confusing.

She settled it for me by grabbing me in a hug and tugging my head down to her, kissing me hard on the cheek, then blowing a fart on my neck. I laughed and pushed her away.

"You want a burrito?" I asked.

"Is that a question or a statement of the obvious?"

"Neither. It's an order."

I bought some funny stickers that said THIS PHONE IS TAPPED which were the right size to put on the receivers on the pay phones that still lined the streets of the Mission, it being the kind of neighborhood where you got people who couldn't necessarily afford a cell phone.

We walked out into the night air. I told Ange about the scene at the park when I left.

"I bet they have a hundred of those trucks parked around the block," she said. "The better to bust you with."

"Um." I looked around. "I sort of hoped that you would say something like, 'Aw, there's no chance they'll do anything about it.'"

"I don't think that's really the idea. The idea is to put a lot of civilians in a position where the cops have to decide, are we going to treat these ordinary people like terrorists? It's a little like the jamming, but with music instead of gadgets. You jam, right?"

Sometimes I forget that all my friends don't know that Marcus and M1k3y are the same person. "Yeah, a little," I said.

"This is like jamming with a bunch of awesome bands."

"I see."

Mission burritos are an institution. They are cheap, giant and delicious. Imagine a tube the size of a bazooka shell, filled with spicy grilled meat, guacamole, salsa, tomatoes, refried beans, rice, onions and cilantro. It has the same relationship to Taco Bell that a Lamborghini has to a Hot Wheels car.

There are about two hundred Mission burrito joints. They're all heroically ugly, with uncomfortable seats, minimal decor—faded Mexican tourist office posters and electrified framed Jesus and Mary holograms—and loud mariachi music. The thing that distinguishes them, mostly, is what kind of exotic meat they fill their wares with. The really authentic places have brains and tongue, which I never order, but it's nice to know it's there.

The place we went to had both brains and tongue, which we didn't order. I got carne asada and she got shredded chicken and we each got a big cup of horchata.

As soon as we sat down, she unrolled her burrito and took a little bottle out of her purse. It was a little stainless steel aerosol canister that looked for all the world like a pepper spray self-defense unit. She aimed it at her burrito's exposed guts and misted them with a fine red oily spray. I caught a whiff of it and my throat closed and my eyes watered.

"What the hell are you doing to that poor, defenseless burrito?"

She gave me a wicked smile. "I'm a spicy food addict," she said. "This is capsaicin oil in a mister."

"Capsaicin—"

"Yeah, the stuff in pepper spray. This is like pepper spray but slightly more dilute. And way more delicious. Think of it as Spicy Cajun Visine if it helps."

My eyes burned just thinking of it.

"You're kidding," I said. "You are *so* not going to eat that."

Her eyebrows shot up. "That sounds like a challenge, sonny. You just watch me."

She rolled the burrito up as carefully as a stoner rolling up a joint, tucking the ends in, then rewrapping it in the tinfoil. She peeled off one end and brought it up to her mouth, poised with it just before her lips.

Right up to the time she bit into it, I couldn't believe that she was going to do it. I mean, that was basically an antipersonnel weapon she'd just slathered on her dinner.

She bit into it. Chewed. Swallowed. Gave every impression of having a delicious dinner.

"Want a bite?" she said, innocently.

"Yeah," I said. I like spicy food. I always order the curries with four chilies next to them on the menu at the Pakistani places.

I peeled back more foil and took a big bite.

Big mistake.

You know that feeling you get when you take a big bite of horseradish or wasabi or whatever, and it feels like your sinuses are closing at the same time as your windpipe, filling your head with trapped, nuclear-hot air that tries to batter its way out through your watering eyes and nostrils? That feeling like steam is about to pour out of your ears like a cartoon character?

This was a lot worse.

This was like putting your hand on a hot stove, only it's not your hand, it's the entire inside of your head, and your esophagus all the way down to your stomach. My entire body sprang out in a sweat and I choked and choked.

Wordlessly, she passed me my horchata and I managed to get the straw into my mouth and suck hard on it, gulping down half of it in one go.

"So there's a scale, the Scoville scale, that we chili-fanciers use to talk about how spicy a pepper is. Pure capsaicin is about fifteen million Scovilles. Tabasco is about twenty-five hundred. Pepper spray is a healthy three million. This stuff is a puny hundred thousand, about as hot as a mild Scotch bonnet pepper. I worked up to it in about a year. Some of the real hardcore can get up to a half million or so, twenty times hotter than Tabasco. That's pretty freaking hot. At Scoville temperatures like that, your brain gets totally awash in endorphins. It's a better body-stone than hash. And it's good for you."

I was getting my sinuses back now, able to breathe without gasping.

"Of course, you get a ferocious ring of fire when you go to the john," she said, winking at me.

Yowch.

"You are insane," I said.

"Fine talk from a man whose hobby is building and smashing laptops," she said.

"Touché," I said and touched my forehead.

"Want some?" She held out her mister.

"Pass," I said, quickly enough that we both laughed.

When we left the restaurant and headed for Dolores Park, she put her arm around my waist and I found that she was just the right height for me to put my arm around her shoulders. That was new. I'd never been a tall guy, and the girls I'd dated had all been my height—teenaged girls grow faster than guys, which is a cruel trick of nature. It was nice. It felt nice.

We turned the corner on 20th Street and walked up toward Dolores. Before we'd taken a single step, we could feel the buzz. It was like the hum of a million bees. There were lots of people streaming toward the park, and when I looked toward it, I saw that it was about a hundred times more crowded than it had been when I went to meet Ange.

That sight made my blood run hot. It was a beautiful cool night and we were about to party, really party, party like there was no tomorrow. "Eat, drink and be merry, for tomorrow we die."

Without saying anything we both broke into a trot. There were lots of cops, with tense faces, but what the hell were they going to do? There were a *lot* of people in the park. I'm not so good at counting crowds. The papers later quoted organizers as saying there were 20,000 people; the cops said 5,000. Maybe that means there were 12,500.

Whatever. It was more people than I'd ever stood among, as part of an unscheduled, unsanctioned, *illegal* event.

We were among them in an instant. I can't swear to it, but I don't think there was anyone over twenty-five in that press of bodies. Everyone was smiling. Some young kids were there, ten or twelve, and that made me feel better. No one would do anything too stupid with kids that little in the crowd. No one wanted to see little kids get hurt. This was just going to be a glorious spring night of celebration.

I figured the thing to do was push in toward the tennis courts. We threaded our way through the crowd, and to stay together we took each other's hands. Only staying together didn't require us to intertwine fingers. That was strictly for pleasure. It was very pleasurable.

The bands were all inside the tennis courts, with their guitars and mixers and keyboards and even a drum kit. Later, on Xnet, I found a Flickr stream of them smuggling all this stuff in, piece by piece, in gym bags and under their coats. Along with it all were huge speakers, the kind you see in automotive supply places, and among them, a stack of . . . car batteries. I laughed. Genius! That was how they were going to power their stacks. From where I stood, I could see that they were cells from a hybrid car, a Prius. Someone had gutted an eco-mobile to power the night's entertainment. The batteries continued outside the courts, stacked up against the fence, tethered to the main stack by wires threaded through the chain-link. I counted two hundred batteries! Christ! Those things weighed a ton, too.

There's no way they organized this without email and wikis and mailing lists. And there's no way people this smart would have done that on the public Internet. This had all taken place on the Xnet, I'd bet my boots on it.

We just kind of bounced around in the crowd for a while as the bands tuned up and conferred with one another. I saw Trudy Doo from a distance, in the tennis courts. She looked like she was in a cage, like a pro wrestler. She was wearing a torn wife-beater and her hair was in long, fluorescent pink dreads down to her waist. She was wearing army camouflage pants and giant gothy boots with steel over-toes. As I watched, she picked up a heavy motorcycle jacket, as worn as a catcher's mitt, and put it on like armor. It probably was armor, I realized.

I tried to wave to her, to impress Ange I guess, but she didn't see me and I kind of looked like a spazz so I stopped. The energy in the crowd was amazing. You hear people talk about "vibes" and "energy" for big groups of people, but until you've experienced it, you probably think it's just a figure of speech.

It's not. It's the smiles, infectious and big as watermelons, on every face. Everyone bopping a little to an unheard rhythm, shoulders rocking. Rolling walks. Jokes and laughs. The tone of every voice tight and excited, like a firework about to go off. And you can't help but be a part of it. Because you are.

By the time the bands kicked off, I was utterly stoned on

crowd-vibe. The opening act was some kind of Serbian turbo-folk, which I couldn't figure out how to dance to. I know how to dance to exactly two kinds of music: trance (shuffle around and let the music move you) and punk (bash around and mosh until you get hurt or exhausted or both). The next act was Oakland hip-hoppers, backed by a thrash metal band, which is better than it sounds. Then some bubblegum pop. Then Speedwhores took the stage, and Trudy Doo stepped up to the mic.

"My name is Trudy Doo and you're an idiot if you trust me. I'm thirty-two and it's too late for me. I'm lost. I'm stuck in the old way of thinking. I still take my freedom for granted and let other people take it away from me. You're the first generation to grow up in Gulag America, and you know what your freedom is worth to the last goddamned cent!"

The crowd roared. She was playing fast little skittery nervous chords on her guitar and her bass player, a huge fat girl with a dykey haircut and even bigger boots and a smile you could open beer bottles with was laying it down fast and hard already. I wanted to bounce. I bounced. Ange bounced with me. We were sweating freely in the evening, which reeked of perspiration and pot smoke. Warm bodies crushed in on all sides of us. They bounced, too.

"Don't trust anyone over 25!" she shouted.

We roared. We were one big animal throat, roaring.

"Don't trust anyone over 25!"

"Don't trust anyone over 25!"

"Don't trust anyone over 25!"

"Don't trust anyone over 25!"

"Don't trust anyone over 25!"

"Don't trust anyone over 25!"

She banged some hard chords on her guitar and the other

guitarist, a little pixie of a girl whose face bristled with piercings, jammed in, going wheedle-dee-wheedle-dee-dee up high, past the twelfth fret.

"It's our goddamned city! It's our goddamned country. No terrorist can take it from us for so long as we're free. Once we're not free, the terrorists win! Take it back! Take it back! You're young enough and stupid enough not to know that you can't possibly win, so you're the only ones who can lead us to victory! *Take it back!*"

"TAKE IT BACK!" we roared. She jammed down hard on her guitar. We roared the note back and then it got really really LOUD.

I danced until I was so tired I couldn't dance another step. Ange danced alongside me. Technically, we were rubbing our sweaty bodies against each other for several hours, but believe or not, I totally wasn't being a horn-dog about it. We were dancing, lost in the godbeat and the thrash and the screaming—TAKE IT BACK! TAKE IT BACK!

When I couldn't dance anymore, I grabbed her hand and she squeezed mine like I was keeping her from falling off a building. She dragged me toward the edge of the crowd, where it got thinner and cooler. Out there, on the edge of Dolores Park, we were in the cool air and the sweat on our bodies went instantly icy. We shivered and she threw her arms around my waist. "Warm me," she commanded. I didn't need a hint. I hugged her back. Her heart was an echo of the fast beats from the stage—break beats now, fast and furious and wordless.

She smelled of sweat, a sharp tang that smelled great. I knew I smelled of sweat, too. My nose was pointed into the top of her head, and her face was right at my collarbone. She moved her hands to my neck and tugged.

"Get down here, I didn't bring a stepladder," is what she said and I tried to smile, but it's hard to smile when you're kissing.

Like I said, I'd kissed three girls in my life. Two of them had never kissed anyone before. One had been dating since she was twelve. She had issues.

None of them kissed like Ange. She made her whole mouth soft, like the inside of a ripe piece of fruit, and she didn't jam her tongue in my mouth, but slid it in there, and sucked my lips into her mouth at the same time, so it was like my mouth and hers were merging. I heard myself moan and I grabbed her and squeezed her harder.

Slowly, gently, we lowered ourselves to the grass. We lay on our sides and clutched each other, kissing and kissing. The world disappeared so there was only the kiss.

My hands found her butt, her waist. The edge of her T-shirt. Her warm tummy, her soft navel. They inched higher. She moaned, too.

"Not here," she said. "Let's move over there." She pointed across the street at the big white church that gives Mission Dolores Park and the Mission its name. Holding hands, moving quickly, we crossed to the church. It had big pillars in front of it. She put my back up against one of them and pulled my face down to hers again. My hands went quickly and boldly back to her shirt. I slipped them up her front.

"It undoes in the back," she whispered into my mouth. I had a boner that could cut glass. I moved my hands around to her back, which was strong and broad, and found the hook with my fingers, which were trembling. I fumbled for a while, thinking of all those jokes about how bad guys are at undoing bras. I was bad at it. Then the hook sprang free. She gasped into my mouth. I slipped my hands around, feeling the wetness of her armpits—which was sexy and not at all gross for some reason—and then brushed the sides of her breasts.

That's when the sirens started.

They were louder than anything I'd ever heard. A sound like a physical sensation, like something blowing you off your feet. A sound as loud as your ears could process, and then louder.

"DISPERSE IMMEDIATELY," a voice said, like God rattling in my skull.

"THIS IS AN ILLEGAL GATHERING. DISPERSE IMMEDIATELY."

The band had stopped playing. The noise of the crowd across the street changed. It got scared. Angry.

I heard a click as the PA system of car speakers and car batteries in the tennis courts powered up.

"TAKE IT BACK!"

It was a defiant yell, like a sound shouted into the surf or screamed off a cliff.

"TAKE IT BACK!"

The crowd *growled,* a sound that made the hairs on the back of my neck stand up. *"TAKE IT BACK!"* they chanted. "TAKE IT BACK TAKE IT BACK TAKE IT BACK!"

The police moved in in lines, carrying plastic shields, wearing Darth Vader helmets that covered their faces. Each one had a black truncheon and infrared goggles. They looked like soldiers out of some futuristic war movie. They took a step forward in unison and every one of them banged his truncheon on his shield, a cracking noise like the earth splitting. Another step, another crack. They were all around the park and closing in now.

"DISPERSE IMMEDIATELY," the voice of God said again. There were helicopters overhead now. No floodlights, though. The infrared goggles, right. Of course. They'd have infrared scopes in the sky, too. I pulled Ange back against the doorway of the church, tucking us back from the cops and the choppers.

"TAKE IT BACK!" the PA roared. It was Trudy Doo's rebel yell and I heard her guitar thrash out some chords, then her drummer playing, then that big deep bass.

"TAKE IT BACK!" the crowd answered, and they boiled out of the park at the police lines.

I've never been in a war, but now I think I know what it must be like. What it must be like when scared kids charge across a field at an opposing force, knowing what's coming, running anyway, screaming, hollering.

"DISPERSE IMMEDIATELY," the voice of God said. It was coming from trucks parked all around the park, trucks that had swung into place in the last few seconds.

That's when the mist fell. It came out of the choppers, and we just caught the edge of it. It made the top of my head feel like it was going to come off. It made my sinuses feel like they were being punctured with ice picks. It made my eyes swell and water, and my throat close.

Pepper spray. Not a hundred thousand Scovilles. A million and a half. They'd gassed the crowd.

I didn't see what happened next, but I heard it, over the sound of both me and Ange choking and holding each other. First the choking, retching sounds. The guitar and drums and bass crashed to a halt. Then coughing.

Then screaming.

The screaming went on for a long time. When I could see again, the cops had their scopes up on their foreheads and the choppers were flooding Dolores Park with so much light it looked like daylight. Everyone was looking at the park, which was good news, because when the lights went up like that, we were totally visible.

"What do we do?" Ange said. Her voice was tight, scared. I didn't trust myself to speak for a moment. I swallowed a few times.

"We walk away," I said. "That's all we can do. Walk away. Like we were just passing by. Down to Dolores and turn left and up toward 16th Street. Like we're just passing by. Like this is none of our business."

"That'll never work," she said.

"It's all I've got."

"You don't think we should try to run for it?"

"No," I said. "If we run, they'll chase us. Maybe if we walk, they'll figure we haven't done anything and let us alone. They have a lot of arrests to make. They'll be busy for a long time."

The park was rolling with bodies, people and adults clawing at their faces and gasping. The cops dragged them by the armpits, then lashed their wrists with plastic cuffs and tossed them into the trucks like rag dolls.

"Okay?" I said.

"Okay," she said.

And that's just what we did. Walked, holding hands, quickly and businesslike, like two people wanting to avoid whatever trouble someone else was making. The kind of walk you adopt when you want to pretend you can't see a panhandler, or don't want to get involved in a street fight.

It worked.

We reached the corner and turned and kept going. Neither of us dared to speak for two blocks. Then I let out a gasp of air I hadn't know I'd been holding in.

We came to 16th Street and turned down toward Mission Street. Normally that's a pretty scary neighborhood at 2 A.M. on a Saturday night. That night it was a relief—same old druggies and hookers and dealers and drunks. No cops with truncheons, no gas.

"Um," I said as we breathed in the night air. "Coffee?"

"Home," she said. "I think home for now. Coffee later."

"Yeah," I agreed. She lived up in Hayes Valley. I spotted a taxi rolling by and I hailed it. That was a small miracle—there are hardly any cabs when you need them in San Francisco.

"Have you got cab fare home?"

"Yeah," she said. The cabdriver looked at us through his window. I opened the back door so he wouldn't take off.

"Good night," I said.

She put her hands behind my head and pulled my face toward her. She kissed me hard on the mouth, nothing sexual in it, but somehow more intimate for that.

"Good night," she whispered in my ear, and slipped into the taxi.

Head swimming, eyes running, a burning shame for having left all those Xnetters to the tender mercies of the DHS and the SFPD, I set off for home.

Monday morning, Fred Benson was standing behind Ms. Galvez's desk.

"Ms. Galvez will no longer be teaching this class," he said, once we'd taken our seats. His voice had a self-satisfied note that I recognized immediately. On a hunch, I checked out Charles. He was smiling like it was his birthday and he'd been given the best present in the world.

I put my hand up.

"Why not?"

"It's Board policy not to discuss employee matters with anyone except the employee and the disciplinary committee," he said, without even bothering to hide how much he enjoyed saying it.

"We'll be beginning a new unit today, on national security. Your SchoolBooks have the new texts. Please open them and turn to the first screen."

The opening screen was emblazoned with a DHS logo and the title: WHAT EVERY AMERICAN SHOULD KNOW ABOUT HOMELAND SECURITY.

I wanted to throw my SchoolBook on the floor.

I'd made arrangements to meet Ange at a cafe in her neighborhood after school. I jumped on the BART and found myself sitting behind two guys in suits. They were looking at the *San Francisco Chronicle,* which featured a full-page postmortem on the "youth riot" in Mission Dolores Park. They were tutting and clucking over it. Then one said to the other, "It's like they're brainwashed or something. Christ, were we ever that stupid?"

I got up and moved to another seat.

Chapter 13

"They're total whores," Ange said, spitting the word out. "In fact, that's an insult to hardworking whores everywhere. They're, they're *profiteers*."

We were looking at a stack of newspapers we'd picked up and brought to the cafe. They all contained "reporting" on the party in Dolores Park and to a one, they made it sound like a drunken, druggy orgy of kids who'd attacked the cops. *USA Today* described the cost of the "riot" and included the cost of washing away the pepper spray residue from the gas-bombing, the rash of asthma attacks that clogged the city's emergency rooms and the cost of processing the eight hundred arrested "rioters."

No one was telling our side.

"Well, the Xnet got it right, anyway," I said. I'd saved a bunch of the blogs and videos and photostreams to my phone and I showed them to her. They were firsthand accounts from people who'd been gassed and beaten up. The video showed us all dancing, having fun, showed the peaceful political speeches and the chant of "Take It Back" and Trudy Doo talking about us being the only generation that could believe in fighting for our freedoms.

"We need to make people know about this," she said.

"Yeah," I said, glumly. "That's a nice theory."

"Well, why do you think the press doesn't ever publish our side?"

"You said it, they're whores."

"Yeah, but whores do it for the money. They could sell more papers and commercials if they had a controversy. All they have now is a crime—controversy is much bigger."

"Okay, point taken. So why don't they do it? Well, reporters can barely search regular blogs, let alone keep track of the Xnet. It's not as if that's a real adult-friendly place to be."

"Yeah," she said. "Well, we can fix that, right?"

"Huh?"

"Write it all up. Put it in one place, with all the links. A single place where you can go that's intended for the press to find it and get the whole picture. Link it to the HOWTOs for Xnet. Internet users can get to the Xnet, provided they don't care about the DHS finding out what they've been surfing."

"You think it'll work?"

"Well, even if it doesn't, it's something positive to do."

"Why would they listen to us, anyway?"

"Who wouldn't listen to M1k3y?"

I put down my coffee. I picked up my phone and slipped it into my pocket. I stood up, turned on my heel and walked out of the cafe. I picked a direction at random and kept going. My face felt tight, the blood gone into my stomach, which churned.

They know who you are, I thought. *They know who M1k3y is.* That was it. If Ange had figured it out, the DHS had, too. I was doomed. I had known that since they let me go from the DHS truck, that someday they'd come and arrest me and put me away forever, send me to wherever Darryl had gone.

It was all over.

She nearly tackled me as I reached Market Street. She was out of breath and looked furious.

"What the *hell* is your problem, mister?"

I shook her off and kept walking. It was all over.

She grabbed me again. "Stop it, Marcus, you're scaring me. Come on, talk to me."

I stopped and looked at her. She blurred before my eyes. I couldn't focus on anything. I had a mad desire to jump into the path of a Muni trolley as it tore past us, down the middle of the road. Better to die than to go back.

"Marcus!" She did something I'd only seen people do in the movies. She slapped me, a hard crack across the face. "Talk to me, dammit!"

I looked at her, and put my hand to my face, which was stinging hard.

"No one is supposed to know who I am," I said. "I can't put it any more simply. If you know, it's all over. Once other people know, it's all over."

"Oh god, I'm sorry. Look, I only know because, well, because I blackmailed Jolu. After the party I stalked you a little, trying to figure out if you were the nice guy you seemed to be or a secret axe-murderer. I've known Jolu for a long time and when I asked him about you, he gushed like you were the Second Coming or something, but I could hear that there was something he wasn't telling me. I've known Jolu for a long time. He dated my sister at computer camp when he was a kid. I have some really good dirt on him. I told him I'd go public with it if he didn't tell me."

"So he told you."

"No," she said. "He told me to go to hell. Then I told him something about me. Something I'd never told anyone else."

"What?"

She looked at me. Looked around. Looked back at me. "Okay. I won't swear you to secrecy because what's the point? Either I can trust you or I can't.

"Last year, I—" she broke off. "Last year, I stole the standardized tests and published them on the net. It was just a lark. I happened to be walking past the principal's office and I saw them in his safe, and the door was hanging open. I ducked into his office—there were six sets of copies and I just put one into my bag and took off again. When I got home, I scanned them all and put them up on a Pirate Party server in Denmark."

"That was *you*?" I said.

She blushed. "Um. Yeah."

"Holy crap!" I said. It had been huge news. The Board of Education said that its No Child Left Behind tests had cost tens of millions of dollars to produce and that they'd have to spend it all over again now that they'd had the leak. They called it "eduterrorism." The news had speculated endlessly about the political motivations of the leaker, wondering if it was a teacher's protest, or a student, or a thief, or a disgruntled government contractor.

"That was YOU?"

"It was me," she said.

"And you told Jolu this—"

"Because I wanted him to be sure that I would keep the secret. If he knew *my* secret, then he'd have something he could use to put me in jail if I opened my trap. Give a little, get a little. Quid pro quo, like in Silence of the Lambs."

"And he told you."

"No," she said. "He didn't."

"But—"

"Then I told him how into you I was. How I was planning

to totally make an idiot of myself and throw myself at you. *Then* he told me."

I couldn't think of anything to say then. I looked down at my toes. She grabbed my hands and squeezed them.

"I'm sorry I squeezed it out of him. It was your decision to tell me, if you were going to tell me at all. I had no business—"

"No," I said. Now that I knew how she'd found out, I was starting to calm down. "No, it's good you know. *You.*"

"Me," she said. "Li'l ol' me."

"Okay, I can live with this. But there's one other thing."

"What?"

"There's no way to say this without sounding like a jerk, so I'll just say it. People who date each other—or whatever it is we're doing now—they split up. When they split up, they get angry at each other. Sometimes even hate each other. It's really cold to think about that happening between us, but you know, we've got to think about it."

"I solemnly promise that there is nothing you could ever do to me that would cause me to betray your secret. Nothing. Screw a dozen cheerleaders in my bed while my mother watches. Make me listen to Britney Spears. Rip off my laptop, smash it with hammers and soak it in seawater. I promise. Nothing. Ever."

I whooshed out some air.

"Um," I said.

"Now would be a good time to kiss me," she said, and turned her face up.

M1k3y's next big project on the Xnet was putting together the ultimate roundup of reports of the DON'T TRUST party at Dolores Park. I put together the biggest, most badass site I could, with sections showing the action by location, by time, by category—police violence, dancing, aftermath, singing. I uploaded the whole concert.

It was pretty much all I worked on for the rest of the night. And the next night. And the next.

My mailbox overflowed with suggestions from people. They sent me dumps off their phones and their pocket cameras. Then I got an email from a name I recognized—Dr Eeevil (three "e"s), one of the prime maintainers of ParanoidLinux.

> M1k3y

> I have been watching your Xnet experiment with great interest. Here in Germany, we have much experience with what happens with a government that gets out of control.

> One thing you should know is that every camera has a unique "noise signature" that can be used to later connect a picture with a camera. That means that the photos you're republishing on your site could potentially be used to identify the photographers, should they later be picked up for something else.

> Luckily, it's not hard to strip out the signatures, if you care to. There's a utility on the ParanoidLinux distro you're using that does this—it's called photonomous, and you'll find it in /usr/bin. Just read the man pages for documentation. It's simple though.

> Good luck with what you're doing. Don't get caught. Stay free. Stay paranoid.

> Dr Eeevil

I defingerprintized all the photos I'd posted and put them back up, along with a note explaining what Dr Eeevil had told me, warning everyone else to do the same. We all had the same basic ParanoidXbox install, so we could all anonymize our pictures. There wasn't anything I could do about the photos that had already been downloaded and cached, but from now on we'd be smarter.

That was all the thought I gave the matter than night, until I got down to breakfast the next morning and Mom had the radio on, playing the NPR morning news.

"Arabic news agency Al-Jazeera is running pictures, video and firsthand accounts of last weekend's youth riot in Mission Dolores Park," the announcer said as I was drinking a glass of orange juice. I managed not to spray it across the room, but I *did* choke a little.

"Al-Jazeera reporters claim that these accounts were published on the so-called 'Xnet,' a clandestine network used by students and Al Qaeda sympathizers in the Bay Area. This network's existence has long been rumored, but today marks its first mainstream mention."

Mom shook her head. "Just what we need," she said. "As if the police weren't bad enough. Kids running around, pretending to be guerillas and giving them the excuse to really crack down."

"The Xnet weblogs have carried hundreds of reports and multimedia files from young people who attended the riot and allege that they were gathered peacefully until the police attacked *them*. Here is one of those accounts."

" 'All we were doing was dancing. I brought my little brother. Bands played and we talked about freedom, about how we were losing it to these jerks who say they hate terrorists but who attack us though we're not terrorists we're Americans. I think they hate freedom, not us.

" 'We danced and the bands played and it was all fun and good and then the cops started shouting at us to disperse. We all shouted take it back! Meaning take America back. The cops gassed us with pepper spray. My little brother is twelve. He missed three days of school. My stupid parents say it was my fault. How about the police? We pay them and they're supposed to protect us but they gassed us for no good reason, gassed us like they gas enemy soldiers.'

"Similar accounts, including audio and video, can be found on Al-Jazeera's website and on the Xnet. You can find directions for accessing this Xnet on NPR's homepage."

Dad came down.

"Do you use the Xnet?" he said. He looked intensely at my face. I felt myself squirm.

"It's for video games," I said. "That's what most people use it for. It's just a wireless network. It's what everyone did with those free Xboxes they gave away last year."

He glowered at me. "Games? Marcus, you don't realize it, but you're providing cover for people who plan on attacking and destroying this country. I don't want to see you using this Xnet. Not anymore. Do I make myself clear?"

I wanted to argue. Hell, I wanted to shake him by the shoulders. But I didn't. I looked away. I said, "Sure, Dad." I went to school.

At first I was relieved when I discovered that they weren't going to leave Mr. Benson in charge of my social studies class. But the woman they found to replace him was my worst nightmare.

She was young, just about twenty-eight or twenty-nine, and pretty, in a wholesome kind of way. She was blonde and spoke with a soft southern accent when she introduced herself to us as Mrs. Andersen. That set off alarm bells right away. I didn't know *any* women under the age of sixty that called themselves "Mrs."

But I was prepared to overlook it. She was young, pretty, she sounded nice. She would be okay.

She wasn't okay.

"Under what circumstances should the federal government be prepared to suspend the Bill of Rights?" she said, turning to the blackboard and writing down a row of numbers, one through ten.

"Never," I said, not waiting to be called on. This was easy. "Constitutional rights are absolute."

"That's not a very sophisticated view." She looked at her seating plan. "Marcus. For example, say a policeman conducts an improper search—he goes beyond the stuff specified in his warrant. He discovers compelling evidence that a bad guy killed your father. It's the only evidence that exists. Should the bad guy go free?"

I knew the answer to this, but I couldn't really explain it. "Yes," I said, finally. "But the police shouldn't conduct improper searches—"

"Wrong," she said. "The proper response to police misconduct is disciplinary action against the police, not punishing all of society for one cop's mistake." She wrote "Criminal guilt" under point one on the board.

"Other ways in which the Bill of Rights can be superseded?"

Charles put his hand up. "Shouting fire in a crowded theater?"

"Very good"—she consulted the seating plan—"Charles. There are many instances in which the First Amendment is not absolute. Let's list some more of those."

Charles put his hand up again. "Endangering a law enforcement officer."

"Yes, disclosing the identity of an undercover policeman or intelligence officer. Very good." She wrote it down. "Others?"

"National security," Charles said, not waiting for her to call on him again. "Libel. Obscenity. Corruption of minors. Child porn. Bomb-making recipes." Mrs. Andersen wrote these down fast, but stopped at child porn. "Child porn is just a form of obscenity."

I was feeling sick. This was not what I'd learned or believed about my country. I put my hand up.

"Yes, Marcus?"

"I don't get it. You're making it sound like the Bill of Rights is optional. It's the Constitution. We're supposed to follow it absolutely."

"That's a common oversimplification," she said, giving me a fake smile. "But the fact of the matter is that the framers of the Constitution intended it to be a living document that was revised over time. They understood that the Republic wouldn't be able to last forever if the government of the day couldn't govern according to the needs of the day. They never intended the Constitution to be looked on like religious doctrine. After all, they came here fleeing religious doctrine."

I shook my head. "What? No. They were merchants and artisans who were loyal to the king until he instituted policies that were against their interests and enforced them brutally. The religious refugees were way earlier."

"Some of the framers were descended from religious refugees," she said.

"And the Bill of Rights isn't supposed to be something you pick and choose from. What the framers hated was tyranny.

That's what the Bill of Rights is supposed to prevent. They were a revolutionary army and they wanted a set of principles that everyone could agree to. Life, liberty and the pursuit of happiness. The right of people to throw off their oppressors."

"Yes, yes," she said, waving at me. "They believed in the right of people to get rid of their kings, but—" Charles was grinning and when she said that, he smiled even wider.

"—they set out the Bill of Rights because they thought that having absolute rights was better than the risk that someone would take them away. Like the First Amendment: it's supposed to protect us by preventing the government from creating two kinds of speech, allowed speech and criminal speech. They didn't want to face the risk that some jerk would decide that the things that he found unpleasant were illegal."

She turned and wrote, "Life, liberty and the pursuit of happiness" on the board.

"We're getting a little ahead of the lesson, but you seem like an advanced group." The others laughed at this, nervously.

"The role of government is to secure for citizens the rights of life, liberty and the pursuit of happiness. In that order. It's like a filter. If the government wants to do something that makes us a little unhappy, or takes away some of our liberty, it's okay, providing they're doing it to save our lives. That's why the cops can lock you up if they think you're a danger to yourself or others. You lose your liberty and happiness to protect life. If you've got life, you might get liberty and happiness later."

Some of the others had their hands up. "Doesn't that mean that they can do anything they want, if they say it's to stop someone from hurting us in the future?"

"Yeah," another kid said. "This sounds like you're saying that national security is more important than the Constitution."

I was so proud of my fellow students then. I said, "How can you protect freedom by suspending the Bill of Rights?"

She shook her head at us like we were being very stupid. "The 'revolutionary' founding fathers *shot traitors* and spies. They didn't believe in absolute freedom, not when it threatened the Republic. Now you take these Xnet people—"

I tried hard not to stiffen.

"—these so-called jammers who were on the news this morning. After this city was attacked by people who've declared war on this country, they set about sabotaging the security measures set up to catch the bad guys and prevent them from doing it again. They did this by endangering and inconveniencing their fellow citizens—"

"They did it to show that our rights were being taken away in the name of protecting them!" I said. Okay, I shouted. God, she had me so steamed. "They did it because the government was treating *everyone* like a suspected terrorist."

"So they wanted to prove that they shouldn't be treated like terrorists," Charles shouted back, "so they acted like terrorists? So they committed terrorism?"

I boiled.

"Oh for Christ's sake. Committed terrorism? They showed that universal surveillance was more dangerous than terrorism. Look at what happened in the park last weekend. Those people were dancing and listening to music. How is *that* terrorism?"

The teacher crossed the room and stood before me, looming over me until I shut up. "Marcus, you seem to think that nothing has changed in this country. You need to understand that the bombing of the Bay Bridge changed everything. Thousands of our friends and relatives lie dead at the bottom of the Bay. This is a time for national unity in the face of the violent insult our country has suffered—"

I stood up. I'd had enough of this "everything has changed" crapola. "National unity? The whole point of America is that we're the country where dissent is welcome. We're a country of dissidents and fighters and university dropouts and free speech people."

I thought of Ms. Galvez's last lesson and the thousands of Berkeley students who'd surrounded the police van when they tried to arrest a guy for distributing civil rights literature. No one tried to stop those trucks when they drove away with all the people who'd been dancing in the park. I didn't try. I was running away.

Maybe everything *had* changed.

"I believe you know where Mr. Benson's office is," she said to me. "You are to present yourself to him immediately. I will *not* have my classes disrupted by disrespectful behavior. For someone who claims to love freedom of speech, you're certainly willing to shout down anyone who disagrees with you."

I picked up my SchoolBook and my bag and stormed out. The door had a gas-lift, so it was impossible to slam or I would have slammed it.

I went fast to Mr. Benson's office. Cameras filmed me as I went. My gait was recorded. The arphids in my student ID broadcast my identity to sensors in the hallway. It was like being in jail.

"Close the door, Marcus," Mr. Benson said. He turned his screen around so that I could see the video feed from the social studies classroom. He'd been watching.

"What do you have to say for yourself?"

"That wasn't teaching, it was *propaganda*. She told us that the Constitution didn't matter!"

"No, she said it wasn't religious doctrine. And you attacked her like some kind of fundamentalist, proving her point. Marcus, you of all people should understand that everything changed when the bridge was bombed. Your friend Darryl—"

"Don't you say a goddamned word about him," I said, the anger bubbling over. "You're not fit to talk about him. Yeah, I understand that everything's different now. We used to be a free country. Now we're not."

"Marcus, do you know what 'zero tolerance' means?"

I backed down. He could expel me for "threatening behavior." It was supposed to be used against gang kids who tried to intimidate their teachers. But of course he wouldn't have any compunction about using it on me.

"Yes," I said. "I know what it means."

"I think you owe me an apology," he said.

I looked at him. He was barely suppressing his sadistic smile. A part of me wanted to grovel. It wanted to beg for his forgiveness for all my shame. I tamped that part down and decided that I would rather get kicked out than apologize.

"Governments are instituted among men, deriving their just powers from the consent of the governed, that whenever any form of government becomes destructive of these ends, it is the right of the people to alter or abolish it, and to institute new government, laying its foundation on such principles, and organizing its powers in such form, as to them shall seem most likely to effect their safety and happiness." I remembered it word for word.

He shook his head. "Remembering things isn't the same as understanding them, sonny." He bent over his computer and made some clicks. His printer purred. He handed me a sheet of warm Board letterhead that said I'd been suspended for two weeks.

"I'll email your parents now. If you are still on school property in thirty minutes, you'll be arrested for trespassing."

I looked at him.

"You don't want to declare war on me in my own school," he said. "You can't win that war. GO!"

I left.

Chapter 14

The Xnet wasn't much fun in the middle of the school day, when all the people who used it were in school. I had the piece of paper folded in the back pocket of my jeans, and I threw it on the kitchen table when I got home. I sat down in the living room and switched on the TV. I never watched it, but I knew that my parents did. The TV and the radio and the newspapers were where they got all their ideas about the world.

The news was terrible. There were so many reasons to be scared. American soldiers were dying all over the world. Not just soldiers, either. National guardsmen, who thought they were signing up to help rescue people from hurricanes, stationed overseas for years and years of a long and endless war.

I flipped around the 24-hour news networks, one after another, a parade of officials telling us why we should be scared. A parade of photos of bombs going off around the world.

I kept flipping and found myself looking at a familiar face. It was the guy who had come into the truck and spoken to severe haircut lady when I was chained up in the back. Wearing a military uniform. The caption identified him as Major General Graeme Sutherland, Regional Commander, DHS.

"I hold in my hands actual literature on offer at the so-called concert in Dolores Park last weekend." He held up a stack of pamphlets. There'd been lots of pamphleteers there, I remembered. Wherever you got a group of people in San Francisco, you got pamphlets.

"I want you to look at these for a moment. Let me read you their titles. 'Without the Consent of the Governed: A Citizen's Guide to Overthrowing the State.' Here's one: 'Did the September 11th Bombings Really Happen?' And another: 'How To Use Their Security Against Them.' This literature shows us the true purpose of the illegal gathering on Saturday night. This wasn't merely an unsafe gathering of thousands of people without proper precaution, or even toilets. It was a recruiting rally for the enemy. It was an attempt to corrupt children into embracing the idea that America shouldn't protect herself.

"Take this slogan: 'Don't Trust Anyone Over 25.' What better way to ensure that no considered, balanced, adult discussion is ever injected into your pro-terrorist message than to exclude adults, limiting your group to impressionable young people?

"When police came on the scene, they found a recruitment rally for America's enemies in progress. The gathering had already disrupted the nights of hundreds of residents in the area, none of whom had been consulted in the planning of this all-night rave party.

"They ordered these people to disperse—that much is visible on all the video—and when the revelers turned to attack them, egged on by the musicians on stage, the police subdued them using nonlethal crowd control techniques.

"The arrestees were ringleaders and provocateurs who had led the thousands of impressionistic young people there to charge the police lines. Eight hundred and twenty-seven of them were taken into custody. Many of these people had prior offenses. More than a hundred of them had outstanding warrants. They are still in custody.

"Ladies and gentlemen, America is fighting a war on many fronts, but nowhere is she in more grave danger than she is here, at home. Whether we are being attacked by terrorists or those who sympathize with them."

A reporter held up a hand and said, "General Sutherland, surely you're not saying that these children were terrorist sympathizers for attending a party in a park?"

"Of course not. But when young people are brought under the influence of our country's enemies, it's easy for them to end up over their heads. Terrorists would love to recruit a fifth column to fight the war on the home front for them. If these were my children, I'd be gravely concerned."

Another reporter chimed in. "Surely this is just an open air concert, General? They were hardly drilling with rifles."

The general produced a stack of photos and began to hold them up. "These are pictures that officers took with infrared cameras before moving in." He held them next to his face and paged through them one at a time. They showed people dancing really rough, some people getting crushed or stepped on. Then they moved into sex stuff by the trees, a girl with three guys, two guys necking together. "There were children as young as ten years old at this event. A deadly cocktail of drugs, propaganda and music resulted in dozens of injuries. It's a wonder there weren't any deaths."

I switched the TV off. They made it look like it had been a riot. If my parents thought I'd been there, they'd have strapped me to my bed for a month and only let me out afterward wearing a tracking collar.

Speaking of which, they were going to be *pissed* when they found out I'd been suspended.

They didn't take it well. Dad wanted to ground me, but Mom and I talked him out of it.

"You know that vice principal has had it in for Marcus for years," Mom said. "The last time we met him you cursed him for an hour afterward. I think the word 'asshole' was mentioned repeatedly."

Dad shook his head. "Disrupting a class to argue against the Department of Homeland Security—"

"It's a social studies class, Dad," I said. I was beyond caring anymore, but I felt like if Mom was going to stick up for me, I should help her out. "We were talking about the DHS. Isn't debate supposed to be healthy?"

"Look, son," he said. He'd taken to calling me "son" a lot. It made me feel like he'd stopped thinking of me as a person and switched to thinking of me as a kind of half-formed larva that needed to be guided out of adolescence. I hated it. "You're going to have to learn to live with the fact that we live in a different world today. You have every right to speak your mind of course, but you have to be prepared for the consequences of doing so. You have to face the fact that there are people who are hurting, who aren't going to want to argue the finer points of Constitutional law when their lives are at stake. We're in a lifeboat now, and once you're in the lifeboat, no one wants to hear about how mean the captain is being."

I barely restrained myself from rolling my eyes.

"I've been assigned two weeks of independent study, writing one paper for each of my subjects, using the city for my background—a history paper, a social studies paper, an English paper, a physics paper. It beats sitting around at home watching television."

Dad looked hard at me, like he suspected I was up to something, then nodded. I said good night to them and went up to my room. I fired up my Xbox and opened a word processor and started to brainstorm ideas for my papers. Why not? It really was better than sitting around at home.

I ended up IMing with Ange for quite a while that night. She was sympathetic about everything and told me she'd help me with my papers if I wanted to meet her after school the next night. I knew where her school was—she went to the same school as Van—and it was all the way over in the East Bay, where I hadn't visited since the bombs went.

I was really excited at the prospect of seeing her again. Every night since the party, I'd gone to bed thinking of two things: the sight of the crowd charging the police lines and the feeling of the side of her breast under her shirt as we leaned against the pillar. She was amazing. I'd never been with a girl as . . . aggressive as her before. It had always been me putting the moves on and them pushing me away. I got the feeling that Ange was as much of a horn-dog as I was. It was a tantalizing notion.

I slept soundly that night, with exciting dreams of me and Ange and what we might do if we found ourselves in a secluded spot somewhere.

The next day, I set out to work on my papers. San Francisco is a good place to write about. History? Sure, it's there, from the Gold Rush to the World War Two shipyards, the Japanese internment camps, the invention of the PC. Physics? The Exploratorium has the coolest exhibits of any museum I've ever been to. I took a perverse satisfaction in the exhibits on soil liquefaction during big quakes. English? Jack London, Beat Poets, science fiction writers like Pat Murphy and Rudy Rucker. Social studies? The Free Speech Movement, Cesar Chavez, gay rights, feminism, the antiwar movement. . . .

I've always loved just learning stuff for its own sake. Just to be smarter about the world around me. I could do that just by walking around the city. I decided I'd do an English paper about the Beats first. City Lights books had a great library in an upstairs room where Allen Ginsberg and his buddies had created their radical druggy poetry. The one we'd read in English class was *Howl* and I would never forget the opening lines, they gave me shivers down my back:

> I saw the best minds of my generation destroyed
>   by madness, starving hysterical naked,
> dragging themselves through the negro streets at
>   dawn looking for an angry fix,
> angelheaded hipsters burning for the ancient
>   heavenly connection to the starry dynamo
>   in the machinery of night. . . .

I liked the way he ran those words all together, "starving hysterical naked." I knew how that felt. And "best minds of my generation" made me think hard, too. It made me remember the park and the police and the gas falling. They busted Ginsberg for obscenity over *Howl*—all about a line about gay sex that would hardly have caused us to blink an eye today. It made me happy somehow, knowing that we'd made some progress. That things had been even more restrictive than this before.

I lost myself in the library, reading these beautiful old editions of the books. I got lost in Jack Kerouac's *On the Road,* a novel I'd been meaning to read for a long time, and a clerk who came up to check on me nodded approvingly and found me a cheap edition that he sold me for six bucks.

I walked into Chinatown and had dim sum buns and noodles with hot sauce that I had previously considered to be pretty hot, but which would never seem anything like hot ever again, not now that I'd had an Ange special.

As the day wore on toward afternoon, I got on the BART and switched to a San Mateo bridge shuttle bus to bring me around to the East Bay. I read my copy of *On the Road* and dug the scenery whizzing past. *On the Road* is a semiautobiographical novel about Jack Kerouac, a druggy, hard-drinking writer who goes hitchhiking around America, working crummy jobs, howling through the streets at night, meeting people and parting ways. Hipsters, sad-faced hobos, con men, muggers, scumbags and angels. There's not really a plot—Kerouac supposedly wrote it in three weeks on a long roll of paper, stoned out of his mind—only a bunch of amazing things, one thing happening after another. He makes friends with self-destructing people like Dean Moriarty, who get him involved in weird schemes that never really work out, but still it works out, if you know what I mean.

There was a rhythm to the words, it was luscious, I could hear it being read aloud in my head. It made me want to lie down in the bed of a pickup truck and wake up in a dusty little town somewhere in the central valley on the way to LA, one of those places with a gas station and a diner, and just walk out into the fields and meet people and see stuff and do stuff.

It was a long bus ride and I must have dozed off a little—staying up late IMing with Ange was hard on my sleep schedule, since Mom still expected me down for breakfast. I woke up and changed buses and before long, I was at Ange's school.

She came bounding out of the gates in her uniform—I'd never seen her in it before, it was kind of cute in a weird way, and reminded me of Van in her uniform. She gave me a long hug and a hard kiss on the cheek.

"Hello you!" she said.

"Hiya!"

"Whatcha reading?"

I'd been waiting for this. I'd marked the passage with a finger. "Listen: 'They danced down the streets like dingledodies, and I shambled after as I've been doing all my life after people who interest me, because the only people for me are the mad ones, the ones who are mad to live, mad to talk, mad to be saved, desirous of everything at the same time, the ones that never yawn or say a commonplace thing, but burn, burn, burn like fabulous yellow roman candles exploding like spiders across the stars and in the middle you see the blue centerlight pop and everybody goes "Awww!" ' "

She took the book and read the passage again for herself. "Wow, dingledodies! I love it! Is it all like this?"

I told her about the parts I'd read, walking slowly down the sidewalk back toward the bus stop. Once we turned the corner, she put her arm around my waist and I slung mine around her shoulder. Walking down the street with a girl—my girlfriend? Sure, why not?—talking about this cool book. It was heaven. Made me forget my troubles for a little while.

"Marcus?"

I turned around. It was Van. In my subconscious I'd expected this. I knew because my conscious mind wasn't remotely surprised. It wasn't a big school, and they all got out at the same time. I hadn't spoken to Van in weeks, and those weeks felt like months. We used to talk every day.

"Hey, Van," I said. I suppressed the urge to take my arm off of Ange's shoulders. Van seemed surprised, but not angry; more ashen, shaken. She looked closely at the two of us.

"Angela?"

"Hey, Vanessa," Ange said.

"What are you doing here?" Van asked me.

"I came out to get Ange," I said, trying to keep my tone neutral. I was suddenly embarrassed to be seen with another girl.

"Oh," Van said. "Well, it was nice to see you."

"Nice to see you, too, Vanessa," Ange said, swinging me around, marching me back toward the bus stop.

"You know her?" Ange said.

"Yeah, since forever."

"Was she your girlfriend?"

"What? No! No way! We were just friends."

"You *were* friends?"

I felt like Van was walking right behind us, listening in, though at the pace we were walking, she would have to be jogging to keep up. I resisted the temptation to look over my shoulder for as long as possible, then I did. There were lots of girls from the school behind us, but no Van.

"She was with me and Jose-Luis and Darryl when we were arrested. We used to ARG together. The four of us, we were kind of best friends."

"And what happened?"

I dropped my voice. "She didn't like the Xnet," I said. "She thought we would get into trouble. That I'd get other people into trouble."

"And that's why you stopped being friends?"

"We just drifted apart."

We walked a few steps. "You weren't, you know, boyfriend/ girlfriend friends?"

"No!" I said. My face was hot. I felt like I sounded like I was lying, even though I was telling the truth.

Ange jerked us to a halt and studied my face.

"Were you?"

"No! Seriously! Just friends. Darryl and her—well, not quite, but Darryl was so into her. There was no way—"

"But if Darryl hadn't been into her, you would have, huh?"

"No, Ange, no. Please, just believe me and let it go. Vanessa was a good friend and we're not anymore, and that upsets me, but I was never into her that way, all right?"

She slumped a little. "Okay, okay. I'm sorry. I don't really get along with her is all. We've never gotten along in all the years we've known each other."

Oh ho, I thought. This would be how it came to be that Jolu knew her for so long and I never met her; she had some kind of thing with Van and he didn't want to bring her around.

She gave me a long hug and we kissed, and a bunch of girls passed us going *woooo* and we straightened up and headed for the bus stop. Ahead of us walked Van, who must have gone past while we were kissing. I felt like a complete jerk.

Of course, she was at the stop and on the bus and we didn't say a word to each other, and I tried to make conversation with Ange all the way, but it was awkward.

The plan was to stop for a coffee and head to Ange's place to hang out and "study," i.e. take turns on her Xbox looking at the Xnet. Ange's mom got home late on Tuesdays, which was her night for yoga class and dinner with her girls, and Ange's sister was going out with her boyfriend, so we'd have the place to ourselves. I'd been having pervy thoughts about it ever since we'd made the plan.

We got to her place and went straight to her room and shut the door. Her room was kind of a disaster, covered with layers of clothes and notebooks and parts of PCs that would dig into your stocking feet like caltrops. Her desk was worse than the floor, piled high with books and comics, so we ended up sitting on her bed, which was okay by me.

The awkwardness from seeing Van had gone away somewhat and we got her Xbox up and running. It was in the center of a nest of wires, some going to a wireless antenna she'd hacked into it and stuck to the window so she could tune in the neighbors' WiFi. Some went to a couple of old laptop screens she'd turned into stand-alone monitors, balanced on stands and bristling with exposed electronics. The screens were on both bedside tables, which was an excellent setup for watching movies or IMing from bed—she could turn the monitors sidewise and lie on her side and they'd be right side up, no matter which side she lay on.

We both knew what we were really there for, sitting side by side propped against the bedside table. I was trembling a little and superconscious of the warmth of her leg and shoulder against mine, but I needed to go through the motions of logging into Xnet and seeing what email I'd gotten and so on.

There was an email from a kid who liked to send in funny phone-cam videos of the DHS being really crazy—the last one had been of them disassembling a baby's stroller after a bomb-sniffing dog had shown an interest in it, taking it apart with screwdrivers right on the street in the Marina while all these rich people walked past, staring at them and marveling at how weird it was.

I'd linked to the video and it had been downloaded like crazy. He'd hosted it on the Internet Archive's Alexandria mirror in Egypt, where they'd host anything for free so long as you'd put it under the Creative Commons license, which let anyone remix it and share it. The U.S. archive—which was down in the Presidio, only a few minutes away—had been forced to take down all those videos in the name of national security, but the Alexandria archive had split away into its own organization and was hosting anything that embarrassed the USA.

This kid—his handle was Kameraspie—had sent me an even better video this time around. It was at the doorway to City Hall in Civic Center, a huge wedding cake of a building covered with statues in little archways and gilt leaves and trim. The DHS had a secure perimeter around the building, and Kameraspie's video showed a great shot of their checkpoint as a guy in an officer's uniform approached and showed his ID and put his briefcase on the X-ray belt.

It was all okay until one of the DHS people saw something he didn't like on the X-ray. He questioned the general, who rolled his eyes and said something inaudible (the video had been shot from across the street, apparently with a homemade concealed zoom lens, so the audio was mostly of people walking past and traffic noises).

The general and the DHS guy got into an argument, and the longer they argued, the more DHS guys gathered around them. Finally, the general shook his head angrily and waved his finger at the DHS guy's chest and picked up his briefcase and started to walk away. The DHS guys shouted at him, but he didn't slow. His body language really said, "I am totally, utterly pissed."

Then it happened. The DHS guys ran after the general. Kameraspie slowed the video down here, so we could see, in frame by frame slo-mo, the general half-turning, his face all like, "No freaking way are you about to tackle me," then changing to horror as three of the giant DHS guards slammed into him, knocking him sideways, then catching him at the middle, like a career-ending football tackle. The general—middle-aged, steely gray hair, lined and dignified face—went down like a sack of potatoes and bounced twice, his face slamming off the sidewalk and blood starting out of his nose.

The DHS hog-tied the general, strapping him at the ankles and wrists. The general was shouting now, really shouting, his face purpling under the blood streaming from his nose. Legs swished by in the tight zoom. Passing pedestrians looked at this guy in his uniform getting tied up, and you could see from his face that this was the worst part, this was the ritual humiliation, the removal of dignity. The clip ended.

"Oh my dear sweet Buddha," I said, looking at the screen as it faded to black, starting the video again. I nudged Ange and showed her the clip. She watched wordless, jaw hanging down to her chest.

"Post that," she said. "Post that post that post that post that!"

I posted it. I could barely type as I wrote it up, describing what I'd seen, adding a note to see if anyone could identify the military man in the video, if anyone knew anything about this.

I hit publish.

We watched the video. We watched it again.

My email pinged.

> I totally recognize that dude—you can find his bio on Wikipedia. He's General Claude Geist. He commanded the joint UN peacekeeping mission in Haiti.

I checked the bio. There was a picture of the general at a press conference, and notes about his role in the difficult Haiti mission. It was clearly the same guy.

I updated the post.

Theoretically, this was Ange's and my chance to make out, but that wasn't what we ended up doing. We crawled the Xnet blogs, looking for more accounts of the DHS searching people, tackling people, invading them. This was a familiar task, the same thing I'd done with all the footage and accounts from the riots in the park. I started a new category on my blog for this, AbusesOf-Authority, and filed them away. Ange kept coming up with new search terms for me to try and by the time her mom got home, my new category had seventy posts, headlined by General Geist's City Hall takedown.

I worked on my Beat paper all the next day at home, reading Kerouac and surfing the Xnet. I was planning on meeting Ange at school, but I totally wimped out at the thought of seeing Van again, so I texted her an excuse about working on the paper.

There were all kinds of great suggestions for AbusesOfAuthority coming in; hundreds of little and big ones, pictures and audio. The meme was spreading.

It spread. The next morning there were even more. Someone started a new blog also called AbusesOfAuthority that collected hundreds more. The pile grew. We competed to find the juiciest stories, the craziest pictures.

The deal with my parents was that I'd eat breakfast with them every morning and talk about the projects I was doing. They liked that I was reading Kerouac. It had been a favorite book of both of theirs and it turned out there was already a copy on the bookcase in my parents' room. My dad brought it down and I flipped through it. There were passages marked up with pen, dog-eared pages, notes in the margin. My dad had really loved this book.

It made me remember a better time, when my dad and I had

been able to talk for five minutes without shouting at each other about terrorism, and we had a great breakfast talking about the way that the novel was plotted, all the crazy adventures.

But the next morning at breakfast they were both glued to the radio.

"Abuses of Authority—it's the latest craze on San Francisco's notorious Xnet, and it's captured the world's attention. Called A-oh-A, the movement is composed of 'Little Brothers' who watch back against the Department of Homeland Security's an- titerrorism measures, documenting the failures and excesses. The rallying cry is a popular viral video clip of a General Claude Geist, a retired three-star general, being tackled by DHS officers on the sidewalk in front of City Hall. Geist hasn't made a state- ment on the incident, but commentary from young people who are upset with their own treatment has been fast and furious.

"Most notable has been the global attention the movement has received. Stills from the Geist video have appeared on the front pages of newspapers in Korea, Great Britain, Germany, Egypt and Japan, and broadcasters around the world have aired the clip on prime-time news. The issue came to a head last night, when the British Broadcasting Corporation's National News Evening program ran a special report on the fact that no Ameri- can broadcaster or news agency has covered this story. Com- menters on the BBC's website noted that BBC America's version of the news did not carry the report."

They brought on a couple of interviews: British media watchdogs, a Swedish Pirate Party kid who made jeering remarks about America's corrupt press, a retired American newscaster liv- ing in Tokyo; then they aired a short clip from Al-Jazeera, com- paring the American press record and the record of the national news media in Syria.

I felt like my parents were staring at me, that they knew what I was doing. But when I cleared away my dishes, I saw that they were looking at each other.

Dad was holding his coffee cup so hard his hands were shaking. Mom was looking at him.

"They're trying to discredit us," Dad said finally. "They're trying to sabotage the efforts to keep us safe."

I opened my mouth, but my mom caught my eye and shook her head. Instead I went up to my room and worked on my Kerouac paper. Once I'd heard the door slam twice, I fired up my Xbox and got online.

> **Hello M1k3y. This is Colin Brown. I'm a producer with the Canadian Broadcasting Corporation's news programme The National. We're doing a story on Xnet and have sent a reporter to San Francisco to cover it from there. Would you be interested in doing an interview to discuss your group and its actions?**

I stared at the screen. Jesus. They wanted to *interview* me about "my group"?

> **Um thanks no. I'm all about privacy. And it's not "my group." But thanks for doing the story!**

A minute later, another email.

> **We can mask you and ensure your anonymity. You know that the Department of Homeland Security will be happy to provide their own spokesperson. I'm interested in getting your side.**

I filed the email. He was right, but I'd be crazy to do this. For all I knew, he *was* the DHS.

I picked up more Kerouac. Another email came in. Same request, different news agency: KQED wanted to meet me and record a radio interview. A station in Brazil. The Australian Broadcasting Corporation. Deutsche Welle. All day, the press requests came in. All day, I politely turned them down.

I didn't get much Kerouac read that day.

"Hold a press conference," is what Ange said as we sat in the cafe near her place that evening. I wasn't keen on going out to her school anymore, getting stuck on a bus with Van again.

"What? Are you crazy?"

"Do it in Clockwork Plunder. Just pick a trading post where there's no PvP allowed and name a time. You can login from here."

PvP is player-versus-player combat. Parts of Clockwork Plunder were neutral ground, which meant that we could theoretically bring in a ton of noob reporters without worrying about gamers killing them in the middle of the press conference.

"I don't know anything about press conferences."

"Oh, just google it. I'm sure someone's written an article on holding a successful one. I mean, if the President can manage it, I'm sure you can. He looks like he can barely tie his shoes without help."

We ordered more coffee.

"You are a very smart woman," I said.

"And I'm beautiful," she said.

"That, too," I said.

Chapter 15

I'd blogged the press conference even before I'd sent out the invitations to the press. I could tell that all these writers wanted to make me into a leader or a general or a supreme guerrilla commandant, and I figured one way of solving that would be to have a bunch of Xnetters running around answering questions, too.

Then I emailed the press. The responses ranged from puzzled to enthusiastic—only the Fox reporter was "outraged" that I had the gall to ask her to play a game in order to appear on her TV show. The rest of them seemed to think that it would make a pretty cool story, though plenty of them wanted lots of tech support for signing onto the game.

I picked 8 P.M., after dinner. Mom had been bugging me about all the evenings I'd been spending out of the house until I finally spilled the beans about Ange, whereupon she came over all misty and kept looking at me like, my-little-boy's-growing-up. She wanted to meet Ange, and I used that as leverage, promising to bring her over the next night if I could "go to the movies" with Ange tonight.

Ange's mom and sister were out again—they weren't real

stay-at-homes—which left me and Ange alone in her room with her Xbox and mine. I unplugged one of her bedside screens and attached my Xbox to it so that we could both login at once.

Both Xboxes were idle, logged into Clockwork Plunder. I was pacing.

"It's going to be fine," she said. She glanced at her screen. "Patcheye Pete's Market has six hundred players in it now!" We'd picked Patcheye Pete's because it was the market closest to the village square where new players spawned. If the reporters weren't already Clockwork Plunder players—ha!—then that's where they'd show up. In my blog post I'd asked people generally to hang out on the route between Patcheye Pete's and the spawn-gate and direct anyone who looked like a disoriented reporter over to Pete's.

"What the hell am I going to tell them?"

"You just answer their questions—and if you don't like a question, ignore it. Someone else can answer it. It'll be fine."

"This is insane."

"This is perfect, Marcus. If you want to really screw the DHS, you have to embarrass them. It's not like you're going to be able to outshoot them. Your only weapon is your ability to make them look like morons."

I flopped on the bed and she pulled my head into her lap and stroked my hair. I'd been playing around with different haircuts before the bombing, dying it all kinds of funny colors, but since I'd gotten out of jail I couldn't be bothered. It had gotten long and stupid and shaggy and I'd gone into the bathroom and grabbed my clippers and buzzed it down to half an inch all around, which took zero effort to take care of and helped me to be invisible when I was out jamming and cloning arphids.

I opened my eyes and stared into her big brown eyes behind

her glasses. They were round and liquid and expressive. She could make them bug out when she wanted to make me laugh, or make them soft and sad, or lazy and sleepy in a way that made me melt into a puddle of horniness.

That's what she was doing right now.

I sat up slowly and hugged her. She hugged me back. We kissed. She was an amazing kisser. I know I've already said that, but it bears repeating. We kissed a lot, but for one reason or another we always stopped before it got too heavy.

Now I wanted to go further. I found the hem of her T-shirt and tugged. She put her hands over her head and pulled back a few inches. I knew that she'd do that. I'd known since the night in the park. Maybe that's why we hadn't gone further—I knew I couldn't rely on her to back off, which scared me a little.

But I wasn't scared then. The impending press conference, the fights with my parents, the international attention, the sense that there was a movement that was careening around the city like a wild pinball—it made my skin tingle and my blood sing.

And she was beautiful, and smart, and clever and funny, and I was falling in love with her.

Her shirt slid off. She arched her back to help me get it over her shoulders. She reached behind her and did something and her bra fell away. I stared goggle-eyed, motionless and breathless, and then she grabbed *my* shirt and pulled it over my head, grabbing me and pulling my bare chest to hers.

We rolled on the bed and touched each other and ground our bodies together and groaned. She kissed all over my chest and I did the same to her. I couldn't breathe, I couldn't think, I could only move and kiss and lick and touch.

We dared each other to go forward. I undid her jeans. She undid mine. I lowered her zipper, she did mine, and tugged my jeans off. I tugged off hers. A moment later we were both naked, except for my socks, which I peeled off with my toes.

It was then that I caught sight of the bedside clock, which had long ago rolled onto the floor and lay there, glowing up at us.

"Crap!" I yelped. "It starts in two minutes!" I couldn't freaking believe that I was about to stop what I was about to stop doing, when I was about to stop doing it. I mean, if you'd asked me, "Marcus, you are about to get laid for the firstest time EVAR, will you stop if I let off this nuclear bomb in the same room as you?" the answer would have been a resounding and un-equivical *NO*.

And yet we stopped for this.

She grabbed me and pulled my face to hers and kissed me until I thought I would pass out, then we both grabbed our clothes and more or less dressed, grabbing our keyboards and mice and heading for Patcheye Pete's.

You could easily tell who the press were: they were the noobs who played their characters like staggering drunks, weaving back and forth and up and down, trying to get the hang of it all, occasionally hitting the wrong key and offering strangers all or part of their inventory, or giving them accidental hugs and kicks.

The Xnetters were easy to spot, too: we all played Clock-work Plunder whenever we had some spare time (or didn't feel like doing our homework), and we had pretty tricked-out char-acters with cool weapons and booby traps on the keys sticking out of our backs that would cream anyone who tried to snatch them and leave us to wind down.

When I appeared, a system status message displayed M1K3Y

HAS ENTERED PATCHEYE PETE'S—WELCOME SWABBIE WE OFFER FAIR TRADE FOR FINE BOOTY. All the players on the screen froze, then they crowded around me. The chat exploded. I thought about turning on my voice-paging and grabbing a headset, but seeing how many people were trying to talk at once, I realized how confusing that would be. Text was much easier to follow and they couldn't misquote me (heh heh).

I'd scouted the location before with Ange—it was great campaigning with her, since we could both keep each other wound up. There was a high spot on a pile of boxes of salt rations that I could stand on and be seen from anywhere in the market.

> Good evening and thank you all for coming. My name is M1k3y and I'm not the leader of anything. All around you are Xnetters who have as much to say about why we're here as I do. I use the Xnet because I believe in freedom and the Constitution of the United States of America. I use Xnet because the DHS has turned my city into a police-state where we're all suspected terrorists. I use Xnet because I think you can't defend freedom by tearing up the Bill of Rights. I learned about the Constitution in a California school and I was raised to love my country for its freedom. If I have a philosophy, it is this:

> Governments are instituted among men, deriving their just powers from the consent of the governed, that whenever any form of government becomes destructive of these ends, it is the right of the people to alter or abolish it, and to institute new government, laying its foundation on such principles, and organizing its powers in such form, as to

```
them shall seem most likely to effect their safety
and happiness.
   > I didn't write that, but I believe it. The DHS
does not govern with my consent.
   > Thank you
```

I'd written this the day before, bouncing drafts back and forth with Ange. Pasting it in only took a second, though it took everyone in the game a moment to read it. A lot of the Xnetters cheered, big showy pirate "Hurrah"s with raised sabers and pet parrots squawking and flying overhead.

Gradually, the journalists digested it, too. The chat was running past fast, so fast you could barely read it, lots of Xnetters saying things like "Right on" and "America, love it or leave it" and "DHS go home" and "America out of San Francisco," all slogans that had been big on the Xnet blogosphere.

```
   > M1k3y, this is Priya Rajneesh from the BBC. You
say you're not the leader of any movement, but do you
believe there is a movement? Is it called the Xnet?
```

Lots of answers. Some people said there wasn't a movement, some said there was and lots of people had ideas about what it was called: Xnet, Little Brothers, Little Sisters and my personal favorite, the United States of America.

They were really cooking. I let them go, thinking of what I could say. Once I had it, I typed,

```
   > I think that kind of answers your question,
doesn't it? There may be one or more movements and
they may be called Xnet or not.
   > M1k3y, I'm Doug Christensen from the Washington
Internet Daily. What do you think the DHS should be
```

doing to prevent another attack on San Francisco, if
what they're doing isn't successful.

More chatter. Lots of people said that the terrorists and the
government were the same—either literally, or just meaning that
they were equally bad. Some said the government knew how to
catch terrorists but preferred not to because "war presidents" got
reelected.

> I don't know

I typed finally.

> I really don't. I ask myself this question a lot
because I don't want to get blown up and I don't want
my city to get blown up. Here's what I've figured out,
though: if it's the DHS's job to keep us safe, they're
failing. All the crap they've done, none of it would
stop the bridge from being blown up again. Tracing us
around the city? Taking away our freedom? Making us
suspicious of each other, turning us against each
other? Calling dissenters traitors? The point of terrorism is to terrify us. The DHS terrifies me.

> I don't have any say in what the terrorists do
to me, but if this is a free country then I should be
able to at least say what my own cops do to me. I
should be able to keep them from terrorizing me.

> I know that's not a good answer. Sorry.

> What do you mean when you say that the DHS
wouldn't stop terrorists? How do you know?

> Who are you?

> I'm with the Sydney Morning Herald.

> I'm 17 years old. I'm not a straight-A student
or anything. Even so, I figured out how to make an

Internet that they can't wiretap. I figured out how to jam their person-tracking technology. I can turn innocent people into suspects and turn guilty people into innocents in their eyes. I could get metal onto an airplane or beat a no-fly list. I figured this stuff out by looking at the web and by thinking about it. If I can do it, terrorists can do it. They told us they took away our freedom to make us safe. Do you feel safe?

> In Australia? Why yes I do

The pirates all laughed.

More journalists asked questions. Some were sympathetic, some were hostile. When I got tired, I handed my keyboard to Ange and let her be M1k3y for a while. It didn't really feel like M1k3y and me were the same person anymore anyway. M1k3y was the kind of kid who talked to international journalists and inspired a movement. Marcus got suspended from school and fought with his dad and wondered if he was good enough for his kick-ass girlfriend.

By 11 P.M. I'd had enough. Besides, my parents would be expecting me home soon. I logged out of the game and so did Ange and we lay there for a moment. I took her hand and she squeezed hard. We hugged.

She kissed my neck and murmured something.

"What?"

"I said I love you," she said. "What, you want me to send you a telegram?"

"Wow," I said.

"You're that surprised, huh?"

"No. Um. It's just—I was going to say that to you."

"Sure you were," she said, and bit the tip of my nose.

"It's just that I've never said it before," I said. "So I was working up to it."

"You still haven't said it, you know. Don't think I haven't noticed. We girls pick up on these things."

"I love you, Ange Carvelli," I said.

"I love you too, Marcus Yallow."

We kissed and nuzzled and I started to breathe hard and so did she. That's when her mom knocked on the door.

"Angela," she said, "I think it's time your friend went home, don't you?"

"Yes, Mother," she said, and mimed swinging an axe. As I put my socks and shoes on, she muttered, "They'll say, that Angela, she was such a good girl, who would have thought it, all the time she was in the backyard, helping her mother out by sharpening that hatchet."

I laughed. "You don't know how easy you have it. There is *no way* my folks would leave us alone in my bedroom until 11 o'clock."

"11:45," she said, checking her clock.

"Crap!" I yelped and tied my shoes.

"Go," she said, "run and be free! Look both ways before crossing the road! Write if you get work! Don't even stop for a hug! If you're not out of here by the count of ten, there's going to be *trouble,* mister. One. Two. Three."

I shut her up by leaping onto the bed, landing on her and kissing her until she stopped trying to count. Satisfied with my victory, I pounded down the stairs, my Xbox under my arm.

Her mom was at the foot of the stairs. We'd only met a couple times. She looked like an older, taller version of Ange—Ange said her father was the short one—with contacts instead of glasses. She seemed to have tentatively classed me as a good guy, I and appreciated it.

"Good night, Mrs. Carvelli," I said.

"Good night, Mr. Yallow," she said. It was one of our little rituals, ever since I'd called her Mrs. Carvelli when we first met.

I found myself standing awkwardly by the door.

"Yes?" she said.

"Um," I said. "Thanks for having me over."

"You're always welcome in our home, young man," she said.

"And thanks for Ange," I said finally, hating how lame it sounded. But she smiled broadly and gave me a brief hug.

"You're very welcome," she said.

The whole bus ride home, I thought over the press conference, thought about Ange naked and writhing with me on her bed, thought about her mother smiling and showing me the door.

My mom was waiting up for me. She asked me about the movie and I gave her the response I'd worked out in advance, cribbing from the review it had gotten in the *Bay Guardian*.

As I fell asleep, the press conference came back. I was really proud of it. It had been so cool, to have all these big-shot journos show up in the game, to have them listen to me and to have them listen to all the people who believed in the same things as me. I dropped off with a smile on my lips.

I should have known better.

Xnet Leader: I Could Get Metal Onto An Airplane
DHS Doesn't Have My Consent To Govern
Xnet Kids: USA Out Of San Francisco

Those were the *good* headlines. Everyone sent me the articles to blog, but it was the last thing I wanted to do.

I'd blown it, somehow. The press had come to my press conference and concluded that we were terrorists or terrorist dupes. The worst was the reporter on Fox News, who had apparently shown up anyway, and who devoted a ten-minute commentary to us, talking about our "criminal treason." Her killer line, repeated on every news outlet I found, was:

"They say they don't have a name. I've got one for them. Let's call these spoiled children Cal Qaeda. They do the terrorists' work on the home front. When—not if, but when—California gets attacked again, these brats will be as much to blame as the House of Saud."

Leaders of the antiwar movement denounced us as fringe elements. One guy went on TV to say that he believed we had been fabricated by the DHS to discredit them.

The DHS had their own press conference announcing that they would double the security in San Francisco. They held up an arphid cloner they'd found somewhere and demonstrated it in action, using it to stage a car theft, and warned everyone to be on the alert for young people behaving suspiciously, especially those whose hands were out of sight.

They weren't kidding. I finished my Kerouac paper and started in on a paper about the Summer of Love, the summer of 1967 when the antiwar movement and the hippies converged on San Francisco. The guys who founded Ben and Jerry's—old hippies themselves—had founded a hippie museum in the Haight, and there were other archives and exhibits to see around town.

But it wasn't easy getting around. By the end of the week, I was getting frisked an average of four times a day. Cops checked my ID and questioned me about why I was out in the street, carefully eyeballing the letter from Chavez saying that I was suspended.

I got lucky. No one arrested me. But the rest of the Xnet weren't so lucky. Every night the DHS announced more arrests, "ringleaders" and "operatives" of Xnet, people I didn't know and had never heard of, paraded on TV along with the arphid sniffers and other devices that had been in their pockets. They announced that the people were "naming names," compromising the "Xnet network" and that more arrests were expected soon. The name "M1k3y" was often heard.

Dad loved this. He and I watched the news together, him gloating, me shrinking away, quietly freaking out. "You should see the stuff they're going to use on these kids," Dad said. "I've seen it in action. They'll get a couple of these kids and check out their friends lists on IM and the speed-dials on their phones, look for names that come up over and over, look for patterns, bringing in more kids. They're going to unravel them like an old sweater."

I canceled Ange's dinner at our place and started spending even more time there. Ange's little sister Tina started to call me "the houseguest," as in "is the houseguest eating dinner with me tonight?" I liked Tina. All she cared about was going out and partying and meeting guys, but she was funny and utterly devoted to Ange. One night as we were doing the dishes, she dried her hands and said, conversationally, "You know, you seem like a nice guy, Marcus. My sister's just crazy about you and I like you, too. But I have to tell you something: if you break her heart, I will track you down and pull your scrotum over your head. It's not a pretty sight."

I assured her that I would sooner pull my own scrotum over my head than break Ange's heart and she nodded. "So long as we're clear on that."

"Your sister is a nut," I said as we lay on Ange's bed again, looking at Xnet blogs. That is pretty much all we did: fool around and read Xnet.

"Did she use the scrotum line on you? I hate it when she does that. She just loves the word 'scrotum,' you know. It's nothing personal."

I kissed her. We read some more.

"Listen to this," she said. "Police project four to six *hundred* arrests this weekend in what they say will be the largest coordinated raid on Xnet dissidents to date."

I felt like throwing up.

"We've got to stop this," I said. "You know there are people who are doing *more* jamming to show that they're not intimidated? Isn't that just *crazy*?"

"I think it's brave," she said. "We can't let them scare us into submission."

"What? No, Ange, no. We can't let hundreds of people go to *jail*. You haven't been there. I have. It's worse than you think. It's worse than you can imagine."

"I have a pretty fertile imagination," she said.

"Stop it, okay? Be serious for a second. I won't do this. I won't send those people to jail. If I do, I'm the guy that Van thinks I am."

"Marcus, I'm being serious. You think that these people don't know they could go to jail? They believe in the cause. You believe in it, too. Give them the credit to know what they're getting into. It's not up to you to decide what risks they can or can't take."

"It's my responsibility because if I tell them to stop, they'll stop."

"I thought you weren't the leader?"

"I'm not, of course I'm not. But I can't help it if they look to me for guidance. And so long as they do, I have a responsibility to help them stay safe. You see that, right?"

"All I see is you getting ready to cut and run at the first sign of trouble. I think you're afraid they're going to figure out who *you* are. I think you're afraid for *you*."

"That's not fair," I said, sitting up, pulling away from her.

"Really? Who's the guy who nearly had a heart attack when he thought that his secret identity was out?"

"That was different," I said. "This isn't about me. You know it isn't. Why are you being like this?"

"Why are *you* like this?" she said. "Why aren't *you* willing to be the guy who was brave enough to get all this started?"

"This isn't brave, it's suicide."

"Cheap teenage melodrama, M1k3y."

"Don't call me that!"

"What, 'M1k3y'? Why not, *M1k3y*?"

I put my shoes on. I picked up my bag. I walked home.

> **Why I'm not jamming**

> **I won't tell anyone else what to do, because I'm not anyone's leader, no matter what Fox News thinks.**

> **But I am going to tell you what _I_ plan on doing. If you think that's the right thing to do, maybe you'll do it too.**

> **I'm not jamming. Not this week. Maybe not next. It's not because I'm scared. It's because I'm smart enough to know that I'm better free than in prison. They figured out how to stop our tactic, so we need to come up with a new tactic. I don't care what the tac-**

tic is, but I want it to work. It's _stupid_ to get
arrested. It's only jamming if you get away with it.

> There's another reason not to jam. If you get
caught, they might use you to catch your friends, and
their friends, and their friends. They might bust
your friends even if they're not on Xnet, because the
DHS is like a maddened bull and they don't exactly
worry if they've got the right guy.

> I'm not telling you what to do.

> But the DHS is dumb and we're smart. Jamming
proves that they can't fight terrorism because it
proves that they can't even stop a bunch of kids. If
you get caught, it makes them look like they're
smarter than us

> THEY AREN'T SMARTER THAN US! We are smarter
than them. Let's be smart. Let's figure out how to jam
them, no matter how many goons they put on the
streets of our city.

I posted it. I went to bed.

I missed Ange.

Ange and I didn't speak for the next four days, including the weekend, and then it was time to go back to school. I'd
almost called her a million times, written a thousand unsent
emails and IMs.

Now I was back in Social Studies class, and Mrs. Andersen
greeted me with voluble, sarcastic courtesy, asking me sweetly
how my "holiday" had been. I sat down and mumbled nothing.
I could hear Charles snicker.

She taught us a class on Manifest Destiny, the idea that the Americans were destined to take over the whole world (or at least that's how she made it seem) and seemed to be trying to provoke me into saying something so she could throw me out.

I felt the eyes of the class on me, and it reminded me of M1k3y and the people who looked up to him. I was sick of being looked up to. I missed Ange.

I got through the rest of the day without anything making any kind of mark on me. I don't think I said eight words.

Finally it was over and I hit the doors, heading for the gates and the stupid Mission and my pointless house.

I was barely out the gate when someone crashed into me. He was a young homeless guy, maybe my age, maybe a little older. He wore a long, greasy overcoat, a pair of baggy jeans and rotting sneakers that looked like they'd been through a wood chipper. His long hair hung over his face, and he had a pubic beard that straggled down his throat into the collar of a no-color knit sweater.

I took this all in as we lay next to each other on the sidewalk, people passing us and giving us weird looks. It seemed that he'd crashed into me while hurrying down Valencia, bent over with the burden of a split backpack that lay beside him on the pavement, covered in tight geometric doodles in Magic Marker.

He got to his knees and rocked back and forth, like he was drunk or had hit his head.

"Sorry buddy," he said. "Didn't see you. You hurt?"

I sat up, too. Nothing felt hurt.

"Um. No, it's okay."

He stood up and smiled. His teeth were shockingly white and straight, like an ad for an orthodontic clinic. He held his hand out to me and his grip was strong and firm.

"I'm really sorry." His voice was also clear and intelligent.

I'd expected him to sound like the drunks who talked to themselves as they roamed the Mission late at night, but he sounded like a knowledgeable bookstore clerk.

"It's no problem," I said.

He stuck out his hand again.

"Zeb," he said.

"Marcus," I said.

"A pleasure, Marcus," he said. "Hope to run into you again sometime!"

Laughing, he picked up his backpack, turned on his heel and hurried away.

I walked the rest of the way home in a bemused fog. Mom was at the kitchen table and we had a little chat about nothing at all, the way we used to do, before everything changed.

I took the stairs up to my room and flopped down in my chair. For once, I didn't want to log in to the Xnet. I'd checked in that morning before school to discover that my note had created a gigantic controversy among people who agreed with me and people who were righteously pissed that I was telling them to back off from their beloved sport.

I had three thousand projects I'd been in the middle of when it had all started. I was building a pinhole camera out of legos, I'd been playing with aerial kite photography using an old digital camera with a trigger hacked out of silly putty that was stretched out at launch and slowly snapped back to its original shape, triggering the shutter at regular intervals. I had a vacuum tube amp I'd been building into an ancient, rusted, dented olive oil tin that looked like an archaeological find—once it was done, I'd planned to build in a dock for my phone and a set of 5.1 surround-sound speakers out of tuna fish cans.

I looked over my workbench and finally picked up the pin-hole camera. Methodically snapping legos together was just about my speed.

I took off my watch and the chunky silver two-finger ring that showed a monkey and a ninja squaring off to fight and dropped them into the little box I used for all the crap I load into my pockets and around my neck before stepping out for the day: phone, wallet, keys, wifinder, change, batteries, retractable cables . . . I dumped it all out into the box, and found myself holding something I didn't remember putting in there in the first place.

It was a piece of paper, gray and soft as flannel, furry at the edges where it had been torn away from some larger piece of paper. It was covered in the tiniest, most careful handwriting I'd ever seen. I unfolded it and held it up. The writing covered both sides, running down from the top left corner of one side to a crabbed signature at the bottom right corner of the other side.

The signature read, simply: ZEB.

I picked it up and started to read.

Dear Marcus

You don't know me but I know you. For the past three months, since the Bay Bridge was blown up, I have been imprisoned on Treasure Island. I was in the yard on the day you talked to that Asian girl and got tackled. You were brave. Good on you.

I had a burst appendix the day afterward and ended up in the infirmary. In the next bed was a guy named Darryl. We were both in recovery for a long time and by the time we got well, we were too much of an embarrassment to them to let go.

So they decided we must really be guilty. They questioned us every day. You've been through their questioning, I know. Imagine it for months. Darryl and I ended up cell-mates. We

knew we were bugged, so we only talked about inconsequential-
ities. But at night, when we were in our cots, we would softly
tap out messages to each other in Morse code (I knew my
HAM radio days would come in useful sometime).

At first, their questions to us were just the same crap as
ever, who did it, how'd they do it. But after a little while, they
switched to asking us about the Xnet. Of course, we'd never
heard of it. That didn't stop them asking.

Darryl told me that they brought him arphid cloners,
Xboxes, all kinds of technology and demanded that he tell them
who used them, where they learned to mod them. Darryl told
me about your games and the things you learned.

Especially: The DHS asked us about our friends. Who did
we know? What were they like? Did they have political feelings? Had they been in trouble at school? With the law?

We call the prison Gitmo-by-the-Bay. It's been a week since
I got out and I don't think that anyone knows that their sons
and daughters are imprisoned in the middle of the Bay. At night
we could hear people laughing and partying on the mainland.

I got out last week. I won't tell you how, in case this falls
into the wrong hands. Maybe others will take my route.

Darryl told me how to find you and made me promise to
tell you what I knew when I got back. Now that I've done that
I'm out of here like last year. One way or another, I'm leaving
this country. Screw America.

Stay strong. They're scared of you. Kick them for me.
Don't get caught.

Zeb

There were tears in my eyes as I finished the note. I had a
disposable lighter somewhere on my desk that I sometimes used

to melt the insulation off of wires, and I dug it out and held it to the note. I knew I owed it to Zeb to destroy it and make sure no one else ever saw it, in case it might lead them back to him, wherever he was going.

I held the flame and the note, but I couldn't do it.

Darryl.

With all the crap with the Xnet and Ange and the DHS, I'd almost forgotten he existed. He'd become a ghost, like an old friend who'd moved away or gone on an exchange program. All that time, they'd been questioning him, demanding that he rat me out, explain the Xnet, the jammers. He'd been on Treasure Island, the abandoned military base that was halfway along the demolished span of the Bay Bridge. He'd been so close I could have swam to him.

I put the lighter down and reread the note. By the time it was done, I was weeping, sobbing. It all came back to me, the lady with the severe haircut and the questions she'd asked and the reek of piss and the stiffness of my pants as the urine dried them into coarse canvas.

"Marcus?"

My door was ajar and my mother was standing in it, watching me with a worried look. How long had she been there?

I armed the tears away from my face and snorted up the snot. "Mom," I said. "Hi."

She came into my room and hugged me. "What is it? Do you need to talk?"

The note lay on the table.

"Is that from your girlfriend? Is everything all right?"

She'd given me an out. I could just blame it all on problems with Ange and she'd leave my room and leave me alone. I opened my mouth to do just that, and then this came out:

"I was in jail. After the bridge blew. I was in jail for that whole time."

The sobs that came then didn't sound like my voice. They sounded like an animal noise, maybe a donkey or some kind of big cat noise in the night. I sobbed so my throat burned and ached with it, so my chest heaved.

Mom took me in her arms, the way she used to when I was a little boy, and she stroked my hair, and she murmured in my ear, and rocked me, and gradually, slowly, the sobs dissipated.

I took a deep breath and Mom got me a glass of water. I sat on the edge of my bed and she sat in my desk chair and I told her everything.

Everything.

Well, most of it.

Chapter 16

At first Mom looked shocked, then outraged, and finally she gave up altogether and just let her jaw hang open as I took her through the interrogation, pissing myself, the bag over my head, Darryl. I showed her the note.

"Why—?"

In that single syllable, every recrimination I'd dealt myself in the night, every moment that I'd lacked the bravery to tell the world what it was really about, why I was really fighting, what had really inspired the Xnet.

I sucked in a breath.

"They told me I'd go to jail if I talked about it. Not just for a few days. Forever. I was—I was scared."

Mom sat with me for a long time, not saying anything. Then, "What about Darryl's father?"

She might as well have stuck a knitting needle in my chest. Darryl's father. He must have assumed that Darryl was dead, long dead.

And wasn't he? After the DHS has held you illegally for three months, would they ever let you go?

But Zeb got out. Maybe Darryl would get out. Maybe me and the Xnet could help get Darryl out.

"I haven't told him," I said.

Now Mom was crying. She didn't cry easily. It was a British thing. It made her little hiccoughing sobs much worse to hear.

"You will tell him," she managed. "You will."

"I will."

"But first we have to tell your father."

Dad no longer had any regular time when he came home. Between his consulting clients—who had lots of work now that the DHS was shopping for data-mining start-ups on the peninsula—and the long commute to Berkeley, he might get home any time between 6 P.M. and midnight.

Tonight Mom called him and told him he was coming home *right now*. He said something and she just repeated it: *right now*.

When he got there, we had arranged ourselves in the living room with the note between us on the coffee table.

It was easier to tell, the second time. The secret was getting lighter. I didn't embellish, I didn't hide anything. I came clean.

I'd heard of coming clean before but I'd never understood what it meant until I did it. Holding in the secret had dirtied me, soiled my spirit. It had made me afraid and ashamed. It had made me into all the things that Ange said I was.

Dad sat stiff as a ramrod the whole time, his face carved of stone. When I handed him the note, he read it twice and then set it down carefully.

He shook his head and stood up and headed for the front door.

"Where are you going?" Mom asked, alarmed.

"I need a walk," was all he managed to gasp, his voice breaking.

We stared awkwardly at each other, Mom and me, and waited for him to come home. I tried to imagine what was going on in his head. He'd been such a different man after the bombings and I knew from Mom that what had changed him were the days of thinking I was dead. He'd come to believe that the terrorists had nearly killed his son and it had made him crazy.

Crazy enough to do whatever the DHS asked, to line up like a good little sheep and let them control him, drive him.

Now he knew that it was the DHS that had imprisoned me, the DHS that had taken San Francisco's children hostage in Gitmo-by-the-Bay. It made perfect sense, now that I thought of it. Of course it had been Treasure Island where I'd been kept. Where else was a ten-minute boat ride from San Francisco?

When Dad came back, he looked angrier than he ever had in his life.

"You should have told me!" he roared.

Mom interposed herself between him and me. "You're blaming the wrong person," she said. "It wasn't Marcus who did the kidnapping and the intimidation."

He shook his head and stamped. "I'm not blaming Marcus. I know *exactly* who's to blame. Me. Me and the stupid DHS. Get your shoes on, grab your coats."

"Where are we going?"

"To see Darryl's father. Then we're going to Barbara Stratford's place."

I knew the name Barbara Stratford from somewhere, but I couldn't remember where. I thought that maybe she was an old friend of my parents, but I couldn't exactly place her.

Meantime, I was headed for Darryl's father's place. I'd never really felt comfortable around the old man, who'd been a Navy radio operator and ran his household like a tight ship. He'd taught Darryl Morse code when he was a kid, which I'd always thought was cool. It was one of the ways I knew that I could trust Zeb's letter. But for every cool thing like Morse code, Darryl's father had some crazy military discipline that seemed to be for its own sake, like insisting on hospital corners on the beds and shaving twice a day. It drove Darryl up the wall.

Darryl's mother hadn't liked it much, either, and had taken off back to her family in Minnesota when Darryl was ten—Darryl spent his summers and Christmases there.

I was sitting in the back of the car, and I could see the back of Dad's head as he drove. The muscles in his neck were tense and kept jumping around as he ground his jaws.

Mom kept her hand on his arm, but no one was around to comfort me. If only I could call Ange. Or Jolu. Or Van. Maybe I would when the day was done.

"He must have buried his son in his mind," Dad said, as we whipped up through the hairpin curves leading up Twin Peaks to the little cottage that Darryl and his father shared. The fog was on Twin Peaks, the way it often was at night in San Francisco, making the headlamps reflect back on us. Each time we swung around a corner, I saw the valleys of the city laid out below us, bowls of twinkling lights that shifted in the mist.

"Is this the one?"

"Yes," I said. "This is it." I hadn't been to Darryl's in months, but I'd spent enough time here over the years to recognize it right off.

The three of us stood around the car for a long moment, waiting to see who would go and ring the doorbell. To my surprise, it was me.

I rang it and we all waited in held-breath silence for a

minute. I rang it again. Darryl's father's car was in the driveway, and we'd seen a light burning in the living room. I was about to ring a third time when the door opened.

"Marcus?" Darryl's father wasn't anything like I remembered him. Unshaven, in a housecoat and bare feet, with long toenails and red eyes. He'd gained weight, and a soft extra chin wobbled beneath the firm military jaw. His thin hair was wispy and disordered.

"Mr. Glover," I said. My parents crowded into the door behind me.

"Hello, Ron," my mother said.

"Ron," my father said.

"You, too? What's going on?"

"Can we come in?"

His living room looked like one of those news segments they show about abandoned kids who spend a month locked in before they're rescued by the neighbors: frozen meal boxes, empty beer cans and juice bottles, moldy cereal bowls and piles of newspapers. There was a reek of cat piss and litter crunched underneath our feet. Even without the cat piss, the smell was incredible, like a bus station toilet.

The couch was made up with a grimy sheet and a couple of greasy pillows and the cushions had a dented, much-slept-upon look.

We all stood there for a long silent moment, embarrassment overwhelming every other emotion. Darryl's father looked like he wanted to die.

Slowly, he moved aside the sheet from the sofa and cleared the stacked, greasy food trays off of a couple of the chairs, carrying them into the kitchen, and, from the sound of it, tossing them on the floor.

We sat gingerly in the places he'd cleared, and then he came back and sat down, too.

"I'm sorry," he said vaguely. "I don't really have any coffee to offer you. I'm having more groceries delivered tomorrow so I'm running low—"

"Ron," my father said. "Listen to us. We have something to tell you, and it's not going to be easy to hear."

He sat like a statue as I talked. He glanced down at the note, read it without seeming to understand it, then read it again. He handed it back to me.

He was trembling.

"He's—"

"Darryl is alive," I said. "Darryl is alive and being held prisoner on Treasure Island."

He stuffed his fist in his mouth and made a horrible groaning sound.

"We have a friend," my father said. "She writes for the *Bay Guardian*. An investigative reporter."

That's where I knew the name from. The free weekly *Guardian* often lost its reporters to bigger daily papers and the Internet, but Barbara Stratford had been there forever. I had a dim memory of having dinner with her when I was a kid.

"We're going there now," my mother said. "Will you come with us, Ron? Will you tell her Darryl's story?"

He put his face in his hands and breathed deeply. Dad tried to put his hand on his shoulders, but Mr. Glover shook it off violently.

"I need to clean myself up," he said. "Give me a minute."

Mr. Glover came back downstairs a changed man. He'd shaved and gelled his hair back, and had put on a crisp military dress uniform with a row of campaign ribbons on the breast. He stopped at the foot of the stairs and kind of gestured at it.

"I don't have much clean stuff that's presentable at the moment. And this seemed appropriate. You know, if she wanted to take pictures."

He and Dad rode up front and I got in the back, behind him. Up close, he smelled a little of beer, like it was coming through his pores.

It was midnight by the time we rolled into Barbara Stratford's driveway. She lived out of town, down in Mountain View, and as we sped down the 101, none of us said a word. The high-tech buildings alongside the highway streamed past us.

This was a different Bay Area to the one I lived in, more like the suburban America I sometimes saw on TV. Lots of freeways and subdivisions of identical houses, towns where there weren't any homeless people pushing shopping carts down the sidewalk— there weren't even sidewalks!

Mom had phoned Barbara Stratford while we were waiting for Mr. Glover to come downstairs. The journalist had been sleeping, but Mom had been so wound up she forgot to be all British and embarrassed about waking her up. Instead, she just told her, tensely, that she had something to talk about and that it had to be in person.

When we rolled up to Barbara Stratford's house, my first thought was of the Brady Bunch place—a low ranch house with a brick baffle in front of it and a neat, perfectly square lawn. There was a kind of abstract tile pattern on the baffle, and an old-fashioned UHF TV antenna rising from behind it. We wandered around to the entrance and saw that there were lights on inside already.

The writer opened the door before we had a chance to ring

the bell. She was about my parents' age, a tall thin woman with a hawklike nose and shrewd eyes with a lot of laugh lines. She was wearing a pair of jeans that were hip enough to be seen at one of the boutiques on Valencia Street, and a loose Indian cotton blouse that hung down to her thighs. She had small round glasses that flashed in her hallway light.

She smiled a tight little smile at us.

"You brought the whole clan, I see," she said.

Mom nodded. "You'll understand why in a minute," she said. Mr. Glover stepped from behind Dad.

"And you called in the Navy?"

"All in good time."

We were introduced one at a time to her. She had a firm handshake and long fingers.

Her place was furnished in Japanese minimalist style, just a few precisely proportioned, low pieces of furniture, large clay pots of bamboo that brushed the ceiling, and what looked like a large, rusted piece of a diesel engine perched on top of a polished marble plinth. I decided I liked it. The floors were old wood, sanded and stained, but not filled, so you could see cracks and pits underneath the varnish. I *really* liked that, especially as I walked over it in my stocking feet.

"I have coffee on," she said. "Who wants some?"

We all put up our hands. I glared defiantly at my parents.

"Right," she said.

She disappeared into another room and came back a moment later bearing a rough bamboo tray with a half-gallon thermos jug and six cups of precise design but with rough, sloppy decorations. I liked those, too.

"Now," she said, once she'd poured and served. "It's very

good to see you all again. Marcus, I think the last time I saw you, you were maybe seven years old. As I recall, you were very excited about your new video games, which you showed me."

I didn't remember it at all, but that sounded like what I'd been into at seven. I guessed it was my Sega Dreamcast.

She produced a tape recorder and a yellow pad and a pen, and twirled the pen. "I'm here to listen to whatever you tell me, and I can promise you that I'll take it all in confidence. But I can't promise that I'll do anything with it, or that it's going to get published." The way she said it made me realize that my mom had called in a pretty big favor getting this lady out of bed, friend or no friend. It must be kind of a pain in the ass to be a big-shot investigative reporter. There were probably a million people who would have liked her to take up their cause.

Mom nodded at me. Even though I'd told the story three times that night, I found myself tongue-tied. This was different from telling my parents. Different from telling Darryl's father. This—this would start a new move in the game.

I started slowly, and watched Barbara take notes. I drank a whole cup of coffee just explaining what ARGing was and how I got out of school to play. Mom and Dad and Mr. Glover all listened intently to this part. I poured myself another cup and drank it on the way to explaining how we were taken in. By the time I'd run through the whole story, I'd drained the pot and I needed to piss like a racehorse.

Her bathroom was just as stark as the living room, with a brown, organic soap that smelled like clean mud. I came back in and found the adults quietly watching me.

Mr. Glover told his story next. He didn't have anything to say about what had happened, but he explained that he was a veteran and that his son was a good kid. He talked about what it felt like to believe that his son had died, about how his ex-wife had had a collapse when she found out and ended up in the hospital. He cried a little, unashamed, the tears streaming down his lined face and darkening the collar of his dress uniform.

When it was all done, Barbara went into a different room and came back with a bottle of Irish whiskey. "It's a Bushmills fifteen-year-old rum-cask aged blend," she said, setting down four small cups. None for me. "It hasn't been sold in ten years. I think this is probably an appropriate time to break it out."

She poured them each a small glass of the liquor, then raised hers and sipped at it, draining half the cup. The rest of the adults followed suit. They drank again, and finished the cups. She poured them new shots.

"All right," she said. "Here's what I can tell you right now. I believe you. Not just because I know you, Lillian. The story sounds right, and it ties in with other rumors I've heard. But I'm not going to be able to just take your word for it. I'm going to have to investigate every aspect of this, and every element of your lives and stories. I need to know if there's anything you're not telling me, anything that could be used to discredit you after this comes to light. I need everything. It could take weeks before I'm ready to publish.

"You also need to think about your safety and this Darryl's safety. If he's really an 'unperson' then bringing pressure to bear on the DHS could cause them to move him somewhere much farther away. Think Syria. They could also do something much worse." She let that hang in the air. I knew she meant that they might kill him.

"I'm going to take this letter and scan it now. I want pictures of all of you, now and later—we can send out a photographer, but I want to document this as thoroughly as I can tonight, too."

I went with her into her office to do the scan. I'd expected a stylish, low-powered computer that fit in with her decor, but instead, her spare bedroom/office was crammed with top-of-the-line PCs, big flat-panel monitors, and a scanner big enough to lay a whole sheet of newsprint on. She was fast with it all, too. I noted with some approval that she was running ParanoidLinux. This lady took her job seriously.

The computers' fans set up an effective white noise shield, but even so, I closed the door and moved in close to her.

"Um, Barbara?"

"Yes?"

"About what you said, about what might be used to discredit me?"

"Yes?"

"What I tell you, you can't be forced to tell anyone else, right?"

"In theory. Let me put it this way. I've gone to jail twice rather than rat out a source."

"Okay, okay. Good. Wow. Jail. Wow. Okay." I took a deep breath. "You've heard of Xnet? Of M1k3y?"

"Yes?"

"I'm M1k3y."

"Oh," she said. She worked the scanner and flipped the note over to get the reverse. She was scanning at some unbelievable resolution, 10,000 dots per inch or higher, and on-screen it was like the output of an electron-tunneling microscope.

"Well, that does put a different complexion on this."

"Yeah," I said. "I guess it does."

"Your parents don't know."

"Nope. And I don't know if I want them to."

"That's something you're going to have to work out. I need

to think about this. Can you come by my office? I'd like to talk to you about what this means, exactly."

"Do you have an Xbox Universal? I could bring over an installer."

"Yes, I'm sure that can be arranged. When you come by, tell the receptionist that you're Mr. Brown, to see me. They know what that means. No note will be taken of you coming, and all the security camera footage for the day will be automatically scrubbed and the cameras deactivated until you leave."

"Wow," I said. "You think like I do."

She smiled and socked me in the shoulder. "Kiddo, I've been at this game for a hell of a long time. So far, I've managed to spend more time free than behind bars. Paranoia is my friend."

I was like a zombie the next day in school. I'd totaled about three hours of sleep, and even three cups of the Turk's caffeine mud failed to jump-start my brain. The problem with caffeine is that it's too easy to get acclimated to it, so you have to take higher and higher doses just to get above normal.

I'd spent the night thinking over what I had to do. It was like running through a maze of twisty little passages, all alike, every one leading to the same dead end. When I went to Barbara, it would be over for me. That was the outcome, no matter how I thought about it.

By the time the school day was over, all I wanted was to go home and crawl into bed. But I had an appointment at the *Bay Guardian,* down on the waterfront. I kept my eyes on my feet as I wobbled out the gate, and as I turned into 24th Street, another pair of feet fell into step with me. I recognized the shoes and stopped.

"Ange?"

She looked like I felt. Sleep-deprived and raccoon-eyed, with sad brackets in the corners of her mouth.

"Hi there," she said. "Surprise. I gave myself French Leave from school. I couldn't concentrate anyway."

"Um," I said.

"Shut up and give me a hug, you idiot."

I did. It felt good. Better than good. It felt like I'd amputated part of myself and it had been reattached.

"I love you, Marcus Yallow."

"I love you, Angela Carvelli."

"Okay," she said breaking it off. "I liked your post about why you're not jamming. I can respect it. What have you done about finding a way to jam them without getting caught?"

"I'm on my way to meet an investigative journalist who's going to publish a story about how I got sent to jail, how I started Xnet and how Darryl is being illegally held by the DHS at a secret prison on Treasure Island."

"Oh." She looked around for a moment. "Couldn't you think of anything, you know, ambitious?"

"Want to come?"

"I am coming, yes. And I would like you to explain this in detail if you don't mind."

After all the retellings, this one, told as we walked to Potrero Avenue and down to 15th Street, was the easiest. She held my hand and squeezed it often.

We took the stairs up to the *Bay Guardian*'s offices two at a time. My heart was pounding. I got to the reception desk and told the bored girl behind it, "I'm here to see Barbara Stratford. My name is Mr. Green."

"I think you mean Mr. Brown?"

"Yeah," I said, and blushed. "Mr. Brown."

She did something at her computer, then said, "Have a seat. Barbara will be out in a minute. Can I get you anything?"

"Coffee," we both said in unison. Another reason to love Ange: we were addicted to the same drug.

The receptionist—a pretty Latina woman only a few years older than us, dressed in Gap styles so old they were actually kind of hipster-retro—nodded and stepped out and came back with a couple of cups bearing the newspaper's masthead.

We sipped in silence, watching visitors and reporters come and go. Finally, Barbara came to get us. She was wearing practically the same thing as the night before. It suited her. She quirked an eyebrow at me when she saw that I'd brought a date.

"Hello," I said. "Um, this is—"

"Ms. Brown," Ange said, extending a hand. Oh, yeah, right, our identities were supposed to be a secret. "I work with Mr. Green." She elbowed me lightly.

"Let's go then," Barbara said, and led us back to a board room with long glass walls with their blinds drawn shut. She set down a tray of Whole Foods organic Oreo clones, a digital recorder and another yellow pad.

"Do you want to record this, too?" she asked.

Hadn't actually thought of that. I could see why it would be useful if I wanted to dispute what Barbara printed, though. Still, if I couldn't trust her to do right by me, I was doomed anyway.

"No, that's okay," I said.

"Right, let's go. Young lady, my name is Barbara Stratford and I'm an investigative reporter. I gather you know why I'm here, and I'm curious to know why you're here."

"I work with Marcus on the Xnet," she said. "Do you need to know my name?"

"Not right now, I don't," Barbara said. "You can be anonymous if you'd like. Marcus, I asked you to tell me this story because I need to know how it plays with the story you told me about your friend Darryl and the note you showed me. I can see how it would be a good adjunct; I could pitch this as the origin of the Xnet. 'They made an enemy they'll never forget,' that sort of thing. But to be honest, I'd rather not have to tell that story if I don't have to.

"I'd rather have a nice clean tale about the secret prison on our doorstep, without having to argue about whether the prisoners there are the sort of people likely to walk out the doors and establish an underground movement bent on destabilizing the federal government. I'm sure you can understand that."

I did. If the Xnet was part of the story, some people would say, see, they need to put guys like that in jail or they'll start a riot.

"This is your show," I said. "I think you need to tell the world about Darryl. When you do that, it's going to tell the DHS that I've gone public and they're going to go after me. Maybe they'll figure out then that I'm involved with the Xnet. Maybe they'll connect me to M1k3y. I guess what I'm saying is, once you publish about Darryl, it's all over for me no matter what. I've made my peace with that."

"As good be hanged for a sheep as a lamb," she said. "Right. Well, that's settled. I want the two of you to tell me everything you can about the founding and operation of the Xnet, and then I want a demonstration. What do you use it for? Who else uses it? How did it spread? Who wrote the software? Everything."

"This'll take a while," Ange said.

"I've got a while," Barbara said. She drank some coffee and ate a fake Oreo. "This could be the most important story of the War on Terror. This could be the story that topples the government. When you have a story like this, you take it very carefully."

Chapter 17

So we told her. I found it really fun, actually. Teaching people how to use technology is always exciting. It's so cool to watch people figure out how the technology around them can be used to make their lives better. Ange was great, too—we made an excellent team. We'd trade off explaining how it all worked. Barbara was pretty good at this stuff to begin with, of course.

It turned out that she'd covered the crypto wars, the period in the early nineties when civil liberties groups like the Electronic Frontier Foundation fought for the right of Americans to use strong crypto. I dimly knew about that period, but Barbara explained it in a way that made me get goose pimples.

It's unbelievable today, but there was a time when the government classed crypto as a munition and made it illegal for anyone to export or use it on national security grounds. Get that? We used to have illegal *math* in this country.

The National Security Agency were the real movers behind the ban. They had a crypto standard that they said was strong enough for bankers and their customers to use, but not so strong that the mafia would be able to keep its books secret from them. The standard, DES-56, was said to be practically unbreakable.

Then one of EFF's millionaire cofounders built a $250,000 DES-56 cracker that could break the cipher in two hours.

Still the NSA argued that it should be able to keep American citizens from possessing secrets it couldn't pry into. Then EFF dealt its death blow. In 1995, they represented a Berkeley mathematics grad student called Dan Bernstein in court. Bernstein had written a crypto tutorial that contained computer code that could be used to make a cipher stronger than DES-56. Millions of times stronger. As far as the NSA was concerned, that made his article into a weapon, and therefore unpublishable.

Well, it may be hard to get a judge to understand crypto and what it means, but it turned out that the average Appeals Court judge isn't real enthusiastic about telling grad students what kind of scholarly articles they're allowed to write. The crypto wars ended with a victory for the good guys when the 9th Circuit Appellate Division Court ruled that code was a form of expression protected under the First Amendment—"Congress shall make no law abridging the freedom of speech." If you've ever bought something on the Internet, or sent a secret message, or checked your bank balance, you used crypto that EFF legalized. Good thing, too: the NSA just isn't that smart. Anything they know how to crack, you can be sure that terrorists and mobsters can get around, too.

Barbara had been one of the reporters who'd made her reputation from covering the issue. She'd cut her teeth covering the tail end of the civil rights movement in San Francisco, and she recognized the similarity between the fight for the Constitution in the real world and the fight in cyberspace.

So she got it. I don't think I could have explained this stuff to my parents, but with Barbara it was easy. She asked smart questions about our cryptographic protocols and security procedures, sometimes asking stuff I didn't know the answer to—sometimes pointing out potential breaks in our procedure.

We plugged in the Xbox and got it online. There were four open WiFi nodes visible from the board room and I told it to change between them at random intervals. She got this, too—once you were actually plugged into the Xnet, it was just like being on the Internet, only some stuff was a little slower, and it was all anonymous and unsniffable.

"So now what?" I said as we wound down. I'd talked myself dry and I had a terrible acid feeling from the coffee. Besides, Ange kept squeezing my hand under the table in a way that made me want to break away and find somewhere private to finish making up for our first fight.

"Now I do journalism. You go away and I research all the things you've told me and try to confirm them to the extent that I can. I'll let you see what I'm going to publish and I'll let you know when it's going to go live. I'd prefer that you *not* talk about this with anyone else now, because I want the scoop and because I want to make sure that I get the story before it goes all muddy from press speculation and DHS spin.

"I *will* have to call the DHS for comment before I go to press, but I'll do that in a way that protects you to whatever extent possible. I'll also be sure to let you know before that happens.

"One thing I need to be clear on: this isn't your story anymore. It's mine. You were very generous to give it to me and I'll try to repay the gift, but you don't get the right to edit anything out, to change it or to stop me. This is now in motion and it won't stop. Do you understand that?"

I hadn't thought about it in those terms but once she said it, it was obvious. It meant that I had launched and I wouldn't be able to recall the rocket. It was going to fall where it was aimed, or it would go off course, but it was in the air and couldn't be changed now. Sometime in the near future, I would stop being Marcus—I would be a public figure. I'd be the guy who blew the whistle on the DHS.

I'd be a dead man walking.

I guess Ange was thinking along the same lines, because she'd gone a color between white and green.

"Let's get out of here," she said.

Ange's mom and sister were out again, which made it easy to decide where we were going for the evening. It was past supper time, but my parents had known that I was meeting with Barbara and wouldn't give me any grief if I came home late.

When we got to Ange's, I had no urge to plug in my Xbox. I had had all the Xnet I could handle for one day. All I could think about was Ange, Ange, Ange. Living without Ange. Knowing Ange was angry with me. Ange never going to talk to me again. Ange never going to kiss me again.

She'd been thinking the same. I could see it in her eyes as we shut the door to her bedroom and looked at each other. I was hungry for her, like you'd hunger for dinner after not eating for days. Like you'd thirst for a glass of water after playing soccer for three hours straight.

Like none of that. It was more. It was something I'd never felt before. I wanted to eat her whole, devour her.

Up until now, she'd been the sexual one in our relationship. I'd let her set and control the pace. It was amazingly erotic to have *her* grab *me* and take off my shirt, drag my face to hers.

But tonight I couldn't hold back. I wouldn't hold back.

The door clicked shut and I reached for the hem of her

T-shirt and yanked, barely giving her time to lift her arms as I pulled it over her head. I tore my own shirt over my head, listening to the cotton crackle as the stitches came loose.

Her eyes were shining, her mouth open, her breathing fast and shallow. Mine was, too, my breath and my heart and my blood all roaring in my ears.

I took off the rest of our clothes with equal zest, throwing them into the piles of dirty and clean laundry on the floor. There were books and papers all over the bed and I swept them aside. We landed on the unmade bedclothes a second later, arms around one another, squeezing like we would pull ourselves right through one another. She moaned into my mouth and I made the sound back, and I felt her voice buzz in my vocal chords, a feeling more intimate than anything I'd ever felt before.

She broke away and reached for the bedstand. She yanked open the drawer and threw a white pharmacy bag on the bed before me. I looked inside. Condoms. Trojans. One dozen spermicidal. Still sealed. I smiled at her and she smiled back and I opened the box.

I'd thought about what it would be like for years. A hundred times a day I'd imagined it. Some days, I'd thought of practically nothing else.

It was nothing like I expected. Parts of it were better. Parts of it were lots worse. While it was going on, it felt like an eternity. Afterward, it seemed to be over in the blink of an eye.

Afterward, I felt the same. But I also felt different. Something had changed between us.

It was weird. We were both shy as we put our clothes on and puttered around the room, looking away, not meeting each other's eyes. I wrapped the condom in a kleenex from a box beside the bed and took it into the bathroom and wound it with toilet paper and stuck it deep into the trash can.

When I came back in, Ange was sitting up in bed and playing with her Xbox. I sat down carefully beside her and took her hand. She turned to face me and smiled. We were both worn out, trembly.

"Thanks," I said.

She didn't say anything. She turned her face to me. She was grinning hugely, but fat tears were rolling down her cheeks.

I hugged her and she grabbed tightly onto me. "You're a good man, Marcus Yallow," she whispered. "Thank you."

I didn't know what to say, but I squeezed her back. Finally, we parted. She wasn't crying anymore, but she was still smiling.

She pointed at my Xbox, on the floor beside the bed. I took the hint. I picked it up and plugged it in and logged in.

Same old same old. Lots of email. The new posts on the blogs I read streamed in. Spam. God did I get a lot of spam. My Swedish mailbox was repeatedly joe-jobbed—used as the return address for spams sent to hundreds of millions of Internet accounts, so that all the bounces and angry messages came back to me. I didn't know who was behind it. Maybe the DHS trying to overwhelm my mailbox. Maybe it was just people pranking. The Pirate Party had pretty good filters, though, and they gave anyone who wanted it five hundred gigabytes of email storage, so I wasn't likely to be drowned any time soon.

I filtered it all out, hammering on the delete key. I had a separate mailbox for stuff that came in encrypted to my public key, since that was likely to be Xnet-related and possibly sensitive. Spammers hadn't figured out that using public keys would make their junk mail more plausible yet, so for now this worked well.

There were a couple dozen encrypted messages from people

in the web of trust. I skimmed them—links to videos and pics of new abuses from the DHS, horror stories about near-escapes, rants about stuff I'd blogged. The usual.

Then I came to one that was only encrypted to my public key. That meant that no one else could read it, but I had no idea who had written it. It said it came from Masha, which could either be a handle or a name—I couldn't tell which.

> M1k3y

> You don't know me, but I know you.

> I was arrested the day that the bridge blew. They questioned me. They decided I was innocent. They offered me a job: help them hunt down the terrorists who'd killed my neighbors.

> It sounded like a good deal at the time. Little did I realize that my actual job would turn out to be spying on kids who resented their city being turned into a police state.

> I infiltrated Xnet on the day it launched. I am in your web of trust. If I wanted to spill my identity, I could send you email from an address you'd trust. Three addresses, actually. I'm totally inside your network as only another 17-year-old can be. Some of the email you've gotten has been carefully chosen misinformation from me and my handlers.

> They don't know who you are, but they're coming close. They continue to turn people, to compromise them. They mine the social network sites and use threats to turn kids into informants. There are hundreds of people working for the DHS on Xnet right now. I have their names, handles and keys. Private and public.

> Within days of the Xnet launch, we went to work on exploiting ParanoidLinux. The exploits so far have been small and insubstantial, but a break is inevitable. Once we have a zero-day break, you're dead.

> I think it's safe to say that if my handlers knew that I was typing this, my ass would be stuck in Gitmo-by-the-Bay until I was an old woman.

> Even if they don't break ParanoidLinux, there are poisoned ParanoidXbox distros floating around. They don't match the checksums, but how many people look at the checksums? Besides me and you? Plenty of kids are already dead, though they don't know it.

> All that remains is for my handlers to figure out the best time to bust you to make the biggest impact in the media. That time will be sooner, not later. Believe.

> You're probably wondering why I'm telling you this.

> I am too.

> Here's where I come from. I signed up to fight terrorists. Instead, I'm spying on Americans who believe things that the DHS doesn't like. Not people who plan on blowing up bridges, but protestors. I can't do it anymore.

> But neither can you, whether or not you know it. Like I say, it's only a matter of time until you're in chains on Treasure Island. That's not if, that's when.

> So I'm through here. Down in Los Angeles, there are some people. They say they can keep me safe if I want to get out.

> I want to get out.

> I will take you with me, if you want to come.
Better to be a fighter than a martyr. If you come with
me, we can figure out how to win together. I'm as
smart as you. Believe.

> What do you say?

> Here's my public key.

> Masha

When in trouble or in doubt, run in circles, scream and
shout.

Ever hear that rhyme? It's not good advice, but at least it's
easy to follow. I leapt off the bed and paced back and forth. My
heart thudded and my blood sang in a cruel parody of the way
I'd felt when we got home. This wasn't sexual excitement, it was
raw terror.

"What?" Ange said. "What?"

I pointed at the screen on my side of the bed. She rolled over
and grabbed my keyboard and scribed on the touchpad with her
fingertip. She read in silence.

I paced.

"This has to be lies," she said. "The DHS is playing games
with your head."

I looked at her. She was biting her lip. She didn't look like
she believed it.

"You think?"

"Sure. They can't beat you, so they're coming after you using Xnet."

"Yeah."

I sat back down on the bed. I was breathing fast again.

"Chill out," she said. "It's just head games. Here."

She never took my keyboard from me before, but now there was a new intimacy between us. She hit reply and typed,

> **Nice try.**

She was writing as M1k3y now, too. We were together in a way that was different from before.

"Go ahead and sign it. We'll see what she says."

I didn't know if that was the best idea, but I didn't have any better ones. I signed it and encrypted it with my private key and the public key Masha had provided.

The reply was instant.

> **I thought you'd say something like that.**

> **Here's a hack you haven't thought of. I can anonymously tunnel video over DNS. Here are some links to clips you might want to look at before you decide I'm full of it. These people are all record-ing each other, all the time, as insurance against a back-stab. It's pretty easy to snoop on them as they snoop on each other.**

> **Masha**

Attached was source code for a little program that appeared to do exactly what Masha claimed: pull video over the Domain Name Service protocol.

Let me back up a moment here and explain something. At the end of the day, every Internet protocol is just a sequence of text sent back and forth in a proscribed order. It's kind of like getting a truck and putting a car in it, then putting a motorcycle in the car's trunk, then attaching a bicycle to the back of the motorcycle, then hanging a pair of Rollerblades on the back of the bike. Except that then, if you want, you can attach the truck to the Rollerblades.

For example, take Simple Mail Transport Protocol, or SMTP, which is used for sending email.

Here's a sample conversation between me and my mail server, sending a message to myself:

```
> HELO littlebrother.com.se
250    mail.pirateparty.org.se    Hello    mail.pi
rateparty.org.se, pleased to meet you
> MAIL FROM:m1k3y@littlebrother.com.se
250    2.1.0    m1k3y@littlebrother.com.se . . .
Sender ok
> RCPT TO:m1k3y@littlebrother.com.se
250  2.1.5  m1k3y@littlebrother.com.se . . . Re-
cipient ok
> DATA
354 Enter mail, end with "." on a line by itself
> When in trouble or in doubt, run in circles,
scream and shout
> .
250 2.0.0 k5SMW0xQ006174 Message accepted for de-
livery
QUIT
221  2.0.0  mail.pirateparty.org.se  closing  con-
nection
Connection closed by foreign host.
```

This conversation's grammar was defined in 1982 by Jon Postel, one of the Internet's heroic forefathers, who used to literally run the most important servers on the net under his desk at the University of Southern California, back in the paleolithic era.

Now, imagine that you hooked up a mail server to an IM session. You could send an IM to the server that said "HELO littlebrother.com.se" and it would reply with "250 mail.pi-rateparty.org.se Hello mail.pirateparty.org.se, pleased to meet you." In other words, you could have the same conversation over IM as you do over SMTP. With the right tweaks, the whole mail server business could take place inside of a chat. Or a web session. Or anything else.

This is called "tunneling." You put the SMTP inside a chat "tunnel." You could then put the chat back into an SMTP tunnel if you wanted to be really weird, tunneling the tunnel in another tunnel.

In fact, every Internet protocol is susceptible to this process. It's cool, because it means that if you're on a network with only web access, you can tunnel your mail over it. You can tunnel your favorite P2P over it. You can even tunnel Xnet—which itself is a tunnel for dozens of protocols—over it.

Domain Name Service is an interesting and ancient Internet protocol, dating back to 1983. It's the way your computer converts a computer's name—like pirateparty.org.se—to the IP number that computers actually use to talk to each other over the net, like 204.11.50.136. It generally works like magic, even though it's got millions of moving parts—every ISP runs a DNS server, as do most governments and lots of private operators. These DNS boxes all talk to each other all the time, making and filling requests to each other so no matter how obscure the name is you feed to your computer, it will be able to turn it into a number.

Before DNS, there was the HOSTS file. Believe it or not, this was a single document that listed the name and address of *every single computer* connected to the Internet. Every computer had a copy of it. This file was eventually too big to move around, so DNS was invented, and ran on a server that used to live under

Jon Postel's desk. If the cleaners knocked out the plug, the entire Internet lost its ability to find itself. Seriously.

The thing about DNS today is that it's everywhere. Every network has a DNS server living on it, and all those servers are configured to talk to each other and to random people all over the Internet.

What Masha had done was figure out a way to tunnel a video-streaming system over DNS. She was breaking up the video into billions of pieces and hiding each of them in a normal message to a DNS server. By running her code, I was able to pull the video from all those DNS servers, all over the Internet, at incredible speed. It must have looked bizarre on the network histograms, like I was looking up the address of every computer in the world.

But it had two advantages I appreciated at once: I was able to get the video with blinding speed—as soon as I clicked the first link, I started to receive full-screen pictures, without any jitter or stuttering—and I had no idea where it was hosted. It was totally anonymous.

At first I didn't even clock the content of the video. I was totally floored by the cleverness of this hack. Streaming video from DNS? That was so smart and weird, it was practically *perverted*.

Gradually, what I was seeing began to sink in.

It was a board room table in a small room with a mirror down one wall. I knew that room. I'd sat in that room, while severe haircut lady had made me speak my password aloud. There were five comfortable chairs around the table, each with a comfortable person, all in DHS uniform. I recognized Major General Graeme Sutherland, the DHS Bay Area commander, along with Severe Haircut. The others were new to me. They all watched a video screen at the end of the table, on which there was an infinitely more familiar face.

Kurt Rooney was known nationally as the President's chief strategist, the man who returned the party for its third term, and who was steaming toward a fourth. They called him "Ruthless" and I'd seen a news report once about how tight a rein he kept his staffers on, calling them, IMing them, watching their every motion, controlling every step. He was old, with a lined face and pale gray eyes and a flat nose with broad, flared nostrils and thin lips, a man who looked like he was smelling something bad all the time.

He was the man on the screen. He was talking, and everyone else was focused on his screen, everyone taking notes as fast as they could type, trying to look smart.

"—say that they're angry with authority, but we need to show the country that it's terrorists, not the government, that they need to blame. Do you understand me? The nation does not love that city. As far as they're concerned, it is a Sodom and Gomorrah of fags and atheists who deserve to rot in hell. The only reason the country cares what they think in San Francisco is that they had the good fortune to have been blown to hell by some Islamic terrorists.

"These Xnet children are getting to the point where they might start to be useful to us. The more radical they get, the more the rest of the nation understands that there are threats everywhere."

His audience finished typing.

"We can control that, I think," Severe Haircut said. "Our people in the Xnet have built up a lot of influence. The Manchurian Bloggers are running as many as fifty blogs each, flooding the chat channels, linking to each other, mostly just taking the party line set by this M1k3y. But they've already shown that they can provoke radical action, even when M1k3y is putting the brakes on."

Major General Sutherland nodded. "We have been planning

to leave them underground until about a month before the midterms." I guessed that meant the midterm elections, not my exams. "That's per the original plan. But it sounds like—"

"We've got another plan for the midterms," Rooney said. "Need-to-know, of course, but you should all probably not plan on traveling for the month before. Cut the Xnet loose now, as soon as you can. So long as they're moderates, they're a liability. Keep them radical."

The video cut off.

Ange and I sat on the edge of the bed, looking at the screen. Ange reached out and started the video again. We watched it. It was worse the second time.

I tossed the keyboard aside and got up.

"I am *so sick* of being scared," I said. "Let's take this to Barbara and have her publish it all. Put it all on the net. Let them take me away. At least I'll know what's going to happen then. At least then I'll have a little *certainty* in my life."

Ange grabbed me and hugged me, soothed me. "I know baby, I know. It's all terrible. But you're focusing on the bad stuff and ignoring the good stuff. You've created a movement. You've outflanked the jerks in the White House, the crooks in DHS uniforms. You've put yourself in a position where you could be responsible for blowing the lid off of the entire rotten DHS thing.

"Sure they're out to get you. 'Course they are. Have you ever doubted it for a moment? I always figured they were. But Marcus, *they don't know who you are*. Think about that. All those people, money, guns and spies, and you, a seventeen-year-old high school kid—you're still beating them. They don't know about Barbara. They don't know about Zeb. You've jammed them in the streets of San Francisco and humiliated them before the world. So stop moping, all right? You're winning."

"They're coming for me, though. You see that. They're going to put me in jail forever. Not even jail. I'll just disappear, like Darryl. Maybe worse. Maybe Syria. Why leave me in San Francisco? I'm a liability as long as I'm in the USA."

She sat down on the bed with me.

"Yeah," she said. "That."

"That."

"Well, you know what you have to do, right?"

"What?" She looked pointedly at my keyboard. I could see the tears rolling down her cheeks. "No! You're out of your mind. You think I'm going to run off with some nut off the Internet? Some spy?"

"You got a better idea?"

I kicked a pile of her laundry into the air. "Whatever. Fine. I'll talk to her some more."

"You talk to her," Ange said. "You tell her you and your girlfriend are getting out."

"What?"

"Shut up, dickhead. You think you're in danger? I'm in just as much danger, Marcus. It's called guilt by association. When you go, I go." She had her jaw thrust out at a mutinous angle. "You and I—we're together now. You have to understand that."

We sat down on the bed together.

"Unless you don't want me," she said, finally, in a small voice.

"You're kidding me, right?"

"Do I look like I'm kidding?"

"There's no way I would voluntarily go without you, Ange. I could never have asked you to come, but I'm ecstatic that you offered."

She smiled and tossed me my keyboard.

"Email this Masha creature. Let's see what this chick can do for us."

I emailed her, encrypting the message, waiting for a reply. Ange nuzzled me a little and I kissed her and we necked. Something about the danger and the pact to go together—it made me forget the awkwardness of having sex, made me freaking horny as hell.

We were half-naked again when Masha's email arrived.

> Two of you? Jesus, like it won't be hard enough already.

> I don't get to leave except to do field intelligence after a big Xnet hit. You get me? The handlers watch my every move, but I go off the leash when something big happens with Xnetters. I get sent into the field then.

> You do something big. I get sent to it. I get us both out. All three of us, if you insist.

> Make it fast, though. I can't send you a lot of email, understand? They watch me. They're closing in on you. You don't have a lot of time. Weeks? Maybe just days.

> I need you to get me out. That's why I'm doing this, in case you're wondering. I can't escape on my own. I need a big Xnet distraction. That's your department. Don't fail me, M1k3y, or we're both dead. Your girlie too.

> Masha

My phone rang, making us both jump. It was my mom wanting to know when I was coming home. I told her I was on my way. She didn't mention Barbara. We'd agreed that we wouldn't talk about any of this stuff on the phone. That was my dad's idea. He could be as paranoid as me.

"I have to go," I said.

"Our parents will be—"

"I know," I said. "I saw what happened to my parents when they thought I was dead. Knowing that I'm a fugitive isn't going to be much better. But they'd rather I be a fugitive than a prisoner. That's what I think. Anyway, once we disappear, Barbara can publish without worrying about getting us into trouble."

We kissed at the door of her room. Not one of the hot, sloppy numbers we usually did when parting ways. A sweet kiss this time. A slow kiss. A good-bye kind of kiss.

BART rides are introspective. When the train rocks
back and forth and you try not to make eye contact with the other riders and you try not to read the ads for plastic surgery, bail bondsmen and AIDS testing, when you try to ignore the graffiti and not look too closely at the stuff in the carpeting. That's when your mind starts to really churn and churn.

You rock back and forth and your mind goes over all the things you've overlooked, plays back all the movies of your life where you're no hero, where you're a chump or a sucker.

Your brain comes up with theories like this one:

If the DHS wanted to catch M1k3y, what better way than to lure him into the open, panic him into leading some kind of big, public Xnet event? Wouldn't that be worth the chance of a compromising video leaking?

Your brain comes up with stuff like that even when the train ride only lasts two or three stops. When you get off, and you start moving, the blood gets running and sometimes your brain helps you out again.

Sometimes your brain gives you solutions in addition to problems.

Chapter 18

There was a time when my favorite thing in the world was putting on a cape and hanging out in hotels, pretending to be an invisible vampire whom everyone stared at.

It's complicated, and not nearly as weird as it sounds. The Live Action Role Playing scene combines the best aspects of D&D with drama club with going to sci-fi cons.

I understand that this might not make it sound as appealing to you as it was to me when I was fourteen.

The best games were the ones at the scout camps out of town: a hundred teenagers, boys and girls, fighting the Friday night traffic, swapping stories, playing handheld games, showing off for hours. Then debarking to stand in the grass before a group of older men and women in badass, homemade armor, dented and scarred, like armor must have been in the old days, not like it's portrayed in the movies, but like a soldier's uniform after a month in the bush.

These people were nominally paid to run the games, but you didn't get the job unless you were the kind of person who'd do it for free. They'd have already divided us into teams based on the questionnaires we'd filled in beforehand, and we'd get our team assignments then, like being called up for baseball sides.

Then you'd get your briefing packages. These were like the briefings the spies get in the movies: here's your identity, here's your mission, here's the secrets you know about the group.

From there, it was time for dinner: roaring fires, meat popping on spits, tofu sizzling on skillets (it's northern California, a vegetarian option is not optional), and a style of eating and drinking that can only be described as quaffing.

Already, the keen kids would be getting into character. My first game, I was a wizard. I had a bag of beanbags that represented spells—when I threw one, I would shout the name of the spell I was casting—fireball, magic missile, cone of light—and the player or "monster" I threw it at would keel over if I connected. Or not—sometimes we had to call in a ref to mediate, but for the most part, we were all pretty good about playing fair. No one liked a dice lawyer.

By bedtime, we were all in character. At fourteen, I wasn't super-sure what a wizard was supposed to sound like, but I could take my cues from the movies and novels. I spoke in slow, measured tones, keeping my face composed in a suitably mystical expression, and thinking mystical thoughts.

The mission was complicated, retrieving a sacred relic that had been stolen by an ogre who was bent on subjugating the people of the land to his will. It didn't really matter a whole lot. What mattered was that I had a private mission, to capture a certain kind of imp to serve as my familiar, and that I had a secret nemesis, another player on the team who had taken part in a raid that killed my family when I was a boy, a player who didn't know that I'd come back, bent on revenge. Somewhere, of course, there was another player with a similar grudge against me, so that even as I was enjoying the camaraderie of the team, I'd always have to keep an eye open for a knife in the back, poison in the food.

For the next two days, we played it out. There were parts of the weekend that were like hide-and-seek, some that were like wilderness survival exercises, some that were like solving crossword puzzles. The game masters had done a great job. And you really got to be friends with the other people on the mission. Darryl was the target of my first murder, and I put my back into it, even though he was my pal. Nice guy. Shame I'd have to kill him.

I fireballed him as he was seeking out treasure after we wiped out a band of orcs, playing rock-paper-scissors with each orc to determine who would prevail in combat. This is a lot more exciting than it sounds.

It was like summer camp for drama geeks. We talked until late at night in tents, looked at the stars, jumped in the river when we got hot, slapped away mosquitos. Became best friends, or lifelong enemies.

I don't know why Charles's parents sent him LARPing. He wasn't the kind of kid who really enjoyed that kind of thing. He was more the pulling-wings-off-flies type. Oh, maybe not. But he just was not into being in costume in the woods. He spent the whole time mooching around, sneering at everyone and everything, trying to convince us all that we weren't having the good time we all felt like we were having. You've no doubt found that kind of person before, the kind of person who is compelled to ensure that everyone else has a rotten time.

The other thing about Charles was that he couldn't get the hang of simulated combat. Once you start running around the woods and playing these elaborate, semimilitary games, it's easy to get totally adrenalized to the point where you're ready to tear out someone's throat. This is not a good state to be in when you're carrying a prop sword, club, pike or other utensil. This is why no one is ever allowed to hit anyone, under any circumstances, in these games. Instead, when you get close enough to someone to fight, you play a quick couple rounds of rock-paper-scissors, with modifiers based on your experience, armaments and condition. The referees mediate disputes. It's quite civilized, and a little weird. You go running after someone through the woods, catch up with him, bare your teeth, and sit down to play a little roshambo. But it works—and it keeps everything safe and fun.

Charles couldn't really get the hang of this. I think he was perfectly capable of understanding that the rule was no contact, but he was simultaneously capable of deciding that the rule didn't matter, and that he wasn't going to abide by it. The refs called him on it a bunch of times over the weekend, and he kept on promising to stick by it, and kept on going back. He was one of the bigger kids there already, and he was fond of "accidentally" tackling you at the end of a chase. Not fun when you get tackled into the rocky forest floor.

I had just mightily smote Darryl in a little clearing where he'd been treasure-hunting, and we were having a little laugh over my extreme sneakiness. He was going to go monstering—killed players could switch to playing monsters, which meant that the longer the game wore on, the more monsters there were coming after you, meaning that everyone got to keep on playing and the game's battles just got more and more epic.

That was when Charles came out of the woods behind me and tackled me, throwing me to the ground so hard that I couldn't breathe for a moment. "Gotcha!" he yelled. I only knew him slightly before this, and I'd never thought much of him, but now I was ready for murder. I climbed slowly to my feet and looked at him, his chest heaving, grinning. "You're so dead," he said. "I totally got you."

I smiled and something felt wrong and sore in my face. I touched my upper lip. It was bloody. My nose was bleeding and my lip was split, cut on a root I'd face-planted into when he tackled me.

I wiped the blood on my pants leg and smiled. I made like I thought that it was all in fun. I laughed a little. I moved toward him.

Charles wasn't fooled. He was already backing away, trying to fade into the woods. Darryl moved to flank him. I took the other flank. Abruptly, he turned and ran. Darryl's foot hooked his ankle and sent him sprawling. We rushed him, just in time to hear a ref's whistle.

The ref hadn't seen Charles foul me, but he'd seen Charles's play that weekend. He sent Charles back to the camp entrance and told him he was out of the game. Charles complained mightily, but to our satisfaction, the ref wasn't having any of it. Once Charles had gone, he gave *us* both a lecture, too, telling us that our retaliation was no more justified than Charles's attack.

It was okay. That night, once the games had ended, we all got hot showers in the scout dorms. Darryl and I stole Charles's clothes and towel. We tied them in knots and dropped them in the urinal. A lot of the boys were happy to contribute to the effort of soaking them. Charles had been very enthusiastic about his tackles.

I wish I could have watched him when he got out of his shower and discovered his clothes. It's a hard decision: do you run naked across the camp, or pick apart the tight, piss-soaked knots in your clothes and then put them on?

He chose nudity. I probably would have chosen the same. We lined up along the route from the showers to the shed where the packs were stored and applauded him. I was at the front of the line, leading the applause.

The Scout Camp weekends only came three or four times a year, which left Darryl and me—and lots of other LARPers—with a serious LARP deficiency in our lives.

Luckily, there were the Wretched Daylight games in the city hotels. Wretched Daylight is another LARP, rival vampire clans and vampire hunters, and it's got its own quirky rules. Players get cards to help them resolve combat skirmishes, so each skirmish involves playing a little hand of a strategic card game. Vampires can become invisible by cloaking themselves, crossing their arms over their chests, and all the other players have to pretend they don't see them, continuing with their conversations about their plans and so on. The true test of a good player is whether you're honest enough to go on spilling your secrets in front of an "invisible" rival without acting as though he was in the room.

There were a couple of big Wretched Daylight games every month. The organizers of the games had a good relationship with the city's hotels and they let it be known that they'd take ten un-booked rooms on Friday night and fill them with players who'd run around the hotel, playing low-key Wretched Daylight in the corridors, around the pool, and so on, eating at the hotel restaurant and paying for the hotel WiFi. They'd close the booking on Friday afternoon, email us, and we'd go straight from school to whichever hotel it was, bringing our knapsacks, sleeping six or eight to a room for the weekend, living on junk food, playing until 3 A.M. It was good, safe fun that our parents could get behind.

The organizers were a well known literacy charity that ran kids' writing workshops, drama workshops and so on. They had been running the games for ten years without incident. Everything was strictly booze and drug free, to keep the organizers from getting busted on some kind of corruption of minors rap. We'd draw between ten and a hundred players, depending on the weekend, and for the cost of a couple movies, you could have two and a half days' worth of solid fun.

One day, though, they lucked into a block of rooms at the Monaco, a hotel in the Tenderloin that catered to arty older tourists, the kind of place where every room came with a gold-fish bowl, where the lobby was full of beautiful old people in fine clothes, showing off their plastic surgery results.

Normally, the mundanes—our word for nonplayers—just ignored us, figuring that we were skylarking kids. But that week-end there happened to be an editor for an Italian travel magazine staying, and he took an interest in things. He cornered me as I skulked in the lobby, hoping to spot the clan-master of my rivals and swoop in on him and draw his blood. I was standing against the wall with my arms folded over my chest, being invisible, when he came up to me and asked me, in accented English, what me and my friends were doing in the hotel that weekend?

I tried to brush him off, but he wouldn't be put off. So I fig-ured I'd just make something up and he'd go away.

I didn't imagine that he'd print it. I really didn't imagine that it would get picked up by the American press.

"We're here because our prince has died, and so we've had to come in search of a new ruler."

"A prince?"

"Yes," I said, getting into it. "We're the Old People. We came to America in the 16th century and have had our own royal family in the wilds of Pennsylvania ever since. We live simply in the woods. We don't use modern technology. But the prince was the last of the line and he died last week. Some terrible wasting disease took him. The young men of my clan have left to find the descendants of his great-uncle, who went away to join the modern people in the time of my grandfather. He is said to have multiplied, and we will find the last of his bloodline and bring them back to their rightful home."

I read a lot of fantasy novels. This kind of thing came easily to me.

"We found a woman who knew of these descendants. She told us one was staying in this hotel, and we've come to find him. But we've been tracked here by a rival clan who would keep us from bringing home our prince, to keep us weak and easy to dominate. Thus it is vital we keep to ourselves. We do not talk to the New People when we can help it. Talking to you now causes me great discomfort."

He was watching me shrewdly. I had uncrossed my arms, which meant that I was now "visible" to rival vampires, one of whom had been slowly sneaking up on us. At the last moment, I turned and saw her, arms spread, hissing at us, vamping it up in high style.

I threw my arms wide and hissed back at her, then pelted through the lobby, hopping over a leather sofa and deking around a potted plant, making her chase me. I'd scouted an escape route down through the stairwell to the basement health club and I took it, shaking her off.

I didn't see him again that weekend, but I *did* relate the story to some of my fellow LARPers, who embroidered the tale and found lots of opportunities to tell it over the weekend.

The Italian magazine had a staffer who'd done her master's degree on Amish antitechnology communities in rural Pennsylvania, and she thought we sounded awfully interesting. Based on the notes and taped interviews of her boss from his trip to San

Francisco, she wrote a fascinating, heart-wrenching article about these weird, juvenile cultists who were crisscrossing America in search of their "prince." Hell, people will print anything these days.

But the thing was, stories like that get picked up and republished. First it was Italian bloggers, then a few American bloggers. People across the country reported "sightings" of the Old People, though whether they were making it up, or whether others were playing the same game, I didn't know.

It worked its way up the media food chain all the way to the *New York Times,* who, unfortunately, have an unhealthy appetite for fact-checking. The reporter they put on the story eventually tracked it down to the Monaco Hotel, who put them in touch with the LARP organizers, who laughingly spilled the whole story.

Well, at that point, LARPing got a lot less cool. We became known as the nation's foremost hoaxers, as weird, pathological liars. The press who we'd inadvertently tricked into covering the story of the Old People were now interested in redeeming themselves by reporting on how unbelievably weird we LARPers were, and that was when Charles let everyone in school know that Darryl and I were were biggest LARPing weenies in the city.

That was not a good season. Some of the gang didn't mind, but we did. The teasing was merciless. Charles led it. I'd find plastic fangs in my bag, and kids I passed in the hall would go "bleh, bleh" like a cartoon vampire, or they'd talk with fake Transylvanian accents when I was around.

We switched to ARGing pretty soon afterward. It was more fun in some ways, and it was a lot less weird. Every now and again, though, I missed my cape and those weekends in the hotel.

———

The opposite of *esprit d'escalier* **is** the way that life's embarrassments come back to haunt us even after they're long past. I could remember every stupid thing I'd ever said or done, recall them with picture-perfect clarity. Any time I was feeling low, I'd naturally start to remember other times I felt that way, a hit parade of humiliations coming one after another to my mind.

As I tried to concentrate on Masha and my impending doom, the Old People incident kept coming back to haunt me. There'd been a similar, sick, sinking doomed feeling then, as more and more press outlets picked up the story, as the likelihood of someone figuring out that it had been me who'd sprung the story on the stupid Italian editor in the designer jeans with crooked seams, the starched collarless shirt and the oversized metal-rimmed glasses.

There's an alternative to dwelling on your mistakes. You can learn from them.

It's a good theory, anyway. Maybe the reason your subconscious dredges up all these miserable ghosts is that they need to get closure before they can rest peacefully in humiliation afterlife. My subconscious kept visiting me with ghosts in the hopes that I would do something to let them rest in peace.

All the way home, I turned over this memory and the thought of what I would do about "Masha," in case she was playing me. I needed some insurance.

And by the time I reached my house—to be swept up into melancholy hugs from Mom and Dad—I had it.

The trick was to time this so that it happened fast enough that the DHS couldn't prepare for it, but with a long enough lead time that the Xnet would have time to turn out in force.

The trick was to stage this so that there were too many present to arrest us all, but to put it somewhere that the press could see it and the grown-ups, so the DHS wouldn't just gas us again.

The trick was to come up with something with the media friendliness of the levitation of the Pentagon. The trick was to stage something that we could rally around, like three thousand Berkeley students refusing to let one of their number be taken away in a police van.

The trick was to put the press there, ready to say what the police did, the way they had in 1968 in Chicago.

It was going to be some trick.

I cut out of school an hour early the next day, using my customary techniques for getting out, not caring if it would trigger some kind of new DHS checker that would result in my parents getting a note.

One way or another, my parents' last problem after tomorrow would be whether I was in trouble at school.

I met Ange at her place. She'd had to cut out of school even earlier, but she'd just made a big deal out of her cramps and pretended she was going to keel over and they sent her home.

We started to spread the word on Xnet. We sent it in email to trusted friends, and IMed it to our buddy lists. We roamed the decks and towns of Clockwork Plunder and told our teammates. Giving everyone enough information to get them to show up but not so much as to tip our hand to the DHS was tricky, but I thought I had just the right balance:

> **VAMPMOB TOMORROW**

> **If you're a goth, dress to impress. If you're not a goth, find a goth and borrow some clothes. Think vampire.**

> **The game starts at 8:00AM sharp. SHARP. Be**

```
there and ready to be divided into teams. The game
lasts 30 minutes, so you'll have plenty of time to
get to school afterward.
    > Location will be revealed tomorrow. Email your
public key to m1k3y@littlebrother.pirateparty.org.se
and check your messages at 7AM for the update. If
that's too early for you, stay up all night. That's
what we're going to do.
    > This is the most fun you will have all year,
guaranteed.
    > Believe.
    > M1k3y
```

Then I sent a short message to Masha.

```
    > Tomorrow
    > M1k3y
```

A minute later, she emailed back:

```
    > I thought so. VampMob, huh? You work fast. Wear
a red hat. Travel light.
```

What do you bring along when you go fugitive? I'd carried enough heavy packs around enough scout camps to know that every ounce you add cuts into your shoulders with all the crushing force of gravity with every step you take—it's not just one ounce, it's one ounce that you carry for a million steps. It's a ton.

"Right," Ange said. "Smart. And you never take more than three days' worth of clothes, either. You can rinse stuff out in the sink. Better to have a spot on your T-shirt than a suitcase that's too big and heavy to stash under a plane seat."

She'd pulled out a ballistic nylon courier bag that went across her chest, between her breasts—something that made me get a little sweaty—and slung diagonally across her back. It was roomy inside, and she'd set it down on the bed. Now she was piling clothes next to it.

"I figure that three T-shirts, a pair of pants, a pair of shorts, three changes of underwear, three pairs of socks and a sweater will do it."

She dumped out her gym bag and picked out her toiletries. "I'll have to remember to stick my toothbrush in tomorrow morning before I head down to Civic Center."

Watching her pack was impressive. She was ruthless about it all. It was also freaky—it made me realize that the next day, I was going to go away. Maybe for a long time. Maybe forever.

"Do I bring my Xbox?" she asked. "I've got a ton of stuff on the hard drive, notes and sketches and email. I wouldn't want it to fall into the wrong hands."

"It's all encrypted," I said. "That's standard with ParanoidXbox. But leave the Xbox behind, there'll be plenty of them in LA. Just create a Pirate Party account and email an image of your hard drive to yourself. I'm going to do the same when I get home."

She did so, and queued up the email. It was going to take a couple hours for all the data to squeeze through her neighbor's WiFi network and wing its way to Sweden.

Then she closed the flap on the bag and tightened the compression straps. She had something the size of a soccer ball slung over her back now, and I stared admiringly at it. She could walk down the street with that under her shoulder and no one would look twice—she looked like she was on her way to school.

"One more thing," she said, and went to her bedside table and took out the condoms. She took the strips of rubbers out of the box and opened the bag and stuck them inside, then gave me a slap on the ass.

"Now what?" I said.

"Now we go to your place and do your stuff. It's time I met your parents, no?"

She left the bag amid the piles of clothes and junk all over the floor. She was ready to turn her back on all of it, walk away, just to be with me. Just to support the cause. It made me feel brave, too.

Mom was already home when I got there. She had her laptop open on the kitchen table and was answering email while talking into a headset connected to it, helping some poor York-shireman and his family acclimate to living in Louisiana.

I came through the door and Ange followed, grinning like mad, but holding my hand so tight I could feel the bones grinding together. I didn't know what she was so worried about. It wasn't like she was going to end up spending a lot of time hanging around with my parents after this, even if it went badly.

Mom hung up on the Yorkshireman when we got in.

"Hello, Marcus," she said, giving me a kiss on the cheek. "And who is this?"

"Mom, meet Ange. Ange, this is my mom, Louisa." Mom stood up and gave Ange a hug.

"It's very good to meet you, darling," she said, looking her over from top to bottom. Ange looked pretty acceptable, I think. She dressed well, and low-key, and you could tell how smart she was just by looking at her.

"A pleasure to meet you, Mrs. Yallow," she said. She sounded very confident and self-assured. Much better than I had when I'd met her mom.

"It's Lillian, love," she said. She was taking in every detail. "Are you staying for dinner?"

"I'd love that," she said.

"Do you eat meat?" Mom's pretty acclimated to living in California.

"I eat anything that doesn't eat me first," she said.

"She's a hot sauce junkie," I said. "You could serve her old tires and she'd eat 'em if she could smother them in salsa."

Ange socked me gently in the shoulder.

"I was going to order Thai," Mom said. "I'll add a couple of their five-chili dishes to the order."

Ange thanked her politely and Mom bustled around the kitchen, getting us glasses of juice and a plate of biscuits and asking three times if we wanted any tea. I squirmed a little.

"Thanks, Mom," I said. "We're going to go upstairs for a while."

Mom's eyes narrowed for a second, then she smiled again. "Of course," she said. "Your father will be home in an hour, we'll eat then."

I had my vampire stuff all stashed in the back of my closet. I let Ange sort through it while I went through my clothes. I was only going as far as LA. They had stores there, all the clothing I could need. I just needed to get together three or four favorite tees and a favorite pair of jeans, a tube of deodorant, a roll of dental floss.

"Money!" I said.

"Yeah," she said. "I was going to clean out my bank account on the way home at an ATM. I've got maybe fifteen hundred saved up."

"Really?"

"What am I going to spend it on?" she said. "Ever since the Xnet, I haven't had to even pay any service charges."

"I think I've got three hundred or so."

"Well, there you go. Grab it on the way to Civic Center in the morning."

I had a big book bag I used when I was hauling lots of gear around town. It was less conspicuous than my camping pack. Ange went through my piles mercilessly and culled them down to her favorites.

Once it was packed and under my bed, we both sat down.

"We're going to have to get up really early tomorrow," she said.

"Yeah, big day."

The plan was to get messages out with a bunch of fake VampMob locations tomorrow, sending people out to secluded spots within a few minutes' walk of Civic Center. We'd cut out a spray-paint stencil that just said VAMPMOB CIVIC CENTER → → that we would spray-paint at those spots around 5 A.M. That would keep the DHS from locking down Civic Center before we got there. I had the mailbot ready to send out the messages at 7 A.M.—I'd just leave my Xbox running when I went out.

"How long . . ." She trailed off.

"That's what I've been wondering, too," I said. "It could be a long time, I suppose. But who knows? With Barbara's article coming out"—I'd queued an email to her for the next morning, too—"and all, maybe we'll be heroes in two weeks."

"Maybe," she said, and sighed.

I put my arm around her. Her shoulders were shaking.

"I'm terrified," I said. "I think that it would be crazy not to be terrified."

"Yeah," she said. "Yeah."

Mom called us to dinner. Dad shook Ange's hand. He looked unshaved and worried, the way he had since we'd gone to see Barbara, but on meeting Ange, a little of the old Dad came back. She kissed him on the cheek and he insisted that she call him Drew.

Dinner was actually really good. The ice broke when Ange took out her hot sauce mister and treated her plate, and explained about Scoville units. Dad tried a forkful of her food and went reeling into the kitchen to drink a gallon of milk. Believe it or not, Mom still tried it after that and gave every impression of loving it. Mom, it turned out, was an undiscovered spicy food prodigy, a natural.

Before she left, Ange pressed the hot sauce mister on Mom. "I have a spare at home," she said. I'd watched her pack it in her backpack. "You seem like the kind of woman who should have one of these."

Chapter 19

Here's the email that went out at 7 A.M. the next day, while Ange and I were spray-painting VAMPMOB CIVIC CENTER →
→ at strategic locations around town.

> **RULES FOR VAMPMOB**

> You are part of a clan of daylight vampires. You've discovered the secret of surviving the terrible light of the sun. The secret was cannibalism: the blood of another vampire can give you the strength to walk among the living.

> You need to bite as many other vampires as you can in order to stay in the game. If one minute goes by without a bite, you're out. Once you're out, turn your shirt around backwards and go referee—watch two or three vamps to see if they're getting their bites in.

> To bite another vamp, you have to say "Bite!" five times before they do. So you run up to a vamp, make eye-contact and shout "bite bite bite bite bite!" and if you get it out before she does, you live and she crumbles to dust.

> You and the other vamps you meet at your rendezvous are a team. They are your clan. You derive no nourishment from their blood.

> You can "go invisible" by standing still and folding your arms over your chest. You can't bite invisible vamps, and they can't bite you.

> This game is played on the honor system. The point is to have fun and get your vamp on, not to win.

> There is an end-game that will be passed by word of mouth as winners begin to emerge. The gamemasters will start a whisper campaign among the players when the time comes. Spread the whisper as quickly as you can and watch for the sign.

> M1k3y

> bite bite bite bite bite!

We'd hoped that a hundred people would be willing to play VampMob. We'd sent out about two hundred invites each. But when I sat bolt upright at 4 A.M. and grabbed my Xbox, there were four hundred replies there. Four *hundred*.

I fed the addresses to the bot and stole out of the house. I descended the stairs, listening to my father snore and my mom rolling over in their bed. I locked the door behind me.

At 4:15 A.M., Potrero Hill was as quiet as the countryside. There were some distant traffic rumbles, and once a car crawled past me. I stopped at an ATM and drew out $320 in twenties, rolled them up and put a rubber band around them, and stuck the roll in a zip-up pocket low on the thigh of my vampire pants.

I was wearing my cape again, and a ruffled shirt, and tuxedo pants that had been modded to have enough pockets to carry all my little bits and pieces. I had on pointed boots with silver-skull buckles, and I'd teased my hair into a black dandelion clock around my head. Ange was bringing the white makeup and had promised to do my eyeliner and black nail polish. Why the hell not? When was the next time I was going to get to play dress-up like this?

Ange met me in front of her house. She had her backpack on, too, and fishnet tights, a ruffled gothic lolita maid's dress, white face-paint, elaborate kabuki eye makeup, and her fingers and throat dripped with silver jewelry.

"You look *great!*" we said to each other in unison, then laughed quietly and stole off through the streets, spray-paint cans in our pockets.

As I surveyed Civic Center, I thought about what it would look like once four hundred VampMobbers converged on it. I expected them in ten minutes, out front of City Hall. Already the big plaza teemed with commuters who neatly side-stepped the homeless people begging there.

I've always hated Civic Center. It's a collection of huge wedding cake buildings: courthouses, museums and civic buildings like City Hall. The sidewalks are wide, the buildings are white. In the tourist guides to San Francisco, they manage to photograph it so that it looks like Epcot Center, futuristic and austere.

But on the ground, it's grimy and gross. Homeless people sleep on all the benches. The district is empty by 6 P.M. except for drunks and druggies, because with only one kind of building there, there's no legit reason for people to hang around after the sun goes down. It's more like a mall than a neighborhood, and the only businesses there are bail bondsmen and liquor stores, places that cater to the families of crooks on trial and the bums who make it their nighttime home.

I really came to understand all this when I read an interview with an amazing old urban planner, a woman called Jane Jacobs who was the first person to really nail why it was wrong to slice cities up with freeways, stick all the poor people in housing projects and use zoning laws to tightly control who got to do what where.

Jacobs explained that real cities are organic and they have a lot of variety—rich and poor, white and brown, Anglo and Mex, retail and residential and even industrial. A neighborhood like that has all kinds of people passing through it at all hours of the day or night, so you get businesses that cater to every need, you get people around all the time, acting like eyes on the street.

You've encountered this before. You go walking around some older part of some city and you find that it's full of the coolest looking stores, guys in suits and people in fashion-rags, upscale restaurants and funky cafes, a little movie theater maybe, houses with elaborate paint jobs. Sure, there might be a Starbucks, too, but there's also a neat-looking fruit market and a florist who appears to be three hundred years old as she snips carefully at the flowers in her windows. It's the opposite of a planned space, like a mall. It feels like a wild garden or even a woods: like it *grew*.

You couldn't get any further from that than Civic Center. I read an interview with Jacobs where she talked about the great old neighborhood they knocked down to build it. It had been just that kind of neighborhood, the kind of place that happened without permission or rhyme or reason.

Jacobs said that she predicted that within a few years, Civic Center would be one of the worst neighborhoods in the city, a ghost town at night, a place that sustained a thin crop of weedy booze shops and flea-pit motels. In the interview, she didn't seem very glad to have been vindicated; she sounded like she was talking about a dead friend when she described what Civic Center had become.

Now it was rush hour and Civic Center was as busy at it could be. The Civic Center BART also serves as the major station for Muni trolley lines, and if you need to switch from one to another, that's where you do it. At 8 A.M. there were thousands of people coming up the stairs, going down the stairs, getting into and out of taxis and on and off buses. They got squeezed by DHS checkpoints by the different civic buildings, and routed around aggressive panhandlers. They all smelled like their shampoos and colognes, fresh out of the shower and armored in their work suits, swinging laptop bags and briefcases. At 8 A.M., Civic Center was business central.

And here came the vamps. A couple dozen coming down Van Ness, a couple dozen coming up Market. More coming from the other side of Market. More coming up from Van Ness. They slipped around the sides of the buildings, wearing the white face-paint and the black eyeliner, black clothes, leather jackets, huge stompy boots. Fishnet fingerless gloves.

They began to fill up the plaza. A few of the business people gave them passing glances and then looked away, not wanting to let these weirdos into their personal realities as they thought about whatever crap they were about to wade through for another eight hours. The vamps milled around, not sure when the game was on. They pooled together in large groups, like an oil spill in reverse, all this black gathering in one place. A lot of them sported old-timey hats, bowlers and toppers. Many of the girls were in full-on elegant gothic lolita maid costumes with huge platforms.

I tried to estimate the numbers. Two hundred. Then, five minutes later, it was three hundred. Four hundred. They were still streaming in. The vamps had brought friends.

Someone grabbed my ass. I spun around and saw Ange, laughing so hard she had to hold her thighs, bent double.

"Look at them all, man, look at them all!" she gasped. The square was twice as crowded as it had been a few minutes ago. I had no idea how many Xnetters there were, but easily a thousand of them had just showed up to my little party. Christ.

The DHS and SFPD cops were starting to mill around, talking into their radios and clustering together. I heard a faraway siren.

"All right," I said, shaking Ange by the arm. "All right, let's *go*."

We both slipped off into the crowd and as soon as we encountered our first vamp, we both said, loudly, "Bite bite bite bite bite!" My victim was a stunned—but cute—girl with spiderwebs drawn on her hands and smudged mascara running down her cheeks. She said, "Crap," and moved away, acknowledging that I'd gotten her.

The call of "bite bite bite bite bite" had scrambled the other nearby vamps. Some of them were attacking each other, others were moving for cover, hiding out. I had my victim for the minute, so I skulked away, using mundanes for cover. All around me, the cry of "bite bite bite bite bite!" and shouts and laughs and curses.

The sound spread like a virus through the crowd. All the vamps knew the game was on now, and the ones who were clustered together were dropping like flies. They laughed and cussed and moved away, clueing the still-in vamps that the game was on. And more vamps were arriving by the second.

8:16. It was time to bag another vamp. I crouched low and moved through the legs of the straights as they headed for the BART stairs. They jerked back with surprise and swerved to avoid me. I had my eyes laser-locked on a set of black platform boots with steel dragons over the toes, and so I wasn't expecting it when I came face to face with another vamp, a guy of about fifteen or sixteen, hair gelled straight back and wearing a PVC Marilyn Manson jacket draped with necklaces of fake tusks carved with intricate symbols.

"Bite bite bite—" he began, when one of the mundanes tripped over him and they both went sprawling. I leapt over to him and shouted "Bite bite bite bite bite!" before he could untangle himself again.

More vamps were arriving. The suits were really freaking out. The game overflowed the sidewalk and moved into Van Ness, spreading up toward Market Street. Drivers honked, the trolleys made angry *dings*. I heard more sirens, but now traffic was snarled in every direction.

It was freaking *glorious*.

BITE BITE BITE BITE BITE!

The sound came from all around me. There were so many vamps there, playing so furiously, it was like a roar. I risked standing up and looking around and found that I was right in the middle of a giant crowd of vamps that went as far as I could see in every direction.

BITE BITE BITE BITE BITE!

This was even better than the concert in Dolores Park. That had been angry and rockin', but this was—well, it was just *fun*. It was like going back to the playground, to the epic games of tag we'd play on lunch breaks when the sun was out, hundreds of people chasing each other around. The adults and the cars just made it more fun, more funny.

That's what it was: it was *funny*. We were all laughing now.

But the cops were really mobilizing now. I heard helicopters. Any second now, it would be over. Time for the endgame.

I grabbed a vamp.

"Endgame: when the cops order us to disperse, pretend you've been gassed. Pass it on. What did I just say?"

The vamp was a girl, tiny, so short I thought she was really young, but she must have been seventeen or eighteen from her face and the smile. "Oh, that's wicked," she said.

"What did I say?"

"Endgame: when the cops order us to disperse, pretend you've been gassed. Pass it on. What did I just say?"

"Right," I said. "Pass it on."

She melted into the crowd. I grabbed another vamp. I passed it on. He went off to pass it on.

Somewhere in the crowd, I knew Ange was doing this, too. Somewhere in the crowd, there might be infiltrators, fake Xnetters, but what could they do with this knowledge? It's not like the cops had a choice. They were going to order us to disperse. That was guaranteed.

I had to get to Ange. The plan was to meet at the Founders' Statue in the Plaza, but reaching it was going to be hard. The crowd wasn't moving anymore, it was *surging*, like the mob had in the way down to the BART station on the day the bombs went off. I struggled to make my way through it just as the PA underneath the helicopter switched on.

"THIS IS THE DEPARTMENT OF HOMELAND SECURITY. YOU ARE ORDERED TO DISPERSE IMMEDIATELY."

Around me, hundreds of vamps fell to the ground, clutching their throats, clawing at their eyes, gasping for breath. It was easy to fake being gassed, we'd all had plenty of time to study the footage of the partiers in Mission Dolores Park going down under the pepper spray clouds.

"DISPERSE IMMEDIATELY."

I fell to the ground, protecting my pack, reaching around to the red baseball hat folded into the waistband of my pants. I jammed it on my head and then grabbed my throat and made horrendous retching noises.

The only ones still standing were the mundanes, the salarymen who'd been just trying to get to their jobs. I looked around as best as I could at them as I choked and gasped.

"THIS IS THE DEPARTMENT OF HOMELAND SECURITY. YOU ARE ORDERED TO DISPERSE IMMEDIATELY. DISPERSE IMMEDIATELY." The voice of god made my bowels ache. I felt it in my molars and in my femurs and my spine.

The salarymen were scared. They were moving as fast as they could, but in no particular direction. The helicopters seemed to be directly overhead no matter where you stood. The cops were wading into the crowd now, and they'd put on their helmets. Some had shields. Some had gas masks. I gasped harder.

Then the salarymen were running. I probably would have run, too. I watched a guy whip a $500 jacket off and wrap it around his face before heading south toward Mission, only to trip and go sprawling. His curses joined the choking sounds.

This wasn't supposed to happen—the choking was just supposed to freak people out and get them confused, not panic them into a stampede.

There were screams now, screams I recognized all too well from the night in the park. That was the sound of people who were scared spitless, running into each other as they tried like hell to get away.

And then the air raid sirens began.

I hadn't heard that sound since the bombs went off, but I

would never forget it. It sliced through me and went straight into my balls, turning my legs into jelly on the way. It made me want to run away in a panic. I got to my feet, red cap on my head, thinking of only one thing: Ange. Ange and the Founders' Statue.

Everyone was on their feet now, running in all directions, screaming. I pushed people out of my way, holding onto my pack and my hat, heading for Founders' Statue. Masha was looking for me, I was looking for Ange. Ange was out there.

I pushed and cursed. Elbowed someone. Someone came down on my foot so hard I felt something go *crunch* and I shoved him so he went down. He tried to get up and someone stepped on him. I shoved and pushed.

Then I reached out my arm to shove someone else and strong hands grabbed my wrist and my elbow in one fluid motion and brought my arm back around behind my back. It felt like my shoulder was about to wrench out of its socket, and I instantly doubled over, hollering, a sound that was barely audible over the din of the crowd, the thrum of the choppers, the wail of the sirens.

I was brought back upright by the strong hands behind me, which steered me like a marionette. The hold was so perfect I couldn't even think of squirming. I couldn't think of the noise or the helicopter or Ange. All I could think of was moving the way that the person who had me wanted me to move. I was brought around so that I was face to face with the person.

It was a girl whose face was sharp and rodentlike, half-hidden by a giant pair of sunglasses. Over the sunglasses, a mop of bright pink hair spiked out in all directions.

"You!" I said. I knew her. She'd taken a picture of me and threatened to rat me out to truant watch. That had been five minutes before the alarms started. She'd been the one, ruthless and cunning. We'd both run from that spot in the Tenderloin as the klaxon sounded behind us, and we'd both been picked up by the cops. I'd been hostile and they'd decided that I was an enemy.

She—Masha—became their ally.

"Hello, M1k3y," she hissed in my ear, close as a lover. A shiver went up my back. She let go of my arm and I shook it out.

"Christ," I said. "You!"

"Yes, me," she said. "The gas is gonna come down in about two minutes. Let's haul ass."

"Ange—my girlfriend—is by the Founders' Statue."

Masha looked over the crowd. "No chance," she said. "We try to make it there, we're doomed. The gas is coming down in two minutes, in case you missed it the first time."

I stopped moving. "I don't go without Ange," I said.

She shrugged. "Suit yourself," she shouted in my ear. "Your funeral."

She began to push through the crowd, moving away, north, toward downtown. I continued to push for the Founders' Statue. A second later, my arm was back in the terrible lock and I was being swung around and propelled forward.

"You know too much, jerk-off," she said. "You've seen my face. You're coming with me."

I screamed at her, struggled till it felt like my arm would break, but she was pushing me forward. My sore foot was agony with every step, my shoulder felt like it would break.

With her using me as a battering ram, we made good progress through the crowd. The whine of the helicopters changed and she gave me a harder push. "RUN!" she yelled. "Here comes the gas!"

The crowd noise changed, too. The choking sounds and scream sounds got much, much louder. I'd heard that pitch of sound before. We were back in the park. The gas was raining down. I held my breath and *ran*.

We cleared the crowd and she let go of my arm. I shook it out. I limped as fast as I could up the sidewalk as the crowd thinned and thinned. We were heading toward a group of DHS cops with riot shields and helmets and masks. As we drew near them, they moved to block us, but Masha held up a badge and they melted away like she was Obi-Wan Kenobi saying "These aren't the droids you're looking for."

"You goddamned *bitch*," I said as we sped up Market Street. "We have to go back for Ange."

She pursed her lips and shook her head. "I feel for you, buddy. I haven't seen my boyfriend in months. He probably thinks I'm dead. Fortunes of war. We go back for your Ange, we're dead. If we push on, we have a chance. So long as we have a chance, she has a chance. Those kids aren't all going to Gitmo. They'll probably take a few hundred in for questioning and send the rest home."

We were moving up Market Street now, past the strip joints where the little encampments of bums and junkies sat, stinking like open toilets. Masha guided me to a little alcove in the shut door of one of the strip places. She stripped off her jacket and turned it inside out—the lining was a muted stripe pattern, and with the jacket's seams reversed, it hung differently. She produced a wool hat from her pocket and pulled it over her hair, letting it form a jaunty, off-center peak. Then she took out some makeup remover wipes and went to work on her face and fingernails. In a minute, she was a different woman.

"Wardrobe change," she said. "Now you. Lose the shoes, lose the jacket, lose the hat." I could see her point. The cops would be looking very carefully at anyone who looked like they'd been a part of the VampMob. I ditched the hat entirely—I'd never liked ball caps. Then I jammed the jacket into my pack and got out a long-sleeved tee with a picture of Rosa Luxembourg on it and pulled it over my black tee. I let Masha wipe my makeup off and clean my nails and a minute later, I was clean.

"Switch off your phone," she said. "You carrying any arphids?"

I had my student card, my ATM card, my Fast Pass. They all went into a silvered bag she held out, which I recognized as a radio-proof Faraday pouch. But as she put them in her pocket, I realized I'd just turned my ID over to her. If she was on the other side . . .

The magnitude of what had just happened began to sink in. In my mind, I'd pictured having Ange with me at this point. Ange would make it two against one. Ange would help me see if there was something amiss. If Masha wasn't all she said she was.

"Put these pebbles in your shoes before you put them on—"

"It's okay. I sprained my foot. No gait recognition program will spot me now."

She nodded once, one pro to another, and slung her pack. I picked up mine and we moved. The total time for the changeover was less than a minute. We looked and walked like two different people.

She looked at her watch and shook her head. "Come on," she said. "We have to make our rendezvous. Don't think of running, either. You've got two choices now. Me, or jail. They'll be analyzing the footage from that mob for days, but once they're done, every face in it will go in a database. Our departure will be noted. We are both wanted criminals now."

She got us off Market Street on the next block, swinging back into the Tenderloin. I knew this neighborhood. This was where we'd gone hunting for an open WiFi access point back on the day, playing Harajuku Fun Madness.

"Where are we going?" I said.

"We're about to catch a ride," she said. "Shut up and let me concentrate."

We moved fast, and sweat streamed down my face from under my hair, coursed down my back and slid down the crack of my ass and my thighs. My foot was *really* hurting and I was seeing the streets of San Francisco race by, maybe for the last time, ever.

It didn't help that we were plowing straight uphill, moving for the zone where the seedy Tenderloin gives way to the nosebleed real estate values of Nob Hill. My breath came in ragged gasps. She moved us mostly up narrow alleys, using the big streets just to get from one alley to the next.

We were just stepping into one such alley, Sabin Place, when someone fell in behind us and said, "Freeze right there." It was full of evil mirth. We stopped and turned around.

At the mouth of the alley stood Charles, wearing a halfhearted VampMob outfit of black T-shirt and jeans and white face-paint. "Hello, Marcus," he said. "You going somewhere?" He smiled a huge, wet grin. "Who's your girlfriend?"

"What do you want, Charles?"

"Well, I've been hanging out on that traitorous Xnet ever since I spotted you giving out DVDs at school. When I heard about your VampMob, I thought I'd go along and hang around the edges, just to see if you showed up and what you did. You know what I saw?"

I said nothing. He had his phone in his hand, pointed at us. Recording. Maybe ready to dial 911. Beside me, Masha had gone still as a board.

"I saw you *leading* the damned thing. And I *recorded* it, Marcus. So now I'm going to call the cops and we're going to wait right here for them. And then you're going to go to pound-you-in-the-ass prison, for a long, long time."

Masha stepped forward.

"Stop right there, chickie," he said. "I saw you get him away. I saw it all—"

She took another step forward and snatched the phone out of his hand, reaching behind her with her other hand and bringing it out holding a wallet open.

"DHS, dickhead," she said. "I'm DHS. I've been running this twerp back to his masters to see where he went. I *was* doing that. Now you've blown it. We have a name for that. We call it 'Obstruction of National Security.' You're about to hear that phrase a lot more often."

Charles took a step backward, his hands held up in front of him. He'd gone even paler under his makeup. "What? No! I mean—I didn't know! I was trying to *help*!"

"The last thing we need is a bunch of high school Junior G-men 'helping' buddy. You can tell it to the judge."

He moved back again, but Masha was fast. She grabbed his wrist and twisted him into the same judo hold she'd had me in back at Civic Center. Her hand dipped back to her pockets and came out holding a strip of plastic, a handcuff strip, which she quickly wound around his wrists.

That was the last thing I saw as I took off running.

I made it as far as the other end of the alley before she caught up with me, tackling me from behind and sending me sprawling. I couldn't move very fast, not with my hurt foot and the weight of my pack. I went down in a hard face-plant and skidded, grinding my cheek into the grimy asphalt.

"Jesus," she said. "You're a goddamned idiot. You didn't *believe* that, did you?"

My heart thudded in my chest. She was on top of me and slowly she let me up.

"Do I need to cuff you, Marcus?"

I got to my feet. I hurt all over. I wanted to die.

"Come on," she said. "It's not far now."

"It" turned out to be a moving van on a Nob Hill side street, a 16-wheeler the size of one of the ubiquitous DHS trucks that still turned up on San Francisco's street corners, bristling with antennas.

This one, though, said "Three Guys and a Truck Moving" on the side, and the three guys were very much in evidence, trekking in and out of a tall apartment building with a green awning. They were carrying crated furniture, neatly labeled boxes, loading them one at a time onto the truck and carefully packing them there.

She walked us around the block once, apparently unsatisfied with something, then, on the next pass, she made eye contact with the man who was watching the van, an older black guy with a kidney-belt and heavy gloves. He had a kind face and he smiled at us as she led us quickly, casually up the truck's three stairs and into its depth. "Under the big table," he said. "We left you some space there."

The truck was more than half full, but there was a narrow corridor around a huge table with a quilted blanket thrown over it and bubble-wrap wound around its legs.

Masha pulled me under the table. It was stuffy and still and dusty under there, and I suppressed a sneeze as we scrunched in among the boxes. The space was so tight that we were on top of each other. I didn't think that Ange would have fit in there.

"Bitch," I said, looking at Masha.

"Shut up. You should be licking my boots, thanking me. You would have ended up in jail in a week, two tops. Not Gitmo by the Bay. Syria, maybe. I think that's where they sent the ones they really wanted to disappear."

I put my head on my knees and tried to breathe deeply.

"Why would you do something so stupid as declaring war on the DHS anyway?"

I told her. I told her about being busted and I told her about Darryl.

She patted her pockets and came up with a phone. It was Charles's. "Wrong phone." She came up with another phone. She turned it on and the glow from its screen filled our little fort. After fiddling for a second, she showed it to me.

It was the picture she'd snapped of us, just before the bombs blew. It was the picture of Jolu and Van and me and—

Darryl.

I was holding in my hand proof that Darryl had been with us minutes before we'd all gone into DHS custody. Proof that he'd been alive and well and in our company.

"You need to give me a copy of this," I said. "I need it."

"When we get to LA," she said, snatching the phone back. "Once you've been briefed on how to be a fugitive without getting both our asses caught and shipped to Syria. I don't want you getting rescue ideas about this guy. He's safe enough where he is—for now."

I thought about trying to take it from her by force, but she'd already demonstrated her physical skill. She must have been a black belt or something.

We sat there in the dark, listening to the three guys load the truck with box after box, tying things down, grunting with the effort of it. I tried to sleep, but couldn't. Masha had no such problem. She snored.

There was still light shining through the narrow, obstructed corridor that led to the fresh air outside. I stared at it, through the gloom, and thought of Ange.

My Ange. Her hair brushing her shoulders as she turned her head from side to side, laughing at something I'd done. Her face when I'd seen her last, falling down in the crowd at VampMob. All those people at VampMob, like the people in the park, down and writhing, the DHS moving in with truncheons. The ones who disappeared.

Darryl. Stuck on Treasure Island, his side stitched up, taken out of his cell for endless rounds of questioning about the terrorists.

Darryl's father, ruined and boozy, unshaven. Washed up and in his uniform, "for the photos." Weeping like a little boy.

My own father, and the way that he had been changed by my disappearance to Treasure Island. He'd been just as broken as Darryl's father, but in his own way. And his face, when I told him where I'd been.

That was when I knew that I couldn't run.

That was when I knew that I had to stay and fight.

Masha's breathing was deep and regular, but when I reached with glacial slowness into her pocket for her phone, she snuffled a little and shifted. I froze and didn't even breathe for a full two minutes, counting one hippopotami, two hippopotami.

Slowly, her breath deepened again. I tugged the phone free

of her jacket pocket one millimeter at a time, my fingers and arm trembling with the effort of moving so slowly.

Then I had it, a little candy bar shaped thing.

I turned to head for the light, when I had a flash of memory: Charles, holding out his phone, waggling it at us, taunting us. It had been a candy bar shaped phone, silver, plastered in the logos of a dozen companies that had subsidized the cost of the handset through the phone company. It was the kind of phone where you had to listen to a commercial every time you made a call.

It was too dim to see the phone clearly in the truck, but I could feel it. Were those company decals on its sides? Yes? Yes. I had just stolen *Charles's* phone from Masha.

I turned back around slowly, slowly, and slowly, slowly, *slowly,* I reached back into her pocket. *Her* phone was bigger and bulkier, with a better camera and who knew what else?

I'd been through this once before—that made it a little easier. Millimeter by millimeter again, I teased it free of her pocket, stopping twice when she snuffled and twitched.

I had the phone free of her pocket and I was beginning to back away when her hand shot out, fast as a snake, and grabbed my wrist, hard, fingertips grinding away at the small, tender bones below my hand.

I gasped and stared into Masha's wide-open, staring eyes.

"You are such an idiot," she said, conversationally, taking the phone from me, punching at its keypad with her other hand. "How did you plan on unlocking this again?"

I swallowed. I felt bones grind against each other in my wrist. I bit my lip to keep from crying out.

She continued to punch away with her other hand. "Is this what you thought you'd get away with?" She showed me the picture of all of us, Darryl and Jolu, Van and me. "This picture?"

I didn't say anything. My wrist felt like it would shatter.

"Maybe I should just delete it, take temptation out of your way." Her free hand moved some more. Her phone asked her if she was sure and she had to look at it to find the right button.

That's when I moved. I had Charles's phone in my other hand still, and I brought it down on her crushing hand as hard as I could, banging my knuckles on the table overhead. I hit her hand so hard the phone shattered and she yelped and her hand went slack. I was still moving, reaching for her other hand, for her now-unlocked phone with her thumb still poised over the okay key. Her fingers spasmed on the empty air as I snatched the phone out of her hand.

I moved down the narrow corridor on hands and knees, heading for the light. I felt her hands slap at my feet and ankles twice, and I had to shove aside some of the boxes that had walled us in like a Pharaoh in a tomb. A few of them fell down behind me, and I heard Masha grunt again.

The rolling truck door was open a crack and I dove for it, slithering out under it. The steps had been removed and I found myself hanging over the road, sliding headfirst into it, clanging my head off the blacktop with a thump that rang my ears like a gong. I scrambled to my feet, holding the bumper, and desperately dragged down on the door handle, slamming it shut. Masha screamed inside—I must have caught her fingertips. I felt like throwing up, but I didn't.

I padlocked the truck instead.

Chapter 20

None of the three guys were around at the moment, so I took off. My head hurt so much I thought I must be bleeding, but my hands came away dry. My twisted ankle had frozen up in the truck so that I ran like a broken marionette, and I stopped only once, to cancel the photo-deletion on Masha's phone. I turned off its radio—both to save the battery and to keep it from being used to track me—and set the sleep timer to two hours, the longest setting available. I tried to set it to not require a password to wake from sleep, but that required a password itself. I was just going to have to tap the keypad at least once every two hours until I could figure out how to get the photo off of the phone. I would need a charger, then.

I didn't have a plan. I needed one. I needed to sit down, to get online—to figure out what I was going to do next. I was sick of letting other people do my planning for me. I didn't want to be acting because of what Masha did, or because of the DHS, or because of my dad. Or because of Ange? Well, maybe I'd act because of Ange. That would be just fine, in fact.

I'd just been slipping downhill, taking alleys when I could, merging with the Tenderloin crowds. I didn't have any destination in mind. Every few minutes, I put my hand in my pocket and nudged one of the keys on Masha's phone to keep it from going asleep. It made an awkward bulge, unfolded there in my jacket.

I stopped and leaned against a building. My ankle was killing me. Where was I, anyway?

O'Farrell, at Hyde Street. In front of a dodgy "Asian Massage Parlor." My traitorous feet had taken me right back to the beginning—taken me back to where the photo on Masha's phone had been taken, seconds before the Bay Bridge blew, before my life changed forever.

I wanted to sit down on the sidewalk and bawl, but that wouldn't solve my problems. I had to call Barbara Stratford, tell her what had happened. Show her the photo of Darryl.

What was I thinking? I had to show her the video, the one that Masha had sent me—the one where the President's Chief of Staff gloated at the attacks on San Francisco and admitted that he knew when and where the next attacks would happen and that he wouldn't stop them because they'd help his man get reelected.

That was a plan, then: get in touch with Barbara, give her the documents and get them into print. The VampMob had to have really freaked people out, made them think that we really were a bunch of terrorists. Of course, when I'd been planning it, I had been thinking of how good a distraction it would be, not how it would look to some NASCAR Dad in Nebraska.

I'd call Barbara, and I'd do it smart, from a pay phone, putting my hood up so that the inevitable CCTV wouldn't get a photo of me. I dug a quarter out of my pocket and polished it on my shirttail, getting the fingerprints off it.

I headed downhill, down and down to the BART station and the pay phones there. I made it to the trolley car stop when I spotted the cover of the week's *Bay Guardian,* stacked in a high pile next to a homeless black guy who smiled at me. "Go ahead and read the cover, it's free—it'll cost you fifty cents to look inside, though."

The headline was set in the biggest type I'd seen since 9/11:

Inside Gitmo-by-the-Bay

Beneath it, in slightly smaller type:

"How the DHS has kept our children and friends in secret prisons on our doorstep.

"By Barbara Stratford, Special to the *Bay Guardian*"

The newspaper seller shook his head. "Can you believe that?" he said. "Right here in San Francisco. Man, the government *sucks*."

Theoretically, the *Guardian* was free, but this guy appeared to have cornered the local market for copies of it. I had a quarter in my hand. I dropped it into his cup and fished for another one. I didn't bother polishing the fingerprints off it this time.

"We're told that the world changed forever when the Bay Bridge was blown up by parties unknown. Thousands of our friends and neighbors died on that day. Almost none of them have been recovered; their remains are presumed to be resting in the city's harbor.

"But an extraordinary story told to this reporter by a young man who was arrested by the DHS minutes after the explosion suggests that our own government has illegally held many of those thought dead on Treasure Island, which had been evacuated and declared off-limits to civilians shortly after the bombing . . ."

I sat down on a bench—the same bench, I noted with a prickly hair-up-the-neck feeling, where we'd rested Darryl after escaping from the BART station—and read the article all the way through. It took a huge effort not to burst into tears right there. Barbara had found some photos of me and Darryl goofing around together and they ran alongside the text. The photos were maybe a year old, but I looked so much *younger* in them, like I was ten or eleven. I'd done a lot of growing up in the past couple months.

The piece was beautifully written. I kept feeling outraged on behalf of the poor kids she was writing about, then remembering that she was writing about *me*. Zeb's note was there, his crabbed handwriting reproduced in large, a half-sheet of the newspaper. Barbara had dug up more info on other kids who were missing and presumed dead, a long list, and asked how many had been stuck there on the island, just a few miles from their parents' doorsteps.

I dug another quarter out of my pocket, then changed my mind. What was the chance that Barbara's phone wasn't tapped? There was no way I was going to be able to call her now, not directly. I needed some intermediary to get in touch with her and get her to meet me somewhere south. So much for plans.

What I really, really needed was the Xnet.

How the hell was I going to get online? My phone's wifinder was blinking like crazy—there was wireless all around me, but I didn't have an Xbox and a TV and a ParanoidXbox DVD to boot from. WiFi, WiFi everywhere . . .

That's when I spotted them. Two kids, about my age, moving among the crowd at the top of the stairs down into the BART.

What caught my eye was the way they were moving, kind of clumsy, nudging up against the commuters and the tourists. Each had a hand in his pocket, and whenever they met one another's eye, they snickered. They couldn't have been more obvious jammers, but the crowd was oblivious to them. Being down in that neighborhood, you expect to be dodging homeless people and crazies, so you don't make eye contact, don't look around at all if you can help it.

I sidled up to one. He seemed really young, but he couldn't have been any younger than me.

"Hey," I said. "Hey, can you guys come over here for a second?"

He pretended not to hear me. He looked right through me, the way you would a homeless person.

"Come on," I said. "I don't have a lot of time." I grabbed his shoulder and hissed in his ear. "The cops are after me. I'm from Xnet."

He looked scared now, like he wanted to run away, and his friend was moving toward us. "I'm serious," I said. "Just hear me out."

His friend came over. He was taller, and beefy—like Darryl. "Hey," he said. "Something wrong?"

His friend whispered in his ear. The two of them looked like they were going to bolt.

I grabbed my copy of the *Bay Guardian* from under my arm and rattled it in front of them. "Just turn to page five, okay?"

They did. They looked at the headline. The photo. Me.

"Oh, dude," the first one said. "We are *so* not worthy." He grinned at me like crazy, and the beefier one slapped me on the back.

"No *way* —" he said. "You're M—"

I put a hand over his mouth. "Come over here, okay?"

I brought them back to my bench. I noticed that there was something old and brown staining the sidewalk underneath it. Darryl's blood? It made my skin pucker up. We sat down.

"I'm Marcus," I said, swallowing hard as I gave my real

name to these two who already knew me as M1k3y. I was blowing my cover, but the *Bay Guardian* had already made the connection for me.

"Nate," the small one said. "Liam," the bigger one said. "Dude, it is *such* an honor to meet you. You're like our all-time hero—"

"Don't say that," I said. "Don't say that. You two are like a flashing advertisement that says, 'I am jamming, please put my ass in Gitmo-by-the-Bay. You couldn't be more obvious."

Liam looked like he might cry.

"Don't worry, you didn't get busted. I'll give you some tips, later." He brightened up again. What was becoming weirdly clear was that these two really *did* idolize M1k3y, and that they'd do anything I said. They were grinning like idiots. It made me uncomfortable, sick to my stomach.

"Listen, I need to get on Xnet, now, without going home or anywhere near home. Do you two live near here?"

"I do," Nate said. "Up at the top of California Street. It's a bit of a walk—steep hills." I'd just walked all the way down them. Masha was somewhere up there. But still, it was better than I had any right to expect.

"Let's go," I said.

Nate loaned me his baseball hat and traded jackets with me. I didn't have to worry about gait-recognition, not with my ankle throbbing the way it was—I limped like an extra in a cowboy movie.

Nate lived in a huge four-bedroom apartment at the top of Nob Hill. The building had a doorman, in a red overcoat with gold brocade, and he touched his cap and called Nate "Mr.

Nate" and welcomed us all there. The place was spotless and smelled of furniture polish. I tried not to gawp at what must have been a couple million bucks' worth of condo.

"My dad," he explained. "He was an investment banker. Lots of life insurance. He died when I was fourteen and we got it all. They'd been divorced for years, but he left my mom as beneficiary."

From the floor-to-ceiling window, you could see a stunning view of the other side of Nob Hill, all the way down to Fisherman's Wharf, to the ugly stub of the Bay Bridge, the crowd of cranes and trucks. Through the mist, I could just make out Treasure Island. Looking down all that way, it gave me a crazy urge to jump.

I got online with his Xbox and a huge plasma screen in the living room. He showed me how many open WiFi networks were visible from his high vantage point—twenty, thirty of them. This was a good spot to be an Xnetter.

There was a *lot* of email in my M1k3y account. Twenty thousand new messages since Ange and I had left her place that morning. Lots of it was from the press, asking for follow-up interviews, but most of it was from the Xnetters, people who'd seen the *Guardian* story and wanted to tell me that they'd do anything to help me, anything I needed.

That did it. Tears started to roll down my cheeks.

Nate and Liam exchanged glances. I tried to stop, but it was no good. I was sobbing now. Nate went to an oak bookcase on one wall and swung a bar out of one of its shelves, revealing gleaming rows of bottles. He poured me a shot of something golden brown and brought it to me.

"Rare Irish whiskey," he said. "Mom's favorite."

It tasted like fire, like gold. I sipped at it, trying not to choke.

I didn't really like hard liquor, but this was different. I took several deep breaths.

"Thanks, Nate," I said. He looked like I'd just pinned a medal on him. He was a good kid.

"All right," I said, and picked up the keyboard. The two boys watched in fascination as I paged through my mail on the gigantic screen.

What I was looking for, first and foremost, was email from Ange. There was a chance that she'd just gotten away. There was always that chance.

I was an idiot to even hope. There was nothing from her. I started going through the mail as fast as I could, picking apart the press requests, the fan mail, the hate mail, the spam . . .

And that's when I found it: a letter from Zeb.

> It wasn't nice to wake up this morning and find the letter that I thought you would destroy in the pages of the newspaper. Not nice at all. Made me feel . . . hunted.

> But I've come to understand why you did it. I don't know if I can approve of your tactics, but it's easy to see that your motives were sound.

> If you're reading this, that means that there's a good chance you've gone underground. It's not easy. I've been learning that. I've been learning a lot more.

> I can help you. I should do that for you. You're doing what you can for me. (Even if you're not doing it with my permission.)

> Reply if you get this, if you're on the run and alone. Or reply if you're in custody, being run by our friends on Gitmo, looking for a way to make the

```
pain stop. If they've got you, you'll do what they
tell you. I know that. I'll take that risk.
 > For you, M1k3y.
```

"Whooooa," Liam breathed. "Duuuuude." I wanted to smack him. I turned to say something awful and cutting to him, but he was staring at me with eyes as big as saucers, looking like he wanted to drop to his knees and worship me.

"Can I just say," Nate said, "can I just say that it is the biggest honor of my entire life to help you? Can I just say that?"

I was blushing now. There was nothing for it. These two were totally starstruck, even though I wasn't any kind of star, not in my own mind at least.

"Can you guys—" I swallowed. "Can I have some privacy here?"

They slunk out of the room like bad puppies and I felt like a tool. I typed fast.

"I got away, Zeb. And I'm on the run. I need all the help I can get. I want to end this now." I remembered to take Masha's phone out of my pocket and tickle it to keep it from going to sleep.

They let me use the shower, gave me a change of clothes, a new backpack with half their earthquake kit in it—energy bars, medicine, hot and cold packs and an old sleeping bag. They even slipped a spare Xbox Universal already loaded with ParanoidXbox on it into there. That was a nice touch. I had to draw the line at a flare gun.

I kept on checking my email to see if Zeb had replied. I answered the fan mail. I answered the mail from the press. I deleted the hate mail. I was half expecting to see something from Masha, but chances were she was halfway to LA by now, her fingers hurt, and in no position to type. I tickled her phone again.

They encouraged me to take a nap and for a brief, shameful moment, I got all paranoid like maybe these guys were thinking of turning me in once I was asleep. Which was idiotic—they could have turned me in just as easily when I was awake. I just couldn't compute the fact that they thought *so much* of me. I had known, intellectually, that there were people who would follow M1k3y. I'd met some of those people that morning, shouting BITE BITE BITE and vamping it up at Civic Center. But these two were more personal. They were just nice, goofy guys, they coulda been any of my friends back in the days before the Xnet, just two pals who palled around having teenage adventures. They'd volunteered to join an army, my army. I had a responsibility to them. Left to themselves, they'd get caught, it was only a matter of time. They were too trusting.

"Guys, listen to me for a second. I have something serious I need to talk to you about."

They almost stood at attention. It would have been funny if it wasn't so scary.

"Here's the thing. Now that you've helped me, it's really dangerous. If you get caught, I'll get caught. They'll get anything you know out of you—" I held up my hand to forestall their protests. "No, stop. You haven't been through it. Everyone talks. Everyone breaks. If you're ever caught, you tell them everything, right away, as fast as you can, as much as you can. They'll get it all eventually anyway. That's how they work.

"But you won't get caught, and here's why: you're not jammers anymore. You are retired from active duty. You're a"—I fished in my memory for vocabulary words culled from spy thrillers—"you're a sleeper cell. Stand down. Go back to being normal kids. One way or another, I'm going to break this thing, break it wide open, end it. Or it will get me, finally, do me in. If you don't hear from me within seventy-two hours, assume that they got me. Do whatever you want then. But for the next three days—and forever, if I do what I'm trying to do—stand down. Will you promise me that?"

They promised with all solemnity. I let them talk me into napping, but made them swear to rouse me once an hour. I'd have to tickle Masha's phone and I wanted to know as soon as Zeb got back in touch with me.

The rendezvous was on a BART car, which made me nervous. They're full of cameras. But Zeb knew what he was doing. He had me meet him in the last car of a certain train departing from Powell Street Station, at a time when that car was filled with the press of bodies. He sidled up to me in the crowd, and the good commuters of San Francisco cleared a space for him, the hollow that always surrounds homeless people.

"Nice to see you again," he muttered, facing into the doorway. Looking into the dark glass, I could see that there was no one close enough to eavesdrop—not without some kind of high-efficiency mic rig, and if they knew enough to show up here with one of those, we were dead anyway.

"You too, brother," I said. "I'm—I'm sorry, you know?"

"Shut up. Don't be sorry. You were braver than I am. Are you ready to go underground now? Ready to disappear?"

"About that."

"Yes?"

"That's not the plan."

"Oh," he said.

"Listen, okay? I have—I have pictures, video. Stuff that really *proves* something." I reached into my pocket and tickled Masha's phone. I'd bought a charger for it in Union Square on the way down, and had stopped and plugged it in at a cafe for long enough to get the battery up to four out of five bars. "I need to get it to Barbara Stratford, the woman from the *Guardian*. But they're going to be watching her—watching to see if I show up."

"You don't think that they'll be watching for me, too? If your plan involves me going within a mile of that woman's home or office—"

"I want you to get Van to come and meet me. Did Darryl ever tell you about Van? The girl—"

"He told me. Yes, he told me. You don't think they'll be watching her? All of you who were arrested?"

"I think they will. I don't think they'll be watching her as hard. And Van has totally clean hands. She never cooperated with any of my—" I swallowed. "With my projects. So they might be a little more relaxed about her. If she calls the *Bay Guardian* to make an appointment to explain why I'm just full of crap, maybe they'll let her keep it."

He stared at the door for a long time.

"You know what happens when they catch us again." It wasn't a question.

I nodded.

"Are you sure? Some of the people that were on Treasure Island with us got taken away in helicopters. They got taken *off-shore*. There are countries where America can outsource its torture. Countries where you will rot forever. Countries where you wish they would just get it over with, have you dig a trench and then shoot you in the back of the head as you stand over it."

I swallowed and nodded.

"Is it worth the risk? We can go underground for a long, long time here. Someday we might get our country back. We can wait it out."

I shook my head. "You can't get anything done by doing nothing. It's our *country*. They've taken it from us. The terrorists who attack us are still free—but *we're not*. I can't go underground for a year, ten years, my whole life, waiting for freedom to be handed to me. Freedom is something you have to take for yourself."

That afternoon, Van left school as usual, sitting in the back of the bus with a tight knot of her friends, laughing and joking the way she always did. The other riders on the bus took special note of her, she was so loud, and besides, she was wearing that stupid, giant floppy hat, something that looked like a piece out of a school play about Renaissance sword fighters. At one point they all huddled together, then turned away to look out the back of the bus, pointing and giggling. The girl who wore the hat now was the same height as Van, and from behind, it could be her.

No one paid any attention to the mousy little Asian girl who got off a few stops before the BART. She was dressed in a plain old school uniform, and looking down shyly as she stepped off. Besides, at that moment, the loud Korean girl let out a whoop and her friends followed along, laughing so loudly that even the bus driver slowed down, twisted in his seat and gave them a dirty look.

Van hurried away down the street with her head down, her hair tied back and dropped down the collar of her out-of-style bubble jacket. She had slipped lifts into her shoes that made her two wobbly, awkward inches taller, and had taken her contacts out and put on her least-favored glasses, with huge lenses that took up half her face. Although I'd been waiting in the bus shelter for her and knew when to expect her, I hardly recognized her. I got up and walked along behind her, across the street, trailing by half a block.

The people who passed me looked away as quickly as possible. I looked like a homeless kid, with a grubby cardboard sign, street-grimy overcoat, huge, overstuffed knapsack with duct tape over its rips. No one wants to look at a street kid, because if you meet his eye, he might ask you for some spare change. I'd walked around Oakland all afternoon and the only people who'd spoken to me were a Jehovah's Witness and a Scientologist, both trying to convert me. It felt gross, like being hit on by a pervert.

Van followed the directions I'd written down carefully. Zeb had passed them to her the same way he'd given me the note outside school—bumping into her as she waited for the bus, apologizing profusely. I'd written the note plainly and simply, just laying it out for her: I know you don't approve. I understand. But this is it, this is the most important favor I've ever asked of you. Please. Please.

She'd come. I knew she would. We had a lot of history, Van and I. She didn't like what had happened to the world, either. Besides, an evil, chuckling voice in my head had pointed out, she was under suspicion now that Barbara's article was out.

We walked like that for six or seven blocks, looking at who was near us, what cars went past. Zeb told me about five-person trails, where five different undercovers traded off duties following you, making it nearly impossible to spot them. You had to go somewhere totally desolate, where anyone at all would stand out like a sore thumb.

The overpass for the 880 was just a few blocks from the Coliseum BART station, and even with all the circling Van did, it didn't take long to reach it. The noise from overhead was nearly deafening. No one else was around, not that I could tell. I'd visited the site before I suggested it to Van in the note, taking care to check for places where someone could hide. There weren't any.

Once she stopped at the appointed place, I moved quickly to catch up to her. She blinked owlishly at me from behind her glasses.

"Marcus," she breathed, and tears swam in her eyes. I found that I was crying, too. I'd make a really rotten fugitive. Too sentimental.

She hugged me so hard I couldn't breathe. I hugged her back even harder.

Then she kissed me.

Not on the cheek, not like a sister. Full on the lips, a hot, wet, steamy kiss that seemed to go on forever. I was so overcome with emotion—

No, that's bull. I knew exactly what I was doing. I kissed her back.

Then I stopped and pulled away, nearly shoved her away. "Van," I gasped.

"Oops," she said.

"Van," I said again.

"Sorry," she said. "I—"

Something occurred to me just then, something I guess I should have seen a long, long time before.

"You *like* me, don't you?"

She nodded miserably. "For years," she said.

Oh, God. Darryl, all these years, so in love with her, and the whole time she was looking at me, secretly wanting me. And then I ended up with Ange. Ange said that she'd always fought with Van. And I was running around, getting into so much trouble.

"Van," I said. "Van, I'm so sorry."

"Forget it," she said, looking away. "I know it can't be. I just wanted to do that once, just in case I never—" She bit down on the words.

"Van, I need you to do something for me. Something important. I need you to meet with the journalist from the *Bay Guardian,* Barbara Stratford, the one who wrote the article. I need you to give her something." I explained about Masha's phone, told her about the video that Masha had sent me.

"What good will this do, Marcus? What's the point?"

"Van, you were right, at least partly. We can't fix the world by putting other people at risk. I need to solve the problem by telling what I know. I should have done that from the start. Should have walked straight out of their custody and to Darryl's father's house and told him what I knew. Now, though, I have evidence. This stuff—it could change the world. This is my last hope. The only hope for getting Darryl out, for getting a life that I don't spend underground, hiding from the cops. And you're the only person I can trust to do this."

"Why me?"

"You're kidding, right? Look at how well you handled getting here. You're a pro. You're the best at this of any of us. You're the only one I can trust. That's why you."

"Why not your friend Ange?" She said the name without any inflection at all, like it was a block of cement.

I looked down. "I thought you knew. They arrested her. She's in Gitmo—on Treasure Island. She's been there for days now." I had been trying not to think about this, not to think about what might be happening to her. Now I couldn't stop myself and I started to sob. I felt a pain in my stomach, like I'd been kicked, and I pushed my hands into my middle to hold myself in. I folded there, and the next thing I knew, I was on my side in the rubble under the freeway, holding myself and crying.

Van knelt down by my side. "Give me the phone," she said, her voice an angry hiss. I fished it out of my pocket and passed it to her.

Embarrassed, I stopped crying and sat up. I knew that snot was running down my face. Van was giving me a look of pure revulsion. "You need to keep it from going to sleep," I said. "I have a charger here." I rummaged in my pack. I hadn't slept all the way through the night since I acquired it. I set the phone's alarm to go off every ninety minutes and wake me up so that I could keep it from going to sleep. "Don't fold it shut, either."

"And the video?"

"That's harder," I said. "I emailed a copy to myself, but I can't get onto the Xnet anymore." In a pinch, I could have gone back to Nate and Liam and used their Xbox again, but I didn't want to risk it. "Look, I'm going to give you my login and password for the Pirate Party's mail server. You'll have to use TOR to access it—Homeland Security is bound to be scanning for people logging into p-party mail."

"Your login and password," she said, looking a little surprised.

"I trust you, Van. I know I can trust you."

She shook her head. "You *never* give out your passwords, Marcus."

"I don't think it matters anymore. Either you succeed or I— or it's the end of Marcus Yallow. Maybe I'll get a new identity, but I don't think so. I think they'll catch me. I guess I've known all along that they'd catch me, some day."

She looked at me, furious now. "What a waste. What was it all for, anyway?"

Of all the things she could have said, nothing could have hurt me more. It was like another kick in the stomach. What a waste, all of it, futile. Darryl and Ange, gone. I might never see my family again. And still, Homeland Security had my city and my country caught in a massive, irrational shrieking freak-out where anything could be done in the name of stopping terrorism.

Van looked like she was waiting for me to say something, but I had nothing to say to that. She left me there.

Zeb had a pizza for me when I got back "home"—to the tent under a freeway overpass in the Mission that he'd staked out for the night. He had a pup tent, military surplus, stenciled with SAN FRANCISCO LOCAL HOMELESS COORDINATING BOARD.

The pizza was a Domino's, cold and clabbered, but delicious for all that. "You like pineapple on your pizza?"

Zeb smiled condescendingly at me. "Freegans can't be choosy," he said.

"Freegans?"

"Like vegans, but we only eat free food."

"Free food?"

He grinned again. "You know—*free* food. From the free food store?"

"You stole this?"

"No, dummy. It's from the other store. The little one out behind the store? Made of blue steel? Kind of funky smelling?"

"You got this out of the garbage?"

He flung his head back and cackled. "Yes indeedy. You should *see* your face. Dude, it's okay. It's not like it was rotten. It was fresh—just a screwed-up order. They threw it out in the box. They sprinkle rat poison over everything at closing time, but if you get there quick, you're okay. You should see what grocery stores throw out! Wait until breakfast. I'm going to make you a fruit salad you won't believe. As soon as one strawberry in the box goes a little green and fuzzy, the whole thing is out—"

I tuned him out. The pizza was fine. It wasn't as if sitting in the Dumpster would infect it or something. If it was gross, that was only because it came from Domino's—the worst pizza in town. I'd never liked their food, and I'd given it up altogether when I found out that they bankrolled a bunch of ultra-crazy politicians who thought that global warming and evolution were satanic plots.

It was hard to shake the feeling of grossness, though.

But there *was* another way to look at it. Zeb had showed me a secret, something I hadn't anticipated: there was a whole hidden world out there, a way of getting by without participating in the system.

"Freegans, huh?"

"Yogurt, too," he said, nodding vigorously. "For the fruit salad. They throw it out the day after the best-before date, but it's not as if it goes green at midnight. It's yogurt, I mean, it's basically just rotten milk to begin with."

I swallowed. The pizza tasted funny. Rat poison. Spoiled yogurt. Furry strawberries. This would take some getting used to.

I ate another bite. Actually, Domino's pizza sucked a little less when you got it for free.

Liam's sleeping bag was warm and welcoming after a long, emotionally exhausting day. Van would have made contact with Barbara by now. She'd have the video and the picture. I'd call her in the morning and find out what she thought I should do next. I'd have to come in once she published, to back it all up.

I thought about that as I closed my eyes, thought about what it would be like to turn myself in, the cameras all rolling, following the infamous M1k3y into one of those big, columnated buildings in Civic Center.

The sound of the cars screaming by overhead turned into a kind of ocean sound as I drifted away. There were other tents nearby, homeless people. I'd met a few of them that afternoon, before it got dark and we all retreated to huddle near our own tents. They were all older than me, rough looking and gruff. None of them looked crazy or violent, though. Just like people who'd had bad luck, or made bad decisions, or both.

I must have fallen asleep, because I don't remember anything else until a bright light was shined into my face, so bright it was blinding.

"That's him," said a voice behind the light.

"Bag him," said another voice, one I'd heard before, one I'd heard over and over again in my dreams, lecturing to me, demanding my passwords. severe haircut woman.

The bag went over my head quickly and was cinched so tight at the throat that I choked and threw up my freegan pizza. As I spasmed and choked, hard hands bound my wrists, then my ankles. I was rolled onto a stretcher and hoisted, then carried into a vehicle, up a couple of clanging metal steps. They dropped me into a padded floor. There was no sound at all in the back of the vehicle once they closed the doors. The padding deadened everything except my own choking.

"Well, hello again," she said. I felt the van rock as she crawled in with me. I was still choking, trying to gasp in a breath. Vomit filled my mouth and trickled down my windpipe.

"We won't let you die," she said. "If you stop breathing, we'll make sure you start again. So don't worry about it."

I choked harder. I sipped at air. Some was getting through. Deep, wracking coughs shook my chest and back, dislodging some more of the puke. More breath.

"See?" she said. "Not so bad. Welcome home, M1k3y. We've got somewhere very special to take you."

I relaxed onto my back, feeling the van rock. The smell of used pizza was overwhelming at first, but as with all strong stimuli, my brain gradually grew accustomed to it, filtered it out until it was just a faint aroma. The rocking of the van was almost comforting.

That's when it happened. An incredible, deep calm that swept over me like I was lying on the beach and the ocean had swept in and lifted me as gently as a parent, held me aloft and swept me out onto a warm sea under a warm sun. After everything that had happened, I was caught, but it didn't matter. I had gotten the information to Barbara. I had organized the Xnet. I had won. And if I hadn't won, I had done everything I could have done. More than I ever thought I could do. I took a mental inventory as I rode, thinking of everything that I had accomplished, that *we* had accomplished. The city, the country, the world was full of people who wouldn't live the way DHS wanted us to live. We'd fight forever. They couldn't jail us all.

I sighed and smiled.

She'd been talking all along, I realized. I'd been so far into my happy place that she'd just gone away.

"—smart kid like you. You'd think that you'd know better than to mess with us. We've had an eye on you since the day you walked out. We would have caught you even if you hadn't gone crying to your lesbo journalist traitor. I just don't get it—we had an understanding, you and me. . . ."

We rumbled over a metal plate, the van's shocks rocking, and then the rocking changed. We were on water. Heading to Treasure Island. Hey, Ange was there. Darryl, too. Maybe.

The hood didn't come off until I was in my cell. They didn't bother with the cuffs at my wrists and ankles, just rolled me off the stretcher and onto the floor. It was dark, but by the moonlight from the single, tiny, high window, I could see that the mattress had been taken off the cot. The room contained me, a toilet, a bed frame and a sink, and nothing else.

I closed my eyes and let the ocean lift me. I floated away. Somewhere, far below me, was my body. I could tell what would happen next. I was being left to piss myself. Again. I knew what that was like. I'd pissed myself before. It smelled bad. It itched. It was humiliating, like being a baby.

But I'd survived it.

I laughed. The sound was weird, and it drew me back into my body, back to the present. I laughed and laughed. I'd had the worst that they could throw at me, and I'd survived it, and I'd *beaten them,* beaten them for months, showed them up as chumps and despots. I'd *won.*

I let my bladder cut loose. It was sore and full anyway, and no time like the present.

The ocean swept me away.

When morning came, two efficient, impersonal guards cut the bindings off my wrists and ankles. I still couldn't walk—when I stood, my legs gave way like a stringless marionette's. Too much time in one position. The guards pulled my arms over their shoulders and half dragged, half carried me down the familiar corridor. The bar codes on the doors were curling up and dangling now, attacked by the salt air.

I got an idea. "Ange!" I yelled. "Darryl!" I yelled. My guards yanked me along faster, clearly disturbed but not sure what to do about it. "Guys, it's me, Marcus! Stay free!"

Behind one of the doors, someone sobbed. Someone else cried out in what sounded like Arabic. Then it was cacophony, a thousand different shouting voices.

They brought me to a new room. It was an old shower room, with the showerheads still present in the mould tiles.

"Hello, M1k3y," Severe Haircut said. "You seem to have had an eventful morning." She wrinkled her nose pointedly.

"I pissed myself," I said, cheerfully. "You should try it."

"Maybe we should give you a bath, then," she said. She nodded, and my guards carried me to another stretcher. This one had restraining straps running its length. They dropped me onto it and it was ice-cold and soaked through. Before I knew it, they had the straps across my shoulders, hips and ankles. A minute later, three more straps were tied down. A man's hands grabbed the railings by my head and released some catches, and a moment later I was tilted down, my head below my feet.

"Let's start with something simple," she said. I craned my head to see her. She had turned to a desk with an Xbox on it, connected to an expensive-looking flat-panel TV. "I'd like you to tell me your login and password for your Pirate Party email, please?"

I closed my eyes and let the ocean carry me off the beach.

"Do you know what waterboarding is, M1k3y?" Her voice reeled me in. "You get strapped down like this, and we pour water over your head, up your nose and down your mouth. You can't suppress the gag reflex. They call it a simulated execution, and from what I can tell from this side of the room, that's a fair assessment. You won't be able to fight the feeling that you're dying."

I tried to go away. I'd heard of waterboarding. This was it, real torture. And this was just the beginning.

I couldn't go away. The ocean didn't sweep in and lift me. There was a tightness in my chest, my eyelids fluttered. I could feel clammy piss on my legs and clammy sweat in my hair. My skin itched from the dried puke.

She swam into view above me. "Let's start with the login," she said.

I closed my eyes, squeezed them shut.

"Give him a drink," she said.

I heard people moving. I took a deep breath and held it.

The water started as a trickle, a ladleful of water gently poured over my chin, my lips. Up my upturned nostrils. It went back into my throat, starting to choke me, but I wouldn't cough, wouldn't gasp and suck it into my lungs. I held onto my breath and squeezed my eyes harder.

There was a commotion from outside the room, a sound of chaotic boots stamping, angry, outraged shouts. The dipper was emptied into my face.

I heard her mutter something to someone in the room, then to me she said, "Just the login, Marcus. It's a simple request. What could I do with your login, anyway?"

This time, it was a bucket of water, all at once, a flood that didn't stop, it must have been gigantic. I couldn't help it. I gasped and aspirated the water into my lungs, coughed and took more water in. I knew they wouldn't kill me, but I couldn't convince my body of that. In every fiber of my being, I knew I was going to die. I couldn't even cry—the water was still pouring over me.

Then it stopped. I coughed and coughed and coughed, but at the angle I was at, the water I coughed up dribbled back into my nose and burned down my sinuses.

The coughs were so deep they hurt, hurt my ribs and my hips as I twisted against them. I hated how my body was betraying me, how my mind couldn't control my body, but there was nothing for it.

Finally, the coughing subsided enough for me to take in what was going on around me. People were shouting and it sounded like someone was scuffling, wrestling. I opened my eyes and blinked into the bright light, then craned my neck, still coughing a little.

The room had a lot more people in it than it had had when we started. Most of them seemed to be wearing body armor, helmets and smoked-plastic visors. They were shouting at the Treasure Island guards, who were shouting back, necks corded with veins.

"Stand down!" one of the body armors said. "Stand down and put your hands in the air. You are under arrest!"

Severe haircut woman was talking on her phone. One of the body armors noticed her and he moved swiftly to her and batted her phone away with a gloved hand. Everyone fell silent as it sailed through the air in an arc that spanned the small room, clattering to the ground in a shower of parts.

The silence broke and the body armors moved into the room. Two grabbed each of my torturers. I almost managed a smile at the look on Severe Haircut's face when two men grabbed her by the shoulders, turned her around and yanked a set of plastic handcuffs around her wrists.

One of the body armors moved forward from the doorway. He had a video camera on his shoulder, a serious rig with blinding white light. He got the whole room, circling me twice while he got me. I found myself staying perfectly still, as though I was sitting for a portrait.

It was ridiculous.

"Do you think you could get me off of this thing?" I managed to get it all out with only a little choking.

Two more body armors moved up to me, one a woman, and began to unstrap me. They flipped their visors up and smiled at me. They had red crosses on their shoulders and helmets.

Beneath the red crosses was another insignia: CHP. California Highway Patrol. They were State Troopers.

I started to ask what they were doing there, and that's when I saw Barbara Stratford. She'd evidently been held back in the corridor, but now she came in pushing and shoving. "There you are," she said, kneeling beside me and grabbing me in the longest, hardest hug of my life.

That's when I knew it—Guantanamo-by-the-Bay was in the hands of its enemies. I was saved.

Chapter 21

They left me and Barbara alone in the room then, and I used the working showerhead to rinse off—I was suddenly embarrassed to be covered in piss and barf. When I finished, Barbara was in tears.

"Your parents—" she began.

I felt like I might throw up again. God, my poor folks. What they must have gone through.

"Are they here?"

"No," she said. "It's complicated," she said.

"What?"

"You're still under arrest, Marcus. Everyone here is. They can't just sweep in and throw open the doors. Everyone here is going to have to be processed through the criminal justice system. It could take, well, it could take months."

"I'm going to have to stay here for *months*?"

She grabbed my hands. "No, I think we're going to be able to get you arraigned and released on bail pretty fast. But pretty fast is a relative term. I wouldn't expect anything to happen today. And it's not going to be like those people had it. It will be humane. There will be real food. No interrogations. Visits from your family.

"Just because the DHS is out, it doesn't mean that you get to just walk out of here. What's happened here is that we're getting rid of the bizarro-world version of the justice system they'd instituted and replacing it with the old system. The system with judges, open trials and lawyers.

"So we can try to get you transferred to a juvie facility on the mainland, but Marcus, those places can be really rough. Really, really rough. This might be the best place for you until we get you bailed out."

Bailed out. Of course. I was a criminal—I hadn't been charged yet, but there were bound to be plenty of charges they could think of. It was practically illegal just to think impure thoughts about the government.

She gave my hands another squeeze. "It sucks, but this is how it has to be. The point is, it's *over*. The Governor has thrown the DHS out of the state, dismantled every checkpoint. The state Attorney General has issued warrants for any law-enforcement officers involved in 'stress interrogations' and secret imprisonments. They'll go to jail, Marcus, and it's because of what you did."

I was numb. I heard the words, but they hardly made sense. Somehow, it was over, but it wasn't over.

"Look," she said. "We probably have an hour or two before this all settles down, before they come back and put you away again. What do you want to do? Walk on the beach? Get a meal? These people had an incredible staff room—we raided it on the way in. Gourmet all the way."

At last a question I could answer. "I want to find Ange. I want to find Darryl."

I tried to use a computer I found to look up their cell numbers, but it wanted a password, so we were reduced to walking the corridors, calling out their names. Behind the cell doors, prisoners screamed back at us, or cried, or begged us to let them go. They didn't understand what had just happened, couldn't see their former guards being herded onto the docks in plastic handcuffs, taken away by California state SWAT teams.

"Ange!" I called over the din, "Ange Carvelli! Darryl Glover! It's Marcus!"

We'd walked the whole length of the cell block and they hadn't answered. I felt like crying. They'd been shipped overseas—they were in Syria or worse. I'd never see them again.

I sat down and leaned against the corridor wall and put my face in my hands. I saw severe haircut woman's face, saw her smirk as she asked me for my login. She had done this. She would go to jail for it, but that wasn't enough. I thought that when I saw her again, I might kill her. She deserved it.

"Come on," Barbara said. "Come on, Marcus. Don't give up. There's more around here, come on."

She was right. All the doors we'd passed in the cell block were old, rusting things that dated back to when the base was first built. But at the very end of the corridor, sagging open, was a new high-security door as thick as a dictionary. We pulled it open and ventured into the dark corridor within.

There were four more cell doors here, doors without bar codes. Each had a small electronic keypad mounted on it.

"Darryl?" I said. "Ange?"

"Marcus?"

It was Ange, calling out from behind the farthest door. Ange, my Ange, my angel.

"Ange!" I cried. "It's me, it's me!"

"Oh God, Marcus," she choked out, and then it was all sobs. I pounded on the other doors. "Darryl! Darryl, are you here?"

"I'm here." The voice was very small, and very hoarse. "I'm here. I'm very, very sorry. Please. I'm very sorry."

He sounded . . . broken. Shattered.

"It's me, D," I said, leaning on his door. "It's Marcus. It's over—they arrested the guards. They kicked the Department of Homeland Security out. We're getting trials, open trials. And we get to testify against *them*."

"I'm sorry," he said. "Please, I'm so sorry."

The California patrolmen came to the door then. They still had their camera rolling. "Ms. Stratford?" one said. He had his faceplate up and he looked like any other cop, not like my savior. Like someone come to lock me up.

"Captain Sanchez," she said. "We've located two of the prisoners of interest here. I'd like to see them released and inspect them for myself."

"Ma'am, we don't have access codes for those doors yet," he said.

She held up her hand. "That wasn't the arrangement. I was to have complete access to this facility. That came direct from the Governor, sir. We aren't budging until you open these cells." Her face was perfectly smooth, without a single hint of give or flex. She meant it.

The captain looked like he needed sleep. He grimaced. "I'll see what I can do," he said.

They did manage to open the cells, finally, about half an hour later. It took three tries, but they eventually got the right codes entered, matching them to the arphids on the ID badges they'd taken off the guards they'd arrested.

They got into Ange's cell first. She was dressed in a hospital gown, open at the back, and her cell was even more bare than mine had been—just padding all over, no sink or bed, no light. She emerged blinking into the corridor and the police camera was on her, its bright lights in her face. Barbara stepped protectively between us and it. Ange stepped tentatively out of her cell, shuffling a little. There was something wrong with her eyes, with her face. She was crying, but that wasn't it.

"They drugged me," she said. "When I wouldn't stop screaming for a lawyer."

That's when I hugged her. She sagged against me, but she squeezed back, too. She smelled stale and sweaty, and I smelled no better. I never wanted to let go.

That's when they opened Darryl's cell.

He had shredded his paper hospital gown. He was curled up, naked, in the back of the cell, shielding himself from the camera and our stares. I ran to him.

"D," I whispered in his ear. "D, it's me. It's Marcus. It's over. The guards have been arrested. We're going to get bail, we're going home."

He trembled and squeezed his eyes shut. "I'm sorry," he whispered, and turned his face away.

They took me away then, a cop in body armor and Barbara, took me back to my cell and locked the door, and that's where I spent the night.

I don't remember much about the trip to the courthouse. They had me chained to five other prisoners, all of whom had been in for a lot longer than me. One only spoke Arabic— he was an old man, and he trembled. The others were all young. I was the only white one. Once we had been gathered on the deck of the ferry, I saw that nearly everyone on Treasure Island had been one shade of brown or another.

I had only been inside for one night, but it was too long. There was a light drizzle coming down, normally the sort of thing that would make me hunch my shoulders and look down, but today I joined everyone else in craning my head back at the infinite gray sky, reveling in the stinging wet as we raced across the bay to the ferry docks.

They took us away in buses. The shackles made climbing into the buses awkward, and it took a long time for everyone to load. No one cared. When we weren't struggling to solve the geometry problem of six people, one chain, narrow bus aisle, we were just looking around at the city around us, up the hill at the buildings.

All I could think of was finding Darryl and Ange, but neither were in evidence. It was a big crowd and we weren't allowed to move freely through it. The state troopers who handled us were gentle enough, but they were still big, armored and armed. I kept thinking I saw Darryl in the crowd, but it was always someone else with that same beaten, hunched look that he'd had in his cell. He wasn't the only broken one.

At the courthouse, they marched us into interview rooms in our shackle group. An ACLU lawyer took our information and asked us a few questions—when she got to me, she smiled and greeted me by name—and then led us into the courtroom before the judge. He wore an actual robe, and seemed to be in a good mood.

The deal seemed to be that anyone who had a family member to post bail could go free, and everyone else got sent to prison. The ACLU lawyer did a lot of talking to the judge, asking for a few more hours while the prisoners' families were rounded up and brought to the courthouse. The judge was pretty good about it, but when I realized that some of these people had been locked up since the bridge blew, taken for dead by their families, without trial, subjected to interrogation, isolation, torture—I wanted to just break the chains myself and set everyone free.

When I was brought before the judge, he looked down at me and took off his glasses. He looked tired. The ACLU lawyer looked tired. The bailiffs looked tired. Behind me, I could hear a sudden buzz of conversation as my name was called by the bailiff. The judge rapped his gavel once, without looking away from me. He scrubbed at his eyes.

"Mr. Yallow," he said, "the prosecution has identified you as a flight risk. I think they have a point. You certainly have more, shall we say, *history,* than the other people here. I am tempted to hold you over for trial, no matter how much bail your parents are prepared to post."

My lawyer started to say something, but the judge silenced her with a look. He scrubbed at his eyes.

"Do you have anything to say?"

"I had the chance to run," I said. "Last week. Someone offered to take me away, get me out of town, help me build a new identity. Instead I stole her phone, escaped from our truck and ran away. I turned over her phone—which had evidence about my friend, Darryl Glover, on it—to a journalist and hid out here, in town."

"You stole a phone?"

"I decided that I couldn't run. That I had to face justice—that my freedom wasn't worth anything if I was a wanted man, or if the city was still under the DHS. If my friends were still locked up. That freedom for me wasn't as important as a free country."

"But you did steal a phone."

I nodded. "I did. I plan on giving it back, if I ever find the young woman in question."

"Well, thank you for that speech, Mr. Yallow. You are a very well-spoken young man." He glared at the prosecutor. "Some would say a very brave man, too. There was a certain video on the news this morning. It suggested that you had some legitimate reason to evade the authorities. In light of that, and of your little speech here, I will grant bail, but I will also ask the prosecutor to add a charge of Misdemeanor Petty Theft to the count, as regards the matter of the phone. For this, I expect another $50,000 in bail."

He banged his gavel again, and my lawyer gave my hand a squeeze.

The judge looked down at me again and reseated his glasses. He had dandruff, there on the shoulders of his robe. A little more rained down as his glasses touched his wiry, curly hair.

"You can go now, young man. Stay out of trouble."

I turned to go and someone tackled me. It was Dad. He literally lifted me off my feet, hugging me so hard my ribs creaked. He hugged me the way I remembered him hugging me when I was a little boy, when he'd spin me around and around in hilarious, vomitous games of airplane that ended with him tossing me in the air and catching me and squeezing me like that, so hard it almost hurt.

A set of softer hands pried me gently out of his arms. Mom. She held me at arm's-length for a moment, searching my face for something, not saying anything, tears streaming down her face. She smiled and it turned into a sob and then she was holding me, too, and Dad's arm encircled us both.

When they let go, I managed to finally say something. "Darryl?"

"His father met him somewhere else. He's in the hospital."

"When can I see him?"

"It's our next stop," Dad said. He was grim. "He doesn't—" He stopped. "They say he'll be okay," he said. His voice was choked.

"How about Ange?"

"Her mother took her home. She wanted to wait here for you, but . . ."

I understood. I felt full of understanding now, for how all the families of all the people who'd been locked away must feel. The courtroom was full of tears and hugs, and even the bailiffs couldn't stop it.

"Let's go see Darryl," I said. "And let me borrow your phone?"

I called Ange on the way to the hospital where they were keeping Darryl—San Francisco General, just down the street from our place—and arranged to see her after dinner. She talked in a hurried whisper. Her mom wasn't sure whether to punish her or not, but Ange didn't want to tempt fate.

There were two state troopers in the corridor where Darryl was being held. They were holding off a legion of reporters who stood on tiptoe to see around them and get pictures. The flashes popped in our eyes like strobes, and I shook my head to clear it. My parents had brought me clean clothes and I'd changed in the backseat, but I still felt gross, even after scrubbing myself in the courthouse bathrooms.

Some of the reporters called my name. Oh yeah, that's right, I was famous now. The state troopers gave me a look, too—either they'd recognized my face or my name when the reporters called it out.

Darryl's father met us at the door of his hospital room, speaking in a whisper too low for the reporters to hear. He was in civvies, the jeans and sweater I normally thought of him wearing, but he had his service ribbons pinned to his breast.

"He's sleeping," he said. "He woke up a little while ago and he started crying. He couldn't stop. They gave him something to help him sleep."

He led us in, and there was Darryl, his hair clean and combed, sleeping with his mouth open. There was white stuff at the corners of his mouth. He had a semiprivate room, and in the other bed there was an older Arab-looking guy, in his forties. I realized it was the guy I'd been chained to on the way off of Treasure Island. We exchanged embarrassed waves.

Then I turned back to Darryl. I took his hand. His nails had been chewed to the quick. He'd been a nail-biter when he was a kid, but he'd kicked the habit when we got to high school. I think Van talked him out of it, telling him how gross it was for him to have his fingers in his mouth all the time.

I heard my parents and Darryl's dad take a step away, drawing the curtains around us. I put my face down next to his on the pillow. He had a straggly, patchy beard that reminded me of Zeb.

"Hey, D," I said. "You made it. You're going to be okay."

He snored a little. I almost said, "I love you," a phrase I'd only said to one nonfamily member ever, a phrase that was weird to say to another guy. In the end, I just gave his hand another squeeze. Poor Darryl.

Epilogue

Barbara called me at the office on July 4th weekend. I wasn't the only one who'd come into work on the holiday weekend, but I was the only one whose excuse was that my day-release program wouldn't let me leave town.

In the end, they convicted me of stealing Masha's phone. Can you believe that? The prosecution had done a deal with my lawyer to drop all charges related to "electronic terrorism" and "inciting riots" in exchange for my pleading guilty to the misdemeanor petty theft charge. I got three months in a day-release program with a halfway house for juvenile defenders in the Mission. I slept at the halfway house, sharing a dorm with a bunch of actual criminals, gang kids and druggie kids, a couple of real nuts. During the day, I was "free" to go out and work at my "job."

"Marcus, they're letting her go," she said.

"Who?"

"Johnstone, Carrie Johnstone," she said. "The closed military tribunal cleared her of any wrongdoing. The file is sealed. She's being returned to active duty. They're sending her to Iraq."

Carrie Johnstone was severe haircut woman's name. It came out in the preliminary hearings at the California Superior Court, but that was just about all that came out. She wouldn't say a word about who she took orders from, what she'd done, who had been imprisoned and why. She just sat, perfectly silent, day after day, in the courthouse.

The feds, meanwhile, had blustered and shouted about the Governor's "unilateral, illegal" shutdown of the Treasure Island facility, and the Mayor's eviction of fed cops from San Francisco. A lot of those cops had ended up in state prisons, along with the guards from Gitmo-by-the-Bay.

Then, one day, there was no statement from the White House, nothing from the state capitol. And the next day, there was a dry, tense press conference held jointly on the steps of the Governor's mansion, where the head of the DHS and the Governor announced their "understanding."

The DHS would hold a closed, military tribunal to investigate "possible errors in judgment" committed after the attack on the Bay Bridge. The tribunal would use every tool at its disposal to ensure that criminal acts were properly punished. In return, control over DHS operations in California would go through the State Senate, which would have the power to shut down, inspect or reprioritize all homeland security in the state.

The roar of the reporters had been deafening and Barbara had gotten the first question in. "Mr. Governor, with all due respect: we have incontrovertible video evidence that Marcus Yallow, a citizen of this state, native-born, was subjected to a simulated execution by DHS officers, apparently acting on orders from the White House. Is the State really willing to abandon any pretense of justice for its citizens in the face of illegal, barbaric *torture*?" Her voice trembled, but didn't crack.

The Governor spread his hands. "The military tribunals will accomplish justice. If Mr. Yallow—or any other person who has cause to fault the Department of Homeland Security—wants further justice, he is, of course, entitled to sue for such damages as may be owing to him from the federal government."

That's what I was doing. Over twenty thousand civil lawsuits were filed against the DHS in the week after the Governor's announcement. Mine was being handled by the ACLU, and they'd filed motions to get at the results of the closed military tribunals. So far, the courts were pretty sympathetic to this.

But I hadn't expected this.

"She got off totally scot-free?"

"The press release doesn't say much. 'After a thorough examination of the events in San Francisco and in the special antiterror detention center on Treasure Island, it is the finding of this tribunal that Ms. Johnstone's actions do not warrant further discipline.' There's that word, 'further'—like they've already punished her."

I snorted. I'd dreamed of Carrie Johnstone nearly every night since I was released from Gitmo-by-the-Bay. I'd seen her face looming over mine, that little snarly smile as she told the man to give me a "drink."

"Marcus—" Barbara said, but I cut her off.

"It's fine. It's fine. I'm going to do a video about this. Get it out over the weekend. Mondays are big days for viral video. Everyone'll be coming back from the holiday weekend, looking for something funny to forward around school or the office."

I saw a shrink twice a week as part of my deal at the halfway house. Once I'd gotten over seeing that as some kind of punishment, it had been good. He'd helped me focus on doing constructive things when I was upset, instead of letting it eat me up. The videos helped.

"I have to go," I said, swallowing hard to keep the emotion out of my voice.

"Take care of yourself, Marcus," Barbara said.

Ange hugged me from behind as I hung up the phone. "I just read about it online," she said. She read a million newsfeeds, pulling them with a headline reader that sucked up stories as fast as they ended up on the wire. She was our official blogger, and she was good at it, snipping out the interesting stories and throwing them online like a short-order cook turning around breakfast orders.

I turned around in her arms so that I was hugging her from in front. Truth be told, we hadn't gotten a lot of work done that day. I wasn't allowed to be out of the halfway house after dinner time, and she couldn't visit me there. We saw each other around the office, but there was usually a lot of other people around, which kind of put a crimp in our cuddling. Being alone in the office for a day was too much temptation. It was hot and sultry, too, which meant we were both in tank tops and shorts, a lot of skin-to-skin contact as we worked next to each other.

"I'm going to make a video," I said. "I want to release it today."

"Good," she said. "Let's do it."

Ange read the press release. I did a little monologue, synched over that famous footage of me on the waterboard, eyes wild in the harsh light of the camera, tears streaming down my face, hair matted and flecked with barf.

"This is me. I am on a waterboard. I am being tortured in a simulated execution. The torture is supervised by a woman called Carrie Johnstone. She works for the government. You might remember her from this video."

I cut in the video of Johnstone and Kurt Rooney. "That's Johnstone and Secretary of State Kurt Rooney, the President's chief strategist."

"The nation does not love that city. As far as they're concerned, it is a Sodom and Gomorrah of fags and atheists who deserve to rot in hell. The only reason the country cares what they think in San Francisco is that they had the good fortune to have been blown to hell by some Islamic terrorists."

"He's talking about the city where I live. At last count, four thousand two hundred fifteen of my neighbors were killed on the day he's talking about. But some of them may not have been killed. Some of them disappeared into the same prison where I was tortured. Some mothers and fathers, children and lovers, brothers and sisters will never see their loved ones again—because they were secretly imprisoned in an illegal jail right here in the San Francisco Bay. They were shipped overseas. The records were meticulous, but Carrie Johnstone has the encryption keys." I cut back to Carrie Johnstone, the footage of her sitting at the board table with Rooney, laughing.

I cut in the footage of Johnstone being arrested. "When they arrested her, I thought we'd get justice. All the people she broke and disappeared. But the President"—I cut to a still of him laughing and playing golf on one of his many holidays—"and chief strategist"—now a still of Rooney shaking hands with an infamous terrorist leader who used to be on "our side"—"intervened. They sent her to a secret military tribunal and now that tribunal has cleared her. Somehow, they saw nothing wrong with all of this."

I cut in a photomontage of the hundreds of shots of prisoners in their cells that Barbara had published on the *Bay Guardian*'s site the day we were released. "We elected these people. We pay their salaries. They're supposed to be on our side. They're supposed to defend our freedoms. But these people"—a series of shots of Johnstone and the others who'd been sent to the tribunal—"betrayed our trust. The election is four months away. That's a lot of time. Enough for you to go out and find five of your neighbors—five people who've given up on voting because their choice is 'none of the above.'

"Talk to your neighbors. Make them promise to vote. Make them promise to take the country back from the torturers and thugs. The people who laughed at my friends as they lay fresh in their graves at the bottom of the harbor. Make them promise to talk to their neighbors.

"Most of us choose none of the above. It's not working. You have to choose—choose freedom.

"My name is Marcus Yallow. I was tortured by my country, but I still love it here. I'm seventeen years old. I want to grow up in a free country. I want to live in a free country."

I faded out to the logo of the website. Ange had built it, with help from Jolu, who got us all the free hosting we could ever need on Pigspleen.

The office was an interesting place. Technically we were called Coalition of Voters for a Free America, but everyone called us the Xnetters. The organization—a charitable nonprofit—had been cofounded by Barbara and some of her lawyer friends right after the liberation of Treasure Island. The funding was kicked off by some tech millionaires who couldn't believe that a bunch of hacker kids had kicked the DHS's ass. Sometimes, they'd ask us to go down the peninsula to Sand Hill Road, where all the venture capitalists were, and give a little presentation on Xnet technology. There were about a zillion start-ups who were trying to make a buck on the Xnet.

Whatever—I didn't have to have anything to do with it, and I got a desk and an office with a storefront, right there on Valencia Street, where we gave away ParanoidXbox CDs and held workshops on building better WiFi antennas. A surprising number of average people dropped in to make personal donations, both of hardware (you can run ParanoidLinux on just about anything, not just Xbox Universals) and cash money. They loved us.

The big plan was to launch our own ARG in September, just in time for the election, and to really tie it in with signing up voters and getting them to the polls. Only 42 percent of Americans showed up at the polls for the last election—nonvoters had a huge majority. I kept trying to get Darryl and Van to one of our planning sessions, but they kept on declining. They were spending a lot of time together, and Van insisted that it was totally nonromantic. Darryl wouldn't talk to me much at all, though he sent me long emails about just about everything that wasn't about Van or terrorism or prison.

Ange squeezed my hand. "God, I hate that woman," she said.

I nodded. "Just one more rotten thing this country's done to Iraq," I said. "If they sent her to my town, I'd probably become a terrorist."

"You did become a terrorist when they sent her to your town."

"So I did," I said.

"Are you going to Ms. Galvez's hearing on Monday?"

"Totally." I'd introduced Ange to Ms. Galvez a couple weeks before, when my old teacher invited me over for dinner. The teacher's union had gotten a hearing for her before the board of the Unified School District to argue for getting her old job back. They said that Fred Benson was coming out of (early) retirement to testify against her. I was looking forward to seeing her again.

"Do you want to go get a burrito?"

"Totally."

"Let me get my hot sauce," she said.

I checked my email one more time—my PirateParty email,

which still got a dribble of messages from old Xnetters who hadn't found my Coalition of Voters address yet.

The latest message was from a throwaway email address from one of the new Brazilian anonymizers.

> **Found her, thanks. You didn't tell me she was so h4wt.**

"Who's *that* from?"

I laughed. "Zeb," I said. "Remember Zeb? I gave him Masha's email address. I figured, if they're both underground, might as well introduce them to one another."

"He thinks Masha is *cute*?"

"Give the guy a break, he's clearly had his mind warped by circumstances."

"And you?"

"Me?"

"Yeah—was your mind warped by circumstances?"

I held Ange out at arm's length and looked her up and down and up and down. I held her cheeks and stared through her thick-framed glasses into her big, mischievous tilted eyes. I ran my fingers through her hair.

"Ange, I've never thought more clearly in my whole life."

She kissed me then, and I kissed her back, and it was some time before we went out for that burrito.

Afterword

by Bruce Schneier

I'm a security technologist. My job is making people secure.

I think about security systems and how to break them. Then, how to make them more secure. Computer security systems. Surveillance systems. Airplane security systems and voting machines and RFID chips and everything else.

Cory invited me into the last few pages of his book because he wanted me to tell you that security is fun. It's incredibly fun. It's cat and mouse, who can outsmart whom, hunter versus hunted fun. I think it's the most fun job you can possibly have. If you thought it was fun to read about Marcus outsmarting the gait-recognition cameras with rocks in his shoes, think of how much more fun it would be if you were the first person in the world to think of that.

Working in security means knowing a lot about technology. It might mean knowing about computers and networks, or cameras and how they work, or the chemistry of bomb detection. But really, security is a mindset. It's a way of thinking. Marcus is a great example of that way of thinking. He's always looking for ways a security system fails. I'll bet he couldn't walk into a store without figuring out a way to shoplift. Not that he'd do it—there's a difference between knowing how to defeat a security system and actually defeating it—but he'd know he could.

It's how security people think. We're constantly looking at security systems and how to get around them; we can't help it.

This kind of thinking is important no matter what side of security you're on. If you've been hired to build a shoplift-proof store, you'd better know how to shoplift. If you're designing a camera system that detects individual gaits, you'd better plan for people putting rocks in their shoes. Because if you don't, you're not going to design anything good.

So when you're wandering through your day, take a moment to look at the security systems around you. Look at the cameras in the stores you shop at. (Do they prevent crime, or just move it next door?) See how a restaurant operates. (If you pay after you eat, why don't more people just leave without paying?) Pay attention at airport security. (How could you get a weapon onto an airplane?) Watch what the teller does at a bank. (Bank security is designed to prevent tellers from stealing just as much as it is to prevent you from stealing.) Stare at an anthill. (Insects are all about security.) Read the Constitution, and notice all the ways it provides people with security against government. Look at traffic lights and door locks and all the security systems on television and in the movies. Figure out how they work, what threats they protect against and what threats they don't, how they fail, and how they can be exploited.

Spend enough time doing this, and you'll find yourself thinking differently about the world. You'll start noticing that many of the security systems out there don't actually do what they claim to, and that much of our national security is a waste of money. You'll understand privacy as essential to security, not in opposition. You'll stop worrying about things other people worry about, and start worrying about things other people don't even think about.

Sometimes you'll notice something about security that no one has ever thought about before. And maybe you'll figure out a new way to break a security system.

It was only a few years ago that someone invented phishing.

I'm frequently amazed how easy it is to break some pretty big-name security systems. There are a lot of reasons for this, but the big one is that it's impossible to prove that something is secure. All you can do is try to break it. If you fail, you know that it's secure enough to keep *you* out, but what about someone who's smarter than you? Anyone can design a security system so strong he himself can't break it.

Think about that for a second, because it's not obvious. No one is qualified to analyze their own security designs, because the designer and the analyzer will be the same person, with the same limits. Someone else has to analyze the security, because it has to be secure against things the designers didn't think of.

This means that all of us have to analyze the security that other people design. And surprisingly often, one of us breaks it. Marcus's exploits aren't far-fetched; that kind of thing happens all the time. Go onto the net and look up "bump key" or "Bic pen Kryptonite lock"; you'll find a couple of really interesting stories about seemingly strong security defeated by pretty basic technology.

And when that happens, be sure to publish it on the Internet somewhere. Secrecy and security aren't the same, even though it may seem that way. Only bad security relies on secrecy; good security works even if all the details of it are public.

And making vulnerabilities public forces security designers to design better security, and makes us all better consumers of security. If you buy a Kryptonite bike lock and it can be defeated with a Bic pen, you're not getting very good security for your money. And, likewise, if a bunch of smart kids can defeat the DHS's antiterrorist technologies, then it's not going to do a very good job against real terrorists.

Trading privacy for security is stupid enough; not getting any actual security in the bargain is even more stupid.

So close the book and go. The world is full of security systems. Hack one of them.

Bruce Schneier
www.schneier.com

Afterword

by Andrew "bunnie" Huang, Xbox Hacker

Hackers are explorers, digital pioneers. It's in a hacker's nature to question conventions and be tempted by intricate problems. Any complex system is sport for a hacker; a side effect of this is the hacker's natural affinity for problems involving security. Society is a large and complex system, and is certainly not off limits to a little hacking. As a result, hackers are often stereotyped as iconoclasts and social misfits, people who defy social norms for the sake of defiance. When I hacked the Xbox in 2002 while at MIT, I wasn't doing it to rebel or to cause harm; I was just following a natural impulse, the same impulse that leads to fixing a broken iPod or exploring the roofs and tunnels at MIT.

Unfortunately, the combination of not complying with social norms and knowing "threatening" things like how to read the arphid on your credit card or how to pick locks causes some people to fear hackers. However, the motivations of a hacker are typically as simple as "I'm an engineer because I like to design things." People often ask me, "Why did you hack the Xbox security system?" And my answer is simple: First, I own the things that I buy. If someone can tell me what I can and can't run on my hardware, then I don't own it. Second, because it's there. It's a system of sufficient complexity to make good sport. It was a great diversion from the late nights working on my Ph.D.

I was lucky. The fact that I was a graduate student at MIT when I hacked the Xbox legitimized the activity in the eyes of the right people. However, the right to hack shouldn't be extended to only academics. I got my start on hacking when I was just a boy in elementary school, taking apart every electronic appliance I could get my hands on, much to my parents' chagrin. My reading collection included books on model rocketry, artillery, nuclear weaponry and explosives manufacture—books that I borrowed from my school library (I think the Cold War influenced the reading selection in public schools). I also played with my fair share of ad-hoc fireworks and roamed the open construction sites of houses being raised in my Midwestern neighborhood. While not the wisest of things to do, these were important experiences in my coming of age and I grew up to be a free thinker because of the social tolerance and trust of my community.

Current events have not been so kind to aspiring hackers. *Little Brother* shows how we can get from where we are today to a world where social tolerance for new and different thoughts dies altogether. A recent event highlights exactly how close we are to crossing the line into the world of *Little Brother*. I had the fortune of reading an early draft of *Little Brother* back in November 2006. Fast-forward two months to the end of January 2007, when Boston police found suspected explosive devices and shut down the city for a day. These devices turned out to be nothing more than circuit boards with flashing LEDs, promoting a show for the Cartoon Network. The artists who placed this urban graffiti were taken in as suspected terrorists and ultimately charged with felony; the network producers had to shell out a $2 million settlement, and the head of the Cartoon Network resigned over the fallout.

Have the terrorists already won? Have we given in to fear, such that artists, hobbyists, hackers, iconoclasts or perhaps an unassuming group of kids playing Harajuku Fun Madness could be so trivially implicated as terrorists?

There is a term for this dysfunction—it is called an autoimmune disease, where an organism's defense system goes into overdrive so much that it fails to recognize itself and attacks its own cells. Ultimately, the organism self-destructs. Right now, America is on the verge of going into anaphylactic shock over its own freedoms, and we need to inoculate ourselves against this. Technology is no cure for this paranoia; in fact, it may enhance the paranoia: it turns us into prisoners of our own devices. Coercing millions of people to strip off their outer garments and walk barefoot through metal detectors everyday is no solution, either. It only serves to remind the population that they have a reason to be afraid, while in practice providing only a flimsy barrier to a determined adversary.

The truth is that we can't count on someone else to make us feel free, and M1k3y won't come and save us the day our freedoms are lost to paranoia. That's because M1k3y is in you and in me—*Little Brother* is a reminder that no matter how unpredictable the future may be, we don't win freedom through security systems, cryptography, interrogations and spot searches. We win freedom by having the courage and the conviction to live every day freely and to act as a free society, no matter how great the threats are on the horizon.

Be like M1k3y: step out the door and dare to be free.

Bibliography

No writer creates from scratch—we all engage in what Isaac Newton called "standing on the shoulders of giants." We borrow, plunder and remix the art and culture created by those around us and by our literary forebears.

If you liked this book and want to learn more, there are plenty of sources to turn to, online and at your local library or bookstore.

Hacking is a great subject. All science relies on telling other people what you've done so that they can verify it, learn from it and improve on it, and hacking is all about that process, so there's plenty published on the subject.

Start with Andrew "bunnie" Huang's *Hacking the Xbox* (No Starch Press, 2003), a wonderful book that tells the story of how bunnie, then a student at MIT, reverse-engineered the Xbox's antitampering mechanisms and opened the way for all the subsequent cool hacks for the platform. In telling the story, bunnie has also created a kind of Bible for reverse engineering and hardware hacking.

Bruce Schneier's *Secrets and Lies* (Wiley, 2000) and *Beyond Fear* (Copernicus, 2003) are the definitive layperson's texts on understanding security and thinking critically about it, while his *Applied*

Cryptography (Wiley, 1995) remains the authoritative source for understanding crypto. Bruce maintains an excellent blog and mailing list at schneier.com/blog. Crypto and security are the realm of the talented amateur, and the "cypherpunk" movement is full of kids, homemakers, parents, lawyers and every other stripe of person, hammering away on security protocols and ciphers.

There are several great magazines devoted to this subject, but the two best ones are *2600: The Hacker Quarterly,* which is full of pseudonymous, boasting accounts of hacks accomplished, and O'Reilly's *MAKE* magazine, which features solid how-tos for making your own hardware projects at home.

The online world overflows with material on this subject, of course. Ed Felten and Alex J. Halderman's Freedom to Tinker (www.freedom-to-tinker.com) is a blog maintained by two fantastic Princeton engineering profs who write lucidly about security, wiretapping, anticopying technology and crypto.

Don't miss Natalie Jeremijenko's "Feral Robotics" at UC San Diego (xdesign.ucsd.edu/feralrobots/). Natalie and her students rewire toy robot dogs from Toys "R" Us and turn them into badass toxic waste detectors. They unleash them on public parks where big corporations have dumped their waste and demonstrate in media-friendly fashion how toxic the ground is.

Like many of the hacks in this book, the tunneling-over-DNS stuff is real. Dan Kaminsky, a tunneling expert of the first water, published details in 2004 (www.doxpara.com/bo2004.ppt).

The guru of "citizen journalism" is Dan Gillmor, who is presently running the Center for Citizen Media at Harvard and UC Berkeley—he also wrote a hell of a book on the subject, *We, the Media* (O'Reilly, 2004).

If you want to learn more about hacking arphids, start with Annalee Newitz's *Wired* article "The RFID Hacking Underground" (www.wirednews.com/wired/archive/14.05/rfid.html). Adam Greenfield's *Everyware* (New Riders Press, 2006) is a chilling look at the dangers of a world of arphids.

Neal Gershenfeld's Fab Lab at MIT (fab.cba.mit.edu) is hacking out the world's first real, cheap "3D printers" that can pump out any object you can dream of. This is documented in Gershenfeld's excellent book on the subject, *Fab* (Basic Books, 2005).

Bruce Sterling's *Shaping Things* (MIT Press, 2005) shows how arphids and fabs could be used to force companies to build products that don't poison the world.

Speaking of Bruce Sterling, he wrote the first great book on hackers and the law, *The Hacker Crackdown* (Bantam, 1993), which is also the first book published by a major publisher that was released on the Internet at the same time (copies abound; see stuff.mit.edu/hacker/hacker.html for one). It was reading this book that turned me on to the Electronic Frontier Foundation, where I was privileged to work for four years.

The Electronic Frontier Foundation (www.eff.org) is a charitable membership organization with a student rate. They spend the money that private individuals give them to keep the Internet safe for personal liberty, free speech, due process and the rest of the Bill of Rights. They're the Internet's most effective freedom fighters, and you can join the struggle just by signing up for their mailing list and writing to your elected officials when they're considering selling you out in the name of fighting terrorism, piracy, the mafia or whatever bogeyman has caught their attention today. EFF also helps maintain TOR, The Onion Router, which is a real technology you can use *right now* to get out of your government, school or library's censoring firewall (tor.eff.org).

EFF has a huge, deep website with amazing information aimed at a general audience, as do the American Civil Liberties Union (aclu.org), Public Knowledge (publicknowledge.org), FreeCulture (freeculture.org), Creative Commons (creativecommons.org)—all of which are also worthy of your support. FreeCulture is an international student movement that actively recruits kids to found their own local chapters at their high schools and universities. It's a great way to get involved and make a difference.

A lot of websites chronicle the fight for cyberliberties, but few go at it with the verve of Slashdot, "News for Nerds, Stuff That Matters" (slashdot.org).

And of course, you *have* to visit Wikipedia, the collaborative, net-authored encyclopedia that anyone can edit, with more than a million entries in English alone. Wikipedia covers hacking and counterculture in astonishing depth and with amazing, up-to-the-nanosecond currency. One caution: you can't just look at the entries in Wikipedia. It's really important to look at the "History" and "Discussion" links at the top of every Wikipedia page to see how the current version of the truth was arrived at, get an appreciation for the competing points of view there and decide for yourself whom you trust.

If you want to get at some *real* forbidden knowledge, have a skim around Cryptome (cryptome.org), the world's most amazing archive of secret, suppressed and liberated information. Cryptome's brave publishers collect and publish material that's been pried out of the state by Freedom of Information Act requests, or leaked by whistle-blowers.

The best fictional account of the history of crypto is, hands down, Neal Stephenson's *Cryptonomicon* (Avon, 2002). Stephenson tells the story of Alan Turing and the Nazi Enigma Machine, turning it into a gripping war novel that you won't be able to put down.

The Pirate Party mentioned in *Little Brother* is real and thriving in Sweden (www.piratpartiet.se), Denmark, the USA and

France at the time of this writing (July, 2006). They're a little out there, but a movement takes all kinds.

Speaking of out there, Abbie Hoffman and the Yippies did indeed try to levitate the Pentagon, throw money into the stock exchange and work with a group called the Up Against the Wall Motherf___ers. Abbie Hoffman's classic book on ripping off the system, *Steal This Book,* is back in print (Four Walls Eight Windows, 2002) and it's also online as a collaborative wiki for people who want to try to update it (stealthiswiki.nine9pages.com).

Hoffman's autobiography, *Soon to Be a Major Motion Picture* (also in print from Four Walls Eight Windows), is one of my favorite memoirs ever, even if it is highly fictionalized. Hoffman was an incredible storyteller and had great activist instincts. If you want to know how he really lived his life, though, try Larry Sloman's *Steal This Dream* (Doubleday, 1998).

More counterculture fun: Jack Kerouac's *On the Road* can be had in practically any used bookstore for a buck or two. Allen Ginsberg's *HOWL* is online in many places, and you can hear him read it if you search for the MP3 at archive.org. For bonus points, track down the album *Tenderness Junction* by the Fugs, which includes the audio of Allen Ginsberg and Abbie Hoffman's levitation ceremony at the Pentagon.

This book couldn't have been written if not for George Orwell's magnificent, world-changing *Nineteen Eighty-Four,* the best novel ever published on how societies go wrong. I read this book when I was twelve and have read it thirty or forty times since, and every time, I get something new out of it. Orwell was a master of storytelling and was clearly sick over the totalitarian state that had emerged in the Soviet Union. *Nineteen Eighty-Four* holds up today as a genuinely frightening work of science fiction, and it is one of the novels that literally changed the world. Today, "Orwellian" is synonymous with a state of ubiquitous surveillance, doublethink and torture.

Many novelists have tackled parts of the story in *Little Brother*. Daniel Pinkwater's towering comic masterpiece, *Alan Mendelsohn: The Boy from Mars* (presently in print as part of the omnibus *5 Novels,* Farrar Straus Giroux, 1997) is a book that every geek needs to read. If you've ever felt like an outcast for being too smart or weird, READ THIS BOOK. It changed my life.

On a more contemporary front, there's Scott Westerfeld's *So Yesterday* (Razorbill, 2004), which follows the adventures of cool hunters and counterculture jammers. Scott and his wife, Justine Larbalestier, were my partial inspiration to write a book for young adults—as was Kathe Koja. Thanks, guys.

Acknowledgments

This book owes a tremendous debt to many writers, friends, mentors and heroes who made it possible.

For the hackers and cypherpunks: Andrew "bunnie" Huang, Seth Schoen, Ed Felten, Alex Halderman, Gweeds, Natalie Jeremijenko, Emmanuel Goldstein, Aaron Swartz

For the heroes: Mitch Kapor, John Gilmore, John Perry Barlow, Larry Lessig, Shari Steele, Cindy Cohn, Fred von Lohmann, Jamie Boyle, George Orwell, Abbie Hoffman, Joe Trippi, Bruce Schneier, Ross Dowson, Harry Kopyto, Tim O'Reilly

For the writers: Bruce Sterling, Kathe Koja, Scott Westerfeld, Justine Larbalestier, Pat York, Annalee Newitz, Dan Gillmor, Daniel Pinkwater, Kevin Pouslen, Wendy Grossman, Jay Lake, Ben Rosenbaum

For the friends: Fiona Romeo, Quinn Norton, Danny O'Brien, Jon Gilbert, danah boyd, Zak Hanna, Emily Hurson, Grad Conn, John Henson, Amanda Foubister, Xeni Jardin, Mark Frauenfelder, David Pescovitz, John Battelle, Karl Levesque, Kate Miles, Neil and Tara-Lee Doctorow, Rael Dornfest, Ken Snider

For the mentors: Judy Merril, Roz and Gord Doctorow, Harriet Wolff, Jim Kelly, Damon Knight, Scott Edelman

Thank you all for giving me the tools to think and write about these ideas.